THE LADY DOTH PROTEST TOO MUCH

Vaguely, Darla was aware that the crowd noise had faded to a murmur, while the sound of her heart beating double time seemed suddenly louder than even the honking horns. She was running toward the van now, while a frantic voice in her head cried, *Don't let it be that, dear God, don't let it be that.*

Some of the teens had spilled over the barricades, and Darla had to shove her way through them. Only then was she close enough to see what the light from the van's one unbroken headlamp revealed upon the asphalt. Her step faltered. For a moment, she feared she might sag to the sidewalk.

She managed to keep her own balance by focusing her attention on Jake, who had her cell phone to his ear and was shouting something unintelligible into it. She didn't want to gaze at the motionless figure tangled in a long black cape that lay sprawled a few feet in front of the van, one limp arm pointing toward a rectangle of white cardboard, the protest sign, farther down the pavement.

Berkley Prime Crime titles by Ali Brandon

DOUBLE BOOKED FOR DEATH
A NOVEL WAY TO DIE

DOUBLE BOOKED
FOR DEATH

ALI BRANDON

BERKLEY PRIME CRIME, NEW YORK

THE BERKLEY PUBLISHING GROUP
Published by the Penguin Group
Penguin Group (USA) Inc.
375 Hudson Street, New York, New York 10014, USA

USA / Canada / UK / Ireland / Australia / New Zealand / India / South Africa / China

Penguin Books Ltd., Registered Offices: 80 Strand, London WC2R 0RL, England
For more information about the Penguin Group, visit penguin.com.

DOUBLE BOOKED FOR DEATH

A Berkley Prime Crime Book / published by arrangement with Tekno Books

Berkley Prime Crime Books are published by The Berkley Publishing Group.
BERKLEY® PRIME CRIME and the PRIME CRIME logo are trademarks of
Penguin Group (USA) Inc.

For information, address: The Berkley Publishing Group,
a division of Penguin Group (USA) Inc.,
375 Hudson Street, New York, New York 10014.

ISBN: 978-0-425-26846-9

PUBLISHING HISTORY
Berkley Prime Crime mass-market edition / December 2011
Read Humane edition / May 2013

PRINTED IN THE UNITED STATES OF AMERICA

10 9 8 7 6 5 4 3 2 1

Cover illustration by Ross Jones.
Cover design by Annette Fiore Defex.
Interior text design by Kristin del Rosario.

For the legions
of dedicated booksellers
out there who do it for the love
and not the money . . .
this one is for you!

ACKNOWLEDGMENTS

Thanks to all the great folks at Tekno Books and Berkley Prime Crime for their support. It is appreciated. Special thanks to my good friend Denise Little and her long-departed but never forgotten black cat, Hamlet. They were the inspiration for my Darla and her Hamlet. As always, thanks to my darling husband, Gerry, who prods me along. And, finally, a fond flick of the whiskers to all my kitties I've loved over the years, starting with Topsey, and continuing with my current orange tabby boys, Butch and Sundance, both of whom kept a close eye on this story as I wrote it. They will tell you that any errors in fact or cat etiquette are mine alone.

ONE

AFTERNOON SUN SPILLED THROUGH THE MOTTLED GLASS of the double front doors leading into Pettistone's Fine Books, the golden light stippling the dark figure sprawled upon the faded Oriental rug that served as a welcome mat. Those customers who'd entered the first-floor brownstone shop within the past half hour had taken the sight of the motionless form in stride—this *was* Brooklyn, after all—and casually stepped over it to head in the direction of the bestseller table. Finally, however, a cardigan-swathed octogenarian halted in the doorway. His expression was one of vexation as he stared down at the body blocking his path.

"Dead, is he?" the old man exclaimed, giving the "he" in question a querulous poke with his rubber-tipped wooden cane.

"No!"

The single panicked word was both an answer and a warning. Darla Pettistone leaped from her perch behind the cash register and rushed toward the door, determined to forestall mayhem. She was too late. A sleek black paw the size of a toddler's hand, but far more dangerously equipped, had already slashed out and caught the lacquered walking stick in five needle-sharp claws.

"Let go, you beast!"

The old man gripped his cane with both arthritic hands as he attempted to wrestle it from a solid black feline the size of a cocker spaniel. The cat answered with a growl that sounded like something from a *When Good Pets Go Bad* television episode. Despite the fact that he had remained prone on the floor and was using but a single paw, the cat appeared to be winning this tug-of-war with the human.

By now, Darla had reached the doorway, her shoulder-length auburn hair swirling about her like a cape. She narrowed her brown eyes and shot the feline her most ferocious look. Unfortunately, given her round face and snub nose with its sprinkling of freckles—all of which combined to make her look a decade younger than her thirty-five years—the result was nothing worse than a peeved expression. Still, Darla's East Texas twang rang with firm authority as she commanded, "Let it go, Hamlet, or I'll break out the pistol."

"Pistol!" a panicked little voice echoed in unexpected response. Rising to a shriek, it continued, "Mom, the lady's gonna shoot the kitty!"

Darla located the source of the outcry. A pigtailed blond girl perhaps ten years old and wearing black-framed eyeglasses too large for her heart-shaped face came flying around the display of Boy Wizard books. Her expression far more fierce than the one Darla had managed, she made a beeline for the spot where Hamlet was still battling the elderly customer for his cane. Before Darla could explain that her weapon was nothing more lethal than a pocket-sized water gun she'd bought for cat disciplinary purposes, the girl flung herself atop the black beast like a soldier diving to cover a live grenade.

Oh no!

Too late to prevent the massacre that would surely result from this action, Darla could only steel herself for the screams of pain and flying droplets of blood that she knew were imminent. On her first day running the store, she'd been the unwitting victim of a lightning-fast swipe from Hamlet's claws. The attack had occurred as she'd moved his downstairs food bowl from its usual spot, in front of the local author showcase, to the corner of the science-fiction section. Hamlet had not approved of the change. It had taken half a bottle of hydrogen peroxide and most of a roll of gauze to patch up the outcome of his displeasure.

Almost half a year later, the food bowl still remained alongside the local author novels, and Darla still had the faint red scars from that particular disagreement.

Spurred by the memory, Darla swooped toward the child, intending to grab her up before any permanently disfiguring damage could be done. Visions of lawsuits, rather than sugar-plums, did the dancing-in-her-head routine while she wondered if her insurance would cover what probably would be a seven-figure settlement. But before she could separate kid from cat, the girl lifted her face from where it was buried in Hamlet's silky fur and declared in a grim tone, "If you want to shoot him, you're going to have to shoot me first."

Darla sagged in relief at the sight of the child's blessedly unblemished flesh, even as she reminded herself that the girl was still within Hamlet's reach. She might be unscratched now, but for how much longer? She needed to talk the child out of range, and fast.

"No real guns, I promise," Darla assured her and raised both hands by way of demonstration. "I was just threatening to squirt the kitty with a little water so he'd give the nice man back his cane. So why don't you come with me, and we'll let the kitty finish his nap?"

Before the girl could reply, Darla heard a rasping sound emanating from beneath the child's huddled form and realized in astonishment that the harsh rumble she heard was Hamlet, purring. She saw, too, that the cat had released the cane from his massive paw and appeared content to be used as a pillow by his would-be rescuer.

How long Hamlet would allow this familiarity, however, none of them was to find out. An exasperated voice drifted from the scrapbooking section, "Callie, quit bothering the lady and get back over here."

"Okay, Mom."

Callie sighed but obediently rose. With a final fond look at Hamlet, and an equally stern stare for Darla, she started back to the aisle where her mother waited.

Darla summoned a weak smile. "Don't worry, honey," she

called after the girl, "the kitty will be fine." Then, recalling the customer whose action had initiated this afternoon's small drama, she turned and prepared to make an apology.

His walking stick once more firmly in his gnarled hands, the old man was squinting at the series of gouges that now marred the lacquer finish. "It's ruined," he decreed with a baleful look that encompassed both her and Hamlet. "Don't think that I won't report to the authorities that you have a wild animal on the loose in your store."

"Wild animal?" Her impulse to apologize faded, but with an ease born of long practice, she kept her proverbial redhead's fiery temper firmly in check. "Hamlet is a *cat*. A domesticated feline," she pointed out, sympathetic to the man's plight but feeling the need to come to the cat's defense. Wasn't he, in a manner of speaking, one of her employees? "And he has resided in this store with the blessing of my late great-aunt for the past ten years, with never a single customer complaint."

Or so she had been told by James, the store's longtime manager when she'd questioned the wisdom of allowing Hamlet—and his claws—to mingle with the paying customers. Surprisingly, the fastidious James had encouraged her to let sleeping cats lie and continue the bookstore cat tradition that her Great-Aunt Dee had started.

The customers enjoy it, and it gives the place a certain ambiance, he'd assured her in his precise tones. But having come to know Hamlet during the brief five months that she had owned the store, Darla wouldn't put it past the wily feline to have disposed of any victims who might have been inclined to make a protest.

Recalling herself to the matter at hand, she went on, "And you must admit that you provoked him. Beating on a sleeping cat with a cane . . . well, let's just say that the local humane society will probably have something to say about that."

"Don't forget PETA," Callie piped up from the rear of the store, apparently deciding to choose the pistol-packing Darla's side over that of the stick-wielding old man.

Faced with the dual threats of an outraged preteen and a radical animal welfare agency, the elderly customer prudently dropped his previous bluster. With a cautious glance at the lounging feline, he conceded, "Perhaps I was a bit out of line, but you must admit your cat did damage my property. Still, I am willing to let bygones be bygones if you and, er, Hamlet will do the same. If you could point me toward the mystery section, I'll pick up a bit of light reading for the weekend and be on my way."

"Certainly."

Darla gave a professional smile as she gestured him forward, suppressing the triumphant grin she'd have preferred. "Mysteries and thrillers are two aisles down next to romance. Why don't I show you a couple of new arrivals that received wonderful reviews this week?"

Giving Hamlet wide berth, the old man started toward the section in question. Darla followed on the man's heels, though she spared a warning look back at the cat in case he planned a rear attack.

But the consternation he'd already caused among the humans was apparently sufficient, for Hamlet merely rose with pantherlike grace and gave a luxurious stretch. Then, noticing Darla's glance, he flopped to one side and thrust a rear leg high over his shoulder. He gave a quick lick to the base of his tail—a gesture that Darla had come to consider the feline equivalent of flipping the bird—before rising again and slipping away like a foul-tempered shadow beneath the display of children's pop-up books.

The remainder of the day proceeded relatively smoothly. The old man made a guilt purchase of two hardcover mysteries plus one large-print paperback. Callie's mother made her way to the register, too. A darker blond version of her daughter—they must have gotten the twofer special on the eyeglasses, Darla thought with a smile—she bought three scrapbook magazines and the latest bestseller romance for herself. She also purchased a paperback version of the latest Boy Wizard tome for Callie, who carried it off with the same reverence with which James handled the store's inventory of rare volumes.

Save for the Hamlet incident, the afternoon's biggest excitement came when she'd had to chase a pair of rambunctious toddlers away from the stairs leading to the shop's second level after they momentarily escaped their frazzled father.

"Sorry, kiddos," she told them with a sympathetic look at

the dad, who was trying with minimal success to round them up again, "upstairs is for grown-ups only." Not that the store's second level was chock-full of dangers, but it wasn't child-proof, and the last thing Darla wanted was for a kid to get injured up there.

She directed the boys to the children's section, wondering not for the first time if she should install one of those kid gates at the foot of the stairs to keep her junior patrons from wandering. "How about you play in the story circle while your father shops?"

The story circle had been one of Darla's innovations. She'd rearranged a couple of shelves to create a cozy open spot in the midst of the children's books. A round, sunflower yellow rug defined the area, while seven kid-sized chairs—each a color of the rainbow—formed the actual circle. In its center was an oversized, electric blue beanbag chair where any adult brave enough to breech the area could find a comfortable if not particularly graceful spot to lounge.

Now, the two boys in question made a beeline for the bean-bag, shrieking and flinging themselves onto it like tiny stunt-men taking a fall. Darla grinned. Great-Aunt Dee would have hated the story circle.

Not that Darla disapproved of the store's original décor. The floor plan itself reminded her of what they called a "shot-gun shack" back home, though the elegant Federal-style building in which it was housed was anything but shacklike. Still, one could walk a straight line—or fire a shotgun—from the front door through the shop's main room (originally the brownstone's parlor), through a broad opening that led to the back room (previously the dining room), and all the way to the back door, which in turn led to a tiny courtyard where she often took lunch. And all without hitting a wall.

Well, one could if not for the maze of oak bookshelves filling both rooms, which practically required a map to negotiate.

For Great-Aunt Dee's decorating style had been a cross between a nineteenth-century library and grandma's attic. Rather than having arranged the shelving so as to make opti-mum use of the available space, the old woman had arranged them in clusters interspersed with the occasional tufted stool or cushioned hardback chair. She also had left most of the rooms' original ornately carved wooden built-ins intact, letting them serve as additional shelves as well as display space for old crockery and bric-a-brac. Sections of the parlor's original mahogany wainscoting had been used to build a narrow, U-shaped counter near the front window where the register was located. The overall effect was intimate if a bit claustrophobic.

The upstairs level allowed a bit more breathing space. It, too, was divided into two rooms. The front section, overlooking the street, was a cozy lounge furnished with a couple of overstuffed love seats and four petite wing chairs. The space served as a combination employee break area and the occasional meeting place for writers' groups and book clubs. Appropriately, the walls were decorated with framed pages from old texts and art books, interspersed with photos of various twentieth-century authors. In one corner, behind an ornate, Asian-inspired folding screen, was a small galley kitchen, just a countertop with a sink and microwave, flanked by a mini refrigerator.

The rear room served as the shop's storeroom and was filled with packing materials and cartons of books awaiting shelving. It was not the most convenient of arrangements, but it was the most logical. On those days when Darla expected new shipments from her distributors, she continued a tradition started by her great-aunt and always brought in fresh pastries and coffee-in-a-box to bribe the drivers. Most were willing to haul one or two hand truck's worth of books up to the second floor in return for bear claws and fresh coffee.

Failing that, there was an old-fashioned dumbwaiter that went between floors. It was sturdy enough to accommodate a case of hardcovers or even, say, a fifth-grader, as Darla had happily discovered during one of her rare childhood visits to her great-aunt. She'd forgotten about the dumbwaiter's existence until her store manager had demonstrated how Darla's octogenarian relative had used it to ferry books from storeroom to shelves. While the process was tedious—Darla could mosey downstairs twice as fast as the well-oiled if primitive electric motor could lower the miniature elevator—it beat risking her and her employees' backs shuffling inventory up and down steps.

But any restocking would wait until the next day. A few more of the store's regulars stopped in for their weekly fix of popular fiction, and a number of first-time teenage customers filtered in and out. In fact each day, this week after school let out, she'd had a steady stream of teen girls coming into the store asking about the upcoming signing. For that Sunday night, Pettistone's was set to host an event for the hugely popular YA author Valerie Baylor, whose first two *Haunted High* books had been at the top of every bestseller list for the past year.

Between sales, Darla managed to pack up a couple of signed first editions for one of their mail-order customers. As for Hamlet, he disappeared to wherever it was that he went when he wasn't busy demanding a meal or serving as a tripping hazard.

When, at seven p.m. she flipped the hand-lettered sign in the door to read "Closed"—her late night was Wednesday, with the shop closed on Mondays—her quick mental tally suggested that this particular Friday had actually been a profitable one. Barring major disaster, however, Sunday night was primed to be the mother lode of all profitable sales days, outstripping even Black Friday and Christmas Eve.

"Hey, you wanna grab some food?"

The question came from Jacqueline Martelli, Darla's tenant-slash-friend. She had stopped in just before closing time and was sprawled on the electric blue beanbag chair in the aforementioned story circle area flipping through a Nancy Drew reprint. Jake, as she was better known to the world at large, freely admitted to being within a stone's throw of middle age and so technically didn't belong among the chapter books. Still, used as Darla was to being mistaken for a twenty-something, she had been surprised upon first meeting her to learn that Jake was a few months shy of her fiftieth birthday.

Good genes, just like you, kid, the older woman had explained with a shrug, her strong, olive-toned features under a short mop of curly black hair displaying only a handful of the so-called character lines one expected to find on a woman her age. She spoke with what Darla had always assumed was a clichéd New Jersey accent but had been surprised to find was genuine . . . a linguistic mash-up that was the Sopranos' "dems" and "dose" overlaid with Archie Bunker's "goils" and "turlets." For her part, Jake had been equally amazed that Darla's twangy East Texas drawl bore such little resemblance to the honeyed Deep South accent most New Yorkers assumed dripped from every mouth south of the Mason-Dixon Line.

Jake had readily spilled the most pertinent details of her background the day Darla had moved into the brownstone. An ex-NYC cop, the older woman had been forced to retire on disability following a shoot-out two years earlier that left her with a permanent limp. Even so, at almost six feet tall with a bodybuilder's physique, she remained an imposing presence, the effect enhanced by the straight-legged blue jeans, battered Doc Martens, and bulky sweaters—never in pastel shades— that she habitually wore.

Darla's late aunt had leased the garden-level apartment below the store to Jake at a reduced rate, pleased with the idea of having what she thought of as her own personal bodyguard. In return, Jake served as unofficial security for the building, which included the bookstore on the first and second floors, and what had been Dee Pettistone's living quarters—and now were Darla's—on the third.

It was an arrangement that Darla had been glad to continue. For one thing, as an unattached woman new to the city, she appreciated the built-in company. For another, Jake's blunt manner and sly sense of humor had done much to offset Darla's occasional bouts of homesickness for her friends and family back in Texas these past few months. Thus, despite their apparent differences, the two women had become fast friends.

Now, Darla gave an eager nod in response to the other woman's suggestion.

"Food would be great. Since I was alone here in the store all afternoon, I didn't have time for more than one of those dinky energy bars for lunch. I am famished with a capital 'F.'"

"Where the hell were Lizzie and James?" Jake asked as she rose somewhat awkwardly from the beanbag chair and limped over to where Darla stood at the cash register.

The Lizzie in question was Lizzie Cavanaugh, an earnest middle-aged woman whom Great-Aunt Dee had hired the previous year to help part-time. Divorced and an empty nester—her only son had recently left home to attend college in Boston—Lizzie had elected to return to school to finish an English literature degree program. According to Lizzie, it was the same degree she had abandoned when she met her future ex-husband, an up-and-coming real estate magnate who turned out to have a wandering eye. Lizzie's alimony settlement now allowed her to be a full-time student, working just a few hours a week for the employee discount to feed her book habit.

"Lizzie started classes again, so she can only manage a couple of days a week anymore," Darla explained as she slid the drawer shut and zipped the cash bag closed. "And I gave James the afternoon off, since he has to stay late Sunday night to work the Valerie Baylor autographing. You should know how he is about working events like that."

For Professor James T. James was, to put it mildly, terminally stuffy. A retired English professor (emphasis on nineteenth-century American literature) who also was an expert in rare volumes, he had worked at Pettistone's Fine Books for more than a decade after finally deciding he'd had enough of the academic world. Upon their first meeting, he had made certain that Darla was aware of his scholastic pedigree: an undergraduate degree from a well-known eastern college, and multiple postgraduate degrees earned at an even more prestigious Ivy League university. He'd also taken pains to make certain that she addressed him in the proper manner, given his repetitious first and last names.

"You may call me Professor James," he had instructed. "Or, as you are my employer, you may address me by my Christian name, James. You may not, however, ever call me by my surname sans any honorific. And trust me," he'd added with the practiced stern mien of college professors everywhere, "I *will* know the difference."

"Fair enough," she'd coolly replied, "just so long as you promise never to call me 'Red.'"

Darla's retort had brought one of the few smiles she had yet seen from him, and if they hadn't exactly bonded at that moment, the ice between them had definitely broken. Now, while Darla gave her head a rueful shake at that memory, Jake allowed herself a grin.

"Not exactly Mr. Gala Night, is he?" she agreed. "But I

have to admit that until I talked to my niece the other night, I had no idea how big a score it was, snagging Valerie Baylor. I swear, the kid about peed her pants when I told her I was handling security for the author of the *Haunted High* series! Apparently, she's even hotter with the teenage girls than the woman who writes those sparkly vampire books."

As if Darla didn't know. "I can't take the credit for getting her," she said as she finished powering down the register. "The publisher and Great-Aunt Dee set things up before she died last January. And apparently, Valerie still lives out in the Hamptons on her parents' estate, so it's not like they have to fly her in or anything."

Jake held up a hand. "Wait. You mean, the woman was already filthy rich before her books made her filthy richer?"

"Pretty much," Darla confirmed with a wry smile. "Not exactly the starving-writer-in-the-garret backstory for her."

As Jake listened with obvious interest, she went on, "I don't think any of her official bios even mention her family. All they talk about is how some assistant agent found her manuscript in a slush pile and somehow managed to get a huge bidding war going for an author who'd only ever published a few category romances years ago. It was the whole J. K. Rowling-scribbling-her-books-in-the-coffee-shop scenario. Then some tabloid got wind that she was from money, and the cat was out of the bag after that. But in a way, I guess she did suffer a bit for her art. Apparently, the rest of the rich folk thought being a writer—especially of genre fiction—was considered a bit . . . common for someone of her background."

"Meh, I could suffer that way," Jake retorted with a snort.

Darla winced a little. Though the bookstore business was making merely a modest profit so far, thanks to her inheritance from Great-Aunt Dee, Darla's actual net worth now was rather substantial . . . a far cry from knocking on bankruptcy's door, as she had been only a few months earlier. Of course, most of said worth was tied up in the brownstone—house poor, her father always called it—meaning she still shopped at the discount stores.

Sidestepping that subject, she went on, "Anyhow, my only role is to play fawning bookstore owner and make sure the whole thing goes off without a hitch . . . with your help, of course."

"No hitches, I promise. So, you think she looks that good in person?"

Jake gestured at the advertising poster propped on an easel and surrounded by a veritable turret of the latest *Haunted High* novel artistically stacked in display. The poster was a blowup of the book's cover, a variation on the same stylized image of a translucent teenage girl against a night sky that appeared on all the books in the series. A big "Meet Author Valerie Baylor!" with the day and time was splashed in gothic lettering across the notice, along with a photo of Valerie herself.

Both Darla and Jake surveyed the photo with varying degrees of appreciation. The author's portrait had been carefully staged to capture the same ghostly feel as the novels. It was a starkly lit three-quarters shot that featured a pale woman in her late thirties with cameo features and a broad forehead. Her wavy black hair fell well past her shoulders and partially obscured her face, while the rest of her was wrapped in a black velvet cape. The scarlet fountain pen she held in one white hand and the slash of crimson lipstick she wore provided the only splashes of color in the photo.

Feeling mousy by comparison in her mint green oxford shirt and khaki slacks, her only makeup a hasty swipe of mascara and bit of pink lip gloss, Darla shook her head.

"Guess we'll find out tomorrow," she answered, though the snarky part of her hoped that there'd been at least a little airbrushing involved in creating such a perfect photo.

Gathering her jacket, keys, and purse, she added, "How about you bodyguard me down to the bank night drop? After that, we can grab a bite. What sounds good?"

Jake had picked up one of the local free papers that Darla kept stacked near the register and was flipping through it. She paused at one ad and replied, "Looks like they've still got that special going at that Thai place you like. Why don't we go there, and we can talk about all the last-minute arrangements for the autograph party?"

Darla finished the closing process: window shades down, bathroom checked a final time, all lights off. Finally, she set the alarm, then rushed Jake to the door while the system did its beeping countdown. They had barely stepped out into the cool night air and started down the half dozen balustraded concrete steps leading to the sidewalk, however, when Darla frowned and halted.

"What in the heck is that?"

At first glance, it appeared that the Valerie Baylor photo had come to life right there on Crawford Avenue. Across the street from the bookstore stood a young woman, perhaps twenty years old. Her dyed black hair rippled over her shoulders, while her bloodred smear of lipstick emphasized full lips and contrasted garishly with her deliberately pale features. Little more of her was discernable, since she wore a black cape that covered her from neck to pointed black boots. Instead of the scarlet pen that the author had brandished in her photo, however, this young woman clutched a hand-painted sign.

The wording was barely visible in the dying light: "Valerie Baylor Plagiarized My Story."

"Yeah, I meant to tell you about that," Jake said, her tone apologetic, while Darla stared in growing dismay. The girl stood there motionless, reminding Darla of one of those living statue performance artists she'd seen busking at an art festival she'd attended down in Austin once. "She's been standing there all afternoon. Guess she's not a *Haunted High* fan, even though she looks like a Valerie Baylor doppelganger."

"But what if she's still there Sunday, when Valerie and her entourage arrive? They might cancel the autographing!" Darla's dismay was now wavering on the brink of mild panic. "Can't you have one of your cop friends arrest her for trespassing or something?"

"Technically, we could probably roust her for loitering or for protesting without a permit, but she'll probably find some ACLU backup who would hit back with that whole free-speech thing and make us all look bad. So if she shows up again on Sunday, I say ignore her."

Darla considered Jake's words for a moment, and then nodded. "Yeah, I guess you're right. Even if she's jumping up and down waving that sign of hers, no one will notice her with five hundred fan girls all clamoring to get Valerie's autograph. Without the sign, she'll look like just another fan in costume."

Half an hour later, having taken care of the night drop, the pair headed back to Thai Me Up for the weekly special Jake had suggested. They managed to score a table by the front window. Seated on high stools, they worked their way through appetizers of coconut milk soup while they waited for the rest of their order. Jake finished first, giving a satisfied smack as she pushed away her now-empty cup. Then she glanced out the window.

"I wonder what that whole plagiarizing thing is about," she mused in the direction of where the anonymous girl had been standing down the block.

Darla reluctantly followed her gaze. It was dark enough now that the girl—assuming she was still there—was hidden in the shadows of the brownstone row. *Good, stay hidden until after the autographing*, she thought, sending "go away" vibes in that direction.

Putting aside her own empty soup cup, Darla replied, "It seems like every time someone comes out of nowhere with a blockbuster book, there's half a dozen other people following after them insisting they wrote the story first. There were those guys who claimed *The Da Vinci Code* was lifted from their research, and a couple of other people who swore they wrote about sparkly vampires and boy wizards and single girls in big cities years before they became bestsellers for someone else. Most of the times, their claims are bogus and the similarities coincidental. After all, how many ways are there to describe a vampire or a love scene?"

"Love scene, eh? Well, how about—"

"Or, sometimes it turns out to be true," Darla rushed to cut her friend short, knowing from the other woman's grin that she was prepared to launch into a blush-inducing recital of adjectives to prove Darla wrong. "An author gets behind on a multibook contract and can't seem to come up with a decent idea, so he—or she—figures why not crib part of their story from someone else's book? Preferably one a dozen or so years old and that came and went without much fanfare. A paragraph here, a paragraph there, just enough to get over the rough parts. Most of the times, no one knows, unless a fan happens to have read the book the author stole from and realizes what's happened. If I recall, there were a few juicy lawsuits with some pretty big romance-genre names back in the nineties."

"You sure know a lot about this sort of thing, for someone who only just inherited a bookstore," Jake said, her surprise evident in her lifted brows.

Darla smiled. "You think Great-Aunt Dee would have left me her store if I didn't know jack about books? I've been a voracious reader since first grade. When I was in high school and all the other girls were reading *Tiger Beat* and other teen magazines, I was reading *Publishers Weekly*. And while I was studying for my business degree, I earned a couple of semesters' tuition money working at a big chain bookstore. Heck, I'll even buy supper if you can stump me on an author or book title."

They played that game for a few minutes, with Darla triumphantly giving correct answers each time, much to Jake's exaggerated dismay. They called it quits only when their teenage waitress returned and set down two heaping plates of beef pad thai.

Darla had noticed earlier that the girl wore a pink T-shirt with the title of the first *Haunted High* novel, *Dead But Still Doing Homework*, emblazoned across the front. The title was appropriate, since the lead character in the series was a high school freshman killed in a freak accident on Homecoming night, but who continued to hang out with her friends despite the fact she was now a ghost.

Darla waited until the waitress was headed back toward the kitchen before remarking to Jake, "I hear that this signing is actually part of Valerie Baylor's 'Up Yours' tour."

"Really? Do tell," Jake urged through a mouthful of noodles.

Darla set down her own fork, having had it drummed into her as a child that one did not chew and talk at the same time.

"Remember I told you before that she had published a few category romances? It was about ten or twelve years ago when the first one came out under the name Val Vixen. The books were well reviewed, but she didn't get any sort of push from her publisher, and most of the big book chains turned her down when she asked to do signings in their stores."

"Val Vixen?" Jake gave a considering frown as she slurped down another forkful. "You know, I think I used to read her books. She had a series featuring lady cops that was decent. The first one was pretty funny. A gal breaks up with her fiancé and goes to the police academy, and when she graduates, her first official bust turns out to be her ex. Oh, don't look so shocked," she added with a snort when Darla raised a brow. "You work a high-stress job, you need a little escapist reading."

"No, I think it's great," Darla protested, quite sincerely. Already, she'd seen her share of customers who would load up on the romances but then insist they be bagged so no one else could see what they were buying. The old written-by-women-for-women-so-it's-got-to-be-sneered-at syndrome, she thought, realizing that becoming a bookseller had also raised her feminist sensibilities a few notches.

"Anyhow, only a few of the independents, including Great-Aunt Dee, bothered to host her anytime she had a new book out," she went on. "The publisher finally dropped her after a few books, and she quit writing romance. But when she hit it big with her *Haunted High* series writing as Valerie Baylor, she remembered which stores had treated her right back in the day, and which ones had blown her off. When her new publisher put together her big tour, Valerie told them that the only places she would make appearances were the independent stores and any place where Val Vixen had been allowed to sign. As for everyone else . . . up theirs."

"Good for her," Jake declared through a bite of egg roll. "Sounds like my kind of girl."

"Well, maybe not. Apparently it's not only the bookstores that snubbed her that get the 'up yours' treatment. Rumor is that all the fame and success has gone to her head, and that she's turned into a real bitch on wheels. She travels with a whole entourage—makeup, publicity, personal assistant, even a bodyguard—and all of them hate her guts."

"Meh, a bitch, I can handle. It's those five hundred teenage girls that have me worried," Jake said with a grin. "By the way, did I tell you I've strong-armed an off-duty cop friend of mine to help me work crowd control for you? I think everything is in place now."

She gave Darla a quick rundown of the steps she was taking to keep the potential chaos down to a workable level that weekend.

Given the bookstore's small size, only the first five hundred people in line would receive one of the coveted numbered wristbands that would allow access to the event. That had been fine by Valerie's publicity representative, who said that the author preferred to limit her crowds, so as not to get overwhelmed. The waiting line would start at the bottom of the bookstore's front steps and stretch down the block, with barricades dividing the sidewalk lengthwise, so that regular pedestrian traffic could pass. Jake had also arranged for traffic control in case the sight of several hundred teenage girls proved a driving distraction. To keep the crowd entertained during their wait, Darla planned to have Lizzie periodically hand out trivia quizzes and raffle tickets for drawings of *Haunted High* memorabilia. Inside, they would keep the fans orderly by means of the old velvet-rope routine.

"If we start right at seven and keep the line moving, we should be able to get everyone through by ten o'clock, latest," Jake finished with a satisfied nod. "The outside stuff is already cleared with the city, and the barricades will be delivered Sunday morning. Reese and I will want to do a final sweep of the shop around six, so if you close early at five, we should be fine. Oh, and I've also made arrangements for a couple of patrol cars to make a few extra drive-bys of the area once the signing begins."

They finalized the details over servings of bean curd ice cream; then, sharing mutual groans at their overindulgence, they each paid their own bill and headed back home. Darla breathed a sigh of relief to see that the Lone Protester, as she'd come to think of the Valerie clone, had apparently abandoned her post for the night.

Once they reached the brownstone, Jake waited on the sidewalk while Darla trotted up a second, smaller set of steps situated to the right of the bookstore's main entry. At the top of that stoop was a more modest glass door that opened into her private entrance hall. It was a convenient arrangement in that she didn't need to cut through the store to reach the two flights of stairs leading up to her apartment but could enter directly from the street. Even better, an inner door connected that hallway to the shop, which meant she could travel from home to business at any time of day or night without ever leaving her building. Talk about an easy commute!

After Darla had locked the outer door behind her, she returned the favor by watching through the mottled glass until Jake made her ungainly way down the half dozen steps to her garden apartment, as Jake had informed her the basement dwelling was euphemistically called. Once Jake had flashed the outside light twice—the older woman's signal that she was safely inside—Darla gave a satisfied nod.

"Goils gotta look out for other goils," she reminded herself with a grin as she managed a fair imitation of her friend's streetwise accent. Then, flipping on the replica Tiffany lamp that sat on the hall table, she unlocked her mailbox and grabbed up the handful of mail. A reflexive glance at the blinking red light on the keypad installed beside the door leading into the shop reassured her that the store alarm was properly set. Tucking the mail beneath her arm, she started up the two flights of stairs leading to her apartment.

TWO

BARELY HAD DARLA TAKEN HER FIRST STEP UP THE STAIRS
when a sleek black shadow dashed between her legs and vanished around the curve at the first landing. Heart pounding,
she grabbed for the banister with her free hand and managed
to avoid stumbling.

"Damn it, Hamlet, you sorry little so-and-so!" she yelled
up the steps after him.

The stair race was one of his favorite tricks, along with
burrowing in her underwear drawer, using her jar of expensive
face cream as a soccer ball, and assorted other mischief
designed to torment a hapless human. Bolstered by fond childhood memories of her family's placid orange tabby Topsey,
whose worst offense had been leaving the occasional dead
mouse on the back step, Darla felt certain that none of this was
instinctual cat behavior, but instead was carefully plotted in
Hamlet's little feline brain. As she'd told Jake only the day
before, if the cat had opposable thumbs, he'd be running a
major corporation . . . that, or ruling a third-world country.

By the time she reached the second landing, Hamlet was
already seated like a small deity in front of her apartment
door: body erect, tail tightly wrapped around his body, and
green gaze focused with luminous intensity upon the knob as

if willing it to open. Which, of course, it did when Darla inserted the key.

"Must be nice to have your own personal doorwoman," she muttered, kicking off her shoes and dropping the mail on the antique sideboard. Then, well-trained human that she was, Darla bypassed the combination foyer/living room/dining nook that comprised most of the third floor and obediently followed Hamlet into the sleek galley kitchen. There, she scrubbed out his cut-glass drinking bowl and refilled it with filtered water.

A sharp meow stopped her just as she was about to set it down on his woven grass place mat there in the tiny butler's pantry.

"Sorry, I forgot," she apologized with exaggerated dismay, punching the button on the refrigerator to dispense a handful of ice—crushed, not cubed—into his lordship's drinking water. After checking to make sure his food bowl was full (surprisingly, he preferred the basic store-brand kibble to the fancy stuff in a can), she left Hamlet to his evening repast and flopped down on Great-Aunt Dee's horsehair couch.

As always, Darla also failed to remember that the century-old hide retained something of its original wild nature, in that it had a tendency to poke through clothing and stab at delicate flesh. Grabbing the well-worn quilt that was folded over its curved back, she spread it over the offending cushions and then flopped again, this time with a sigh. She'd not yet eased into a formal evening ritual; in fact, though she'd lived there almost half a year now, the apartment still felt unfamiliar enough to her that she often felt she was merely house-sitting for her aunt and would be hopping on a plane for home in the next few days.

Part of the problem was that, when she'd moved into the place, it had been pretty much as her great-aunt had left it . . . not surprisingly, since the old woman had simply passed away one night in her sleep. Luckily, James and her aunt's friend, Mary Ann, had cleared the kitchen of all perishables and tact-fully disposed of the mattress where she'd breathed her last. But Dee's personal effects had still filled the drawers and shelves for Darla to sort through. She had dutifully taken on the task, alternately chuckling and raising her brows over various of her aunt's possessions she had discovered in the process. She'd also taken an immediate vow to destroy or dispose of anything of her own that she would be embarrassed to have found should *she* suddenly depart life without any warning.

Of course, her late great-aunt's brownstone had not been totally unknown to her when she'd taken up residence there. Back when she was in grade school, she and her mother had occasionally paid visits to New York to see the original Darla Pettistone, after whom Darla had been named. By then, however, her great-aunt was on her third well-to-do husband and had long since shortened her given name to Dee, claiming that "Darla" was too quaint for a woman of her status. She had also abandoned the blond beehive that every good Texas female of her generation had proudly sported, instead wearing her hair cropped fashionably short and hennaed a blinding shade of red that made Darla's auburn hair appear positively subdued in comparison.

Tellingly, though, the old woman had never lost her twangy, and somewhat grammatically challenged, manner of speech.

Those grade-school-era visits had comprised most of perhaps a dozen times that Darla had ever actually met her great-aunt in person, but the two of them had always had a rapport. Even so, learning that, save for several charities, she'd been named the sole heir to the woman's sizeable estate had been such a shock.

But a welcome one, Darla reminded herself. Especially given that after losing her job and having her snake of an ex-husband conveniently declare bankruptcy, leaving her responsible for what remained of their mutual debt, she'd been a couple of weeks from having her home foreclosed upon at the time.

Not wanting to dwell on that unpleasant past, or worry about Sunday night's stellar event, Darla sat up again and took a look at her to-be-read pile on the end table. At the top lay an advance reader copy of the latest *Haunted High* novel, *Ghost of a Chance*, which had languished there for the past couple of weeks. It was the book that Valerie Baylor would be signing Sunday night.

Might as well find out what I'll be selling a thousand copies of this weekend, she told herself with a shrug.

Darla hadn't read the previous two books in the series, but she had read the reviews, so she knew the basic story line: In Book One, *Dead But Still Doing Homework*, the main character, Lani, was killed in a bleacher collapse during a homecoming football game with her school's biggest rivals. Even though the now-ghostly teen realized that she was dead, she found herself unable to move on to her appropriate afterlife destination.

Instead, for reasons Lani didn't understand—at least, not until Book Two, *School Spirit*—the teen ghost was stuck there in the school. She was not alone, however. Her otherworldly companions included other phantom classmates who also had died in strange accidents on school grounds over the years. A few of Lani's grieving friends could actually see her, but her own family and almost everyone else had no clue that her spirit still remained trapped in the school.

"Yep, sound just like my old high school days," Darla muttered with a snort as she flipped open the cover of *Ghost of a Chance* and began to read.

What she expected was a frothy, teen-angsty read enlivened by spooky doings and targeted to a junior high through high school audience . . . entertainment light for the under-twenty set. She got the froth, angst, and scares. But what she also discovered, as she delved deeper into those pages, was a sly and often poignant send-up of the teen years, replete with themes of loss and marginalization designed to resonate with readers of all ages.

About fifty pages in, Darla came up for figurative air and a literal diet cola. Hamlet had long since finished his evening meal and lay sprawled alongside the refrigerator, taking advantage of the marginal heat its energy-efficient motor put out. His snores matched the appliance's soft rumble. The dual sound lent the apartment a surprisingly homey ambiance, she thought with a small smile as, glass in hand, she made her way back to the couch and took up her book again.

As she settled in, however, she couldn't help recalling the girl who'd been standing across the street from the shop. Did the girl really have cause to think that Valerie Baylor had plagiarized her work, as her handmade sign proclaimed? Or was she instead a fan who had crossed the line into angry obsession and now sought to bring down the woman she'd once admired?

"Not my business," she decided.

Darla turned back to the page where she'd left off and read straight through for the next hour. She'd just started the chapter where the ghostly Lani was being pursued through the high school hallways by malevolent beings that had sprung from the frightening Janitor's closet, when the retro princess phone on the end table beside her abruptly rang. The unexpected sound almost sent her leaping off the horsehair couch.

Realizing on the second ring that the obnoxious trill wasn't caused by anything supernatural, Darla swiftly fumbled for the receiver. "Hello?" she gasped out, pressing her free hand to her chest to help slow her heartbeat.

Jake's voice answered. "Darla, are you all right? I just wanted to see if you were in the apartment, or down in the store."

"Nope, just lying here on the couch. Actually, I'm reading the new *Haunted High* book, and it's pretty—"

"Did you go back downstairs recently?" Jake cut her short, sounding concerned. "Maybe to check on something, unpack a few more books?"

"No, why?" Darla sat up, the book forgotten in her lap. "What's wrong?"

"Probably nothing, since the alarm hasn't gone off, but a few minutes ago I thought I heard what sounded like someone walking around upstairs in the store. I went outside to take a look, and I saw a light in the back room go on. And I could have sworn I saw someone moving around in there."

A shiver that had as much to do with her ghostly reading as it did with Jake's troubled words sent gooseflesh down both Darla's arms. Then, almost as swiftly, an explanation occurred to her, and anger supplanted fear. "Oh, crap, do you think one of those fan girls managed to hide out in the store after all?"

"That, or your Great-Aunt Dee is haunting the place. I'm going to grab the spare key and take a look."

"I'll be right down," Darla replied, hanging up before Jake could tell her not to.

Grabbing her keys, she didn't bother with her shoes but hurried out her front door and down the two flights of stairs to the entrance hall below. The LED on the keypad next to the door leading from hall to store now glowed with a solid green light, indicating that Jake must have already deactivated the alarm and gone in. Opening the door slowly, Darla stuck her head inside the shop.

From what Jake had said, she'd expected to see lights blazing. Instead, the only illumination came from the yellow streetlights trickling through the store's front window and from the soft glow from her Tiffany lamp in the hall. Softly she called, "Jake, are you in there?"

"Right here," came the other woman's voice practically in her ear, causing Darla to have her second mini heart attack in almost as many minutes. Jake waved Darla inside the shop, then closed the door after her.

"You hung up on me before I could tell you to stay the hell outside," Jake accused her in the same hushed tone, sounding pretty well ticked. "Rule number one, Nancy Drew . . . never go barging into a dark place when there's an intruder running around. Let the cops do their thing."

"Okay, okay," Darla muttered back. "But what's with the lights? I thought you told me they were on?"

"When I went back outside after calling you, all of them were off again. Now, stay put and don't move!"

With that whispered demand, Jake stepped to the side of the *Haunted High* display and clicked on an oversized police-issue flashlight, sending a blinding stream of white light across the store. She swung the beam toward the back room, where the first editions and collectible volumes were shelved, and then back toward the front door, while Darla strained her eyes and ears to catch any sight or sound. As far as she could tell, however, the floor was empty save for the two of them.

Of course, that didn't mean someone hadn't moved up to the second-floor lounge and storeroom area while Jake was on the phone to her a few moments earlier.

"I'm going to hit the main lights," Jake murmured. "You wait here."

Darla did as instructed, one hand on the doorknob behind her in case she needed to make a strategic retreat. Not that she'd leave Jake alone with an intruder, she told herself. But if someone came flying out from behind the stacks and somehow overpowered Jake, despite the flashlight the size of a club that she was packing, Darla wanted to be able to go for help. On the other hand, if it *was* Great-Aunt Dee's ghost skulking around . . . well, Jake was on her own.

A line of incandescent light fixtures—Great-Aunt Dee had not approved of fluorescent bulbs—abruptly sprang to life above her. Darla squinted against the onslaught of brilliance and scanned the store. Everything appeared in place, and as far as she could see, no one was lurking in the stacks. A glance at the cash register showed it was turned off and closed, just as she'd left it. Jake took a quick look at the register herself before making a swift tour of the back room and then the restroom. Darla made her own brief rounds, peering into those odd corners behind various shelves where she'd known the occasional child customer to conceal himself while his distracted parent was shopping.

"No one here," Jake confirmed as she rejoined Darla a moment later. "I'll try upstairs. Stay by the phone, just in case. If I yell 9-1-1, start dialing."

"Gotcha."

Darla gave a firm nod and hurried over to the register, where the phone was. On the off chance that someone *was* in the store, it had to be one of the fan girls who would doubtless find the formidable Jake more terrifying than any *Haunted High* phantom and give herself up without a fight. She couldn't image a run-of-the-mill burglar breaking in; a bookstore was hardly the place anyone would expect to find significant cash. Even the rare books weren't something one could run down to the pawnshop with and expect to get more than a few dollars for in return. Still, she couldn't help a tremor of nervousness as she watched Jake make her awkward yet resolute way up the steps.

This staircase ran along the wall shared with Darla's hallway and paralleled the one there, save that it went only one floor up. Once, there had been access from the second-floor rooms onto the adjoining landing on Darla's personal stairway. That doorway had been plastered over to separate the four stories into two separate apartments long before Great-Aunt Dee had converted the lower half into her bookstore. This meant that anyone hiding on the second floor would be trapped there, unless she—or he—had squeezed out one of the windows overlooking the street and climbed down the fire escape.

Darla heard the muffled sound of Jake's uneven gait above her, mentally followed the progress of her Docs as they made a zigzag sweep of both rooms above. A few moments later, Jake appeared at the head of the stairs.

"All clear up here," she declared, tucking the flashlight into the back waistband of her jeans and making her careful way down the stairs again. As she reached the bottom step, Darla noticed that Jake clutched a length of dark fabric in one hand.

"The only explanation I can think of is that maybe Hamlet found his way into the shop from your apartment and some-how managed to bump a light switch while playing around on the displays," Jake said. "The alarm was still set when I unlocked the door, and nothing appeared out of place. Well, except this."

She held up the fabric, which turned out to be a hooded black cape similar to the one that the girl on the street had been wearing, and which echoed the one Valerie Baylor wore in her author photo. Except that this cape sported a large "Made in China" tag along one inner seam, and was made of lightweight velour.

"I found this at the top of the stairs," she went on, tossing the cloak to Darla. "Any chance it belongs to you?"

Darla nodded. "Yes, actually. Valerie Baylor's publisher sent us all manner of *Haunted High* promotional items so we employees could join in the dress-up fun during Valerie's appearance."

Darla had managed to lay hands on three of these capes, which had arrived via courier only that morning. Though somehow, she just could not picture the natty James wearing a cheap knockoff cloak over his usual cable-knit vest, hand-made Oxford shirt, and sharp-creased wool trousers. She added, "There should be two more of them hanging up in the storeroom, which is where this one should have been. I don't know how it ended up on the stairs."

"I'm putting in another vote for Hamlet," Jake promptly

replied. "He probably saw it hanging off the peg and managed to drag it down. In fact"—she paused and grinned a little—"I bet that's what I saw moving around the store. He must have gotten wrapped in the cloth and then went racing up and down the stairs trying to untangle himself. The top step is where the cape must finally have fallen off."

"That makes sense . . . at least, more sense than my great-aunt haunting the place," Darla said, shaking out the cape and studying it for signs of damage. The cloth appeared to have escaped unharmed. Folding it over her arm, she went on, "But how did he get into the store? He was upstairs with me the whole time."

Or had he been? Come to think of it, had she seen him since she'd gone into the kitchen for her soda an hour earlier?

Jake shrugged. "A place this old and remodeled a time or two always has a few cat-sized ins and outs. He probably has his own private tunnels all through the building. You think he's snug on his cushion, and he's really out on the town . . . or, rather, out on the town house," she finished with another grin.

Darla grinned back, feeling uncommonly relieved that it was neither ghost nor fan girl who'd been prowling about the place. Still, if Hamlet managed to start setting off the alarm during one of his forays, it could become a problem.

Setting down the cape on the register counter, she said, "Sorry to waste your time, but thanks for coming to the rescue."

"Hey, kid, coming to the rescue is why I pay half the going rate for rent around here," the older woman replied. "But I've got a glass of a nice red waiting on me downstairs, so why don't we lock up the place so I can get out of here?"

"Sounds good. I'll lock up after you and reset the alarm from my hall. Then I'm going to head back upstairs and finish reading my book." Darla paused and gave a sheepish grin. "I can't believe it, but I think I've turned into a Valerie Baylor fan myself."

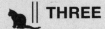 **THREE**

"JAMES, TAKE A LOOK AT THIS."

Darla rose from her spot behind the cash register and handed her store manager a single-spaced, typewritten page, its demure, oyster-colored stock matching its accompanying envelope. The letter had been part of the stack she'd collected the night before but was only now getting to this morning. While the return address had been an unfamiliar one, the Dallas postmark had prompted her to open that correspondence first.

Someone writing from home, had been her first pleased thought.

And so it had been, though the letter's contents had been anything but homey.

James took the proffered page and adjusted his gold-rimmed reading glasses, and then began to read aloud.

Dear Darla: You do not know me, but I am a neighbor of your sister, Linda. She has told me much about you, and the fact that you left your husband and now own a bookstore in New York City, of all places. While I do not APPROVE of such a lifestyle, I myself am also a SINNER and so do not stoop to casting stones. But I cannot remain silent now that I have heard your young nephews telling my children that you have actually invited the author VALERIE BAYLOR to your store to sign her books.

James paused in his narrative to shoot Darla a wry look and then continued reading.

As a Christian, it is my DUTY to warn you that you are about to bring EVIL into your life by allowing THAT WOMAN into your store. Her books are of SATAN! She corrupts YOUNG MINDS with her stories of supernatural beings. If you allow this, then you are as GUILTY as she is in spreading THE DEVIL'S WORD! I have been praying daily that you will see GOD'S LIGHT and cancel this sinful affair. And I must warn you that, if you don't, members of The Lord's Blessing Church will be there to protest MOST VOCIFEROUSLY against you and that woman. Take care for your own soul! Yours in the LORD, Mrs. Bobby Jennings (Marnie).

Darla stood in shocked silence a moment after he'd finished reading. Hearing the words spoken aloud had an even greater impact than seeing them on paper. Finally, she took a calming breath and asked, "So, what do you think?"

"I think the woman has a fixation with the uppercase," James remarked in his usual understated manner as he handed back the letter to her. "But I am confused. I thought you had told me your sister ran off to Seattle, married a grunge musician, and became a corporate lawyer while her spouse stayed home to care for their three children. What is she doing befriending this odd churchwoman?"

"Actually, my sister Brenda is the lawyer . . . and it's Portland, not Seattle. Linda is still back home in Texas. She's the stay-at-home mom with two boys, and her husband is a financial analyst."

Darla grimaced at that last. Said brother-in-law, though a decent enough guy, also happened to be Darla's ex-husband's cousin. That inconvenient relationship had led to a few tense moments those times that her sister had hosted any extended-family get-togethers in the two years following Darla's divorce.

Darla sighed. She had left Texas and taken on the responsibility of her late great-aunt's store knowing full well that times were tough for independent booksellers. It had been a gamble . . . but, as far as she could see, a reasonable one. With nothing but debt (courtesy of her deadbeat ex) and a dwindling job market left to her in Dallas, she had jumped at the opportunity of owning both a home and a business, free and clear.

She hadn't realized just how tough things actually were, however, until she'd started keeping the shop's books. Each month, the gap between black ink and red continued to narrow. While she was still turning a modest profit—James's rare-books expertise and her push into Internet sales had been proving the difference—one bad month and the red ink would begin spurting. The rent she collected from Jake was a nice little bonus, but since the lease terms as negotiated with Great-Aunt Dee were far below the going rate, those payments didn't do much to offset any real drop in store revenues.

The last thing she needed now was a boycott to run off the customers she had!

"Anyhow, I'm sure Linda isn't involved with these Lord's Blessing people," Darla went on, shoving aside her unpleasant memories to concentrate on the new bad stuff. "She and her family attend your basic garden-variety Methodist church. But I did read something about this church in the Dallas paper last year. The congregation decided that a movie theater in a town about thirty miles north of the city was busy doing the devil's work. Apparently, the place showed horror-movie marathons on Friday and Saturday nights. It was a real draw for the local teens."

"Ah, let me guess," James interjected. "Mrs. Jennings and her fellow churchgoers saw evil incarnate and decided that a little soul saving was in order."

"Exactly. They picketed the theater every weekend for two months until most of the kids gave up and quit going to the movies. The owner finally had to shut the place down," Darla finished with a disgusted shake of her red mane.

James gave a genteel snort. "It sounds as if Mrs. Jennings and her fellow fanatics have forgotten that both Old and New Testaments are rife with supernatural happenings far more outlandish than anything you will find in movie theaters or

Ms. Baylor's books. But do not worry. In my estimation, your immortal soul is safe even if you refuse to cancel the signing."

"It isn't exactly my soul that I'm worried about," Darla replied as she took back the offending letter and shoved it into its envelope. "It's my livelihood that concerns me. It's bad enough that we had a girl outside the store yesterday waving a sign accusing Valerie Baylor of plagiarism. What if those church people really do show up here this weekend and raise a stink about the signing? The same thing might happen to us that happened to the theater owner."

"My dear Darla, I can assure you that in this part of the world, such a protest would only increase business. But if you are uncomfortable with that sort of publicity, I will be happy to deal with them for you should they make an appearance."

That last brought a weak smile to Darla's lips. If anyone could handle a group of chanting fanatics, it would be James. Countless semesters of dealing with college students had endowed him with a no-nonsense attitude, while his own self-confessed stint as a sixties activist had taught him all the tricks of the protester trade. And his years in retail had prepared him for anything.

Darla's smile broadened as she recalled James's history with the store. He had assumed the management reins from Great-Aunt Dee after she suffered her first stroke half a dozen years earlier, taking on the responsibility for the day-to-day running of the store right up until her death. Per a provision in the old woman's will, he had continued in that role during the weeks it took to sort out her estate and, eventually, turn the store over to her great-niece.

Quite understandably, he had been somewhat reluctant to relinquish those responsibilities to Darla, no matter that he had reached official retirement age and could easily have supported himself on what he'd once hinted was a generous university pension. But Darla considered herself fortunate that James preferred to keep working. He'd not hesitated to inform her that his expertise buying and selling rare volumes brought in a nice revenue stream, doing much to keep the store going in an era when numerous independent bookstores were shutting their doors. Moreover, he had quite a customer following, despite his acerbic manner and barely veiled disdain for anything he personally did not view as worthy literature.

Recognizing his value to the business, Darla had made the first move by paying him a substantial bonus in recognition of his past contributions. Mollified, he had allowed her to take on the administrative role after a week's intensive training, though she'd insisted he retain the title of manager.

"Perhaps it is better this way, after all," he had conceded once he'd turned over the passwords to the various accounting and inventory spreadsheets. "Now, I can concentrate on fine literature and no longer have to pretend to enjoy selling genre fiction and tell-all books."

With his rich, cultured tones reminiscent of a Richard Burton or a James Earl Jones, James could have easily had a career in voice-overs had he not opted to teach. A couple of decades earlier, he might even have landed a leading man's role had he been interested in a stage career. Now, however, his short-cropped hair and beard were completely gray in stark contrast to his mahogany features, though many of the older female customers—and even some of the younger ones—still considered him quite debonair. And although he was proud to say he'd been active in the Civil Rights movement in his twenties, he did not coddle the current crop of youth who hung out on the various street corners nearby looking menacing and occasionally poking a head inside the store.

"If you wish to shop in this store, you will pull up your pants and shut off your iPods so as not to disturb the other customers," was his standard speech to any young person bold enough to step over the threshold. "And if you would like a recommendation on some uplifting literature, I will be glad to provide it. Otherwise, you may take your business elsewhere."

Darla had watched this scenario perhaps twenty times in her first weeks there, at first with trepidation, and later with appreciation. Usually, the youth in question would spew a few choice epithets before turning on a heel and leaving without incident. A few times, however, the kid in question would actually pull up, shut off, and then come inside. About half of those young folk left with a purchase in hand—perhaps one of Ralph Ellison's works, or something from Twain or Austen or a similar author.

One or two of them had even become regular, discount-card-carrying customers.

Yes, if anyone could handle the Lord's Blessing people, it was Professor James James, Darla reassured herself. Besides, it was already Saturday, and no busload of church people had yet spilled out into the street in front of her store. She glanced at the letter's envelope and saw the postmark was from two days ago. Not much time to organize a cross-country boycott. Perhaps it had all been an empty threat. But as for the Lone Protester . . .

"Lizzie," Darla called as her other employee made a timely if breathless entry through the front door that sent the bells jangling. "Is that girl out there this morning, the one dressed like Valerie Baylor and carrying a sign?"

"Oh, Darla, I am so sorry I'm late," the woman exclaimed, ignoring the question and almost knocking over a display of celebrity cookbooks in her rush to reach the counter.

Lizzie's plump face beneath a chin-length brown bob was flushed, and her pink lipstick was half gone already from her nervous habit of gnawing her lips. She stuffed the oversized canvas tote that held the manuscript she was perpetually rewriting beneath the register; then, with an exaggerated shudder, the middle-aged woman turned back to Darla.

"The bus took forever to get to my stop, and this man there kept watching me the whole time we were waiting," she declared. "Then, when the bus finally showed up, the same creepy guy sat down right behind me, even though there were plenty of other seats. The last straw was when he started breathing on my neck. He made me so nervous that I got off two stops early and walked the rest of the way. Seriously, I'm still looking over my shoulder to make sure he's not there."

"How very unsettling for you," James commented. "Perhaps once you recover from the shock of it, you might take a look at the genre shelves. They could use a bit of restocking." To Darla, he added, "I'll be up in the storeroom finishing inventory if you need me."

So saying, he picked up his coffee cup and started toward the stairs. Lizzie waited until his back was turned and then stuck out her tongue in his direction.

Darla sighed and suppressed the urge to chastise the pair

with a stern, "Play nicely, children." Both were older than she—Lizzie by a decade, and James by a good thirty years!—and yet it seemed that she was the one playing the parental role.

Darla had noticed that over the past few weeks, Lizzie had grown increasingly snippy toward James while he, in turn, had become even more patronizing than usual in his dealings with Lizzie. When previously questioned, each had denied any friction existed between them. Still, looking back, Darla was pretty sure the trouble had begun when Lizzie resumed her college classes and started working only part-time at the store, leaving more of the burden to James.

She suspected the turning point had come when Lizzie had declared one morning that she would soon be a professor just like James had been. What Darla had overheard of James's response had owed more to good old Anglo-Saxon than Latin or Greek, camouflaged though it had been among numerous polysyllabic words. By way of response, Lizzie had turned on the waterworks, and Darla had found herself playing peacekeeper.

Part of the problem, she knew, was that while James retained the store manager title, Darla reserved for herself the final word on hiring and firing. And since Lizzie had been a loyal employee for a couple of years prior to Darla's tenure, and seemed to genuinely enjoy dealing with their customers, Darla was loath to let her go strictly to assuage James's considerable ego. But that didn't mean that Lizzie's drama-llama tendencies didn't get on her nerves on occasion, too.

"I'm sorry you had a fright, Lizzie," she said in a mollifying tone, "but that's to be expected if you use public transportation. What I'm more concerned about is that girl I asked you about. Was she out there?"

"Girl?" Lizzie opened her eyes wide and shook her head, sending the bob swinging. "Cross my heart, Darla, I don't know anything about her. Ooh, customers," she added as the bells on the door jangled, and a young couple walked in. "Gotta go help them out!"

"I didn't ask if you—oh, never mind," Darla muttered to Lizzie's departing form and marched toward the front window to take a look for herself.

The street had been empty of all save the usual Saturday traffic when she'd finally dragged herself out of bed that morning after having stayed up until well after midnight finishing Valerie Baylor's book. Darla allowed herself a rueful smile. The story had sucked her in, pure and simple, and it had been all she could do not to sneak back down to the store and grab copies of the first two in the series so that she could catch up. *Later, after the signing*, she promised herself as she warily peered out onto the street.

She heaved a relieved sigh when she saw no sign of the Lone Protester. Of course, it was only quarter after ten on a Saturday morning. The girl was probably still sleeping, like any normal kid her age. Darla would have slept in even later herself, save that by eight a.m. an unsympathetic Hamlet had reached the caterwauling stage as far as demanding breakfast.

She turned from the window again and shook her head. Just like Lizzie and her bus-stop guy, she'd be peering over her shoulder the rest of the day lest the Lone Protester or the Lord's Blessing congregation make a surprise appearance outside her door.

But over the next few hours, things were busy enough in the store that Darla didn't have much time for over-shoulder peering. Between finalizing arrangements for the Valerie Baylor appearance and a glut of teen customers all trying to snag a copy of *Ghost of a Chance* early—"Sorry, no sales until the autographing tomorrow"—she and her staff kept busy well past lunch. Even Hamlet stayed relatively civil toward the shoppers, save for a small incident with a teacup poodle traveling in its Paris-Hilton-wannabee owner's purse.

The girl—in her midtwenties, and wearing exaggerated eye makeup and a pink dress that, to use one of Jake's expressions, barely covered her lady parts—made the unfortunate error of setting down said purse next to a stack of books. Unfortunately, Hamlet had chosen the spot behind that stack for his postlunch nap.

What happened next was pure Hamlet. The teacup pup had sensed the cat's presence and promptly let loose with a high-pitched bark of challenge. The obnoxious sound caused the feline to open one baleful green eye. He'd not bothered responding, however . . . at least, not until the poodle barked again. This time, Hamlet emitted a hiss that sounded like a cross between a ticked-off lion and a set of air brakes being released. And he'd accompanied that threatening sound with the swipe of a single oversized black paw from around the stack, hitting the purse square on.

The bag had already been sitting dangerously close to the counter's edge. The force of Hamlet's blow sent it skittering so that it now hung halfway off. It took but a single bound from the frightened pup for the inevitable to happen.

Darla had seen what was coming, though, and was already in full-swoop mode. She reached the counter in time to catch the handbag in midfall, saving the feisty dog from a tumble.

"Oh. My. God!" the Paris clone exclaimed in outrage, wheeling about to snatch the purse with its yelping occupant from Darla's grasp. "Your cat nearly killed my puppy!"

"He did no such thing," came Darla's stern rebuke. She pointed to a standup sign on the counter, right next to where the purse had been sitting, and went on, "And if you'd read our policy, you would have known that any pet brought into the store must be held at all times. That same notice is on our front door, too."

"Well, I didn't see it." The young woman gave her head a careless toss and slipped her purse strap over her shoulder, so that the pup was now tucked under her arm. "I think I'd better leave now, before that beast of yours attacks again. You'll be lucky if I don't sue for pain and suffering."

"Pain and suffering, my butt," Darla muttered as the girl stalked her way to the front door. The only one in pain and suffering was the poor dog that was being carted around like an accessory. Why, she had half a mind to—

"Wait!" Lizzie called, trotting past the girl and beating her to the door. Smile bright, she went on, "With all the excitement, you must have forgotten that lovely blue fountain pen you picked up. I know you'll enjoy using it. It's such an elegant writing instrument."

Then, when the girl made no response, Lizzie added, "Cash or charge?" and held out an expectant hand.

The girl hesitated; then, a blush mottling her powdered cheeks, she reached down the neckline of her dress and plucked out a flat, red-velvet-covered case. Thrusting it at

Lizzie, she sputtered, "I forgot to grab a shopping bag and had to put it somewhere while I was looking around. But I've changed my mind. Here," she finished, and then pushed past Lizzie and rushed out the door.

Her smile triumphant now, Lizzie sashayed her way back to the counter while Darla stared at her, openmouthed. "How—how did you know she was shoplifting?" she asked as Lizzie laid the expensive pen upon the counter.

The other woman shrugged. "She didn't look at the back cover of a single book, so I knew right off she wasn't a reader. Then, when I went by the pen display, I saw that one of them was missing. Really, Darla, you need to get a lock for that, no matter what Ms. Pettistone said," she scolded.

Darla nodded her agreement. Great-Aunt Dee had been big on the whole touchy-feely concept for her customers, figuring they were more inclined to purchase a high-end item if they didn't have to track down someone to unlock a case. But given that the pens in question retailed from one hundred dollars on the low end—with the almost-stolen blue one worth more than twice that—Darla had to agree with Lizzie on this one.

"And the dog was part of it, too," the other woman went on with a wise nod. "Even if Hamlet hadn't smacked the purse, she'd put it so close to the edge of the counter that the puppy was bound to make it fall. She was already planning to use it as an excuse to leave, and figured we'd be so upset about the dog that we'd let her go without paying much attention. It's an old shoplifter's trick."

"Wow, good job," Darla told her, most sincerely. "The only shoplifters I ever came across when I worked at the chain were ten-year-old boys sticking comics down the backs of their pants. I guess I'll have to start being a little less trusting."

"Yeah, well." Lizzie shrugged, her smile slipping. "You never know who's going to steal something from you until they do. And then you can't always prove it."

With those cryptic words, she grabbed up the pen once more and headed off to return it to its rightful spot. Darla didn't have time to puzzle over her meaning, for the door jangled again, and another gaggle of teen girls entered, determined looks in their overly made-up eyes. She did, however, discuss the afternoon's events with Jake that night after she'd closed the store and sent her employees home with strict instructions to rest up for tomorrow night.

"Lizzie's right, you never know who might be a shoplifter," Jake agreed as she sipped a diet soda—she told Darla that she never drank the night before a job—rather than her usual glass of red. "That was pretty sharp-eyed of her, catching the woman like that."

They were in Jake's garden apartment, sitting at the 1950s-era chrome kitchen table in her combination living and dining room. That piece of furniture would have looked out of place, except that Jake's entire apartment was decorated with a distinct mid-twentieth-century vibe that reminded Darla of old television sitcoms. From what Jake had told her, the previous tenant had left behind a mishmash of furniture dating from that era. Rather than hauling it all to the curb, however, she'd embraced the style and tied everything together with finds from various thrift shops. From the starburst wall clock to the mod floor-to-ceiling lamp with its three shades that looked like melted red plastic bowls, the décor had a funky kitschy look that usually made Darla smile.

This night, however, any smile was forced as she contemplated how the Valerie Baylor autographing might play out. In her fantasies, it would be a triumph of execution, with La Baylor begging to return to her store with every new book published. But in her nightmares, the dual threats that were the Lone Protester and the Lord's Blessing congregation shut down the event before it even started, reducing Pettistone's Fine Books to pariah status in the eyes of readers and authors alike.

"Don't sweat it, kid," Jake reassured her after she'd voiced those last concerns aloud. "Even if those church people do manage to make their way to Brooklyn, there are plenty of laws saying how they can and can't conduct their protests. We'll handle it for you. Besides, Valerie has probably seen her share of wackaloons claiming that she's written the second coming of *The Satanic Verses*. Like they say, there's no such thing as bad publicity."

Yeah, tell that to the theater owner these particular wackaloons shut down, was Darla's first reflexive thought. But those defeatist words were crowded out by an image that flashed in her mind of Great-Aunt Dee as she'd last seen her almost twenty years ago: short-cropped hair dyed an impossible shade of red that verged on purple, and wrinkled features so heavily powdered that her ruddy complexion looked almost white. Her blue eyes had still been clear as a summer sky in Texas, however, and they'd snapped with intelligent impatience anytime something—or someone—stood in her way. How else had she managed to snag and outlive three wealthy husbands?

Darla hesitated a moment as she contemplated WWDD: *What Would Dee Do?* For sure, the old woman wouldn't sit around dwelling on a bunch of what-ifs and maybes. She'd forge ahead with her own plans and steamroll right over anyone who tried to throw a monkey wrench into the works. Darla could almost hear the woman's unmistakable twang echoing in her mind.

Hell, girl, are you gonna let folks like them tell you how to run this here store of ours?

Feeling abruptly cheered, Darla shook her head. Not just no, but, hell no!

"You're right," she told Jake with a grin and a toast of her diet soda. "There's no such thing as bad publicity. So let's hear it for the Lone Protester and the Lord's Blessing Church."

"To wackaloons," Jake agreed with a clink of her glass. Then she gave Darla a wry smile. "And don't forget the five hundred teenagers who are going to start lining up outside your store at the crack of dawn. Mix them all together, and something tells me that tomorrow's going to be a long, long day."

FOUR

"SOMETHING TELLS ME THAT TODAY IS GOING TO BE A long, long day."

The curt words came from James as he hung up the phone, which had been ringing almost nonstop all morning. The majority of the calls had been from teenage girls wanting to know a) how long the line was already, and b) would Valerie sign more than two books for her since she was Valerie's Biggest Fan Ever. The clipped answers James gave to these questions were a) *very* and b) *no*.

"I know it's a pain, James, but just keep being polite," Darla told him, feeling more than a bit harried herself.

It was barely noon, and already yesterday's positive thoughts were drifting perilously back toward negative territory. Was the payoff for this night's event going to be worth the agony they all already were feeling? The first fans had already been in line at seven a.m. when Darla's alarm clock went off. Girlish squeals had reached all the way to the third floor, sending her rushing to the window to see close to twenty black-caped girls of indeterminate age already queued up at the bottom step.

Fortunately, Valerie's fans had been the only ones lined up. Darla had resigned herself to finding a busload of Bible-carrying activists milling about, so she'd been pleasantly surprised to find the sidewalk free of both Mrs. Bobby Jennings's (a.k.a. Marnie's) fellow congregation members and the presumably unaffiliated but equally unwelcome Lone Protester.

By ten o'clock, when the barricade guy finally showed up, the line of fans had reached the end of the block. Now, with the official barrier in place to keep the crowd in check, Jake had started handing out the coveted wristbands guaranteeing access to the signing that evening.

But though the fans may have been physically contained behind the barricades, their exuberance was not. The sound of laughing and shouting teenage girls was audible inside the store, drowning out the New Age soundtrack Darla had playing. Which meant the actual noise level outside must be getting up there in decibels. Adding to the ruckus were the occasional honks from passing vehicles—traffic control wasn't due for a few more hours—with the inevitable shouted question, "Early for Halloween, aren't you?" The occasional answering middle finger from one of the black-draped girls brought a few pithy comments in return, but none worse than Darla normally heard on a walk through the neighborhood.

Thank God, no one is complaining . . . yet, she thought, mentally crossing her fingers that her fellow shop owners would continue to take the situation in stride.

She'd forewarned her neighbors of the event so they could make their own preparations for the expected crush. Some were fans of Valerie Baylor's and were thrilled to have her in the proximity; others simply saw the influx of hundreds of people, plus the inevitable press that would be covering the event, as a positive. The few who were not with the program simply gritted their teeth and chose to close early rather than weather the fan-girl storm.

"Wow, check this out!"

Lizzie, wearing her official *Haunted High* black cape over a sensible smocked blouse and a pair of mom jeans, held up her phone to display its small screen. A self-proclaimed middle-aged techno geek, she'd had her phone out most of the morning, checking the various social networks to see if word of Valerie's appearance was making the rounds. Hers was one of those high-end models that surfed the Internet, served as a

GPS, took photos and videos . . . and occasionally even was used to make calls.

"Darla, you should be proud. As of now, Pettistone's Fine Books is one of the top trends on Twitter, and we're showing as a hot topic on Alexa," she confirmed. "Oh, and we've had the same number of hits on our website in just the past two hours as we usually get in a month. And that Facebook page for the store that I set up last week already has almost a thousand fans now."

"Well, let's just hope some of that momentum keeps up after Valerie has come and gone," Darla muttered as she rang up the latest celebrity diet book for a bleached blond matron dressed two decades too young for her likely true age. "We could use an infusion of new customers. Not that we don't love all our regular folks," she clarified with a smile for the woman before her.

The customer rolled her heavily made-up eyes. "These teenage girls, what's with them and their ghosts and vampires and wizards? They should try reading something more wholesome like we did when we were kids. Like Nancy Drew."

"So long as they're reading, I'm happy," Darla replied. That catchphrase had become her mantra and kept her from succumbing to James-like snobbery anytime a customer hauled the latest blockbuster movie novelization to the register.

The woman sniffed again in disapproval; then, catching a glimpse of Hamlet lounging behind the counter, her demeanor promptly changed.

"Oh, how cute," she squealed, drawing a cold green squint from the feline in question. "Kitty gets to go to work with Mommy. I bet she's a hard worker, too. What's her name?"

"*His* name is Hamlet," Darla replied, managing not to laugh at the gender confusion and the presumed cuddly relationship between the two of them.

The woman looked suitably impressed. "Oh, is he named after those cats at the Algonquin Hotel?"

Darla had heard this question before. Her customer was referring to the successive feline mascots that had been a tradition for several decades at the New York City landmark hotel. Most of those cats had been named Hamlet, too—though the most recent female holder of that post had broken tradition by being dubbed Matilda. Darla recalled reading of the famous Algonquin cats as a child, but she had forgotten about that quaint tradition until she moved to New York.

Now, she shook her head. "Nope, no relation," she said with a smile. "Our Hamlet came by his name on his own."

The story James had told her was that Hamlet, then a scrawny little kitten, had simply shown up in the store one day. Somehow, without anyone noticing him, he'd managed to pull a volume of Shakespeare down from one of the shelves and made himself a little bed. He was fast asleep on it when Great-Aunt Dee found him, his little paws pointing to the word "Hamlet" on the cover. So, Hamlet he became.

Darla finished checking out the woman, whose Hamlet sighting had seemingly blunted her pique over Valerie Baylor's black-clad fans. Then she excused herself to sign for a UPS package. Lizzie, meanwhile, tucked her cell back into her pocket and began ringing up the next person. James had abandoned his post at the main phone—*I refuse to speak with another crazed sixteen-year-old*, he'd said—and was helping the handful of noncrazed customers who were actually shopping.

Returning from the stockroom after dropping off the package, Darla glanced at her watch again to see that time was doing a pretty fair semblance of freezing. The words "a long, long day" echoed in her mind. Sometimes it was the anticipation and not the actual event that was the killer, she thought with an inner grimace.

"Hold down the fort. I'll be back," Darla told the others and headed out the front door to see how things were going outside.

Controlled mayhem was the best description of what awaited her. All five hundred allowed fans must have been already standing in the line, which wrapped from the front of the store and around the block.

Oh my God, it's like an undertakers' convention, was Darla's first thought upon seeing the sea of black . . . not that the color wasn't already the official uniform of a large percentage of New York City's women. That had been one of the first things she'd noticed after her move there; though, as Jake had pointed out with a grin, the pastels and earth tones that Darla favored made it easy to spot her in a crowd.

But few of the city's stylish black-clad working women wore hooded black capes over long black shifts as did almost every one of these girls of various ages and ethnicities. Darla spotted several random teen boys among the crowd—fans, she wondered, or simply there to pick up girls?—dressed in black to match their female counterparts. And where in the heck had they all found these cloaks, anyhow? She sure hadn't seen any Capes R Us stores back in the malls in Dallas. Clearly New York City had more shops catering to goth outerwear.

Although relatively well behaved, the waiting fans shouted back and forth to each other, swapping red lipsticks and comparing outfits. Since, at Jake's direction, stoops were off-limits for seating, many of the fans were using the barricades as makeshift benches. Most, however, had simply plopped on the concrete sidewalk, their young bones apparently impervious to the late September chill that still seeped from the ground. At regular intervals, the hubbub would be split by one of those distinctive high-pitched shrieks characteristic of pubescent girls, causing nearby window glass to practically vibrate and Darla to fear her ears would spontaneously start bleeding.

Standing guard a few yards down the line was Jake's off-duty cop friend, Reese. He was a tall guy with curly blond hair who looked like he spent a lot of time in the gym. Darla guessed he was a few years younger than she, probably no more than thirty. No doubt when he was in his twenties, he'd been considered a pretty boy.

Still would be, in Darla's opinion, had his nose not been broken in the past and apparently never properly reset, maybe for that very reason. Like Jake and everyone else in line, he was dressed all in black: long-sleeved black denim shirt with sleeves rolled to expose a hint of oversized biceps, black jeans, and black motorcycle boots. Darla figured the attire was less an homage to Valerie Baylor and more a nod to the boys in S.W.A.T. back at the office. His expression, or what she could see of it behind the wraparound sunglasses, reminded her of the blank mien cultivated by the Buckingham Palace guards. She noticed, too, that the older girls in line were shooting him appreciative looks in between arguing over *Haunted High* trivia with their friends.

Darla had met Reese earlier but there hadn't been time for any chitchat, since the barricades were being delivered as he'd showed up. By then the crowd had begun to take on a girlishly moblike air. After a quick hello, he'd swiftly gotten to work, unloading the bright blue sawhorses from the truck and setting them up. Jake, a small electronic megaphone in hand, had begun organizing the waiting fans into a fair semblance of a line behind the ever-lengthening barrier.

"Hey, only about ten more hours of this. Think you can handle it?" Darla called to Reese now, over the sound of the crowd.

The palace guard cracked a smile. "Yeah, what every cop dreams of, spending a day riding herd on hundreds of teenage girls. How about you?"

"I'll tell you that tomorrow, when I know if this day is going to go on the books as a fond memory to savor, or a nightmare to relive again and again."

"As far as crowd control goes, this one's a piece of cake," he assured her. "I could tell you about some genuine nightmares, but this ain't one of them. Don't worry . . . Jake and I have it under control."

His accent was a toned-down version of Jake's, and amusingly at odds with his corn-fed, midwestern looks. His smile revealed a chipped front tooth, possibly a result of the same blow that had done the deed on his nose. Though Darla had always preferred dark-haired, dark-eyed men, she was finding herself more than mildly attracted to this cop. Unfortunately, now was neither the time nor the place to indulge in it.

A tug at her shirtsleeve dispelled any lingering doubt that today was all about business. She looked down to see a familiar pair of large black-framed glasses set on a heart-shaped face staring up at her in concern. The pigtails were absent this day. Instead, the girl's wavy blond hair streamed over the shoulders of her scaled-down black cape, the effect only slightly spoiled by her pink backpack. A crooked application of red lipstick made her look less a vamp, however, and more like she'd just chowed down on one of those big red candied apples from the Texas State Fair.

"Hi, Callie," Darla said with a smile, refraining from commenting on how cute the girl looked dressed as a mini-Valerie. Callie, she suspected, would not appreciate it. "Are you here for the autographing?"

The girl extended one thin wrist to display the bloodred band she wore. "I'm number 137. My sister is number 138. My mom made her and her friends take me with them, but they're pretending they're not with me. That's okay, though, because I brought stuff to read."

Callie's serious expression morphed into one of preteen disdain. "Susanna says I'm too young for the *Haunted High* books, but I read at a college-freshman level. *She* only reads at grade ten. I think she's only ever read about five books in her whole life."

"So long as your mom says it's okay for you to be here, you're fine," Darla replied, feeling a sudden kinship with this über-solemn girl.

She hoped that Susanna was responsible enough to keep an eye on her little sister all day long, as Darla could not. Indicating the man beside her, she added, "I have to get back inside the store now, but if you need anything, this is Reese. He and my friend, Ms. Martelli"—she pointed at Jake, who was heading down the walk toward them, her limp less noticeable because of the stacked boots she wore—"they're in charge of security. If you need help for any reason, you go to them, okay?"

Reese gave the girl a noncommittal nod, obviously wavering between wanting to look accessible yet needing to keep up his tough-guy image. Callie, however, appeared suitably impressed.

"I will." Then, turning to Darla again, she said, "But what about Hamlet? That's what I came to ask. I'm worried he'd be scared by all the people."

"Don't worry about Hamlet. He's been lounging around the store happy as a clam despite the noise. I'll run him back upstairs to my apartment in a little bit. He'll probably sleep the rest of the day and not bother anyone."

Or so she hoped. The last thing this event needed was Mr. Hell on Paws racing about, no matter that he was properly dressed for it. And if he escaped out the front door . . . well, she wasn't sure who she feared for more, Hamlet or the outside world.

Mollified, Callie trudged back to her spot in line.

"Cute kid," Reese commented after her. "But I sure hope for her sake she lightens up by the time she gets to high school. That bookworm thing doesn't go over much with the guys."

"What's wrong with being a bookworm?" Darla demanded, bristling on the girl's behalf. She had been a bookworm herself and had managed to get a few dates despite that.

Reese seemed to realize he'd stepped in it, for he raised both hands in surrender. "Sorry, I didn't mean anything. I'm just not much on wasting my time on books . . . not that there's anything wrong with selling them or anything . . ." He trailed off as he obviously recalled that books were the livelihood of the woman paying his check this day. "Uh, no offense."

"None taken," Darla replied with a brilliantly fake smile.

Barbarian, she inwardly groused, recalling why she never had been attracted to corn-fed blond musclemen. Most of them looked upon a book as nothing more than a handy item to prop up the leg of an uneven couch.

"I'll send Lizzie out with some sandwiches and drinks for you and Jake in a few minutes. In the meantime, keep up the good work, and let me know if any spontaneous outbursts of reading occur, okay?"

Still smiling, she drew aside Jake, who had joined them in time to overhear the last exchange, and muttered in her ear, "So where did you say you found Mr. Literary Guild, here?"

"Hey, he's a good guy," Jake protested mildly as they headed toward the store entrance. "He might not settle in with a book every night like some people, but he has a photographic memory and better street smarts than most cops I know. Not only that, he was the guy who jumped out from behind a squad car and pulled me out of the line of fire the day I was shot. I owe him my life."

Feeling abruptly and suitably chastened, Darla spared another look back at Reese. He'd resumed his tough-guy stance and was dutifully ignoring the occasional "Oooh, baby!" shouted his way by one or another of the girls. In the brief time she'd known Jake, the woman had never given more than the barest details of what had happened that day that ended her police career, but Darla guessed it had been pretty bad. She was more than willing to give Reese the benefit of the doubt now, knowing his role in the affair.

"Besides," Jake added, giving her a friendly nudge in the ribs, "he's damn good-looking. If nothing else, I keep him around just so I can drool over him."

Darla gave a surprised little laugh. Jake had never hinted at any sort of personal relationship, and the only people she'd seen visit the woman besides herself were James and Lizzie. Truth be told, she'd assumed upon their first meeting that Jake batted for the other team, as Darla's terminally unenlightened ex-husband would have put it. Not that Darla cared about the older woman's orientation, nor had Jake ever even hinted at wanting anything more than friendship between the two of them, but she'd just . . . assumed. Now, seeing Jake's obvious appreciation for a guy who reasonably could be termed a hunk, Darla reconsidered. Had she fallen into the age-old trap of stereotyping a strapping female cop?

Aloud, she merely said, "Well, he seems to have everything under control here. You did warn him we might have some unwelcome visitors, didn't you?" she added, referring to the possibility of protesters from two different camps.

Jake nodded. "Don't worry, kid, he's been briefed. Though if any of those people were going to show, they probably would be here by now."

"You're probably right." Darla breathed a small sigh of relief. Surely Jake knew more about this sort of thing than she did. "Anyhow, I'll have those sandwiches out to you in just a bit, after I take Hamlet back upstairs."

The remainder of the afternoon inched by without any incident, save for a steady influx of black-caped girls needing to use the restroom. All too aware of how customers could treat the facilities, Darla had made the girls go in one at a time, threatening to revoke the wristband of anyone who left the area in less-than-pristine condition.

It'll be one hell of a water bill the next month, she thought in resignation, but at least she was pretty sure there would be no need to call out the hazmat crew to take care of things later.

Around four p.m., a brief flurry of shouting and honking almost sent her into a panic until she saw the source was not the

Lord's Blessing gang. Instead—though almost as annoying—a local television news team had showed up to interview some of the fans about the upcoming arrival of their author heroine. *Any publicity* . . . Darla reminded herself, knowing she should welcome what amounted to free advertising.

After about twenty minutes, the reporter and her camerawoman rushed up the steps and into the store. They attempted to buttonhole James first, but he stopped them short with his patented look and pointed in Darla's direction. Taking the hint, the pair hurried over to where Darla was unpacking more copies of *Ghost of a Chance*. Before she could make a pitch for Pettistone's Fine Books, however, the perky blond reporter leaped right into her questions

"It seems not everyone here is a fan of Valerie Baylor. What can you tell us about the girl standing outside holding the sign?" she demanded as she shoved a microphone in Darla's direction.

The Lone Protester was back! Darla felt a sudden surge of panic that manifested itself as a figurative punch to her gut. She managed, however, to hide her dismay as she answered, "Sorry, I don't know anything about it. I suggest you ask her."

"I already did," Perky persisted, her cap-toothed smile widening. "She claims that she found some of the old Val Vixen romances in a used book store and admired her work, so she sent her ghost manuscript to the author to get her opinion. Next thing she knew, her story was being published under Valerie Baylor's name as the first *Haunted High* book."

"That sounds like something you need to ask Valerie or her attorneys," Darla countered, her bright smile matching the reporter's. "I'm just the bookstore owner. That's Pettistone's Fine Books," she reiterated, looking squarely into the camera. "We're in Brooklyn at the intersection of Crawford and—"

"Thanks, that's all we need," the reporter broke in, flipping off the smile as she gave the "cut" signal. "Check out the eleven o'clock news tonight and maybe you'll see yourself."

To her camerawoman, she added, "C'mon, let's go back outside. There was the cutest girl in black glasses all dressed up like the big kids. I want to interview her."

"Sic 'em, Callie," Darla muttered as the pair hightailed it to the door. With any luck, the blunt little girl would keep the reporter occupied for a while. Setting down her box cutter, Darla followed more slowly after them, peering out the window for a look. Sure enough, the Lone Protester stood across the street clutching her sign. This one, however, read, "Valerie Baylor Will Be SORRY She Stole My Book."

"Wow, sounds like a threat," Darla exclaimed. "I hope Valerie brings those bodyguards of hers with her."

"Yeah, well, maybe she deserves something bad to happen to her."

The snide words came from Lizzie, who had joined her at the window. Her normally pleasant features looked downright outraged, and Darla stared at her employee in surprise. True, Lizzie tended to be overdramatic, but Darla had never before seen any true venom from the woman.

Catching her expression, Lizzie gave her chin a stubborn lift. "Really, Darla, don't you keep up with the industry news? I've read more than one rumor that Valerie's lifted plots from other writers. In fact, I, uh, might happen to know someone who, uh, has personal knowledge of it."

Darla frowned as she glanced from Lizzie to the protester and back again. "Do you mean you know that girl out there?"

"Oh no. Certainly not!" Lizzie waved her hands in the universal erase-everything-I-just-said gesture. "Sorry, I was overreacting. I'm just feeling sorry for myself, I guess. I—I got another rejection on my romance novel query yesterday."

Lizzie's brown bob dipped as she lowered her head, and Darla heard an unmistakable sniffle. Impulsively, she gave the woman a hug.

"I'm so sorry. I knew you were still working on your manuscript, but I thought you'd decided to concentrate on getting your master's in feminist literature so you could teach."

"Yeah, well." Lizzie made a furtive swipe at her eyes and managed a crooked smile. "I figured I'd give it one last shot. After all, I've been trying to get that book published for the last ten years, so I didn't want to call it quits until I knew there wasn't any more hope."

"Maybe you can start again in another semester or two with a different project, something new for your thesis," Darla tactfully suggested. "You've got talent. It's just a matter of the right place and right time. You know that."

Her words weren't strictly meant as a balm. A couple of weeks ago, she had read a chapter of Lizzie's book. Darla had found it to be surprisingly well written. Unfortunately for Lizzie and her hopes of publication, though, the plotline and writing style were dated, more typical of the romances that Val Vixen and other writers had put out back when Darla was in college. If Lizzie had been trying to sell the same book for a decade, as she said, chances were she was out of step with the market now.

Lizzie was nodding. "I know. I guess seeing that poor girl standing out there with her sign brought up some bad feelings."

"That poor girl, as you call her, is likely just a delusional fan who made up this whole thing in her head. I'd bet money she's never even been in contact with Valerie Baylor before. If she's not careful, she's going to get slapped with a restraining order."

"You're probably right," Lizzie agreed. Then, with a small self-conscious smile, she added, "Well, I suppose I should 'fess up. Did I ever tell you that *I* know Valerie Baylor? We were in English composition class together back in college."

"Wow," Darla replied, suitably impressed. "The best I've got is that I went to high school with the guy who invented the Eggspert Egg Slicer . . . you know, the commercial you see on late-night television?"

"Of course, she was still Valerie Vickson—*V-i-c-k-s-o-n*—back then," Lizzie went on, apparently underwhelmed by Darla's egg-slicer inventor. "This was before she got married to some snooty rich guy whose last name was Baylor. Of course, the marriage didn't last, but I heard she got a big juicy settlement in the divorce. Not that she needed it, because her family already was richer than God."

Her tone took on a sour note again. "I don't know what she was doing at a state university, slumming with the rest of us," she added. "Maybe she thought it would look better in her author's bio, or maybe she was just researching the little people for her books. Oh, and that whole 'Vixen' thing as her pseudonym was a play on her maiden name. She always told us she thought 'Val Vixen' would look great on a romance novel cover."

Darla had been listening with interest to Lizzie doing her

version of the Biography Channel. Recalling the woman's earlier outburst, she said sympathetically, "I'm guessing you and Valerie weren't best friends, were you? You think she'll remember you?"

"She'd better," Lizzie proclaimed, her smile now bright.

They continued chatting as they finished restocking the display, with Darla keeping an eye on the clock. "James," she called a few minutes later, "can you remind the folks back in the mystery section that we're closing early to get ready for the autographing? Oh, and is Mary Ann here yet?"

Mary Ann Plinski, the same old friend of Great-Aunt Dee's who'd helped out after her death, had volunteered to run the register during the event. She lived next door in an apartment over her brother's antique store, so she could pop in at a moment's notice, and since she'd helped out Dee before, she needed no training on the equipment. She would be the first stop once the eager fans finally made their way inside the store. Each would pay her for up to two books and then present the receipt to Lizzie or James at the signing table, where Valerie would sign their copies.

Mary Ann showed up just as they escorted out the last customer.

"My goodness, those kids are having a wonderful time out there," she exclaimed with a smile after greeting everyone. Though she wore her pewter-hued hair in its usual French twist, she'd gotten into the spirit of things and had donned a vintage 1940s-era black gown that Darla suspected was borrowed from her brother's inventory.

Darla locked the door after the older woman. "Are you sure we won't be keeping you up too late tonight?" she asked her. "We'll probably be here until eleven, maybe later."

"Oh gracious, don't worry about that," Mary Ann declared, waving away Darla's concerns with one wrinkled hand. "You get to be my age, and you don't sleep too much, anyway. I'm always up at all hours, so tonight won't be any different."

The clamor on the sidewalk outside had risen as the time drew closer to the magical Valerie hour. Darla felt her temples begin to thrum, though she wasn't sure if it was from lack of food or from nerves. This was, after all, her first major event since taking ownership of the place. But just in case it was the former, she had that covered.

"Thai food is on the way," she said, earning sounds of gratified approval from her staff. "In the meantime, let's get those bookshelves moved so we can set up the autographing area."

In a bit of clever carpentry, the shelves in the center of the store were all on casters. A flick of a lever unlocked each wheel, so an entire unit could be rolled away without unloading the books, allowing the store's floor plan to be reconfigured with only a bit of effort. Soon enough, they had cleared a broad path down the center of the store. That accomplished, they created a mazelike pathway with the stanchions.

"Pack 'em in here like sardines," Mary Ann said approvingly.

"Ooh, it's like the waiting line for a ride at Disney World," Lizzie declared in satisfaction.

"Or the line going through airport security," James countered, drawing a disapproving moue from the woman, while Darla merely shook her head.

At the rear of the main room, they swiftly set up a table that they covered in black and red cloths, behind which Valerie would sit as she signed books. Lizzie arranged an artful pile of books on either end of the table—they'd be replenishing books all night long from displays and a few dozen more boxes still unopened along the back wall—while Darla moved the easel with its poster into place. For a finishing touch, Mary Ann draped black cloth over the shelving behind the table and covered the folding chair with a properly spooky black slipcover.

"The Thai has arrived," James proclaimed as the women stepped back to admire their handiwork.

Over the next hour, the four of them took turns standing watch over the crowd while Jake and Reese made a runthrough of the store and managed a final break to eat before the evening's excitement began. Lizzie, meanwhile, went outside to hand out the first of the giveaways, an official *Haunted High* trivia sheet. Later would come the silicone bracelets with the various book titles on them, and then the *Haunted*

High pins. When it was her turn to play security guard, Darla pulled on her black cloak and went to check on Callie first thing.

It was almost dark now, but the nearby streetlamps and security lights from the surrounding buildings provided adequate illumination to see what was going on. She found Callie sitting propped against the wall, her pink backpack in her lap as a makeshift table to hold the paperback she was reading. She looked up at Darla's greeting and gave a lopsided smile that showed most of her red lipstick had worn off.

"I'm almost finished reading my second book," she proclaimed over the noise of the teens surrounding her. "It's a good thing I brought three with me. Is Valerie going to be here soon?"

"Any minute now. Did you get something to eat?"

Callie nodded. "Mom packed me enough for lunch and dinner, plus I've got a chocolate bar for dessert. Susanna"— she motioned to the petulant-looking brunette teen standing next to her huddled with two other girls, all three dressed in the requisite black capes—"she had one, too, but she said it would make her fat, so she gave hers to Mr. Reese."

While Darla considered this, Callie scrunched up her small face in concern. "Is Mr. Reese your boyfriend?"

"No, he's just a friend of my friend."

"Whew," the girl exclaimed, making an exaggerated swipe of her hand across her brow. "That's good, because I heard Susanna tell Mimi and Janna that she'd like to jump his bones. That didn't sound very polite, especially not if he already has a girlfriend."

Darla glanced over at the teen in question and smiled sweetly, though she discovered to her surprise that she had to suppress a sudden impulse to give Susanna a good shake. "Don't worry, Callie," she replied through gritted teeth, "Mr. Reese is way too old for your sister. Now, sit tight, and when the line starts moving, I want you to hold on to your sister's hand so you don't get shoved or stepped on. Got it?"

"Got it."

Satisfied for the moment that Callie was taken care of, Darla made her way down the line. She was pleased to see that the crowd continued to be civilized, save for those occasional earsplitting shrieks. She wondered if Jake and Reese had pre-intimidated the crowd into good behavior, or if Valerie's fans were naturally well behaved. Either was fine by her.

Then she glimpsed the Lone Protester in her usual spot, and her good mood dissolved.

FIVE

DARLA TAPPED THE SHOULDER OF ONE OF THE CLOAK-
wearing girls in line. The teen turned her way, displaying a
moderate case of acne and a shock of bleached hair so overly
processed that it would probably ignite if it came within ten
feet of an open flame.

"Yeah."

It was less a question than a statement, but Darla took it as
a conversational opening. "See that girl across the street?" she
asked, pointing. "Do you know who she is, or why she's protesting Valerie?"

The girl smacked her gum and shot a bored look at the still
figure. "I dunno. Some loser, I guess. Why don't you go ask
her?"

A reasonable enough question, Darla wryly told herself.
She had half a mind to march over there and have a few words
with the girl—or send Lizzie out to do the dirty work—but
she wasn't sure what that would accomplish. The last thing
she needed was to get into a brawl with some disgruntled teen
just as Valerie and her entourage were pulling up.

And then there was the problem of physically getting over
there to her.

Valerie Baylor's upcoming appearance was bringing out all

the gawkers, with traffic picking up rather than dwindling as it usually did on a Sunday evening. At least the police were doing a great job with traffic control, and the passing vehicles were moving along at a brisk pace, Darla thought in approval. But that meant crossing the street would be an even dicier prospect than usual. No point risking her life just for the satisfaction of telling off a teenager.

She received similar responses from a few other girls that she questioned, though the last teen added, "She must be stupid. Everyone knows Valerie wrote all those books."

Conceding defeat, Darla started back toward the store, pausing under a streetlight to check her watch. Quarter to seven. Surely, Valerie should be there by now!

Jake met her coming down the stairs. "Any idea where the big star is?"

"No clue, but they have the store's number if they need to call." Glancing up at her apartment window, where a light was burning, she said, "I'm going to run upstairs real fast and check on Hamlet. It's nearly his suppertime, and you know how he gets."

A few moments later, she was unlocking her apartment door. She'd half expected a fleeting swipe of a p.o.'d paw when she walked in, but it seemed his highness had decided against exacting punishment for her tardiness. She flipped on the kitchen light, prepared to see him there by his bowl. Instead, there was no sign of the cat, in the kitchen or anywhere else.

Darla quickly put out food and fresh water and headed back to the door, calling over her shoulder, "You'd better be in here, Hamlet, and not wandering around downstairs. Back soon."

The sound began drifting up to her as she hit the second landing. Frowning, she made it to the first floor, and then realized what it was. Chanting.

"We want Valerie! We want Valerie! We want Valerie!"

"Great," she muttered as, using her key, she let herself into the store via her hallway entrance. No way was she going to run that gauntlet from outer door to outer door! Inside, Lizzie, Mary Ann, and James had their faces pressed to the window. They turned as one when she asked, "Any word?"

James shook his head. "Neither the publicist nor the driver

has called. I put on the radio and heard nothing about any traffic backups. So it seems that they are, in a word, late."

"Great," Darla repeated, managing not to modify the word with the universal adjective. "How are Jake and Reese holding out?"

"Except for the chanting, everything appears under control. But perhaps if you have a contact phone number, you might wish to—"

A cheer erupted from the crowd outside, cutting short James's suggestion. Lizzie, who had still been glued to the window, spun about. Cheeks flushed and black cape swirling, she rushed toward the door while exclaiming the obvious.

"Valerie Baylor is here!"

"YOU WILL FIND PLENTY OF EXTRA PENS HERE, MS. BAYLOR," JAMES said, pointing to a box on the black and red draped table, "and we have a selection of bottled water, as you requested. We also have soft drinks stocked, if you would care for one, or there is freshly brewed coffee, if you prefer. Oh, and the strawberry yogurt and whole wheat bagels with butter you requested are waiting upstairs in our lounge area."

"Actually, what I really want to do is to take a pee and have a smoke, preferably in that order. Point me to the ladies', would you?"

Long black velvet cape swirling, Valerie Baylor sauntered off in the direction James indicated. Darla's first less-than-kind thought upon meeting Valerie had been the satisfied realization that the author's publicity photo had definitely been retouched. Not that Valerie wasn't an attractive woman, despite her theatrical spill of black hair and pale features. In person, however, her cameo features showed the beginnings of middle-aged sag, while the slash of red lipstick emphasized the trademark smoker's wrinkles that radiated from her mouth. But she was dressed for the role, with tight black leather pants and a black silk blouse, along with three-inch red satin pumps that Darla guessed came from Manolo Blahnik or some other trendy designer.

Valerie's entourage included a young woman in a too-short yellow sweater dress who looked like a brunette, grown-up version of Callie, and a chunky Asian man in his fifties, who was wearing designer jeans that appeared to have been both starched and then ironed into sharp-creased submission. It didn't take much imagination to guess that the second man in the group—a bald, buff African American sporting wrap-around shades similar to those Reese was wearing—was the official bodyguard.

"Name's Everest, ma'am, like the mountain," he introduced himself to Darla before taking up position at the front door to serve as a living roadblock.

The final member of Valerie's posse was a model-thin woman with broad shoulders and sleek blond hair almost as long as the author's. Her apparent Botox addiction had left her gaunt face almost expressionless, though her liberal application of makeup was flawless. She opened a satchel from which she now was pulling various pots and tubes of cosmetics and laying them like surgical tools upon the signing table.

The Asian man, meanwhile, stuck out an uncertain hand in Darla's direction.

"Hi, Darla, right? I'm Koji Foster, Valerie's publicist. We've been emailing back and forth." Indicating first the brunette and then the blonde, he went on, "That's Hillary Gables, Valerie's agent, and Mavis, her personal assistant. So sorry we weren't here earlier, but traffic was bad. We'll be ready to start in just a few minutes, I promise."

"Don't worry, we understand. And I'm sure the kids outside do, too," Darla answered, glancing over at the wall clock and noting that it was only quarter after seven. But then, with another look at the cosmetic counter's worth of products the assistant had by now unloaded, she wondered, just how much prep time was the author going to need before she was ready to meet her public?

The screams that had risen from the crowd as Valerie's limo pulled up had rivaled those of the audience at the boy-band concert to which Darla had taken her preteen niece a few years earlier. Flanked by her bodyguard and agent, and wrapped in her signature black cape, the author had graciously waved to the line of ecstatic young women before rushing up the steps to the store, Koji and Mavis trotting after her. She'd favored Darla with a limp handshake and brief greeting before eyeing the autographing area with a jaundiced look in her pale blue eyes that made Darla regret she hadn't sprung for a red carpet or something equally over-the-top.

"The store looks lovely," Hillary spoke up, as if she sensed Darla's concerns, though her distracted gaze was fixed on the closed bathroom door Valerie had disappeared behind. She pulled a tissue from her jacket pocket and snuffled into it. "Sorry, allergies," she explained, tucking the tissue away again. "And I was so sorry to hear about your aunt. I met her once before during another event here and thought she was charming."

"Well, I'm sure she would have gotten a kick out of Val Vixen returning to her store as the famous Valerie Baylor after all these years."

"Much better," Valerie declared as she burst from the restroom and headed back toward the table. Plopping into the slipcovered chair, she added, "Koji, you did make sure the people here know my rules about what I will and won't sign, didn't you? For Chrissakes, we don't need a bunch of little twerps selling scraps of paper with my signature on them all over eBay. And if the press show up, no interviews. They can read what I have to say in my blog. C'mon, Mavis, I need a touch-up."

This last was directed toward the silent assistant, who obediently plucked an oversized satin bib from her bag of tricks and tied it about Valerie's neck before she began applying dramatic smudgy color to the author's lids. She used her array of brushes with the swift expertise of one of those artists on the old PBS how-to-paint television shows, much to Darla's admiration. She herself was still trying to perfect the art of applying mascara without leaving behind a few clumps and smears.

Darla noted in passing that Mavis's hands seemed unusually large for her thin frame, though they fluttered about her client's neck with practiced grace as she adjusted the bib. And she couldn't help but admire the heavy gold puzzle ring the woman wore on one long finger. Darla recalled a far cheaper version of that ring that she'd once bought for herself, having been intrigued by the series of thin interlocked bands that linked together to form what resembled a Celtic knot. Unfortunately, she'd succumbed to temptation and had taken it apart, only to concede after several fruitless hours that she had no clue how to put the darn thing back together again. In frustration, she had given the ring to her then six-year-old niece—and within five minutes, the girl was triumphantly sporting her auntie's reassembled ring on one chubby finger, leaving Darla to shake her head in amazement.

"And make sure you keep things moving this time, Koji," Valerie instructed the publicist as, shadow applied, she rolled her eyes upward for an application of mascara. Shutting them for a dusting of powder, she went on, "I want these kids in and out again as quickly as possible . . . not like the last event. We spent way too much time in that store in Boston. Christ, I had one girl talking to me for almost three minutes before you managed to get her out of my face."

"Don't worry, we'll be moving your readers through here lickety-split," Darla hastened to assure her, not sure whether to laugh or simply be appalled at the woman's cavalier manner toward her fans. "In fact, I have a stopwatch that we use for the writers' critique group that meets here. Maybe I can let Koji borrow it."

She smiled as she said it, intending the suggestion as a mild joke to take the tension down a notch. To her surprise, however, the writer nodded.

"Not a bad idea. Dig it out, why don't you, and we'll get this down to a science." Then, snatching a hand mirror from Mavis, who had finally set aside her brushes, Valerie stared at her retouched reflection a moment before making a sound of disgust.

"For Chrissakes, I'm supposed to look ethereal, not like the Crypt Keeper. No, no, leave it alone," she went on as Mavis attempted a bit of repair with a cosmetic puff. "We don't have time to fix it. I'll just look a hot mess, and who the hell cares?"

Yanking off the bib, she tossed it and the mirror onto the table and shoved back her chair. "God, I need that cigarette now," she announced in Darla's direction. "Is there a place out back I can smoke?"

"Right this way, Ms. Baylor," James smoothly interjected. "We have an enclosed courtyard just behind the store that you can use."

Darla suppressed a smile. The word "courtyard" was a bit fancy for what basically was a walled rectangle of brick-paved space five feet wide and perhaps twice as long that stretched from back door to alley. At its far end was one of those open-style walls—the kind with every other brick missing—which flanked a wrought-iron gate that opened onto the alley. The accoutrements were equally simple: a wrought-iron table with two matching chairs, and a pair of stone urns holding some sort of evergreens topiaried into three stacked balls. Here, Darla and her employees took lunch when the weather was nice, and here Jake indulged in the occasional cigarette herself; that was, when she wasn't in the middle of another attempt to quit.

"Uh, sir, if you don't mind?" This interjection came from the bodyguard, Everest. "I need to check it out first, sir, just to make sure no fans will see her and try to get in that way."

"The space is hardly large enough to fit a mob," James responded, "and the gate locks from the inside. But I understand your concern. You are welcome to make your inspection."

"Jeez, I'm sorry, I forgot that Grandma Everest sees danger lurking behind every lamppost," Valerie said with exaggerated politeness. Then, giving him a proprietary pat on his beefy arm, she added, "Just kidding, Ev. Come along, if you must, but for Chrissakes make it fast so I can hurry up and suck down a bit of nicotine, okay?"

Led by James, the odd couple made their way to the back of the store. Darla could almost hear a collective sigh of relief from everyone—herself included—in the wake of Valerie's departure. What she definitely *did* hear, however, was a single soft word: "Bitch."

Muttered in an unmistakable baritone that seemingly was meant only for her ears, the descriptive made her jump . . . not so much because she disagreed with the sentiment, but because it had come not from Koji, but Mavis. She—or, rather, he—shrugged a skinny shoulder.

"I call them as I see them," he explained in the same soft yet manly tones as he began packing up his gear again.

While Darla struggled a moment in uncomfortable silence—had anyone else heard or noticed what had just happened?—Lizzie shook out the folds of her black cape and brightly proclaimed, "All righty, then. Why don't I bring out some of those refreshments, like James suggested?"

"Good idea," Darla said with a grateful nod in the other woman's direction. To Hillary and Koji, who were pulling on black cloaks of their own, she added, "I'm going to give my folks outside the heads-up that we're almost ready to begin. Can I get anything for you?"

"You might want to grab that stopwatch," Hillary answered with a sour little smile, while Koji blinked nervously. "I can guarantee that if you don't, she'll ask about it."

Could be worse, Darla told herself as she headed to the front. At least Valerie hadn't asked for a bevy of male strippers and a tub of M&Ms with all the yellow ones picked out. She peered out the door only to wince as the fans' Valerie chant began anew.

"Almost ready," Darla yelled to a waiting Jake. "Give us five, okay?"

Having apparently blessed the miniscule courtyard as being safe for his charge, Everest had now returned to his post. A few minutes later, Valerie also returned, trailing a noticeable odor of cigarette smoke after her but looking surprisingly cheerful. Settling into her chair, she said to Darla, "That's one cute kitty you have out there. We had a nice little chat."

"You mean Hamlet?" she asked in dismay. *How in the hell did the little bugger get out?* "Solid black with green eyes, about the size of a small horse?"

"That's him. What a sweetheart." Glancing over at her assistant, she added, "Mavis adores cats, too. May, darling, you really should go out and take a look at him. He's a cutie."

Valerie's smile was genuine, and Darla reluctantly found herself revising her opinion of the woman. If she liked cats, she couldn't be all bad. Then again, she was talking about Hamlet . . . maybe the pair of them had simply recognized kindred evil spirits and had bonded over some secret blood ritual.

"Sure, maybe later," Mavis agreed with a hint of a smile and in a soft soprano that made Darla do a mental double take. Surely she hadn't imagined the masculine voice that had come from the assistant just a few minutes earlier? "Excuse me,

Valerie," Lizzie interjected, a stack of the author's books in her arms. "James asked if you'd sign a few of these for the store real quick while we queue up the first group of readers."

"Sure, sure."

Flipping open the first one, Valerie scrawled her name in sharp letters. Lizzie, meanwhile, expertly ran through the rest of the stack, tucking each dust jacket flap like a bookmark at each title page so that the author didn't have to fumble for the right spot in the book to sign her name. As for James, he had pulled a camera from his vest pocket and clicked away while Valerie wielded her pen.

Always get the author to sign some store copies first, James had reminded them both earlier in the day. *Otherwise, if you wait until the end of the event, your author invariably has writer's cramp and the signatures are almost illegible.*

Which made sense, Darla thought. After three hours of dashing off one's name, it was inevitable that the quality control would go down. Despite James's disdain for genre fiction, he knew the value of a signed first edition to fans of a particular author. Valerie finished signing the last one with a flourish and then set down her pen. She frowned a bit at Lizzie, who stood clutching the signed stack, an expectant look on her face. "Was there something else?"

Lizzie gave an eager nod, though it seemed to Darla that her expression had taken on a strained air. "Actually, I wanted to see if you remembered me. I'm Lizzie Cavanaugh. We took an Intro to Novel Writing class together back in college. Professor Jardin's night class."

"I recall the class, but I'm afraid I don't remember you. Did we ever talk?"

"I sat right next to you. We were in the same critique group for the class project." When Valerie continued to stare blankly, Lizzie persisted in a sharp tone, "You read my work in process, about a girl who breaks up with her fiancé and decides to go to the police academy. I'm sure you remember that."

"If you say so, Lisa," the author agreed with a careless shrug, while Darla cringed a little on her employee's behalf, "but I'm afraid I don't recall your book, or you. Of course, that was quite some time ago, and it was a large class, wasn't it?"

"It's Lizzie. And, yes, twenty people . . . really large."

Head high and cape swirling, Lizzie marched over to the register and tucked the signed books under the counter. Recalling their earlier conversation about her college days, Darla could imagine that if Valerie had treated Lizzie the same casually cruel way when they were students together, no wonder Lizzie had a chip on her shoulder about the woman.

Valerie merely blinked, and turned to her publicist.

"For Chrissakes, what are we waiting for? Let's get this show on the road."

Darla didn't wait for further encouragement. Grabbing up her own black cape and pulling it on, she propped open the store's front door and called down to Jake and Reese, "We're ready."

Spontaneous applause rose from those closest to the front of the line, and though it was not meant for her, Darla felt a small thrill sweep her anyhow. *So this is what it's like to have a fan base*, she thought with a grin. Maybe being famous wasn't a half-bad gig after all.

From her post at the top of the stairs, Darla could see the movement begin at the rear of the line and ripple forward. The sight reminded her of the train station scene in the old Hitchcock movie where Cary Grant's falsely accused character disguises himself as a redcap and disappears into a veritable sea of scarlet-hatted porters, to the dismay of the police in pursuit. She could picture a teen on her cell phone trying to get hold of her BFF to let her know where she was this night.

Hey, Tiff, I'm here in line at the bookstore. You'll find me, no problem. Look for the girl wearing a long black cloak and red lipstick.

But as the whooping and laughing fans began rushing toward the door, Darla realized with a jolt that perhaps she'd made a tactical error in not getting out of the way sooner. Everest, however, had obviously done this kind of thing before. Before she could move, he had slid into place in front of her. At more than six feet tall and well over three hundred pounds, his mere presence was enough to halt the girls at the threshold.

"Ladies, show me your bracelets," he ordered, getting what looked like a Black Power salute in return as the front of the pack simultaneously raised their fists to display the bands in question. "Thank you. Now, we're going to do this quietly, and in order. You young ladies walk inside in a nice line, hear?"

They heard. As soon as Everest stepped aside, the girls marched into the store with almost military precision, walking two abreast to the register to pay, and then winding through the maze toward the table where Valerie awaited. Darla saw him doing a head count as well, allowing in perhaps forty of them before cutting off the procession at the threshold.

"You'll have a maximum occupancy here, ma'am," he told her with a professional nod, his single diamond earring catching the light. "Don't want any problems with the fire marshal."

Darla gave him a grateful smile and went inside. The air of orderliness that Everest had imposed continued to hold, though within half an hour the noise level had risen substantially. That was to be expected, so she grinned and bore it. Lizzie and James were working the table, passing books down to Valerie with almost automated precision, while the constant camera flashes lit up the place like a disco. Mary Ann played the register with professional panache while chatting up the teens, several of whom proposed to buy her dress on the spot. The elderly woman smilingly declined all offers but passed out business cards with her brother's store's website so they could join her special vintage clothing email newsletter.

"Oh yes, I'm quite the social networker," Darla overheard her tell one teen who had expressed surprise that someone of Mary Ann's generation had an email address, let alone actually communicated in that fashion.

And so, with all positions filled, Darla was left with little to do but supervise.

"I'm going to go check on Jake and Reese," she called to Mary Ann, and then squeezed her way through the caped throng to the door.

A cool breeze swept her like a literal breath of fresh air, and she inhaled deeply. Though her black cape was but a cheap knockoff, it made a pretty effective blanket . . . nice out here in the early autumn night, but stifling in the crowded store. At the bottom of the stairs, she spied a familiar pink backpack and waved to Callie, who jumped up and down and waved back. With a final smile for the girl, Darla turned her attention to the rest of the line.

While it seemed that Hillary and Koji—stopwatch or not—were keeping things moving in the store, the line here on the street didn't seem to be getting much shorter. Though the barricades still remained in place, it appeared from Darla's vantage point that the blue sawhorses had steadily shifted. The line was no longer a neat, single file affair, but rather an untidy column three and four abreast in some spots.

Moreover, a new wrinkle had been added to the festivities. The Lone Protester had abandoned her post across the street and was now walking up and down the line of Valerie's fans, her sign held high. That one-woman demonstration was not going unnoticed by the faithful, for Darla could hear a few vulgarities being shouted over the general backdrop of noise.

She barely had time to tell herself, *Trouble waiting to happen*, when it did.

SIX

TWO OF THE FAN GIRLS REACHED OVER THE BARRICADE
and grabbed at the Lone Protester's poster. The tug-of-war
that ensued was over almost before it began, however, for Jake
was already headed in that direction.

As Darla watched in relief, the woman swooped down
upon the girls and promptly broke up what might have turned
into a small melee. Darla was too far away to hear what was
said afterward, but from the resulting pantomime, it was clear
that Jake was laying down the law to the two who'd instigated
the incident. As for the protester, Jake didn't let her off
unscathed, either, but was pointing her back toward the opposite side of the street.

Let this night be over, and soon, Darla found herself praying to the gods of literature.

She waited awhile longer to see if any other disasters
might befall the crowd. When relative peace seemed to be
reigning, however, she went back inside, only to discover that
the earlier snail-like pace of the line had slowed to positively
glacial. The party atmosphere, however, had not abated. She
noticed with an inner grin that Callie, who was now halfway
through the line, was busy snapping a covert picture of her
sister, who had bent to look at another fan's tattooed ankle.

"Why did the line quit moving? Is everything okay?" Darla asked Mary Ann.

The older woman nodded. "Ms. Baylor said she needed a break."

She glanced around to see if the girls nearby were paying attention; then, in an exaggerated stage whisper, she added, "I think she went out back to have a smoke."

"She just had one!" Darla pointed out and shook her head. If Valerie was going to take a smoke break every hour, it would make an already long night longer.

She headed toward the back and found the signing table abandoned except for James. As for Lizzie, Darla thought she saw her at the front of the line, chatting with a couple of the teens. Of course, since everyone was cloaked and hooded, it was hard to know for sure. Neither Hillary nor Koji were anywhere to be seen. Probably on a bathroom break while the boss lady was doing her thing, she guessed. Mavis had vanished as well . . . hiding upstairs away from the crowds? Darla stood tapping her foot for a few minutes longer. Tempted as she was to head out to the courtyard and drag the author back inside, she knew that tactic would not go over well. Better she head out front again and let Jake and Reese know they might be in for a longer stint than they'd anticipated.

As she opened the door, another welcome breeze swept past her, carrying with it the familiar shrieks of laughter and waves of chatter. Passing traffic and the incessant flash of phone cameras lent a strobe effect to the scene. Darla was reminded of those horror movies deliberately filmed to look like home videos taken by someone with a bad case of the shakes. She could feel a headache coming on; fortunately, she had an almost full bottle of aspirin tucked under the counter.

Darla had just popped two tablets and squeezed her way past Everest, when over the ambient noise, she heard a single, earsplitting squeal of rubber.

It took her only a heartbeat to realize what that sound meant. By then, a small passenger van was stopped about halfway down the block on the side of the street closest to where Valerie's fans were gathered. Behind it, half a dozen other cars had plowed to a halt, horns blaring. Reese was sprinting from one direction toward the van, while Jake was rushing from the other. Vaguely, Darla was aware that the crowd noise had faded to a murmur, while the sound of her heart beating double time seemed suddenly louder than even the honking horns. She was running toward the van now, while a frantic voice in her head cried, *Don't let it be that, dear God, don't let it be that.*

Some of the teens had spilled over the barricades, and Darla had to shove her way through them. Only then was she close enough to see what the light from the van's one unbroken headlamp revealed upon the asphalt. Her step faltered. For a moment, she feared she might sag to the sidewalk.

She managed to keep her balance by focusing her attention on Jake, who had her cell phone to his ear and was shouting something into it. Darla noted that the van's front two doors had sprung open, with the driver and several passengers now huddling behind the twin shields of steel as if warding off the sight before them. Darla didn't blame them. Just like them, she didn't want to gaze at the motionless figure tangled in a long black cape that lay sprawled a few feet in front of the van, one limp arm pointing toward a rectangle of white cardboard farther down the pavement.

A few girlish screams promptly rose from those closest to the scene. The cries echoed down the length of the line and were punctuated now by the repeated pulse of a police siren, no doubt courtesy of the traffic-control cop. One of the caped fans, more responsible than the others, had already leaped into the street to check on the fallen girl. Reese pushed the fan aside and knelt beneath the headlight's harsh gleam. After a quick check, he glanced back up at Jake to give a swift shake of his head.

Darla stared in disbelief. Shouldn't he be giving her mouth-to-mouth or chest compressions or something? But when Reese scrambled to his feet, she realized that the girl must already be past saving.

She watched as he stripped off his black denim shirt, revealing a tight black T-shirt printed with the words NYPD and POLICE, as well as a gold badge that dangled from a lanyard around his neck. The sight spurred her back to action. She shoved her way to the curb and caught his eye.

"Can I help?" she called in a tremulous voice, hoping she could be heard over the hubbub.

He shook his head but tossed his long-sleeved shirt in her direction. She caught it and tucked the garment under one arm, not sure whether to be insulted or relieved that apparently her only role in this catastrophe would be to serve as valet.

Reese, meanwhile, raised his badge at the crowd, the metal gleaming as it reflected the van's single headlight beam.

"Quiet down!" he commanded, his free hand making the universal take-it-down-a-notch gesture. "This is now a police investigation. I need everyone to back up and take a seat on the sidewalk. No talking above a whisper, and remain in line until we say you can go. Anyone who saw the accident or what happened beforehand, we'll be coming by in a bit to take your statements."

He swiftly moved down the line repeating the same instructions, his voice all but drowned out by the shriek of still more sirens and the occasional blast of a horn from someone who hadn't yet figured out that traffic wasn't going anywhere anytime soon. Luckily, the majority of the fan girls appeared too stunned by what had just occurred to do anything other than obey orders. Sitting cross-legged and tightly wrapped in their cloaks—the evening had taken on a distinct chill now—they huddled in small groups.

Jake, meanwhile, was dragging some of the barricades from the sidewalk to block off the accident site. Tying Reese's shirt around her waist, Darla rushed to help her.

"I can't believe this happened," the older woman exclaimed in a low tone as they maneuvered another sawhorse into place. "I sent that girl back across the street not ten minutes ago. What in the hell was she doing back on this side?"

"It's not your fault, Jake. You told her to stay away. It was her choice to come back," Darla protested in a voice that was little better than a gasp.

The small exertion of hauling the barricade combined with her earlier light-headedness, so that she felt as if she'd just run a marathon. She felt perilously close to collapsing onto the asphalt in a puddle of tears. Jake, who likely had seen such reactions around accident scenes before, took note of Darla's faltering composure and promptly pointed her back toward the shop.

"Kid, you're not going to do me a damn bit of good if you pass out here on the street," the woman told her, not unkindly.

"Get your butt back inside and let Valerie and her people know what's happened. They can finish up with the girls already in the store, but we'll be shutting things down after that. Besides, more help than we'll ever need will be here in a minute."

Right on cue, a pair of highway patrol cars with their distinctive high-rise light bars on their roofs nosed past the stopped traffic and joined the first police vehicle parked now alongside the van. A minute later, two motorcycle officers roared up, the rumble of their Harleys echoing off the buildings. Thankfully, they'd all shut off their sirens, but their blue and red lights continued to strobe off the rows of brownstones on either side of the street. Their headlights further illuminated the area, so that the entire accident scene now was visible in harsh relief. The ambulance hadn't yet arrived, but under the circumstances, there was no big hurry . . . not anymore.

Darla took a deep, steadying breath and nodded. "I'm okay now," she insisted. "But you're right. I've got to tell them what's going on."

She headed at a quick pace back toward the shop, hearing behind her the sounds of the uniformed police taking control of the situation, while still more sirens howled in the distance. Pushing her none-too-gentle way past the girls camped out on the steps, she all but stumbled into Everest, who was still keeping guard at the door.

"Bad news, ma'am?" he asked in a resigned voice that said he already knew that answer.

His height, combined with his position on the stairway, would easily have given him a bird's-eye view of the accident scene. Darla glanced back in that same direction to see another police car had arrived, while the ambulance was now at the end of the block. The boxy vehicle eased its way through the street with the occasional pulse of its siren to clear the way. She noted that the news truck, which earlier had been parked across the way while the reporter interviewed the waiting fans, had returned. In another fifteen minutes, news of the accident would be all over television, not to mention the Internet. Hell, doubtless most of the girls in line were already Tweeting comments and pictures that were being read and seen by millions.

Darla bit back a few choice curses. Horrible as she felt at the knowledge that a young woman had died almost on her doorstep, she couldn't suppress an equal surge of dismay at the realization that all this was going to be very, very bad for business. Death had a way of scaring off paying customers. Why in the hell hadn't the girl pulled her stunt over at Barnes and Noble?

Tamping down that unworthy thought, she turned back to Everest and nodded. "The girl who was protesting the autographing was hit and killed by a van. I need to tell Valerie and the others. Don't let any more fans go inside the store, okay?"

Everest grunted his assent, his stern dark features settling into grim lines. No doubt he figured this was bad for his business, too, no matter how peripherally he was involved. Leaving him to stand guard, Darla slipped past the door and into the shop.

Mary Ann was right there, and her small soft hand promptly clutched Darla's arm. "My gracious, what's going on?" she whispered in alarm. "We heard all the sirens and could see the flashing lights through the windows."

In fact, the emergency lights still flashed like blue and red lightning beyond the glass, while the muffled sounds of a distant siren and the brief bark from a bullhorn could be heard even inside the store. "I'm afraid there was an accident," she replied, gently prying the old woman's fingers from her wrist. "Come with me, and you can hear the details when I tell Valerie and her people."

Sidestepping the maze, she took the direct route toward the back of the room, swiftly assessing the small crowd as she passed them. The fans murmured restively as they waited in line, aware that something was amiss but not knowing what. Darla spotted Callie, looking very young in her severe black cape as she clutched her copy of Valerie's latest novel. The official entourage had returned from their respective breaks, and everyone was in his or her proper place around the table. The only one still missing was the author.

"Where's Valerie?" Darla asked Hillary, who was busy checking her iPhone.

"Still outside polluting the air," she replied with a shrug. "What's going on out front?"

Darla eyed the nearby fans and pulled Hillary and Koji aside. "There's been a bad accident. Let me run and get Valerie, and I'll make the announcement to everyone in the store at one time."

She hurried toward the back door, Koji on her heels. Like Everest, he doubtless considered any incident part of his job.

The pungent odor of cigarette smoke assailed her as they slipped outside. "Valerie? Ms. Baylor?" Darla softly called as she peered about the small courtyard, "Can you come in for—"

She broke off at the twin realizations that the darkened enclosure was empty and that the gate leading into the alley was wide open. Very slowly, she turned to Koji and said in a small voice, "Are you sure she didn't come back into the store?"

The publicist gave her a stricken look. "She said she wanted a cigarette. Sh-she does that a lot."

He stood there uncertainly, but Darla didn't hesitate. Pushing past him, she rushed to the gate and went running into the small alley. The faint odors of old garbage and recent urine assailed her, but she ignored them as she ran the short distance to the street and then hooked a turn back toward Crawford Avenue and the kaleidoscope of emergency lights. The ambulance was there at the accident scene now, its two EMTs preparing to make what likely was a perfunctory check of the victim still sprawled prostrate on the road.

The same earlier voice of doom was shrieking in Darla's head again. *No way,* she tried to reassure herself, even as she knew with sudden dread and certainty where her missing author had disappeared to. She reached Jake's side just as one of the paramedics rolled the still form to one side, and the array of headlights illuminated the victim's face, along with a pair of red Manolo Blahnik pumps that lay nearby.

Darla's reflexive scream was muffled by her hands as she clamped numb fingers over her mouth, but half a dozen of the closest fan girls were not so inhibited. A collective shriek of anguish rose from the direction of the sidewalk. Louder still was a single heartrending cry from one of the girls who'd also caught a glimpse of the dead woman's slack features.

"Oh my God, it's Valerie Baylor!"

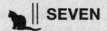 **SEVEN**

THREE EMPTY TISSUE BOXES SAT IN THE CENTER OF THE table, while the tiny wastebasket Darla had commandeered from the restroom overflowed now with soggy Kleenex. The refuse served as mute testament to the torrent of emotion that had washed through the store a couple of hours earlier, right after Darla announced in somber tones that Valerie Baylor had just been killed after stepping into the path of a van while outside taking a break.

Darla sighed, remembering the reaction to her pronouncement: total pandemonium. A communal shriek rose from the three dozen or so fan girls there in the store. A good third of them collapsed onto the floor upon hearing the news, causing Lizzie and Mary Ann to rush to their collective aid with motherly words of comfort. Most of the remainder simply gave way to noisy sobs, though a few of the girls hurried for the door, apparently intent on mourning at their idol's dead feet.

Ever the professional, Everest had blocked the exit with his substantial bulk, and Koji had joined him, though the tears running down the publicist's round cheeks had made him look anything but formidable beside the larger man. Fearing that the girls still might struggle past and tumble into the street just as Valerie had, Darla had rushed to assist the pair. With a bit of strong-arm help from the bodyguard, she had managed to convince the weeping girls to sit in a circle on the floor and take deep breaths until they had sufficiently recovered themselves to be trusted not to make some melodramatic gesture.

Her next concern had been for Callie. The girl's sister, Susanna, and Susanna's two BFFs had promptly joined in the general wailing. Callie, however, had stood silently by, looking like one of those hooded medieval cemetery statues as she clutched her unsigned novel. Tears ran down her thin cheeks and washed away the last traces of her red lipstick. Unsure how best to comfort the girl, Darla had gone with the tried and true, and given her a hug.

Callie had allowed this familiarity for a few moments. Then, firmly if politely pulling away, she said in a small voice, "I want my mommy."

Since Darla had been thinking along much the same lines herself, she gave the girl a sympathetic nod. "Hold on a few minutes longer, honey, and I'll ask Mr. Reese if it's OK for you and Susanna to go home."

It took longer than a few minutes, however, for Darla to keep that promise. Between the police and EMTs and reporters, not to mention almost five hundred teenage girls in various states of hysteria, Reese and Jake had plenty on their hands outside for the moment. Darla decided to let things settle down before seeing about sending everyone in the store home.

She next turned her attention to Valerie's entourage. Both Hillary and Koji had whipped out their respective cell phones, and from snippets of overheard conversation Darla assumed they were notifying various people of the situation. She'd expected shock, or even dismay—after all, at least two of the four had just lost their respective jobs with no Valerie to guard or gussy up—but to her surprise, they all seemed struck by genuine grief.

Mavis had broken down into delicate sobs, his broad shoulders shaking as he buried his face in his large hands, while Hillary sniffled into the tissues that Lizzie had prudently fetched from the storeroom. Though he remained dry-eyed as befitted his job, Everest wore the guilty expression of a man who realized that he had, in the end, failed to keep his charge safe. Darla noticed him give a discreet honk into his crisp linen handkerchief. As for Koji, the lost expression he wore better befitted a boy than a middle-aged man.

Had she been mistaken in her judgment regarding the author? Had Valerie actually been a paragon rather than a pain?

Darla swiped at an unexpected tear of her own, while a glance at Lizzie and Mary Ann showed both women dabbing at their eyes, too. Mass hysteria, perhaps? It was hard *not* to be swept away by the emotion permeating the room, she rationalized, given the sheer volume of tears being shed by the author's fans.

For now, however, her mission was to keep the teen fans under control. At her urging, James had begun reading aloud from Valerie's latest novel. While no fan of the *Haunted High* series, the retired professor could never resist an audience; the soothing tones of his melodious baritone soon reduced the chorus of sobs to muffled sniffles.

After perhaps an hour, a grim-faced Jake had come into the shop to advise Darla that the fans could all be on their way. "But the police will have some questions for the rest of you," she added, her gaze encompassing Darla's people as well as Valerie's. "So make yourselves comfortable here awhile longer."

Most of the fans outside had dispersed, save for a handful of those who'd been closest to the spot where Valerie had met her dramatic end. Reese was still taking notes, and Darla wondered how many pages he'd gone through so far. The reports doubtless would make for some substantial reading for someone who professed never to crack open a book, Darla thought with a momentary lapse into snark. Then, chiding herself for being petty at such a time, she concentrated on escorting out the fans, particularly Callie and the other three girls.

Traffic outside had slowed to near glacial upon reaching the flashing police lights. Those seeking a quick thrill would be disappointed, for the police vehicles and a hastily erected barrier assembled from sawhorses covered with tarps blocked their view. To Darla's relief, Valerie's body had been removed.

Unfortunately, the area where she'd landed was now marked with Day-Glo spots of spray paint, and the accident investigators were still measuring and photographing the scene.

At least they didn't draw one of those cliché body silhouettes, Darla thought in relief as she deliberately kept Callie to her far side in order to spare her the sight of the death scene. Unfortunately, Susanna and her friends had shrieked with sufficient vigor upon glimpsing the lonely pair of red pumps still lying in the street that Callie had looked, too. She'd said nothing, however, but merely clutched Darla's hand more tightly.

Somewhat to Darla's surprise, Susanna politely protested Darla's plan to call a taxi for them. "It's, like, not necessary," the teen said with a shrug, managing a blasé tone despite the twin trails of tear-spilled black eyeliner that now bisected either pale cheek. "We can totally walk home."

Before they walked off, Callie lingered behind her sister for a moment. "I never even got my book signed," she said, her soft tone filled with resigned sorrow.

Darla gave her an encouraging smile. "Tell you what. Give it a few days for things to settle down, and then have your mom bring you by the store. I'll see if I can make it up to you."

Satisfied the girls were safely on their way, Darla had returned inside to wait with the others. By then, the worst of the grief storm had passed, replaced by a general air of defeat. Someone had brought the food down from upstairs and arranged it neatly on the counter near the register, but it didn't appear anyone was hungry. Not feeling much of an appetite herself, Darla spent the next half hour straightening stock, until, tiring of the busywork, she'd settled herself at the far side of the signing table. No one, it seemed, wanted to sit in the black-draped chair that had been Valerie's.

What would Great-Aunt Dee have done had this happened on her watch? Darla frowned, considering. Knowing Dee, she probably would've sponsored some big memorial event at the store for her customers: a splashy-yet-tasteful party that would make all the papers. It was a good idea, Darla thought. Maybe she should consider something similar.

She sighed. For the moment, her only plan was to snag a signed copy of Valerie's book for Callie, assuming that the girl ever returned to the store. The memory of the girl's pinched features and silent tears haunted Darla almost as much as the image of Valerie's slack, waxen face thrown into harsh relief under the headlights' glare. Perhaps an auto-graphed copy would ease a bit of her young pain.

The *ching* of the cash register roused her from her state of mental exhaustion.

"James, what in the heck are you doing?"

Darla stared in dismay at the sight of her employee, casu-ally ringing up an armful of books. Valerie Baylor's books, to be exact. And they'd not come from the remaining stacks that now waited forlornly for autographs that would never be penned. Instead, they were from the under-counter stash of books that Valerie had signed at the beginning of the night, which had been tagged as store copies.

"Employee discount purchase," he replied, his crisp tone unapologetic as he ran his American Express card through the reader, then, per policy, handed the receipt to her, along with a pen. "I do have my retirement to consider, if you would be so kind as to oblige?"

Darla stared at the slip of paper for a moment before sigh-ing. "Sure," she replied, aware she probably should put her foot down about such a ghoulishly opportunistic buy, but not caring. She had more to worry about than James making a few bucks selling books that more properly ought to remain store stock. Her bigger concern was how this was going to affect the shop's business from here on out. She still had sev-eral hundred copies of Valerie's new book in boxes and on display. Would people want to buy their books from the place that, for all intents and purposes, had been the site of the country's most popular author's death?

Then again, James was probably right. Darla could remem-ber quite clearly how, the day after the Princess of Wales's tragic death in Paris, she'd impulsively headed to her local bookseller to pick up one of those Diana coffee-table books as a memento. Everyone else in town apparently had had the same idea. By the time she got there, every Diana tell-all bio and picture book had been wiped from the shelves, along with every gossip magazine that might have contained a scandalous photo or two of the prin-cess. Darla had counted herself fortunate to score a week-old copy of a news magazine with an article on Diana that she'd found stashed behind the napkins in the coffee bar area of the store. In fact, she'd been so stoked that she had not even bothered to ask for a discount to account for the coffee rings on the front cover.

Given that, chances were that Valerie's books, even the unsigned ones, would fly off the shelves come Tuesday, when she opened again.

That was, *if* she decided to reopen the store at all, after what had happened.

Hillary broke the silence as she watched James's transaction.

"Put a couple on eBay tonight," the agent advised in a glum tone. "You'll get the first wave of hysterical fandom that'll be glad to bid away their entire college fund for a piece of Valerie."

Then, when everyone else stared with faintly horrified looks at her choice of words, she gave an inelegant snort. "Oh, for Chrissakes, I don't mean literally," she clarified, seemingly channeling her dead client for a moment. To James, she went on, "Hang on to the others for later, and you'll catch the serious collectors. If the books have tonight's date along with her signature, so much the better."

While James reviewed the title page of each and nodded in satisfaction, Darla rose. "I'll check with Jake and see if they're ready to take our statements now," she told the others. "It's almost eleven, so hopefully they're about done out there."

And, outside, things did finally seem to be winding down. The police appeared finished with photographing the scene and taking measurements, though the light show from the emergency vehicles continued on. The death van, as Darla morbidly found herself thinking of it, already had been loaded onto a flatbed wrecker. The wrecker, in turn, now idled impatiently as the police began removing the barricades still blocking off that lane.

She wondered what had happened to the driver who'd hit Valerie, until she noticed a handful of people who must have been that van's passengers huddled near one of the police cruisers. Another figure—presumably the driver—was barely visible behind the officer who appeared to be questioning him. Darla felt sorry for the guy, for chances were he'd never even seen Valerie coming. Now, given her rabid fans, he might end up needing to change his name and leave town—heck, leave the country!—as soon as the law let him.

She glanced back to the action on the sidewalk. Reese was taking a statement from a final pair of black-caped girls, both of whom were gesturing with exaggerated animation. Jake stood removed from it all, leaning against one of the blue sawhorses still on the sidewalk. The red glow of her cigarette somehow seemed a fitting punctuation point to the night's events.

Darla headed in Jake's direction. "So what's the word with my staff and Valerie's people?" she asked as she settled on the wooden support alongside her.

"Reese or one of the other cops will want to get brief statements from them first, and then they'll be free to go." Jake took another deep drag on her cigarette, then exhaled an impatient cloud of secondhand smoke. "The police will be sticking around a bit longer. It's never quick and dirty when it's a pedestrian fatality."

"I still don't understand that part," Darla protested. "Traffic was moving, but it wasn't going that fast. How can she be dead?"

Jake flicked an ash and glanced Darla's way.

"You don't have to be hit by Speed Racer to be killed by a moving vehicle. Even if the van was going only thirty miles an hour or so, that's still a pretty good smack. She probably flew at least fifteen feet. All it takes is landing headfirst on the pavement, and you're dead on scene. We'll know the exact cause later."

Darla suppressed a shudder. "So has anyone figured out why she ended up in the street in the first place?"

"Since I'm not a cop anymore, kid, I'm pretty much on the outside here. They took my statement just like they did with your fan girls."

She paused for another draw on her cigarette.

"Unofficially, from what I've overheard of our witness statements, it looks like Valerie decided to confront your Lone Protester, and the two of them struggled," she went on. "Of course, at the time, no one realized it was Valerie herself doing the confronting. She was wearing the same hooded black cape that everyone else and their dog had on. As far as anyone who noticed that little smackdown knew, she was just another fan who didn't like seeing her pet author being dissed. It seems Valerie managed to grab the sign, but lost her footing in the process and stumbled off the curb just as that poor SOB in the van was driving past. At least, that's what our witnesses say they saw."

Darla frowned. "What, do you think there's more to it than that?"

"Like I said, I'm on the outside here. But from all the publicity I've read about her, I have to wonder why in the hell Valerie would've abandoned her adoring masses just to lay down the law to some kook. If it worried her that much, she could have sent her bodyguard out to do the old intimidation routine. I don't even see how she knew that protester was out here."

"Probably one of the fans mentioned it when she was autographing, and it ticked her off," Darla reasoned. "So she made up the excuse about needing another smoke break, and instead she snuck out to deal with the girl."

She was about to ask if the police had tracked down this unknown antifan who'd been the root cause of the tragedy. Before she could, however, the officer who had been interviewing the driver began herding all the van's occupants away from the accident site and toward where Darla and Jake were leaning.

Darla, who had given the passengers only a cursory look before, now stared in surprise. While Valerie's fans had all been dressed in black capes, this group was attired in white robes that billowed behind them as they walked and which gleamed beneath the artificial light. The effect was even more pronounced, given the crisp black precision of the officer's tapered motorcycle breeches and tall boots.

"Must have been running late for a KKK meeting," Jake observed with a snort as she stood and stubbed out her cigarette on one leg of the barricade. Flicking away the tobacco remains, she straightened and stuck the filtered butt into her back pocket.

"How's it going, Harry?" she addressed the cop, who had

halted before them, the van passengers hanging back in a small uncertain knot behind him.

The officer pulled off his cap to reveal a balding pate. Wiping a sleeve across his brow, he resettled his hat and shrugged. "You know how it is, Jake. Good as it gets under the circumstances." Then, with a look at Darla, he added, "You're Ms. Pettistone, the bookstore owner?"

"That's me," Darla said, wondering which of his five white-clad charges was the ill-fated driver. Best she could make out, there were three women and two men, all dressed in the same odd fashion.

The cop thrust a beefy thumb over one shoulder. "We've got the driver's and passengers' statements, so these folks are free to go for the moment. But the driver wanted to talk to you . . . claims she knows you."

She?

That was Darla's first surprised thought. Somehow, she had expected that the driver would have been male. On the heels of that came confusion. How in the world did the driver know her, unless maybe she was a bookstore customer who'd had the horribly unfortunate bad luck to be driving past at the same moment that Valerie stepped off the curb? But before she had much more than a moment to wonder, one of the white-robed women pushed past the cop to stand toe-to-toe with her.

She was about Darla's age, with blond hair that had been teased and sprayed into a magnificent concoction that rose a good three inches at the crown of her head. But despite the woman's exaggerated hairdo, Darla was surprised to note that she wore almost no makeup, just a touch of mascara on her wide blue eyes. And as soon as the woman opened her mouth and Darla heard a familiar twangy drawl, she knew this was no Snooki wannabe.

"This is so unfortunate," she exclaimed in a soft voice that wavered on the edge of tears. "You don't know how sorry I am"—she gestured at her companions—"how sorry we all are for this terrible accident. I was just trying to find us a parking spot—I swear, there's not one to be had in this city!— and I never saw that poor woman until she was right in front of me. You can be sure that our entire congregation will be praying that she repented of her sins in those last precious moments of life. Eternal damnation is not a pleasant fate, I do assure you."

Eternal damnation? Darla's confusion deepened . . . and then, abruptly, she realized just who this woman might be.

"You're my sister Linda's neighbor, the one who wrote me that letter," she choked out in disbelief.

The wavering lips firmed into a small smile that didn't quite reach those wide blue eyes.

"Why, yes. Yes, I am," she replied and stuck out a small, neatly manicured hand from the oversized sleeve of what Darla realized now was a choir robe. "I'm Marnie Jennings. My fellow brothers and sisters in Christ drove all the way here from the Lord's Blessing Church in Dallas, Texas, to help you and all those poor children find salvation."

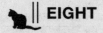 **EIGHT**

"JAMES, YOU WON'T BELIEVE THIS," DARLA MUTTERED IN her store manager's ear, casually drawing him aside from the others still inside the bookshop. She waited until they were near the front door, and softly added, "You know the driver of the van that killed Valerie Baylor? It turns out she is that same crazy woman who wrote the letter I showed you."

"You mean, Mrs. Bobby Jennings of the Lord's Blessing Church? You actually talked to her?" James stared at her, one eyebrow raised . . . for him, an indication of extreme surprise.

She nodded. "The highway patrol officer brought her over to me. He was taking her statement about the accident, and she told him that she knew me."

Darla went on to relate her mercifully brief encounter with Marnie and the other congregation members a few minutes earlier. With their church van impounded by the police, they were stranded, at least for the night. For a single awful moment, Darla had feared that the woman was going to ask if she and her church posse could stay with her. Relief had swept her when Marnie had told her they had already been in contact with a local church who'd agreed to put them up until their van was returned to them.

"And thank God for that," Darla finished, the words as

heartfelt as any prayer of Marnie's. "You should have heard the things she was saying about hellfire and damnation. I was serious when I told you she was a crazy woman."

"So do the police think this was a deliberate attack on her part?"

"Surely not, or they would have arrested her . . . or at least held her longer for questioning."

Darla hesitated. *But, could it have been?*

"No," she repeated more firmly, "no way could she have known that Valerie would step out onto the street, and no way could she have timed it so exactly. Heck, no one even realized the dead woman was Valerie at first, with all those girls and their black capes. Awful as it is, I would guess Marnie's not going to be charged with anything."

Though Darla cynically wondered if all the nasty vibes Marnie and her gang had sent Valerie's way could be considered a contributory factor in the tragedy. Changing the subject, she asked, "So how are things going in here?"

"Your Detective Reese has already taken my statement, as well as those of Lizzie, Mary Ann, Mavis, Mr. Foster, and Ms. Gables. Ms. Baylor's bodyguard is the last person waiting to be interviewed . . . that is, besides you."

Darla nodded. She saw that Everest now sat with Reese at the signing table, while everyone else was gathered near the register, where someone had arranged a few of the chairs in an impromptu circle. Mavis slumped desolately in one, flanked by Koji and Mary Ann, both of whom were murmuring words of consolation. Lizzie sat slightly apart, her nose in a new paperback romance, while Hillary sat texting away on her phone. The agent looked up as Darla and James approached. "I don't know why they're bothering to take our statements," she said with more than a hint of pique. "We were all here inside when it happened."

"Not necessarily," was James's smooth rejoinder. "Busy as we all were, I venture to say that no one was taking attendance. Besides which, almost everyone in the store with the exception of myself and those two gentlemen"—he gestured at Everest and then Koji—"was wearing a black cape, making it difficult to know who was where, and when."

"And what the hell does that mean?" Hillary snapped back.

"Yes, what does that mean?" Lizzie echoed, a quaver in her voice as she looked up from her novel. "Are you saying one of us might have followed her outside?"

"I am merely pointing out that the police are obliged to check out all possibilities when someone is killed. But it does seem apparent that what happened to Ms. Baylor was, in fact, nothing more than a tragic accident."

"Are you certain about that, James?"

This came from Mary Ann, who had left Mavis's side and now was busy wrapping the uneaten food. As all eyes turned her way, she calmly went on, "I heard there was some girl who was causing trouble out there on the street. In fact, I overheard Officer Reese say that she might have pushed Valerie into traffic on purpose."

"It's Detective Reese, ma'am," the man in question corrected as he approached the group. "And all I said was that one of the witnesses claimed she saw what she believed to be a deliberate push. We don't know for certain yet exactly what happened tonight."

"But are you saying that maybe it *was* murder?" Lizzie's quaver had morphed into a squeak, while her fingers fluttered at the ties that held her black cape around her throat.

Reese shook his head. "That's not my call. Unless we come up with some hard evidence that points to criminal intent, it's up to the medical examiner to decide if Ms. Baylor's death was an accident or not. So it would help me out"—his sharp blue gaze swept the whole group—"if all of you kept that kind of talk under your hats until after we have a formal ruling." He paused. "But you're all free to go now, all except for Ms. Pettistone. I still need her statement. We'll let you know if we need anything more from any of you. Oh, and sir—er, ma'am," he added as Mavis began scooping up Valerie's purse and cigarettes, "if those belonged to Ms. Baylor, leave them here. We'll see that her property gets couriered over to her family in the morning."

Mavis stared blankly at him for a moment and looked as if she'd protest, but then nodded. Gathering up the oversized makeup bag, the assistant joined Hillary and Koji as Darla—after assuring Reese that she would be right back—walked the somber group to the door and waited with them on the outer steps. Everest had walked on ahead to retrieve the limo parked farther down the block.

Darla glanced down the street and was relieved to see that the last police car was pulling away from the scene. The crews from the satellite trucks emblazoned with various local news station logos were packing up their equipment. Very soon, traffic would be back to its usual late-Sunday-night pattern, with no sign that a death had occurred there on the pavement a few hours earlier.

"There goes the rest of the tour," Hillary said with a sharp sigh as she tapped her foot on the concrete step with ill-concealed impatience.

Indeed, to Darla, she now sounded less grief stricken and more aggrieved when it came to her recently deceased client. She'd shed the earlier reticent air that had hung about her as she had catered to Valerie and now seemed snappishly capable in manner. Perhaps the subdued version of Hillary had been but an act she'd put on for the author's benefit.

"What about Valerie's family?" Darla asked, knowing only what she'd told Jake, that the author supposedly lived on the family estate in the Hamptons. "Did she have a husband, or any children?"

"No kids," Hillary confirmed, "just an ex-husband who's been out of her life for the last twenty years or so. But she's got parents and a brother who still live in the area. Koji drew the short straw, so he gets to ride out there with the cops to let them know what happened."

Darla gave a puzzled frown. Somehow, she would have expected Valerie's agent to have taken on that particular duty. But Darla saw that the same officer that Jake had called Harry was signaling the publicist to join him. Koji nodded and then turned to Darla.

"Good-bye, Ms. Pettistone," he told her in a glum tone as he held out a hand. "It was a pleasure meeting you. And I will be sure to inform everyone at Ibizan Books that your arrangements here tonight had no bearing on this tragedy."

Not sure if a "thank you" was an appropriate response to that last, Darla merely nodded.

Hillary waited until he was just out of earshot and then snorted. "He is *so* fired tomorrow, I guarantee you."

"Oh no! Surely the publisher won't blame him?"

Hillary gave her a pitying look, and Darla hurriedly changed the subject. "I'm guessing the burial will be private?"

"God, can you imagine the circus if it isn't? Ibizan Books is sure to sponsor some sort of public memorial for her fans later on, but I can guarantee the actual service will be just relatives and the important people in the business."

She went on to tick off the names of current and past *New York Times* bestselling authors and their respective publishers, and then dropped a few Hollywood names as well.

"Since they're still casting the movie version of *Haunted High*," she explained. "We're hoping to get Miley to play Lani, but we've got a couple of backups in case she goes Lindsay on us." She paused and gave Darla a shrewd look. "I'll do what I can to get you a seat at the service, if that's what you're asking."

"I'd like to pay my respects, that's all," she replied, trying not to sound offended. "I can't help but feel somehow responsible for what happened."

Everest pulled up in the limo just then, so she followed the remainder of Valerie's entourage as they trouped down the steps to where he was holding open the car door. Before slipping inside, Hillary paused to give Darla a quick air kiss.

"If I do get you in, promise me you won't tell anyone who you are. You think Koji's butt is in the fire? Just wait until you get introduced to the CEO of Ibizan as the person who killed off their golden goose."

While Darla pictured that last unpleasant scenario and Hillary settled herself in the limo, a red-eyed Mavis extended a large pale hand in Darla's direction. "I appreciate your kindness tonight," he said in a tone so low that she barely made out the words. "And ignore Hillary. Don't worry, no one blames you for any of this."

"Thanks, Mavis. I appreciate it," she replied, most sincerely.

By then, however, he already had folded himself into the limo, dragging his wheeled makeup kit in next to him. Everest gave her a polite "Ma'am," and after closing the rear door, took his seat behind the wheel. She heard the soft purr of the stretch vehicle's engine, and then the limo made a smooth merge into the late-night traffic. Its twin red taillights gleaming in the darkness reminded her of Hamlet.

"Oh my God, Hamlet!" So saying, Darla rushed over to where the blue sawhorses that earlier extended down the sidewalk had now been gathered into several neat stacks for the barricade guy to retrieve come morning. Jake had just finished chaining the lot together against theft in the interim, padlocking the final length of chain to the wrought-iron railing in front of her basement apartment. She was brushing her palms against her black-denim-clad hips to knock off the worst of the grime as a breathless Darla joined her.

"I forgot about Hamlet," she hurried to explain. "Valerie said he was out in the courtyard with her the first time she took a smoke break. He was probably still there the second time she went out, too. Damn it, and she left the gate wide open. I need to make sure that he didn't wander out after her. He's never left the courtyard before . . . but then, the gate has never been left open for him, either."

"Go ahead," Jake told her. "I'll take a look out here, just in case he snuck around the front. Reese can take your statement later, if need be. It's not like we don't know where to find you."

With a quick word of thanks, Darla took off at a run toward the store. With luck, Hamlet would be lounging in a darkened corner of the courtyard prepared to treat her with lordly disdain once she found him and fawned over him in relief. That, or she'd find him skulking about the alley looking for something furred or feathered he could chomp on. She didn't want to think about him wandering the streets of Brooklyn, where chances were he'd meet Valerie's same fate beneath some vehicle's tires.

"Gotta find the cat," she told James and Lizzie as she scrambled beneath the counter for a flashlight. "Back in a minute."

Reese, who was chatting with Mary Ann, half rose out of his chair at the sight of Darla flying past him, flashlight now in hand. Whatever he might have called after her, she did not hear as she slipped into the dark courtyard and snapped on her light.

Its feeble yellow beam did not so much pierce the shadows

as bounce right over them. Making an annoyed mental note to see about adding a security light over the door ASAP—that, and buying new batteries—she waved the flashlight in a regular pattern from corner to corner of the enclosure. An oversized glass ashtray sat in the table's center, filled with several lipstick-stained cigarette butts. Even with the passage of a few hours, the odor of stale cigarette smoke hung heavily in the air, and she suppressed the sneeze that threatened.

"Here, Hamlet! Kitty, kitty, kitty."

She was certain Hamlet would not deign to come to her on command—particularly not if she called him "kitty"—but with any luck he'd shoot her an evil glare that would reflect back to her should the flashlight's beam happen to skim over him.

"C'mon, fellow," she urged in a slightly louder tone, trying not to sound desperate.

She'd always heard that animals were experts at sensing fear. Mr. Beelzebub in Fur Pants was probably a black belt in fear detection and would doubtless laugh his cat self silly if he thought she was worried about his safety. While she'd gotten used to the obnoxious beast, Darla could not in any honesty claim to be fond of him. But he had been Great-Aunt Dee's beloved pet, and he was a store fixture.

Consider it keeping tabs on inventory, she told herself as she searched the final shadowy corner. Other than a few scuttling roaches and spiders, she found nothing.

Muttering a curse, she turned her beam on the gate. It was still just as she and Koji had found it when they'd gone in search of the missing author: wide open so that any vagrant could slip in. Or any cat slip out.

Damn that woman! The least she could have done was shut the freakin' gate, Darla silently fumed as she peered into the alley again. Odd, though, that a presumed cat lover such as Valerie would have left Hamlet in such potential peril. She must have been revved up, indeed, to have gone storming out without realizing she'd left her new feline friend at risk.

Darla started down the alley in the opposite direction from which she'd run a few hours earlier. While no fan of rodents and other crawlies, she hoped there might be a sufficient number of them lurking there to hold Hamlet's interest should he have ventured that way. Gingerly tiptoeing lest those same rodents and crawlies take an interest in her, she shone the rapidly fading flashlight beam down the narrow passage. No eyes reflected back to her, and no meows answered her calls.

She bit her lower lip and gave herself a quick mental pep talk. For all she knew, Hamlet might never have left the courtyard for the alley at all. He might be lounging somewhere in the store now, or else had long since returned to his comfortable digs upstairs in the apartment. Heck, he might even be watching her out the bathroom window that overlooked the courtyard, his green eyes bright with evil satisfaction at her obvious distress.

The flashlight chose that moment to peter out. Darla gave it a brisk slap against her palm, trying to revive the beam, but to no avail. She was halfway down the alley now, wrapped in shadows and not a stone's throw distance from where a woman had been tragically killed but a few hours earlier.

A shiver that had nothing to do with the night's chill sent gooseflesh down her arms. Not that she believed in ghosts, she assured herself; still, under the circumstances she couldn't help being reminded of the *Haunted High* book she'd read last night, packed full of specters and hauntings. It would be just like Valerie to emulate her heroine and hang around tormenting the living instead of going into the light, or wherever it was that dead folks were supposed to go.

Then there was that little business about someone—something?—that had been stomping about her store in the night and flicking lights on and off. What if Stompy Foot and Valerie had joined forces in the afterlife? Darla winced. Great, that's just what she needed, her bookstore being turned into phantom central for all local ghosts.

Something skittered in the darkness behind her. Darla gave a startled yelp and then looked around in embarrassment in case someone—something?—was watching. Heck, in another minute, she was going to be sobbing out the Cowardly Lion's famous declaration, *I do believe in spooks. I do believe in spooks. I do, I do, I do!*

Though she managed not to make a run for it, her pace still was brisk as she made her way back up the alley and through the courtyard. The tingling on the back of her neck didn't cease until she was inside the shop again.

"Did you find Hamlet?" Lizzie wanted to know as Darla locked the door behind her.

Darla shook her head. "I'm hoping he's hiding somewhere inside and just being obnoxious about not showing himself."

She had debated during her foray through the alley whether or not to leave the gate open overnight, just in case Hamlet *was* still out there. Prudence had trumped concern, and she'd ultimately decided to lock it. Hers wasn't exactly a bad neighborhood, but neither was it small-town Texas. And while she'd never seen the cat exert himself unduly unless it was strictly necessary, Hamlet was certainly athletic enough to scale the wall or else slip between the bars if he was outside and decided he wanted back in.

She saw that Lizzie and Mary Ann were gathering their respective purses and exchanging black capes for sweaters. Lizzie gave an apologetic shrug.

"Sorry, we're both beat. I hope you don't mind if we leave things the way they are. James said he'd come in early on Tuesday morning to straighten up. That is, if—"

"If we're even open Tuesday," Darla finished for her. At least since she was always closed on Mondays, that would give her a day to recoup. "Under the circumstances, I'm wondering if we ought to close for an extra day. Or maybe a week."

Lizzie nodded. "You mean, out of respect."

"My gracious, don't be silly, Darla," Mary Ann interjected while giving Lizzie a severe look. "Losing a week of profit won't do anything to bring back the dead. Go ahead and stay closed tomorrow, as you normally would, but no more than that—not to be morbid about it, but the shop will probably have more business than you can handle on Tuesday. You know how ghoulish people are. Everyone will want to see the spot where the famous Valerie Baylor met her grisly end, and then buy one of her books as a souvenir."

Darla sighed. Things could go either way . . . a full-blown boycott or a sales blowout. It occurred to her, too, that she ought to give her insurance agent a call. Technically, the accident didn't happen on her property, but the last thing she needed was to be hit with a civil suit from Valerie's family. If the late author's relatives were anything like Valerie, they likely kept a lawyer on staff for just such contingencies.

Suddenly, Hamlet and his infamous claws didn't seem like such a liability anymore.

Aloud, she merely said, "You're probably right, Mary Ann. James"—she glanced over to where the older man was chatting quietly with Reese—"we'll reopen on Tuesday, as usual."

"A reasonable decision," he agreed as he gathered his stack of Valerie's books. "And now, since the good detective has dismissed us, I need to hurry home and set up my auctions. I believe I will start with a reserve price of five hundred dollars and see where things go from there."

A few moments later, he and the two women had departed the store, leaving Darla alone with Reese.

NINE

"UH, THINK I MIGHT GET MY SHIRT BACK NOW?" THE DE-
tective asked.

Darla frowned in confusion; then, with a blush, she realized that she still had his denim shirt wrapped around her
waist. Feeling uncomfortably like a high school girl who'd
been parading about wearing her boyfriend's clothes to
impress the other girls, she hastily handed over the shirt with
a mumbled, "Sorry."

She plopped into the seat at the table beside him, not caring it was the same black-covered chair where Valerie had sat.
Neither did she care that her wavy red hair now was fairly
bristling out of the French braid that, hours before, had lain so
sleekly against her neck.

"I guess you need to do the question routine with me, too."

"We'll make it fast," the detective assured her, his effort at
a smile reflecting her own tired state of mind.

He began with the expected queries as to her name, profes-
sion, and connection to "the deceased," as the author had now
become known. From there, he made her recount her actions
up to the time of the accident. Most of the questions she
replied to, but a few she had to answer with an "I don't know."
One question, in particular, gave Darla momentary pause.

"The books the deceased wrote had to do with ghosts, right?" he asked, getting a nod in return from her. "So, I'm curious. Why are all her fans wearing black capes? That's a vampire thing, isn't it?"

"Or goth, or steampunk," Darla replied, having been educated somewhat on the subject by her younger relatives. "A lot of her readers apparently subscribe to those lifestyles. But you're right . . . I wondered that, too. I know that Valerie wears—wore—a black cape in her publicity photos, so that's probably why all her fans do, too. Besides, they'd look pretty silly wearing white sheets."

Which reminded her of Marnie and the other Lord's Blessing people in their white choir robes. She fleetingly wondered if she should tell him about the letter she'd received from Marnie, threatening a boycott. Maybe later, she decided. Reese could find out about the Lord's Blessing people from the highway patrol officer, if he hadn't already. For now, she was suddenly too weary to want to drag things out any longer than she had to.

Reese, meanwhile, appeared still to be mulling over the black versus white costuming issue, but to his credit he made no further comment on the subject. A few minutes and a few more questions later, he flipped his notebook shut and capped his pen.

"Done," he declared ungrammatically, but Darla didn't bother to correct him. She stood, instead, and headed toward the door.

"No offense, but if you have everything you need, I'm going to kick you out," she said, hand on knob. "It's been a hell of a night and I'm tired. Besides, I still have to find Hamlet."

Reese followed her to the front of the store. Now, he nodded in recognition, for the missing obnoxious feline had been part of her official statement to him.

"I can help you look for Hamlet," he offered. "I'm pretty much a dog man myself, but my sister had a cat when we were growing up. Pain in the butt, he was . . . probably could give your little guy a run for the money. But I got pretty good at cat wrangling."

"Thanks, but I'd better handle it on my own. The way my luck's going tonight, he'd probably gnaw a chunk out of your leg for your trouble. I'm already anticipating Valerie's family coming after me with a wrongful death suit or something. I can't afford the city taking me to court to cover your pain and suffering, too."

"Hey, I'm off the clock. And I promise, I won't sue."

Reese gave her the same chip-toothed smile that she'd seen from him earlier that night. It occurred to her then that maybe his offer wasn't totally altruistic. Had he decided to overlook her lamentable interest in the printed word and hit on her?

Darla managed not to succumb to a reflexive eye roll at the thought.

Talk about cliché. How better to get on a woman's good side than return her missing pet to her? And even if they didn't find the wily beast, she'd be in her apartment alone with a man she just met. Though Jake had pretty much vouched for Reese's character, Darla still remembered her Single Girl 101 training. Rule number one: the easier it is for a guy to get into a woman's apartment, the harder it is to convince him he can't get into something else! Rules number two and three: see Rule number one.

"Truly, I appreciate the offer," she repeated, pulling open the door, "but between me and Jake I think we have it covered. If Hamlet hasn't shown up by morning, I'll call you to put out an APB on him."

"Suit yourself."

His attitude all professional now, Reese stuffed the notebook into his back pocket. "Sorry about how things turned out tonight," he added. "Jake and I have done this kind of thing a hundred times before. I don't know how—"

"Don't worry, Jake already gave me the apology," she cut him short, stifling a yawn. "All I want is for you to find out for sure that Valerie's death was accidental."

"I'll be on the computer the rest of the night looking for uploads of video and photos," he assured her. "With the crowd you had, I can almost assure you that we'll find something to make the case, one way or the other. 'Night, Darla," he said and headed down the front steps.

He passed Jake, who was sitting on the stoop finishing off another cigarette. So much for her friend's latest attempt at quitting, Darla thought, though after tonight's events she wasn't about to fault her. Reese paused long enough to exchange a few words with the woman, and then headed off. Darla waited until she was certain he was on his way, and then took the few steps down to join her.

"You ready to call it a night?" she asked sympathetically.

Jake sighed and shook her head as she stared out onto the darkened street in the direction of the accident scene.

"I think I'll spend awhile on the computer looking for pictures and video of the event. We still need to find out who your Lone Protester is. Even if your religious friend doesn't face any charges, chances are that girl is looking at some jail time if they find proof she shoved Valerie. And since I'm the only one who got a good look at her face, I'll be giving Reese a hand on this."

She paused and glanced Darla's way. "Any luck finding Hamlet?"

"The little beggar's still on the lam," she replied, drawing a faint smile from her friend, "but he's a big boy, so I'm not going to agonize over it any more tonight. I'll check out back one more time, and if he's not back inside by then, that's his tough luck. I'm going to go to bed and pull the covers over my head until morning."

"He'll be fine. Text me if you find him all snuggled up on the sofa, would you?"

"Will do."

Darla started to rise, only to pause again as Jake put a restraining hand on her arm.

"Listen, Darla, you don't know how sorry I am about all this," the older woman said, her usual brassy tones heavy now with contrition. "I did off-duty security lots of times when I was still a cop, with crowds two and three times the size of what we had tonight. Believe me, nothing like this ever happened before."

"Don't worry, no one blames you," Darla hurried to assure her, echoing Mavis's earlier sentiment and knowing just how her friend felt. "You and Reese had everything down to a science. Not to point fingers at the victim, but if Valerie had just stayed put, she'd have been riding off in that limo with the rest of them right now. It's her own damn fault for getting into a shoving match. Truly, it's Marnie who I feel most sorry for, even if she is a wackaloon. She's got to live with this."

Jake, however, seemed unconcerned with the church-woman. She shook her head, shaggy curls bouncing. "I swear, kid, I don't know how it happened. I all but frog-marched your protester back across the street. I can't figure out how she got back over on this side again without me noticing."

"Might have been the fact there were four hundred ninety-nine other girls all dressed in black capes standing around on that same street. Do you think the police will be able to track her down and get any sort of confession out of her?"

"It's the age of Twitter and cell phone cameras," Jake said with a shrug. "That many teenagers around, odds are good someone snapped a picture or took a video that caught at least part of the action. Between YouTube and Facebook, some-thing's bound to show up . . . assuming there *is* something."

"Okay, that's the same thing that Reese said."

She left Jake and headed back into the store, where she finished her closing routine more quickly than usual; then, after another look in the courtyard and then setting the alarm code, she slipped through the side door connecting to her pri-vate hall and locked the shop door behind her.

As she mounted the first stair, she half expected Hamlet to go flying between her feet in his typical kamikaze kitty rou-tine. In fact, tonight she would have welcomed his bad behav-ior. But she made it up both flights unhampered by fleet paws trying to trip her. Neither was he sitting at the top of the main landing trying to open the door by pure force of his cold green stare.

The little beast is probably lounging by the refrigerator, she reassured herself as she turned the key. But once inside her apartment, a quick sweep through the living room and kitchen did not reveal Hamlet in any of his usual spots.

"Hey, boy, I'm home," she called out experimentally, even though she would have fainted on the spot had she received a cheerful meow in return. Hamlet never greeted her when she came home. He waited for her to come to him bearing food, water, or the occasional catnip mouse. Coming when called was something that lower forms of life, like dogs, did.

"Fine, stay outside all night," she muttered into the result-ing silence and headed toward her bedroom. If he was still gone come morning, she'd enlist Jake's help and slap up a couple of "lost cat" signs in the neighborhood. Otherwise, she had enough troubles without having to worry where Mr. Prince of Darkness, Jr., was going to lay his feline head this night.

That decided, Darla flipped on the bedroom light, glanced at her bed, and let out a muffled shriek.

Hamlet lay sprawled upon his back in the center of her blue and gold comforter. His sleek black legs stuck out in the direction of all four compass points, while his head was turned at an unnatural angle. His eyes were green slits, and his jaw hung open to reveal sharp white teeth and a pink tongue that lolled to one side. She'd never noticed the thumbnail-sized diamond of white fur on his lower belly before.

"Oh my God," she breathed, taking a cautious step closer toward the motionless form.

In the few months that she'd lived in the apartment, Hamlet had never once set paw in what was now her bedroom. Since he seemed to think the rest of the place belonged to him, she'd wondered if this was a nice little cat courtesy on his part, or if his marked boycott of her personal space simply was some sort of veiled feline insult. But now, he lay on her bed, looking like that guy in the opening scene of *The Da Vinci Code*. All he needed was the circle drawn around him and a few more fuzzy legs to be the quintessential Vitruvian Cat.

"Hamlet, are you okay?" Darla whispered, realizing the question likely was futile. She'd driven past enough roadkill on Texas highways to know it when she saw it.

A cold little blade of guilt pierced her. She should have dragged his furry butt out of the courtyard the minute Valerie said she'd seen him there. But she hadn't, and as a result maybe he'd found something toxic in the alley—a puddle of antifreeze or one of those plastic trap things filled with rat poison. Or maybe he'd been hit and run over by Marnie and her gang, and stubbornly managed to hang on long enough to crawl home and die. Or perhaps all the dark stars had aligned at once, and it simply had been his time to go to the big litter box in the sky.

Or maybe he witnessed something he should not have seen, a little voice whispered in her head, *and curiosity—or rather, its human equivalent—actually killed this cat!*

Shoving aside that last thought as way over the top, Darla sighed and started toward the bed. If she could find an old towel or something to wrap him in, she could bury him in the courtyard tomorrow and then hold a little service for him with Lizzie and James and Jake the day after. Maybe she'd even buy one of those pet memorial stones with his name and date, she told herself, surprised to realize that a tear had drizzled down one cheek. Brushing it away, she reached down to lift the furry limp form.

A sleek black paw whipped toward her with the speed of a striking cobra. Two fanglike claws snagged the sleeve of her blouse before she could move out of range.

"Hamlet!"

Her shriek held equal parts relief and outrage as she stared down at the obviously hale and hearty feline. After that initial attack he had flipped onto his belly and swiftly gathered together his limbs and his dignity. Now, he sat crouched with his tail wrapped tightly around him, green eyes daring her to remind him that she'd caught him in a vulnerable position.

Darla's indignation faded into unwilling sympathy. Poor cat, he was smart enough to know that something bad had happened. Needing comfort, he'd put aside feline self-esteem for the security of her room, doubtless feeling he would be safe there. It was only bad luck on his part that she had caught him in the act.

"It's okay, Hamlet," she softly told him. "We've all had a rotten night tonight. If you want to sleep on the bed with me, I don't mind."

She half expected him to hiss and stalk out of the room at this impertinent suggestion. When he didn't, she left him where he sat, and, after sending Jake a quick text message— *Hamlet safely home!*—she headed for the bathroom. She returned a few minutes later, wearing one of the oversized T-shirts that served as her usual sleep attire. She saw in amusement that, in the interim, Hamlet had moved to the far-thermost corner of the queen-sized bed. He lay curled so tightly that she could barely tell head from tail.

"You scooch down any farther away from me, and you're going to fall off," she warned, feeling an unwilling rush of fondness for the ornery beast. Truth be told, she would welcome a little company, even Hamlet's. Careful not to disturb him, she slipped under the comforter and snapped off the light.

"Sleep tight," she told him, though she doubted she herself would be able to do any such thing. Every time she shut her eyes, she saw Valerie Baylor sprawled on the asphalt.

Okay, so think of something pleasant.

Abruptly, Reese's face flashed through her mind, and she grimaced into the darkness. *No, not him!* Deliberately, she settled her imagination on a cute little bed-and-breakfast located deep in the Piney Woods of East Texas where she'd once spent a restful three-day weekend. The tranquil mental scene made her smile, until she recalled she'd made that trip with her slimeball ex-husband.

She gave a frustrated groan and, managing not to dislodge the cat at her feet, settled on her back. She still remembered some of the yoga relaxation techniques she'd learned in the beginner's class she used to attend. Maybe they'd help her block out the night's events and get some shut-eye.

The technique must have worked. The next thing Darla knew, she had struggled awake from a confusing dream where she was wearing earmuffs while mowing the lawn. She glanced over at the LCD alarm clock on the table beside her bed and saw it was almost three thirty a.m. But for some reason she could still hear the lawn mower that she had been pushing in her dream. Moreover, something very warm and furry was definitely pressed against her ear.

Hamlet.

Sometime after she'd fallen asleep, he had abandoned his sulky post at the bottom of the bed and crept his way onto her pillow, where he now lay snoring beside her. Apparently, the little hell-raiser had deigned to forge a truce between them . . . at least, while no one else was looking. And she had to admit that his presence in the dark of night was surprisingly comforting. She gave a sleepy smile and shut her eyes again. Doubtless in the morning they'd be back to their mutually adversarial ways, but for now the lion was lying down with the lamb.

Just to play it safe, however, tomorrow she'd do a little research in the religion section of the store and make sure that Hamlet's unexpected lapse into feline civility was not one of the lesser known signs of a coming apocalypse.

TEN

DESPITE THE RESTLESS START TO HER NIGHT, DARLA DID
not wake until almost nine o'clock Monday morning, well
past her usual rising time, even for her day off. Between her
pounding headache and queasy stomach, she felt hungover,
despite not touching a single drop of alcohol the night before.
Bleary-eyed, she stumbled to the kitchen, where Hamlet sat
beside his empty food bowl. At her approach, he turned a
baleful green gaze upon her, their détente apparently forgotten in the wake of his empty stomach.

"Hold your horses," she muttered, knowing she'd be use-
less until she had at least one cup of coffee in her.

She made swift work of filling her small coffeemaker and
punched the "On" button with the fervor of an acolyte awaiting
divine intercession. That begun—the coffee-making process,
not the blessing—she dragged out the canister of dry cat food
from the cabinet. Hamlet continued his disdainful regard of
her until she'd poured the kibble and refilled his crystal bowl
with water. Then, with what had to be a deliberate curl of his
lip, he turned his back on her and commenced crunching away
at his breakfast.

"And good morning to you, too," she answered the snub,

taking one of Great-Aunt Dee's antique chintz-patterned tea-cups from the cabinet.

The smell of brewing coffee revived her somewhat. It also brought back into sharp focus memories of the previous night's tragedy, and concern about what this day would bring. She'd seen at least three news trucks filming the scene in the hours after the accident, but maybe dead authors didn't rate national coverage. With any luck, the story had made last night's eleven o'clock news and was already played out.

She waited until she had a steaming cup of coffee liberally laced with cream in hand, however, before she dared turn on one of the cable news channels to test that theory. Would Valerie's death still be an item of interest?

It was.

Remote in hand, Darla winced as she clicked back and forth among the major news channels. Every minute or so, the ubiquitous headline tickers scrolled an abbreviated account of the fatality across the bottom of the screen, the story sandwiched between the most recent political scandal and a foreign sports triumph. She breathed a bit easier when she saw that the crawl did not mention her store by name. She groaned, however, and paused in her channel surfing when she recognized on one of the stations the same blonde who'd interviewed her the afternoon before. And she almost dropped her chintz cup into her lap when the camera swung away from the reporter, and the familiar gilded words, *Pettistone's Fine Books*, abruptly filled the television screen, along with the banner proclaiming, "Live Report."

"Holy crap, Hamlet, they're right outside," she shrieked as she rushed to the window and twitched aside the curtain.

Sure enough, the same news van from yesterday was parked on the street right below her apartment, with the same reporter and female camera operator posed on the step outside Darla's store. Apparently, the local affiliate station had been tapped to give its take on the dramatic death. Standing at the window, Darla divided her disbelieving gaze between the live drama below and the broadcast going on there in her living room.

On-screen, the reporter was recounting Valerie's final minutes, her blond bob quivering with sincerity as she shook her head over the tragedy. While she continued to speak in voice-over, scenes from the previous night played: a discreet view of a covered figure lying in the street; a close-up of the church van's front end; a long shot of the crowd of weeping, black-cape-clad teens . . . and all illuminated by the strobing lights of half a dozen emergency vehicles. The scene looked like something out of an end-time movie.

The voice-over continued, "The driver of the vehicle responsible for this fatal accident has been identified as thirty-two-year-old Marnie Jennings of Dallas, Texas."

A grainy shot of Marnie, her mouth wide in midshout, flashed on-screen.

"Ms. Jennings and her fellow members of the Lord's Blessing Church out of Dallas were on their way to protest the Valerie Baylor autographing when the tragedy occurred," the reporter continued. Abruptly, the television screen was filled with footage of a chanting group of picketers all dressed in white choir robes. "This same church has previously been responsible for protests against what they consider, quote, Satan-based events, unquote, in the Dallas area, but it now appears they are attempting to extend their influence nation-wide. For the moment, however, no charges have been filed against Ms. Jennings, and unconfirmed eyewitness accounts suggest that an unrelated sidewalk scuffle might have precipitated the accident."

The newscast switched back to the live feed, and the camera panned right, sliding past the iron railing of Jake's basement apartment and in the direction of Mary Ann's brother's antique shop. Just beyond that point, at the approximate spot where Valerie and the van had had their fatal encounter, Darla could see that a shrine of sorts had been erected.

She gasped. Heedless of the news crew below, she shoved up her window and craned her neck for a better look. From above, the shrine was even more impressive than it appeared on the small screen. A veritable florist shop's worth of flowers—a few carnations and daisies, but mostly red roses—interspersed with candles and stuffed animals, lay against the building and covered a large section of sidewalk. The display rivaled the spontaneous tributes to Lennon and Jackson and other pop culture icons that Darla recalled seeing on TV.

Quickly, lest the reporter catch sight of her and turn the camera in her direction, she slammed her window shut again. She returned her attention to the television in time to see two more teens walk into the shot and lay another fistful of red roses atop the mound of blossoms.

"Last night, five hundred adoring fans—mostly teenage girls—were lined up on this sidewalk waiting for the chance to see Ms. Baylor in person," came the reporter's words while the camera zoomed in on a single red rose tied with a black ribbon. "Now, those same fans have been visiting the site of her untimely death over the last few hours to leave flowers, candles, and notes of condolence."

The camera pulled back, and the reporter maneuvered herself into the shot once again. "It's obvious that this tragedy has struck a large segment of the reading public to the heart," she went on. "Valerie Baylor's previous *Haunted High* books have sold more than ten million copies to date. For now, her fans are contenting themselves with buying up Valerie's final novel while the authorities continue to investigate."

The reporter allowed herself a final dramatic pause and stared straight into the camera. "Reporting live from the scene of Valerie Baylor's untimely death, this is Juanita Hillburn, Channel Twelve News. Back to you, David."

Barely had Darla let the curtain drop than her phone began to ring. Her first frantic thought was that the media had tracked her down and that someone wanted a statement from her. A glance at the caller ID, however, showed it was Jake on the other end.

"Any chance you were watching television just now, or looking out the window?" the other woman asked before Darla could manage a hello.

"Both."

Darla muted the television and sank onto the couch, clutching the phone in one hand and holding her head with the other. "My God, they even showed the front door of the store. And that mountain of flowers is unbelievable."

"Yeah, I heard people tromping past my place all night long." Jake's raspy voice held more than a note of weariness. "I'm waiting for the swarm of honeybees next."

"It's not the flowers that worry me, it's the media," Darla

replied. Summoning a hopeful tone, she added, "Do you think this was it as far as news reports?"

"Not a chance, kid. You just missed the folks from the Spanish-language station. The other major networks have already come and gone, and the smaller cable channels are circling the block now like vultures. Famous author plus grisly death equals news. If I were you, I'd stay inside until tomorrow."

"Great," Darla answered forlornly.

"Listen, I'm going back to bed, kid. Didn't get much sleep last night, you know? But I'll yell if Reese calls with any updates."

Darla hung up and shut off the television, and then peered out the window again. By now, two more news trucks had stopped in the curbside lane and were blocking traffic as they scrambled for some quick shots of the scene. The passing drivers either responded with a blare of a horn and rude gestures, or else slowed to gawk at the floral tribute, further snarling traffic. A few more fans had gathered now, joining hands in what appeared to be a gothic ring-around-the-rosy.

Jake has the right idea, she thought with a groan, abandoning the window as she contemplated heading right back to bed, too. Since the store was closed today anyhow, she had nowhere to be for the rest of the day. Camping out under the covers seemed the best plan.

Darla contemplated that bit of self-indulgence for a few more minutes and then shook her head. The apartment needed a good vacuuming, laundry needed washing, and a stack of store paperwork awaited her. Mundane tasks to be sure, but unless the good fairies paid her an unexpected visit, none of it would get done unless she did it.

Giving the bed a final longing look, she dragged herself to the shower. Thirty minutes later, her auburn hair was freshly braided and she was wearing her official lounge-around-the-house uniform of sweatpants and a T-shirt. Since the apartment held a bit of a chill, she also pulled on an oversized black sweater to complete her less-than-stunning ensemble and then headed back to the kitchen for more coffee and a yogurt.

Hamlet had long since finished his own breakfast and lay stretched out full length on the back of the horsehair couch, watching her from the living room. He contented himself with a protracted baleful green stare in her direction, until she finished off the last bite of lemon-cream yogurt. Then he rose in an elegant move and gave a single sharp meow.

"What?" Darla demanded in a grumpy voice.

Hamlet did not waste his delicate lungs on a repeat but merely hopped off the couch and strolled to the front door. There, he planted his furry butt and stared in fierce concentration at that section of heavy wood paneling that led to the great outdoors. He was still seated there a few moments later after Darla had washed her spoon and coffee cup. She shot him a baleful look of her own and then sighed.

"Fine, we'll head down to the store first," she agreed, grabbing up her keys. "I need to review a whole pile of invoices. But you'd better mind your manners. And no going outside into the courtyard."

Hamlet took the lead, his long black tail held aloft as he negotiated the steps in a series of graceful bounds, rather than padding properly one riser at a time. By the time Darla reached the lower landing, he was already at the door leading from hall to shop, standing on his hind legs with both front paws wrapped around the cut-glass knob.

"Sorry, buddy, you can't open the door without a key," she reminded him as she unlocked the door and stepped inside the shop. While she shut off the alarm system, Hamlet flew past her, his momentum leaving a fleeting feline hurricane in his wake.

Darla followed more slowly, flipping on only a couple of necessary lights lest the store appear open for business. It was cool inside without the heat turned on, but not unpleasantly so. Otherwise, the place was just as she'd left it, the moveable shelves still pushed to either side of the main room to form a broad aisle down the center. The red and black draped table was still piled with neat stacks of brand-new books and looked eerily abandoned behind the empty maze where Valerie's fans had waited with such anticipation. From the easel near the table, Valerie's dramatic image continued to hold court, her carefully composed features seeming to stare out from her publicity poster with more than a bit of malice.

Suppressing a shiver, Darla hurried over to the easel and

pulled down the poster. Great-Aunt Dee had kept similar promotional posters of famous authors hanging in the upstairs loft
and storeroom as reminders of past events. But the last thing
Darla wanted was the late *Haunted High* author hanging around
her store—even in the figurative sense—laying a guilt trip on
her every time she happened to glance at the photo. She'd tuck
away the poster behind the counter for now and let James haul it
off tomorrow. Chances were he could get a tidy bit of cash for it
on one of his online auctions.

Suddenly impatient to return the place to normal, Darla
decided not to wait for James to do the heavy lifting in the
morning but to tackle the job herself, here and now.

Restoring order took perhaps an hour, requiring a moderate amount of sweat and the unfortunate breakage of one fin-
gernail. She doffed the oversized sweater a few minutes into
it, since hauling around the loaded shelves was sufficient
activity to raise a good sweat. Hamlet supervised her work
from atop the bestseller shelf, looking like a small panther as
he lay draped along one wooden edge. She had just folded the
last of the table throws and was ready for a break when she
heard frantic tapping on the front glass.

Startled, she glanced in that direction to see a hooded dark
figure looming on the other side of the door. Her reflexive
gasp was released as a small groan when she realized on second look that the intruder was one of the ubiquitous black-
caped teens. No doubt the girl had come to pay her respects at
the impromptu Valerie shrine and had noticed Darla moving
about inside the store.

Pantomiming *sorry, go away* gestures, she headed toward
the door and called through the glass, "I'm afraid we're closed
today. Try us again tomorrow."

"But tomorrow will be too late!" the fan wailed back, her
breath frosting the glass. "I'm the only one I know who didn't
get a copy of *Ghost of a Chance* yet. If I can't read it along
with everyone else, I'll die."

Darla's first impulse was to tell the girl she'd just have to
make funeral arrangements, but a second look at the teen's
pleading face did her in. After all, she could have been putting
on a hysterical display out there on the stoop, blaming Darla
for her idol's death, instead of wanting to put money into the

store's coffers. With a reluctant nod, she turned the lock and opened the door.

"Okay, just this once," she agreed as the girl, with a little skip of joy, slipped in past her. "Grab a book off the display while I power up the register."

A few minutes later, she was letting the teen out the door again, the book gleefully clutched to her chest. "Don't tell anyone else I did this for you," Darla called after the girl as she hurried down the steps toward the street.

Whether or not the teen heard that directive, Darla wasn't sure. What she could see was the teen waving her newly acquired book in triumph as she rushed toward a cluster of Valerie's fans kneeling by the growing mountain of flowers. *Remember what she said: everyone else already has a copy*, Darla thought with a shrug. She locked the door again and caught Hamlet's cool green gaze as she headed back toward the register.

"So sue me, I did something nice," she told him as she grabbed up a sheaf of invoices that needed reconciling to orders. "Besides, it was just that one time."

Barely had the words left her lips, however, when she heard more tapping at the front glass. This time, it was two fan girls, both plump with spiked black hair and silver rings in their respective noses. Seeing that Darla had noticed them, they began frantically waving.

"Lindsay said you were open for Valerie's fans," one of them called through the glass as Darla approached, intent on putting a stop to this nonsense once and for all. "That is so, like, chill. No one else understands."

Darla sighed. Since she was there in the store anyhow, she might as well make some money. And she needed Valerie's readers on her side, in case things turned nasty with the glut of news stories that was sure to fill the airwaves the next few days.

Besides, how could she resist being thought of as "chill" by the high school set?

Over the next two hours, she sold almost fifty copies of *Ghost of a Chance*, along with a few copies of Valerie's first two *Haunted High* books. She felt like she was operating a speakeasy, with her teen customers being admitted one or two at a time into the darkened store. Moreover, entry was granted only after she scrutinized them through the front-door glass to make sure Juanita Hillburn or one of the other reporters wasn't trying to sneak in under cover of cape. Some of the fans sobbed with happiness as they scrambled in; others maintained a proper goth-girl stoicism as they paid for their books, though their reddened eyes betrayed their inner emotions. And before letting them out again, Darla gave each a stern warning not to let anyone but true Valerie fans know about this special event.

"We don't want the press barging in," she cautioned. "They don't respect Valerie like her readers do. I'm keeping the store open a couple of hours today just for you, and not the public."

To a girl, each swore only to tell her BFFs who truly loved Valerie and her books. Fans of the Boy Wizard novels were pointedly scorned as not worthy of sharing in the secret.

Between customers and invoices, Darla glanced out occasionally to see what was happening down the street. The parade of mourners continued slow but unabated, as did the caravans of press vehicles. Fortunately, the latter seemed more concerned with the shrine to Valerie and interviewing the fans who came to pay their respects, rather than checking out the bookstore that had been the catalyst for the tragedy. As for Hamlet, he proved surprisingly well behaved. Having abandoned his earlier ceiling-high perch for the checkout counter, he lounged there casually grooming his sleek black coat and accepting the respectful compliments of the similarly attired customers.

Around eleven thirty, when almost twenty minutes had passed since the last teen had sought entry, Darla decided that it was time to shut down the clandestine operation. But barely had she powered off the register again when another tap at the glass drew her attention. Determined now to hold firm, she went to the door ready to send away the newcomer, when she recognized Jake's frizzy mane through the glass.

"Oh no, did I wake you?" she asked in concern as she ushered in her friend.

Jake, she saw, was wearing an identical barely-out-of-bed outfit of sweatpants and T-shirt, topped with oversized sweater. Somehow on her the über-casual clothes didn't look quite so frumpy. *Probably because she's tall*, Darla assured herself. Aloud, she went on, "I kept getting Valerie's fans coming by looking for her latest, and I couldn't turn them down."

"You're a real Mother Teresa," Jake replied with a weary grin, following Darla toward the register. "But, no, it wasn't you. Every time I closed my eyes, another one of those crazy kids was tromping past my place to go pay homage to the glorious Valerie. It's Monday. Shouldn't they all be in school or something?"

"They probably cut class to come out here," Darla guessed, wondering if "Valerie flu" was running rampant throughout all the local schools.

Jake snorted. "I wouldn't mind it so much except, I swear, they must all have feet the size of dinner plates."

"I know what you mean. The little ninety-eight-pounders are the worst." Darla smiled at this last, and then added, "But, seriously, I really did feel like I was performing a public service, seeing how they were all so thrilled to get their books."

"Worth getting slapped with an unexcused absence from school, right?"

"Don't look at me, I'm not the truant officer," Darla said with a shrug and an even broader smile. Then, sobering, she added, "Any news trucks still outside?"

"Last one left about thirty minutes ago. I think we're safe for the moment."

"Great." Darla paused and glanced at her watch. "It's almost noon. How about I finish up here real quick, and we head down to the deli for lunch, my treat?"

"Have you ever seen me pass up a free meal, kid? Don't worry, I can entertain myself for a few minutes." With a look around the store, she added, "Fast work getting the place back in shape. And Hamlet decided to lend a hand, I see."

Hearing his name, the cat looked up from his countertop perch where he was luxuriating in obvious comfort. He sneezed twice and then deliberately hopped down onto the floor.

"I think he caught the sarcasm," Darla explained as she filed the rest of her paperwork into designated folders. "Actually, he's been pretty well behaved since he gave me my latest heart attack."

She went on to describe finding Hamlet on her bed looking like he'd just been visited by the feline Grim Reaper. Jake laughed and shook her head. "He's what, ten years old now? Ornery creature that he is, I bet he hasn't used up more than one of his lives so far. I think he'll be with you for the long haul.

"Oh, but look," she added with another chuckle, pointing toward the rear of the main room, "I think my guilt trip worked. The little beggar is actually playing janitor."

In fact, Hamlet had discovered a crumpled piece of paper sticking out from beneath one of the shelves that Darla had just rolled back into place. As she and Jake watched in amusement, he snagged it with a claw and dragged it out into the open; then, with the skill of a professional soccer player, he batted the wad from paw to paw so that it skittered across the smooth wooden floor. With a final swipe of one large paw, he sent the paper ball flying so that it landed squarely between Jake's booted feet.

"And he scores!" Jake said, giving Hamlet a round of applause while Darla grinned in appreciation. "I wonder how he is at softball. Reese said they need a couple of fielders for the precinct team." She bent and retrieved the paper, and smoothed the sheet and held it up in the dim light.

"It looks like one of those *Haunted High* trivia sheets Lizzie was passing out to the fans yesterday," she confirmed. *Tsk*ing a little, she added, "It's not like you don't have trash cans in here. If someone didn't want their copy, they could have—"

Jake broke off as she apparently realized that Darla was now frowning in her direction. "What . . . do I have something stuck in my teeth?"

"Not that I noticed," Darla answered, unable to keep the sudden urgency from her tone, "but you might want to take a look at the back of that page you're holding."

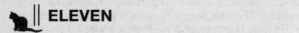

ELEVEN

JAKE FLIPPED THE PAPER OVER. ON WHAT SHOULD HAVE been the blank reverse side, she saw what Darla already had noticed in some alarm . . . someone had scrawled a few words in what appeared to be dark red lipstick.

"We need to talk. Now," the older woman read aloud. Frowning, she glanced from the paper to Darla. "So someone wrote a note last night. What's the big deal?"

"Maybe nothing. On the other hand, think about it. Wasn't it a bit odd how Valerie spontaneously decided to abandon her book signing to go after the Lone Protester, and accidentally got herself run over in the process? Maybe this note was meant for her, to deliberately get her out onto the street."

"You mean someone lured her out there?" Jake gave the page a doubtful look and shook her head. "Kid, I think you've been spending too much time in the mystery section. I know you feel guilty about Valerie—hell, we all do—but this is grasping at straws. There were hundreds of these trivia sheets floating around last night, and just about everyone in the vicinity had a red lipstick with them. Any one of the girls waiting in line could have written that note to one of her friends. Beside, who would want to knock off Valerie Baylor?"

"Well, the Lone Protester, for a start. And don't forget,

Valerie was mean to Mavis and condescending to Koji and Everest. And she pretended not to know Lizzie, when the two of them had taken a college writing class together. Oh, and you might as well toss Marnie and her friends into the pot. I think the only one she didn't tick off was Hamlet."

"Which is why he's digging up clues to prove the author's accidental death was actually a ghastly murder?" Jake finished for her, not bothering to hide a friendly smirk. She reached down to scratch the ersatz detective behind his ears, but he was having none of it. With a hiss and a flick of one paw—that last for show only, since he didn't bother to unsheathe his claws—Hamlet stalked off in the direction of the classics.

Inspecting her hand for damage and finding none, Jake went on, "Look, if being a bitch was a killing offense, half the world's women would be dead, and the other half behind bars. Same thing with the men. So if you and Hamlet want to play Nancy Drew and Ned, you need to dredge up some better clues than this."

"Fine. As of this moment, Hamlet and I are officially retired from the detective biz." Darla smiled, however, as she said it. She picked up the quiz and made a show of depositing it in the wastebasket under the counter. Then, displaying empty hands, she added, "But don't come crying to me when you need DNA evidence off the lipstick, and it's not here."

"Fine, hang onto it, and I'll mention it to Reese. Speaking of which, I ought to ring him up while we're walking to lunch."

"Right, lunch." She'd almost forgotten her offer. She dug the paper out of the trash again; then she continued, "I've got to head upstairs and get my wallet before we go. Let me check on Hamlet, and then you can wait in the foyer after I lock up here."

While Jake amused herself with the Jane Austen action figures next to the register, Darla walked over to the classics section. Hamlet was seated at the foot of the "A through H" section, in seeming contemplation of Hemingway's collective oeuvre.

"Hey, Hammy, Ms. Ex-Cop doesn't think much of our detecting skills," she told him. "But I'm still going to buy her lunch, anyhow. You want to stick around down here while we're out, or go upstairs?"

She paused, expecting either a hiss—he understood the words "go upstairs"—or else his trademark leg-over-the-shoulder kiss-off in response. Instead, he gave a little chirp of a meow and stretched at full length against the bookshelf. With seeming deliberation, he used one large paw to snag the spine of a volume on the C–D shelf and pull it out of its slot. The book landed on the polished wood floor with a gunshot-loud splat that made her jump.

"Darn cat," Darla muttered, reaching down to retrieve the volume. She stopped short, however, as she flipped it over in her hands and saw the book's title and stark, iconic cover art. Surely it had to be a coincidence. But, still . . .

"Jake," she called.

Raising the book, she read the title aloud. "*In Cold Blood*, by Truman Capote. Here I tell Hamlet that you think his clue is bogus, and he drops this book at my feet. Maybe he really did see something last night, and he's trying in his own way to let us know there's something fishy about Valerie's accident."

Barely were the words out of her mouth than she realized just how lame they sounded. A cat communicating by way of book titles? Still, it was too late to call back what she'd said. And so it was left for her to cringe a little when Jake gave her the expected bright smile . . . the kind people used to humor small children and mental patients.

"Uh-huh. Kid, I don't know how to break it to you, but the only thing fishy around here is Hamlet's food. So far as the officers on the scene were able to tell, Valerie's death was an accident. Your Lone Protester might have gotten into a shoving match with her, but worst that makes it is manslaughter. Assuming they find the girl, and assuming they uncover some sort of video or eyewitness testimony to convince a grand jury to take it to trial."

"I know, I know," Darla muttered, torn between a grin and a groan at Jake's unassailable logic. She settled for a blush as she stuck the book back in place, adding, "I think I'm a bit punchy from all that's happened. Pretend you never heard what I said, okay?" To Hamlet, she added, "Come on, let's get out of here before I make a bigger idiot of myself."

To her surprise, the feline followed her upstairs without protest. A few minutes later, having settled Hamlet comfortably in the apartment, Darla rejoined Jake. From the foyer, they made a quick visual reconnoiter of the sidewalk beyond and then, seeing no media sorts, started toward the deli. Unfortunately, they had to pass the Valerie shrine in the process.

"Holy crap, wouldja look at that," Jake said in an undertone as they approached the still-growing mound of tribute candles and flowers. "The whole street smells like a florist shop. I bet the local flower sellers are making money hand over fist today. What do you want to bet that the kid who played the Boy Wizard in all those movies wouldn't get half this attention if he dropped dead tomorrow?"

Darla could only shake her head by way of response as she stared in equal amazement.

The spread had doubled in size since she'd seen it from her window a couple of hours earlier. And Jake was right: the perfume of roses and carnations and burning candles did overwhelm the usual street smells of exhaust and restaurant food. The tribute made one thing perfectly clear: unpleasant as she might have been one-on-one, Valerie Baylor had obviously touched untold numbers of readers with her books. *And perhaps that fact outweighed the other*, she thought, feeling suddenly humble.

Jake, however, appeared untroubled by sentiment but had seemingly succumbed to her more ghoulish nature. Heedless of the dozen or so silent, sobbing teens who stood respectfully by, she knelt alongside the mound and began methodically pawing through the notes and cards that had been left there.

"Hey, dude, not cool!" one of them protested, drawing murmurs of resentful assent from the other fans gathered there.

Jake shot the girls a stern look as they began moving toward her and Darla. "Police business, ladies. I'll need you to keep your distance until I'm finished." Darla eyed the girls with some trepidation. Last thing they needed was a band of grieving high school kids going after them.

To her relief, however, the authority in her friend's voice held the teens at bay as Jake continued her search, though what she was looking for, Darla couldn't guess. Finally, the older woman stood and dusted her knees, then reached into her back pocket for a slightly crushed cigarette.

"All right, let's get that lunch."

Leaving behind the scowling girls, the two of them skirted the remainder of the blossom mountain and continued down the street. Darla waited until they were out of hearing range of Valerie's fans before asking, "Okay, I'll bite. What were you looking for back there?"

"Clues, Ms. Drew."

Then, at Darla's sour look, Jake went on, "I'm not saying I think there's anything more to Valerie's death than what we know, but I'll admit that note did set off my hinky meter just a bit. I figured since we were standing right there, I'd check to see if there were any other lipstick notes or any writing that looked like what we saw back in the store."

"And did you see any?"

"Not a one."

They traveled the final block to their destination in mutual thoughtful silence, Darla planning a look at the flower tribute herself. *Her* hinky meter had been running at the high end of the scale since the moment Hamlet had dropped that book at her feet, no matter that she'd tried to pretend otherwise.

Outside the deli door, they paused while Jake pulled out her phone. "Since you're buying, go ahead and order me the usual. I'm going to call Reese about any updates, and then I'll meet you."

Darla nodded and headed inside to order two mile-high turkey Reubens with extra sauerkraut, potato salad, and diet colas. By the time she paid for the full tray, Jake had already claimed a table and was waving her over.

"So what did Reese know?" Darla asked once they'd both made significant progress with their sandwiches.

Jake took another large bite, chewed, and swallowed before replying.

"Well, it looks like there won't be any criminal charges filed against your buddy Marnie. There's no evidence that she was negligent or impaired, and she didn't flee the scene, so she's pretty much in the clear . . . unless the family goes after her with a civil suit. As far as anything else, Reese was being a typical damn cop and playing it cagey. But it sounded like he might have found something interesting posted on the Internet. He wants to drop by later this afternoon, if that's all right by you."

"Works for me," Darla mumbled through a mouthful of turkey. "Which reminds me, I never did find out what his first na—"

Jake's phone abruptly let loose with a few riffs from the ominous "Imperial March" from the original *Star Wars* movie, cutting short Darla's question.

"Sorry, kid, I gotta take this one," Jake exclaimed, her expression wry. Flipping open the phone, she said, "Hi, Ma, how's it going down there in Florida? Yeah, yeah, I know I call you every Sunday by noon, but I got tied up yesterday morning and forgot."

By now, Darla had wrapped the other half of her sandwich for later and was piling her empties on the tray. At her questioning look, Jake shrugged and rolled her eyes. "Don't wait on me," she whispered, the hand over her phone not blocking out her mother's tinny voice coming through the speaker. "This might take a while."

Grinning, Darla left her friend and headed out alone. Once on the sidewalk again, however, her grin thinned to a firm look of determination. She hadn't forgotten her plan to do a little snooping herself through the mound of flowers. By the time Darla reached the makeshift shrine again, a new group of mourners was paying homage. Keeping her distance, she knelt as Jake had done and began a quick survey of the written tributes. Most were written by hand—some on traditional condolence cards, others on girlish stationery or even lined notebook paper. A few had been printed off computers with an almost professional élan, featuring photos of Valerie and her book covers with garish red text the same font as in the *Haunted High* graphics. All of them, however, were brimming with heartfelt sentiments of love and loss, as if Valerie had been a sister or a mother unfairly taken from them.

"Hey, lady," a girl's peevish voice abruptly said, "leave this stuff alone."

"Yeah, it's like, sacred," a young male chimed in, sounding equally put out.

Darla looked up to see a pair of teens in full goth

regalia—kohled eyes, black lipstick, and yards of black lace and velvet—advancing on her. While she'd learned during her brief retail tenure that the badass emo goth reputation was, for the most part, unfounded, these particular representatives looked as if they meant business.

She scrambled to her feet and tried out Jake's line. "Sorry, kids, police business. Move along now, you hear?"

"Yeah, right. If you're a cop, where's your freakin' badge?" the girl demanded, her face a black and white mask of disdain.

Her companion gave a cold little smile. "She don't need no freakin' badges, just like in that movie. But that's because she's not a cop. Right, lady? You're probably some religious freak who thinks we're going to hell for liking Valerie's books. You just want to mess things up for everyone because you don't like anyone who dresses like us."

"That's not true," Darla protested, truly stung. "I'm a big fan of Valerie. In fact, I'm the one who set up the autographing at the store last night so everyone could meet her in person."

She realized as soon as the words left her lips that she'd made a tactical error. The teens made the connection just as swiftly. The bored expression on the girl's face promptly morphed into a look of genuine horror—likely the first emotion she'd allowed herself to show in an adult's presence for months.

"Oh my Gawd, you're the reason Valerie is dead! If you hadn't made her come here, like, she'd still be all alive!"

"Yeah, it's your fault," her companion hotly agreed, tossing the single inky lock that dangled from his otherwise shaved hairline. His drawn-on black brows dove into an accusing frown as he jabbed his forefinger in Darla's direction. "So how ya gonna fix it? We're already telling everyone we know to boycott your store."

"Yeah," the girl chimed in, snapping her gum, "I already posted on my Facebook page."

"But it wasn't my fault! It was an accident. The police already said as much," Darla countered. Between the goth kids and the Christian crowd, she seemingly couldn't win for losing. As for the boy's threatening demeanor, that had her glancing back the way she'd come to see if Jake was nearby. Unfortunately, it looked like she was on her own, with only half a turkey Reuben to use as a defensive weapon.

"Look, er, kids," she tried again. "We can't bring Valerie back, but there's a chance I might be able to get my hands on some signed books from her." Seeing a spark of interest replace their hostility, she went on, "I can't guarantee anything, of course, but—"

"Sunny, Robert, how are you?" a familiar voice called.

Glancing back at the buildings behind her, Darla saw Mary Ann waving from the front door of her brother's shop, Bygone Days Antiques. "What are you two doing out of school so early?"

"We declared it a day of mourning," Sunny answered for them, her tone appropriately doleful. "Like, no way I could sit through social studies thinking about Valerie."

"I understand," the old woman answered with a sympathetic click of her tongue. "I felt the very same way when I heard that Carole Lombard had died."

While the teens exchanged blank glances at the mention of one of Hollywood's most famous Golden Age actresses, Mary Ann went on, "Be sure to stop by the store this weekend. We just unpacked some vintage mourning jewelry that you might like."

"Sick," the obviously misnamed Sunny replied in apparent approval.

"Ill," Robert added, seemingly agreeing with his girlfriend. "Thanks for the heads-up, Ms. Plinski."

"Oh, no problemo, it's chill," the elderly woman exclaimed, her garbled attempt at hipness drawing tolerant snickers from both teens. Then she turned her attention to Darla, gesturing her to join her. "Darla, I need your help here in the store. When you say good-bye to your friends, can you stop in for a moment?"

"Sure, Mary Ann, I'm on the way," Darla called back, realizing she'd just been tossed a life preserver, in a manner of speaking. To the goth pair, she brightly added, "We'll talk more later. Bye!"

She turned on her heel and took the dozen or so steps to the antique shop at a brisker pace than usual. Once past the shop door, she glanced back for a final look. The teens were still eyeing her with suspicion but did not appear inclined to pursue. She closed the door behind her and turned to Mary Ann with a sigh.

"Thanks for the rescue. I was afraid it might get a bit nasty out there."

"Oh, surely not," the old woman said with a smile. "Sunny and Robert are perfectly nice children and good customers, to boot. But I happened to look out the window and saw everyone standing there outside. They did seem rather upset, so I thought I should defuse the situation. My gracious, aren't all those flowers something?"

"They're something, all right," Darla agreed with a sigh. "I imagine it's been pretty unnerving for you today, too. Did you see the cable news people circling like hawks this morning? And you were right about people wanting to buy. I ended up opening the store for a couple of hours. But good old Sunny and Robert said that they're organizing a boycott against me."

She gave Mary Ann an overview of her morning, including the fact that the police had determined not to charge Marnie in connection with the author's death. She left out the part about Hamlet's finding the lipstick note, however, as well as her debate with Jake as to whether or not it constituted a clue. The older woman nodded sympathetically as she listened, and Darla felt herself relax just a bit. Something about the woman's briskly cheerful attitude seemed to dial down her own feeling of doom.

The store itself added to that homey feel. Unlike other similar establishments with their emphasis on overpriced European antiquities, Bygone Days Antiques specialized in eighteenth- and nineteenth-century Americana, the sort of items that one might find in one's grandparents' house. Though she'd only visited the store a couple of times, the faintly musty scents of old wooden furniture and vintage clothing and linens always made Darla feel at home.

"Well, I'm glad the poor driver won't have to face any charges," Mary Ann said. "As for the rest, it's my opinion that when it's our time to leave this world, it's our time to go, and nothing can stop us. So consider yourself absolved of any fault. Now, would you like to come upstairs for a cup of tea?"

Darla considered the offer a moment and then shook her

head. "Normally, I would, but Detective Reese is supposed to stop by later to discuss a few things. I probably should clean the apartment a little before he arrives."

"Ah."

The old woman's knowing smile made Darla blush despite herself, but she figured any protest would only add fuel to the fire. Cripes, couldn't she have a casual chat with a good-looking guy without people trying to read something into it?

With a glance out the shop window, she deflected that subject and instead said, "Looks like Sunny and Robert are gone, so I'd better duck out now while the getting is good. Too bad there's no connecting door between your place and mine, so I wouldn't have to go back out onto the street in case another news van drives past."

The other woman chuckled, and pointed to a display of wide-brimmed, beribboned women's chapeaux, saying, "If you want, you can borrow a shawl to wrap around your head, or one of those big picture hats."

"No, I'm good."

That last was said with just a tinge of regret. Another time, Darla wouldn't mind trying out the black straw number with a matching veil . . . the one sitting rakishly atop a mannequin head that sported a painted bob the same red color as her own dark auburn hair.

Bidding Mary Ann farewell, she slipped out the shop door and made hasty tracks to her own stoop. She couldn't tell from a glance at the basement apartment if Jake had made it home yet, but she'd catch up with her when Reese showed up. In the meantime, Darla took the lipstick letter she'd snagged from the store trash, tucked it carefully into a clear sheet protector, and then headed upstairs to give her place the once-over.

Hamlet was waiting at the door when she let herself back into the apartment. The timbre of his meow indicated displeasure with something she'd apparently done . . . or not done.

"All right, Hamlet, spit it out. You've got food, fresh water, and I even took your side on this whole note thing"—she waved the plastic-wrapped flier in his direction—"when Jake laughed at us. So what more do you need? And, no, you're not getting my sandwich."

By way of response, the cat padded over to the front

window overlooking the street below. He reared up onto his hind legs, just as he'd done with the bookcase earlier, stretching so that his front paws were on the windowsill. Black nose pressed almost to the glass and tail twitching, he meowed again.

"What is it, fellow?"

Frowning, Darla tossed the sandwich into the fridge and made her own way to the window. In the short time that they'd shared space together, she had never seen Hamlet demonstrate interest in the activity on the street below. He preferred things up close and personal, be it in the store or underneath her feet. A glance outside at the mountain of flowers showed little change from the scene she'd left only a little while earlier. A new group of mourners was busy paying their respects, a few dressed much like Robert and Sunny, and the rest in the classic teen uniform of jeans, tops, and jackets.

"Just your typical *Haunted High* fans," she muttered. So what was it that had attracted the cat's attention? She shrugged and started to turn away, when abruptly she found herself staring just like Hamlet.

One of the jean-clad teens stood slightly apart from the rest, holding what appeared from Darla's vantage point to be an oversized card. Her black hair was well below shoulder length, and so straight that Darla guessed that she must use one of those ceramic flat irons on it. Something about her posture, the way she tilted her head, looked oddly familiar. Darla squinted, her own nose a bare inch from the glass, trying for a better look as she struggled to recall where she might have seen the girl before.

As she watched, the girl bent and propped her card on a pile of black carnations alongside a lit red pillar candle. The action sent the shawl-like black scarf she wore sliding forward, momentarily hooding her features. The sight sparked an even stronger sense of familiarity, and Darla frowned.

And then it came to her.

"Oh my God, it's the Lone Protester!"

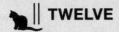 **TWELVE**

"LET ME GET THIS STRAIGHT, DARLA. YOU CHASED A strange girl because your cat gave her a funny look?"

Reese was giving her a funny look of his own, and Darla bit back a frustrated groan. She knew her instincts had been right. The problem would be convincing Reese.

The detective had shown up on her stoop not long after she had dragged herself, sweating and gasping for breath, back to the store after a fruitless sprint down Crawford Avenue. Her quarry had looked up from the wall of flowers just in time to see a determined Darla advancing on her.

Either the girl had recognized her, or else she'd seen the purpose in Darla's expression. Either way, she had promptly fled the scene with Darla in hot pursuit, but had managed to put sufficient distance between them long enough to catch one of the borough's few cabs and make good her escape.

Watching the taxi speed off with the girl inside, Darla had made an immediate vow to join a gym and get back into shape.

Now, back in her apartment, she was fortifying herself with a tall glass of sweet tea as she related the details of her missed encounter to the detective and Jake. Both were perched on the prickly horsehair couch while Darla paced impatiently about the small room. Reese had exchanged last night's head-to-toe black for a fashionably tight and faded pair of jeans topped by a short-sleeved, navy Henley. He'd stripped off the black motorcycle jacket that he'd walked in wearing—a jacket that looked like it had seen the asphalt at some point—giving her a good look at the bulging biceps she recalled from the previous evening. Remembering, too, that she was still ticked at the guy for his attitude last night, she made a point of not paying attention to said muscles, or the fact that this vaguely retro look suited him.

To her credit, Jake hadn't yet cracked a smile over the situation, though she was surveying Darla with a tolerant expression that spoke volumes. She set down her own tea glass on the coffee table and propped her Docs-clad feet beside it.

"All right, kid, let me catch up here, since I came to the party late," the older woman began. "You say you saw this girl from a third-story window half a block away, but you're sure she's the same girl from the other day who you also saw only from a distance. No offense, but that's pretty thin as far as eye-witness testimony goes. How could you be sure it was her?"

"Right," Reese interjected, jabbing his pen in the air for emphasis. Though technically off-duty, he had whipped out a notebook and was scribbling in it as she described her encounter. "I was there last night and saw the same girl, too—except I didn't really see her face, because she was wearing some sort of hood. No way could I pick her out of a crowd. Jake's the only one who actually ever talked to her, as far as I know."

"I know it was her," Darla insisted. "I could tell from her body language, from the way she stood."

When the pair merely looked at her expectantly, she shook her head.

"Look, back in high school I had a friend who was near-sighted. She couldn't wear contact lenses for some reason, and she was too vain to wear glasses. But it didn't matter. She told me she could see someone clear down the hall and tell who it was, even though they were blurry, just by the way they moved. Same principle here. Besides, isn't it telling that the girl took off running when I tried to talk to her?"

"Uh-huh." Reese flipped his notebook shut. "Which is what I'd do if I had a crazy woman chasing after—ouch!"

Clapping a hand to his neck, he swung around to glare at Hamlet. The feline lay sprawled atop the sofa back, conveniently within paws' reach of the man but with both those appendages neatly tucked against his chest.

"Your damn cat scratched me," the detective claimed in an accusing tone. Hamlet stared back at him, green eyes unflinching and round with innocence. Darla knew from experience that this likely meant the hardheaded feline indeed was guilty as charged, despite none of them having actually witnessed the supposed attack.

She suppressed a smile as she fleetingly reflected on the concept of instant karma as it applied to Reese. Hamlet was owed a nice treat for that one. She and Hamlet might not be bosom buddies, but apparently he didn't care for a stranger dissing his human roommate.

Aloud, however, she made the appropriate noises of concerned dismay.

"Bad kitty!" she declared and shook a finger in the cat's direction. Then, to Reese, she added, "Are you bleeding? Here, let me take a look. I've got bandages if you need them."

"Don't be such a big baby, Reese," Jake said before he could answer. "I can see from here it's just a nick. Hell, I've had worse paper cuts than that. Believe me, you'll live."

From the expression on the detective's face, Darla guessed he was counting to ten. After a few seconds of silence, and through gritted teeth, he said, "Thanks for everyone's concern . . . and yes, I'll live. But that spawn of Garfield better hope I don't come down with cat scratch fever."

The detective shot the spawn in question a cold look and removed himself to one of a pair of ladder-back chairs situated a safe distance from the feline. Straddling it—chair, not cat—and tapping his notebook against his knee, he said, "So let's assume the girl you saw *is* your Lone Protester. That could be interesting in light of some things I found online last night. Problem is, your sighting doesn't do us much good, not unless you got the cab number."

"Gotcha covered." Darla rattled off the information, which she had taken care to memorize as soon as she realized that the girl had escaped her. While Reese scribbled that down, Jake gave her a smile of approval.

"First-rate work, kid. Now, I don't suppose your girl conveniently dropped her wallet or anything, did she?"

"Not her wallet . . . but I have something almost as good."

Setting down her tea, Darla went over to her old-fashioned rolltop desk. Propped atop it was a large white note card illustrated with a single red rose. Careful to hold it by one corner, she handed off the note to Jake, who'd dragged herself up from the couch to follow.

"I saw her put this on a pile of black carnations along with a bunch of other cards," she explained, trying to sound blasé, though in fact her discovery had only bolstered her earlier suspicions. "I stopped to pick it up, and that's how she got away from me."

Which sounded better than admitting she'd been outrun.

Jake squinted at the card a moment and then read aloud, *"Sorry for what I did, I needed the money."*

"I told you there was something fishy going on," Darla exclaimed. "Maybe everyone was wrong about Marnie and her gang being innocent victims, too. Maybe the Lord's Blessing Church paid her to help bump off Valerie."

Her enthusiasm for her hypothesis building, Darla rushed on, "It all makes sense now. The girl lured Valerie outside with the whole protest act, waited for the right moment and, *pow* . . . off the curb Valerie went. Marnie and her van do the dirty work, the girl vanishes into the crowd of fans, and the police chalk off Valerie's death as an accident. Case closed. So what do you think?"

"I think you need to take a deep breath and leave the investigating to the professionals," Reese answered her, not bothering to suppress a dismissive snort that promptly burst Darla's sleuthing bubble. "There's a little thing called evidence . . . and a random Hallmark card isn't enough to convict someone with."

"Whatever," Darla muttered. "But you have to admit, that card is more than the police have."

"Now, now, children . . . play nice," Jake said with an absent frown, still studying the card in question. Darla noted that she, too, was taking care not to touch more than a corner of it. She reviewed it a moment longer and then looked back up at Darla.

"I hate to ask, but how about we take a look at the lipstick note that Hamlet found?"

While Jake explained to Reese how Hamlet had found the discarded paper, Darla opened the desk's top drawer and triumphantly handed over the page, still in its plastic protector.

Jake scrutinized both documents side by side before walking them over to Reese. "Doesn't look like the same handwriting, but it's kind of a coincidence that we found this, too. Take a look."

Reese did as ordered, and a flicker of interest replaced his previous expression of forced tolerance. "Okay, let's see if we can track down that cab."

He pulled out his cell phone and dialed. His muttered conversation with the person on the other end took only a few seconds before he hung up and addressed the women again.

"I've got a buddy at the cab company who'll call me back in a minute. Now, don't get your hopes up," he cautioned as Darla allowed herself a celebratory fist pump. "Even together, all this isn't exactly what I'd call a confession, but maybe your hellcat over there"—he gestured at Hamlet, who responded with a yawn—"has a knack for police work. Darla, do you have a computer here with Internet access we could use?"

"Sure."

Feeling vindicated, Darla slid up the rolltop's slatted panel to reveal a sleek laptop within the oversized cubby. She booted up the computer as Reese abandoned his seat and headed in her direction.

"I assume you want to drive?" she said with a deliberately bright smile, vacating her seat.

Appearing not in the least chastened, he simply nodded and sat down. While Jake and Darla both peered over his shoulders, he entered the address of a popular video-upload site.

"Like I said before, with all the kids and their camera phones, I figured there'd be plenty of video from the autographing floating around. I checked when I got home last night and found at least fifty new Valerie Baylor clips that had been uploaded to YouTube. I must have watched forty-nine of them before I found something."

He typed in a search string, and a series of tiny screen shots appeared on the page. He clicked on one, which pulled up a black rectangle tagged at eleven minutes, seven seconds that was labeled "Me and Alexa and Bridgette and Emily waiting for Valerie Baylor." The clip loaded to focus on a red-lipsticked, braces-filled mouth that presumably belonged to the "me" of the title. The lips pursed in a series of air kisses, while girlish shrieks and giggles served as an audio backdrop.

After a few seconds, the amateur videographer turned her camera from her dental work to the grainy, close-up faces of several other shrieking teens, equally red-lipped and grinning. Wincing a little, Reese dialed down the volume. Now, the clip was a silent show of black-caped girls chattering, dancing, and mugging for the camera. Despite the nighttime venue, however, the ambient light along the street had provided a surprisingly decent view of the action.

While Darla and Jake watched expectantly, Reese took on the role of voice-over narrator. "You've got the one girl filming her three friends"—he pointed out two blondes and one brunette, all of whom appeared about fourteen years old—"and you can see the antique store behind them. That's our establishing shot. Now, the girl with the camera phone swings around to show the steps leading up to Darla's store, and then goes back to her friends."

"Ugh, I'm getting dizzy," Jake complained as the video swirled just as he predicted. "Another Spielberg, the kid ain't."

"It goes on like this for a while," Reese said. "Now, around the nine-minute mark is where we get down to business. You'll see Ms. Baylor walking toward us in a minute. Watch."

Darla and Jake obediently leaned closer as the camera girl apparently ducked beneath the barricade. The video jumped about again for a few dizzying seconds, and Darla felt a bit of momentary queasiness herself. Then the camera focused in again, showing a long view of the street leading away from the store.

The line of blue barricades was clearly visible, though the youthful fans lining the sidewalk behind those sawhorses were almost indistinguishable from each other with their uniform black garb. Just as Darla recalled it, they had managed by this point in the evening to edge the barricade closer to the street, leaving barely enough space on the walk for a pedestrian to squeeze by.

Knowing what was to come, she focused on the street traffic with an uneasy eye. A steady stream of vehicles rushed toward the camera, the view unimpeded because of alternate-side parking restrictions on that side of the street. While not traveling at expressway speeds—and, in fact, they were going slower than the posted speed limit due to the gawking factor—it was apparent that those cars and trucks were moving swiftly enough that no amount of emergency braking could stop them in sufficient time should a pedestrian dart into traffic.

"There," Reese said, diverting her attention back to the sidewalk.

He pointed toward a black-caped figure walking on the wrong side of the sawhorses, moving toward the camera. The figure sidestepped a concrete trash container at the curb, the movement revealing a second similarly caped figure following behind the first. A flash of white broke the latter's black silhouette, and by dint of squinting Darla recognized a large rectangular shape that appeared tucked beneath the second figure's arm.

The protest sign.

"Which one's Valerie?" Jake demanded, her nose almost touching the screen now.

Darla had leaned closer, too.

"That must be her in the back, because she was holding the sign when she was hit." Then, remembering the witness statements that Jake had mentioned, she amended, "But maybe that's her in the front, since some of the kids said they saw her struggling with the protester."

"Uh, it's hard to say, since you still can't see any faces," Reese admitted, cranking up the volume again so that the sounds of laughing and shrieking girls filled the room again. "Now, watch. The one with the sign is going to grab the other one."

As he spoke, the first caped figure paused and turned, as if sensing trouble. The pursuer swiftly closed the gap between them and reached out to grab her quarry's arm with her free hand. With the other, she gesticulated with the sign that she clutched, seemingly forcing the other to read it. The pair was perhaps a dozen feet from the camera now, Darla judged—close enough to tell both pursuer and pursued were of similar height, though the billowing capes made it difficult to distinguish their builds. The first figure shook off the other's grasp and made as if to turn.

And that was when a trio of grinning teenage faces shoved their way into a close-up, all but blocking the scene going on behind them.

"Oh, for cryin' out loud," Jake exclaimed, the words echoing Darla's own annoyed reaction. She thrust a strong finger toward the screen, pointing at a gap between two of the mugging girls. "There. You can see Valerie and your protester, but I still can't tell which one is which. But it does look like some sort of a struggle going on. And, wait, they're moving closer to the curb. Crud, and now the damn kids are blocking the view again!"

Listening to Jake's blow-by-blow description, Darla gnawed her lower lip in equal frustration. Not that she was looking forward to watching Valerie Baylor's grisly end; she simply wanted to know the full story of what had happened to the author. Accident, or something more sinister? And where was the white van being driven by Marnie?

Sure enough, in the line of oncoming traffic Darla spied a large white vehicle headed on its inevitable path toward what would be the accident scene. She glanced at the progress bar again and saw that only a few seconds now remained of the video. She sucked in a deep breath and steeled herself for what she knew was coming.

The moment of truth proved distinctly anticlimactic.

Darla managed another glimpse of the grappling pair when one of the mugging teens bent with exaggerated laughter. The girl bounced back into the frame almost immediately, however, once more blotting out the action behind her. Then, so swiftly that she almost missed it, Darla saw a flutter of black that must have been Valerie's cape spiral out of camera range behind the girl. At the same instant, though barely audible over the block-party bedlam, Darla heard the unmistakable squeal of automobile brakes being frantically applied.

"Hey, I think something just happened," the camera girl's

puzzled voice overrode the background noise just before the video went black.

The three of them stared in mutual silence for a few moments at the screen, which now displayed an invitation either to share or replay the clip. Jake was the first to speak up.

"Interesting, but not exactly helpful. All this does is corroborate some of your witness statements. I think you need to find that girl."

Reese's phone rang just then. He answered, interspersing a few "uh-huh's" with the scribbled notes he was making while Darla and Jake replayed the final few moments of the video. Next event like this, Darla grimly told herself, she'd have a camera on the crowd the whole time, just in case.

Reese had already hung up by the time the screen went black again. Eagerly, the pair turned to him.

"Got it," he confirmed. "My buddy was able to get hold of the driver who picked up your girl. He said he just dropped off a fare matching her description at a coffee joint in the Village. If we're lucky, maybe she's planning to camp there the rest of the afternoon like all the kids do. Jake, you feel like reliving the good old days and heading out for a cuppa joe? Strictly off the clock . . . you know how the department is about OT these days."

"Fine by me, since I'm off the clock permanently," the woman replied with a grin. She rose from her spot on the couch. "I'll be bad cop, okay?"

"Not so fast, Dirty Harriet. Guess you retired right about the time they hit us with all that sensitivity training. These days, it's 'good cop, mildly disapproving cop.' Don't want to hurt the perp's feelings, you know."

"Fine. I'll stand behind you and look annoyed. Now let's get moving."

"Hey, what about me?" Darla wanted to know. Jake and Reese exchanged glances. Then, before either of them could protest, she added in a casually offhanded tone, "I have a car. A Mercedes."

From the reaction she got from Reese, her words might as well have been punctuated by a sudden beam of sunlight accompanied by a harp glissando.

"A Mercedes?" he echoed with the sort of reverent awe usually reserved for weeping statues of saints and angelic visitations.

"Great-Aunt Dee left the car to me along with the apartment. Jake's ridden with me before. It's parked in a garage a few blocks away."

That particular bequest had been, to her mind, a godsend. If there was one thing she'd yet to grow used to living in New York, it was being so dependent on public transportation. Not that she didn't understand the whole New York car-free thing from a practical point of view. The simple act of trying to snag a parking space on the crowded city streets could take up to an hour on a good day. Moreover, once said spot was snagged, it usually ended up being a couple of blocks' hike from one's final destination. And this didn't even take into consideration the veritable game of musical chairs that was alternate-side street parking, which might or might not be enforced on a particular day, depending on the vagaries of weather, politics, and official holidays.

But coming from the wide open spaces of Texas, one was almost a nonentity without a gas-powered vehicle at one's beck and call. A car was not so much a privilege as a birthright. Darla couldn't envision life without her own personal wheels. Especially since the car was hers, free and clear, and the exorbitant garage fees were already paid for the next year.

Reese had apparently already calculated the advantages of having a car at his disposal—particularly one that was likely eight or ten steps above what he normally drove when on duty—for he nodded as he grabbed his jacket. "Sure, Red. You can come, but you're only there to ID the girl if Jake doesn't spot her first. No chasing suspects on foot. Or running them over."

Darla was already digging into her purse for her keys, when she halted and gave Reese a stony look. Jake, who knew the cause of her sudden ire, grinned broadly.

"Hey, Reese," she said, "you'd better retract that, or you're gonna be walking the whole way to the Village."

"Retract what?" he demanded, looking from her to Darla in bemusement.

Before Darla could explain, Jake cheerfully went on, "You

just broke the first commandment of Darla: thou shalt not *ever* call her 'Red.' That is, not if you value your man parts."

Reese's bemused look turned faintly disbelieving, but he took a prudent step back anyhow as he asked, "Okay, and why not?"

"Because my ex-husband used to call me that," Darla spoke up in a tight voice.

Reese shrugged and raised both hands in mock surrender. "Good enough reason for me. Sure, *Darla*, you can come."

"Fine."

She jangled the keys, feeling a bit embarrassed at her abrupt reaction to the nickname, which she knew had been meant in a comradely way. *Face it*, she told herself, *with hair this color, there's always someone who's going to call you that. Time to toughen up.*

Summoning a conciliatory smile to smooth things over, she added, "So, what are we waiting for?"

They walked quickly over to the garage, where Darla took the service elevator to the level where her late aunt's sleek, midnight blue sedan sat patiently parked. She unlocked it and slipped behind the wheel, not bothering to suppress the reflexive "ahh" as she sunk into the cushy leather seat in contrasting gray. A hint of Dee's favorite perfume still lingered, despite the fact it had been half a year since the last time the old woman had driven it.

Darla had never owned a car this nice. Her ex had somehow always ended up with the more expensive vehicle in the family. His excuse had been that his job often entailed whisking customers about town, and he couldn't very well pick them up in a cloth-seated compact. Whenever it came time for her to purchase a new car, however, he invariably laid the whole environmentally conscious guilt trip on her and insisted that, since her commute was longer, she should opt for a cheaper, more fuel-efficient model. And so she'd spent most of her adult life driving cars that sipped fuel but did little to nourish her inner diva. By contrast, her inherited Mercedes barely got double-digit mileage in town, but compensated for that lack with its air of pure luxury that made her feel to the manner born.

Darla had last driven the car about two weeks earlier, and

so she held her breath as she waited for the engine to turn over. To her relief, it caught with a purr that would have put Hamlet to shame. She slid open the moonroof and then put on the eighties-era pair of black-framed Wayfarers that she had found tucked behind the visor the first time she drove the car.

She wasn't sure if said sunglasses had belonged to Great-Aunt Dee or the last of her late husbands. Still, in Darla's opinion the retro eyewear added a nice, adventurous vibe to her usual sedate fashion choices. She didn't have time this day, however, to admire the effect in the rearview mirror. Instead, she hastily put the Mercedes into gear, and a few moments later she was downstairs again at the entry where Reese and Jake awaited her. Both had donned sunglasses as well, though theirs were the mirrored, police-issue variety.

She powered down the driver's side window and frowned in Reese's direction.

"No way," she told him when he appeared headed toward her door. "The computer's one thing, but no one drives May-belle except me. You can ride shotgun."

She thought for a moment he'd argue the point. To his credit, however, he only said, "Nice shades," and opened the rear passenger door for Jake. Then, politely closing it after her, he walked around to the front passenger side.

Jake, meanwhile, had leaned over the front seat, chin almost on Darla's shoulder. "That was pretty bold of you, telling a Jersey boy he has to sit there and let a broad drive him around," she said with a grin. "Now, show a little compassion and don't rub it in."

"I won't," she promised as Reese opened his door and slid in. He shot her a look. Or so she presumed, since she technically couldn't see his eyes behind the sunglasses.

"You won't what?" he said.

"I won't break any traffic laws getting there. Now, how about some directions, before the Lone Protester flies the coop again?"

Reese gave her the name of their destination, which was literally "A Cuppa Joe"—she had thought he was indulging in cop-speak before—and pointed her in the direction of the expressway. Once they were well on their way, he settled back in his seat and gave an experimental sniff.

"Smells like Chanel No. 5."

"Yep. That was Great-Aunt Dee's favorite."

Darla managed a fond smile even as she negotiated a tricky lane change and then ignored sign language from the driver she passed.

"I can remember her wearing it from the time I was a little girl," she went on. "I think the scent permanently permeated the seat leather of this car after ten years of her driving it. The apartment used to smell the same way, but now it's dissipated. I kind of miss it, though."

"Yeah, my ma liked Chanel No. 5, too. She'd save up a whole year to buy herself one of those little bitty bottles, and she'd make it last until the next year. I always told her someday I'd buy her a whole vat of it, so she could bathe in it if she wanted, but I never got the chance."

Darla glanced Reese's way in time to see him shrug. From the way he let the subject trail off, she had to assume his mother was long dead. She didn't know him well enough yet to broach a potentially awkward subject like that, so instead, she took the safe way out and asked, "Is this my turn coming up?"

"Next block," he told her. "And while we've got a minute, how about a description of your girl? Jake's already given me hers, but we'd better compare notes in case she changed her hair or put on glasses or something."

As Darla relayed what she'd noticed, another thought occurred to her.

"Wait. I know someone else who has seen her up close and personal. Juanita Hillburn." When he merely stared at her, expression quizzical, Darla added, "She's one of the local television news people. You know, blond, obnoxious, in-your-face."

"Reese doesn't watch anything except ESPN and the History Channel," Jake interjected with a grin.

Reese gave her a quelling look over his shoulder and then asked Darla, "This Hillburn woman . . . when would she have seen the girl?"

"The day of the autographing. She was interviewing me and mentioned she'd also talked to the Lone Protester. You must have noticed her news van on the street."

"Yeah, well, I was kinda busy then, and that was before your author got herself killed," he said with a shrug as he reached for his cell phone again. "I'll have someone check that out with Hillburn. Maybe she's got some tape we can pull. What station did you say she was on?"

Darla gave him the call letters while he dialed his precinct. Once he'd relayed that bit of information, he snapped the phone shut again with a satisfied nod. "If we need it, it's ours. Now, turn here."

They reached the coffee shop a few minutes later. A young couple and a college-aged boy sat at two of the three outdoor tables, meaning the Lone Protester—if she was still there— must be enjoying her brew inside the café. As to be expected, every parking spot on the block was taken, except for one Mercedes-sized opening in a restricted loading zone.

"Park there," Reese instructed, pointing to said illegal space. When she gave him a questioning look, he added, "Don't worry, we're on police business. Anyone tries to tow you, I'll show 'em my badge."

"Works for me," Darla replied, secretly hoping a tow driver *would* try to drag Maybelle off, just so she could watch that badge-flashing action in person. After all, it always looked pretty cool and official on the television cop shows.

She slid into the spot with a brisk efficiency that earned her a nod of approval from the detective. His next words, however, took some of the glow off that unspoken praise.

"You wait here in the car while Jake and I go inside to see if anyone matches your girl's description. If we find someone, we'll have you ID her through the window. But in the meantime, keep your head down. You've already scared her off once. We don't want you spooking her a second time. Got it?"

"Got it," Darla agreed, tone resigned as she switched off the key. "You two play good cop and bad cop, and I'll just hang out here and play sit-on-my-ass cop."

"Don't worry, kid," Jake assured her as she unfolded herself from the backseat, "sitting on your ass is one of the first things they teach you at the academy. It's a vital skill, but hardly anyone ever fails that course. I'm sure you can handle it."

The pair of them exited the car. Jake hastily lit a cigarette, took a couple of quick puffs, then tamped it out and tucked her arm through Reese's. This presumably was so they'd look more like a couple stopping in for lattes than a cop and his retired partner out prowling about for suspects. In Darla's opinion, however, the effort ranked as an *epic fail*, as her teen customers have would put it.

"Talk about scaring off suspects," she muttered as she watched the two enter the coffee shop. The pair might as well have had "Police" stenciled on their foreheads, trailing as they both did a whole kick-butt aura about them. The sunglasses didn't help, either.

Still, Darla obediently scooched down in her seat, window cracked to admit ventilation without allowing more than the top of her head to be seen. She also slid over to the passenger side, not so much for a better view as to look like she was waiting for the driver to return. It was a trick she'd seen on one of those police procedural television shows years ago, and she figured it wouldn't hurt to try. Then, peering intently from behind her Wayfarers, she studied the coffee shop.

From the outside, at least, A Cuppa Joe seemed like one of those trendy spots that tried hard not to be one. A trio of battered wrought-iron bistro tables with matching chairs served as outdoor dining, while the wooden sign hanging beside the door with a crude rendition of a steaming coffee cup looked as if the owner had painted it himself. The interior likely carried on that same "just folks" casual air, no doubt with mismatched furniture and crockery. But Darla had an idea of what property in this area leased for . . . knew, too, that every vehicle parked nearby would have sported a hefty price tag on the dealer's lot. Success on this block would require a loyal and substantial following.

Sure enough, more people began drifting toward its doors, so that now a line had spilled out onto the sidewalk. Darla frowned and glanced at her watch. Jake and Reese had been inside a good five minutes, ample time to have determined whether or not the Lone Protester was there. Either the girl had long since come and gone, or else her destination had been somewhere other than the coffee shop.

As if on cue, the door to the consignment shop next door opened, and the Lone Protester stepped out onto the sidewalk, shopping bag in hand.

"Oh no!" Darla sat up straight and shot a look at the coffee shop door. The line was no shorter, and Jake and Reese were still nowhere to be seen. And the Lone Protester was strolling right toward where the Mercedes was parked!

 **THIRTEEN**

SCRUNCHING DOWN AGAIN, DARLA GRABBED HER CELL AND quickly dialed Jake's phone, only to hear the "Yellow Rose of Texas"—the tune Jake had downloaded as the default ring for Darla's number—playing behind her. Jake's phone must have fallen out of her pocket and onto the seat when she squeezed out of the back door.

Darla shut her phone in frustration. She didn't know Reese's number, and since she already knew that Jake's phone couldn't be unlocked without the correct password, she couldn't search her friend's contacts for that information. That meant she'd have to wait until the protester was safely past and then run inside the coffee shop to find them. The problem with that plan was that, in the meantime, the Lone Protester might grab another cab or disappear into another shop. It seemed that her only choice would be to follow the girl once again . . . but this time, in such a way that the teen didn't know she was being tailed.

Darla frowned. Though her Wayfarers would serve as something of a disguise, it would be hard to hide her red hair unless Great-Aunt Dee had tucked a convenient scarf a la Audrey Hepburn into the glove box. She made a quick, hopeful rummage through the compartment but came up empty.

No matter. The Lone Protester couldn't be expecting to be followed a second time today, anyhow, right?

By this time, the girl had passed the car and was continuing at a casual pace down the sidewalk. Darla swiftly made her decision. She'd follow the girl and go on the assumption that her quarry wasn't packing a weapon or fists of fury, or anything else that might require Darla needing immediate backup should she be spotted and recognized. Not the ideal plan, she conceded, but no way she was leaving Maybelle alone and unlocked. This meant that if Jake showed up at the Mercedes before Darla returned, the most she could do was stare through the car window at her cell phone, which was still lying on the back seat. She could only hope that Jake had her cell number memorized so she could use Reese's phone to call her and find out what was going on.

She had just grabbed her purse and was about to reach over and pull the keys from the ignition when a sharp rapping against the driver's side window glass made her jump. Choking back a surprised gasp, she glanced up to see a beefy uniformed police officer staring at her through the tinted glass, his expression one of extreme disapproval.

Bad cop.

That was Darla's reflexive categorization of the broad-faced, mustachioed officer as she recalled Reese's earlier take on this new kinder, gentler breed of law enforcement. As for Reese, he fell into the infamous never-one-around-when-you-need-one cop category. Here, he'd instructed her to park illegally, and now he wasn't available to do the promised badge flashing to get her out of it. Frantic, she glanced from the coffee shop door to the Lone Protester's retreating figure. Not only were they going to lose their sole suspect in Valerie Baylor's possibly suspicious death, but she was about to get slapped with a substantial fine as well. She needed to talk her way out of this ticket, and quickly.

She took a deep breath and powered down the driver's side window via the center console, and then leaned toward the uniformed man.

"Hello, Officer," she said with a broad smile, deliberately thickening her East Texas twang into even more honeyed southern tones. She'd found that most middle-aged New York men responded positively to that accent. "Gorgeous day, isn't it? Is there something I can help you with?"

"Yeah," he replied, still disapproving and apparently immune to sweetness and light. He flipped open his citation book and started to scribble. "You can make sure whosever's car this is gets this little love note. In case you didn't notice, lady, you're in a loading zone."

"Are we? Oh dear, and here my friend, Detective Reese, said it was fine for us to park here while he checked out a suspect."

"Suspect?"

The cop paused to squint at her, and Darla anxiously pointed to the Lone Protester, who now was peering into the window of a shop a few doors down.

"That girl with the long dark hair and black scarf, right near the red awning," she said, giving up the southern-girl routine and cutting to the chase. "I was just about to go after her. She knows something about a murder. If we lose her now, we might never find her again."

"Yeah? So where's this detective friend of yours, and where's his parking placard? And why isn't *he* following this so-called murder suspect?"

"He would be, but he's still checking out the coffee shop," she exclaimed, not bothering to correct his assumption about who owned the Mercedes. Shaking her head in frustration, she grabbed the keys from the ignition. "Look, if you need to write a ticket, write it, but I really need to go now."

"Lady, where you really need to go is out of this loading zone. You've got the keys, so do your friend a favor and move his car for him. I still see it parked here a minute from now, I'm booting it and calling a tow truck."

Baring oversized teeth in what probably was supposed to be a smile, he ripped the citation from the book and tucked it under the windshield wiper. "Now, you have a nice day," he told her and climbed back inside his patrol car.

Biting back a groan of frustration, Darla powered up the window again and yanked open the passenger door, almost falling out it in her haste. She climbed up on the door frame for a better look at her quarry. The Lone Protester had moved on down the block now and was approaching the busy intersection.

The familiar orange hand flashed on the pedestrian crosswalk sign, meaning Darla still had several seconds to catch up before the light changed again. Otherwise, the girl likely would escape her a second time. She hopped down again and slammed the door, only to hear Reese's voice behind her.

"I told you to wait in the car. Your protester sees you hanging around here, and she'll take off again."

Darla whipped about to find him and Jake surveying her with the same disapproving look Officer Bad Cop had just used on her. The needle on her own disapproval meter promptly swung way over into the totally p.o.'d zone.

"Where in the hell were you two, roasting your own coffee beans?" she demanded. "The Lone Protester wasn't in the coffee shop, she was next door in the consignment store. And now she's standing on the corner about to vanish again as soon as the light changes."

Though, in fact, the light had already switched over from orange hand to walking man. As Darla pointed in the girl's direction, the latter stepped off the curb and headed down the crosswalk with another dozen or so pedestrians.

Reese said nothing but dashed off in that direction. Jake was on his heels, though not before she ordered, "Wait here, Darla. We'll be back in a minute."

"I can't wait," Darla called after her, waving the ticket like a flag. "I just got fined for parking in a loading zone. The cop is going to call a tow truck on me."

"We'll take care of it," Jake's voice drifted back to her.

Despite her limp, the older woman was swiftly closing the gap between her and Reese. He, in turn, had already reached the corner. Unfortunately, from what Darla could see through the passing traffic, the Lone Protester had already made her way safely across the street and was headed down the next block, oblivious to any chase going on behind her.

By now, Jake had joined Reese there on the corner. Darla watched the distant pantomime as the pair seemed to confer for a moment, Reese gesturing in the girl's direction. Then, shaking off the restraining hand that Jake had put on his arm, he plunged into the stream of cross traffic.

"No!" Darla gasped and shut her eyes, certain a repeat of last night's deadly accident was imminent. Sure enough, horns blatted, and more than one set of brakes squealed. When a few more seconds passed and she didn't hear the impact of steel against human flesh, however, she assumed he must have made it across the street safely.

She sighed and opened her eyes again, only to find herself nose to nose with the same policeman who'd just given her a parking ticket.

"Maybe I didn't make myself clear, lady. I told you if you didn't move your friend's car, I was gonna slap a boot on it and call a tow truck. Well, you didn't, so I am."

"Wait!" she told him, urgently pointing down the street. "Here he comes . . . and he has the suspect."

For the Lone Protester, looking tiny and defeated, was indeed walking between Reese and Jake. Leaving her to stand alongside the Mercedes, Officer Hallonquist—she'd finally gotten a good look at the name pinned to his uniform— hurried to join them.

The four halted a short distance from her. She saw Jake speak to Reese for a few moments before breaking away to head back in Darla's direction. The two men remained where they were, the girl between them as they conferred. A moment later, they hustled the girl into Hallonquist's patrol car, which was double-parked a few cars from Darla, and then climbed in after her. The car took off down the street, presumably headed to the nearest precinct.

Jake, meanwhile, had made it back to the Mercedes. She grinned and thrust a fist at Darla for the obligatory bump.

"Good work, Nancy," she exclaimed as their knuckles collided. "You were right about your Lone Protester, whose name is Janie, by the way. She admitted right off that she was the one holding up the anti-Valerie signs. Of course, she denied shoving her into the street to be squashed like a bug, but she agreed to go in for questioning. We'll let Reese worry about getting a confession out of her."

Rather than joining Jake's moment of triumph, however, Darla felt herself gripped by a nagging sense of guilt. Anyone who'd had a hand in killing someone else deserved prison time, at the very least; still, the girl looked awfully young to go to jail for the next twenty-odd years. And something about her defeated air seemed unlike the attitude one would expect of a brazen murderer. Could the girl's claim of innocence be legitimate?

Jake seemed not to notice Darla's dismay. Instead, after ruefully snagging her abandoned phone from the rear of the Mercedes, she hopped into the front seat, furtively massaging her bad leg while pretending to do an after-workout stretch. "Jeez, I didn't realize how much I missed the old running-down-a-perp routine," she exclaimed as Darla slid behind the wheel. Snatching the citation Darla still clutched, she added, "I'll see that Reese takes care of this. Your friend Officer Hallonquist won't mind, not after he's had the chance to help collar a murderer."

"Alleged murderer," Darla sourly corrected as she turned the key. "Isn't that what you're supposed to say until someone is actually convicted?"

Jake waved away such trivialities, though she gave Darla a keen look. "So what's got your panties in a twist, kid? I thought you'd be thrilled that Hamlet and you have a knack for detecting."

"I am."

Darla pulled out into traffic again and turned Maybelle back toward Brooklyn. "What was going on inside the coffee shop?" she asked instead, deciding she needed to wait until she was alone to contemplate the other topic. "Unless it's a heck of a lot bigger than it looks, you should have been in and out of there in a couple of minutes."

"Yeah, the kid behind the counter played us, I think. He claimed your girl had been in the shop but had to leave to find an ATM, and that she'd be back any minute. It sounded kinda fishy to me, but it was all we had, so we decided to wait it out for a while. Good thing you were keeping an eye on things from here."

"So much for street smarts," Darla muttered, recalling how Jake had praised Reese's innate instincts the day before. Apparently, his intuition had taken a vacation this afternoon. "What happens to Janie now? I guess she's under arrest?"

"Not at this point. Like I said, right now she's going in for questioning. We'll see what happens after that. And who knows, maybe they won't find anything to charge her with after all."

The remainder of the trip back to the brownstone focused on whether or not Darla would be open for business as usual in the morning. "It wouldn't be fair for James to lose a day's pay," she finally decided. "Besides, if we get the kind of sales tomorrow that I had in just a few hours today, I can't afford *not* to be open."

"Business is business, kid," Jake agreed. "And you know that if the situation had been reversed, Valerie Baylor darn sure wouldn't have taken a day off touring out of respect for you."

Darla swung by the brownstone first before heading to the garage, telling Jake she was worried about how things were going at the Valerie shrine. In truth, she was more concerned about her friend. She'd noticed the older woman still massaging her bum leg when she thought Darla wasn't looking her way. The impromptu sprint outside the coffeehouse hadn't done her any good, and Darla didn't want her to walk back from the garage while still in obvious pain.

She'd halfway expected Jake to protest this special treatment, but she agreed to have Darla drop her off outside the building. As they approached their block, they could see that the shrine had continued to grow exponentially in their short absence. Now only a narrow strip of sidewalk remained for pedestrians to pass by, and the tribute's length almost reached the antique shop. The shrine had become a gawking hazard for drivers as well, with most of them slowing as to stare in amazement at the profusion of candles and flowers. Pretty soon, the city would have to send some sort of traffic control down to keep things moving . . . that, or assign a front-end loader to clear it all away!

Darla took advantage of the confusion by pulling right up to the store's curb. "I'll be back in a few," she told Jake.

She waited until the other woman climbed out, and then pulled back into Monday afternoon traffic. A few minutes later, she had situated Maybelle in her usual spot in the parking garage and was headed back to the brownstone on foot.

Normally, the walk would have been a pleasant one. The weather was fine, and the handful of crazies who wandered her neighborhood had apparently decided to stay inside for the duration. But Darla couldn't stop thinking about Valerie

Baylor and the Lone Protester—Janie—who might well be
responsible for the author's death.

More unsettling than that, however, was a selfish concern.
Though she had tried at the time to dismiss it, she couldn't
help but worry that Robert and Sunny's threatened boycott
might come to pass. Chances were the teens had several hundred so-called friends each on their respective pages, meaning it wouldn't be hard for them to drum up a few dozen
people to march around just for the fun of it. It was hard work
keeping a bookstore afloat these days. Should too many people jump on their emo bandwagon, Pettistone's Fine Books
might meet much the same fate as Valerie.

Jake was waiting for her on the stoop, seated on the concrete steps leading up to the quaint wood and glass door. She
apparently had been talking on her cell, for she snapped her
phone shut at Darla's approach.

"That was Reese," she announced. "Seems Janie sang like
a canary. Problem is, she only knew one verse."

"What do you mean?"

"She admits to the whole protest routine, but she said
someone paid her to do it. And she swears she wasn't the one
who tossed your author under the bus . . . er, church van. She
claims she ditched her sign in the alley and left the scene
almost half an hour before the accident, and had no idea what
happened until she saw the news story online."

"Did Reese believe her?"

The older woman shrugged. "He's hedging his bets, but I
think he's inclined to accept her at her word. All I know for
sure is that they didn't charge her with any crime, so she's free
to do her own thing for the moment."

"So who's the person who hired her?" Darla persisted.

Jake rose from the steps and gave an elaborate stretch. The
routine reminded Darla of Hamlet, minus any legs thrown
over any shoulders. Kink-free now, she said, "That's where it
gets interesting. Your girl claims she answered a help-wanted
ad for a performance artist on TheEverythingList."

TheEverythingList, Darla knew, was a popular Internet
want-ad site that listed, well, everything. It was a place where
people bought and sold and hired and advertised availability
by means of online postings. Darla had used the site herself,

or, rather, she'd had Lizzie post some of the store's old fixtures for sale and found it an easy way to unload unwanted goods.

"Since she's a theater major at Tisch," Jake went on, referring to the well-known school of the arts in New York City proper, "this gig was right up her alley. She got her instructions by email, and only met the person who hired her when it came time to collect her first payment. They hooked up at a fast-food joint."

"Don't tell me," Darla interrupted with a snort, "the guy she met was in disguise."

"Actually, the guy was a woman, but otherwise you're right. Janie says she was wearing a scarf and dark glasses, so Reese didn't get much of a description out of her. From what she said, the woman claimed to work for Valerie's publisher. The whole protest thing was supposed to be a publicity stunt."

"But Valerie didn't need publicity," Darla pointed out. "Besides, Koji Foster was her publicist, and he certainly didn't indicate he was in on the joke the night of the signing."

Jake nodded. "I think we can pretty well eliminate the possibility that Scarf Lady was legit. The emails were sent from one of those free email accounts, not from the publishing house. And, of course, the payment was all in cash. Janie's a little ticked, too, because she's still owed fifty bucks for last night, and the so-called publicist wasn't at the fast-food place this morning to pay like she said she'd be. Reese said he'd passed on the email address to one of the department's IT guys to track. But here's the real kicker—"

Her words were cut short by a sudden chorus of angry horns as someone slowed a bit too long while passing the Valerie shrine. The driver who'd drawn the ire of his fellows responded with a single-finger salute. Jake shook her head and shouted a few choice Jersey-isms at them all.

"We're going to be pulling more bodies off the street if this keeps up. I'm going to call a friend of mine in Traffic and see what they can do. So, where was I?"

"The real kicker," Darla helpfully supplied.

Jake hesitated, and then went on, "According to Reese, Janie claims that Scarf Lady spoke with a southern accent."

Something in her tone made Darla hesitate as well. Then

understanding dawned, and she gasped. "Don't tell me that Reese thinks *I'm* Scarf Lady?"

"Well, he did kinda float that theory for about five seconds, until I told him he was being an idiot," Jake admitted.

At Darla's yelp of disbelief, she grinned a little before continuing. "Of course, if you think about it, it's not that farfetched. I mean, drumming up a publicity stunt like that in advance of the signing could get people talking, which equals you selling more books. Besides, the first rule of police work is that everyone's a suspect until they're not. But I told him how upset you were over the whole protest thing, and that I was pretty sure you weren't the second coming of Meryl Streep who could fool me. I think I convinced him, but heads up in case he wants to put you in a photo lineup."

"Great," Darla muttered. Then the obvious thought hit her. "What about Marnie? Talk about a prime suspect. Southern accent, hated Valerie Baylor, *ran her over with her van*," she persisted, ticking off the points on her fingers.

Jake shrugged. "True, but Janie's first meeting with the Scarf Lady was a week before the autographing. Even if Marnie had someone else mail that letter for her to throw us off with the postmark, she drove up here with a carful of other people. The timeline's off. Nope, we gotta keep looking." She glanced at her watch and added, "Reese is going to drop by my place with pizza and an update around six. You're welcome to join us if you want, listen to his theories, protest your innocence and all."

"Sure, why not? Nothing better than spending an evening dodging suspicion with your friends."

So saying, she stood and spared a final look at the most recent worshippers gathered at the spontaneous Church of Valerie. Jake could have them and the traffic snarl. Darla was going to grab some quiet downtime in the peaceful confines of her third-story apartment.

Peace, however, was not quite what she found when she unlocked her front door.

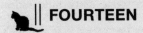 **FOURTEEN**

"HAMLET!"

Darla stared in dismay at the havoc that had been wrought in her short absence from the apartment. To be fair, the chaos was limited to one corner of her living room, right in front of the ceiling-height bookcase along the wall. Still, it was significant.

Fully half the books—classics, mostly, along with a few biographies and trendy self-help volumes—had been pulled down from the upper shelves and lay in piles upon the floor. As for the culprit, he'd not bothered to make tracks. Instead, he sat with regal stiffness between two neat stacks of volumes tall as he, his green eyes fixed upon her as if daring her to say anything.

She dared.

"You little hellion! What possessed you? You're a book-store cat—you should have more respect for the written word. I swear it's going to take me an hour to put everything back in the proper order."

Still huffing, she set down her purse and started toward the jumble. She should have taken the squirt gun to him earlier in the store, when he'd pulled down the Capote book. Given that there had been no consequences that first time, he apparently had decided that snagging books from shelves was an entertaining way to pass an afternoon.

Her irritation mingled with dismay, however, as another explanation occurred to her—since she'd never seen him be destructive just for the fun of it before, what if there had been mice in the bookcases, and Hamlet had been trying to catch them? She might have to call in an exterminator for the entire building. After all, where there's one nasty little rodent, there's bound to be—

She abruptly halted, swept by one of those something's-wrong-but-I-can't-quite-put-my-finger-on-it moments. Hamlet had not moved, but remained seated like an Egyptian statue, the books on either side of him serving as matching columns. She swore he was trying to communicate something . . . something other than his usual disdain, that was.

Then it struck her.

Hamlet could easily leap to the uppermost shelf, and he had already demonstrated that he could pull books out of a bookcase. But even a cat as clever as he lacked the facility to stack those volumes into such carefully arranged towers. So if he hadn't been playing architect with the collected works of Austen, Brontë, and Dickens, then who had?

"Hamlet?" she repeated, far more softly this time. With a small shiver, she gazed about the room. Someone had been in her apartment while she was gone, and for some reason had searched her bookcase. The question was, why? And, more important, was that person still in the apartment with her?

A prudent woman would have left the place posthaste. Jake had a gun and would know how to search a house for a possible intruder. But Darla remembered the way the ex-cop had surreptitiously coddled her bad leg after her impromptu sprint. While the other woman would not hesitate to make the round-trip up and down two narrow flights of stairs to guarantee Darla's safety, Darla was loath to put her through the pain. Besides, Hamlet had now abandoned the books for the back of the sofa, which meant whoever might have broken in was probably long since gone.

Probably.

Cell phone in one hand and a clublike wooden rain stick that Great-Aunt Dee had brought back from a Chilean vacation in

the other, Darla checked out the rest of the apartment. Her first
thought was for her laptop and television. Both were in their
usual places, as was her jewelry and the small stash of cash she
kept in a mug in an upper kitchen cabinet. Her aunt's valuable
nineteenth-century glassware and a lesser-known example of
Jackson Pollock's early work were untouched as well.

The bedroom appeared equally intact. No drawers were
dumped onto the floor, no mattress was flipped, and no crazed
book stackers leaped out of any closets at her. She ended the
hunt back in the living room a few minutes later, feeling
relieved yet somewhat foolish. After all, what kind of thief
limited his ransacking to overstuffed shelves of highly uncol-
lectible volumes? Just to be certain, she checked the windows.
All were locked, so that even if the intruder had scaled the
front of the building or somehow had managed to crawl onto
the fire escape in the back, he'd not come in that way. The
deadbolt on the apartment door had been locked, as had the
ground-level door. As for extra keys, Jake had the only other
one. Unless Hamlet had opened the door to a stranger, there
was no way someone had entered from the outside.

Setting the rain stick back in its spot in one corner, Darla
flipped open her cell phone and dialed Mary Ann's number.
Something still didn't seem right about the situation. She'd
run it past Jake and Reese at supper. In the meantime, it didn't
hurt to find out if Mary Ann or her brother had seen someone
lurking around the building.

"Why, Darla, it's been so long since we've spoken," the old
woman answered her call on the first ring, chuckling at her
mild joke. "What can I do for you?"

Mary Ann sounded frailer and a bit more breathless over
the phone than she did in person, and Darla hesitated. She
didn't want to upset the woman unnecessarily by carrying on
about a possible intruder. On the other hand, Mary Ann might
have noticed someone hanging about the place, and, at the
very least, she should be aware if something untoward was
going on in her neighborhood.

"I don't want to worry you, but something odd just happened. I went out for a few hours with Jake and Detective
Reese, and when I got back, I found half the books in my
bookcase lying on my living room floor."

"Oh dear, was Hamlet misbehaving?" Not surprisingly, Mary Ann sounded puzzled, but she gamely went on, "He's usually such a civilized cat, but he's probably upset with everything that's happened since yesterday. I'm sure he won't do it again."

"No, it's more than that. Don't be alarmed, but I think someone broke into my apartment while I was out."

When she heard a gasp from the old woman, she hurried to add, "Like I said, no need to worry. Nothing's been taken that I can see, and Hamlet's fine. It's just some books that got scattered around. But I was wondering if maybe you saw someone who didn't belong hanging out by my door this afternoon."

"Oh my gracious, let me think. No, no one in particular, my dear, though all those young people have been wandering down the sidewalk all day bringing their flowers. Oh, but wait."

Darla heard a pause and shuffle of footsteps before Mary Ann went on, "I almost forgot, there was a woman out chatting with some of the young people a bit earlier—a pretty young thing, and in such a respectable suit. She was there for about an hour and then left, but I'm looking out my window and she's back again."

A woman? A bad feeling swept her, and Darla promptly headed for her own window to take a look. Since the Lone Protester had only just been released from custody from what Jake had said, then it had to be . . .

Marnie!

Darla set her jaw as she stared down at the woman in a pink jacket and skirt handing out what appeared to be tracts to a pair of teen girls near the Valerie shrine. She was going to have a word with her, no doubt.

"I see her," Darla replied, "and I'm pretty sure it's the same woman who was driving the van that killed Valerie Baylor."

"Gracious!" was Mary Ann's shocked response. "Whatever is she doing back here?"

"I don't know, but admittedly she doesn't look like my idea of a break-and-enter artist."

"Maybe you should call that nice Detective Reese if you're worried," Mary Ann suggested, sounding more than a bit concerned herself. "And I can send Brother up to repair your door for you."

"Thanks, but the door's fine. Everything was locked up tight as a drum when I got back."

Mary Ann made a small, polite sound of confusion. "I'm sorry, dear, I must be missing something. If everything was locked up, and nothing is missing, why are you certain it wasn't Hamlet being a little devil?"

"Because the books were stacked neatly."

Almost hearing Mary Ann's questioning look through the phone, Darla gazed at the volumes on the floor in front of her and went on, "I know it doesn't sound like much . . . I guess you have to see it to understand. Some of the books were scattered on the floor, but most of them were arranged in perfect columns about a dozen high. Hamlet is clever, but he doesn't know how to use a carpenter's square."

Mary Ann was silent a moment. "Well, that *is* very strange," she finally said. "Maybe you have a poltergeist."

A poltergeist!

Now, it was Darla's turn to fall silent as she eyed the books with even greater misgivings. She'd read enough ghost stories to recall that strangely stacked items *were* a hallmark of a poltergeist haunting. She hadn't forgotten that Great-Aunt Dee had died in this very apartment—in her very own bed, to be specific, though Darla had made certain to replace that particular piece of furniture before moving in—and Valerie had been killed just outside her building. That added up to at least two possible unruly spirits right there.

That was, if one were inclined to believe in such things.

Darla frowned. While she considered herself a skeptic when it came to the occult, Valerie's *Haunted High* books *had* occupied her thoughts for the past few days. Moreover, she couldn't forget Jake's reports of mysterious footsteps in the store after hours, and the lights turning on and off by themselves. Were Hamlet's stacked books but the latest incident in a string of other strange occurrences?

"Darla? Darla, are you there?" came Mary Ann's worried voice breaking through her unsettling reverie. "My dear, I was only joking about a poltergeist," the woman said, punctuating those words with a nervous-sounding chuckle. "I hope you didn't take me seriously. I've lived in this building all my life, and believe me, there are no ghosts here. Would you like me to come over, just to make you feel better?"

"Well . . ."

Darla hesitated, tempted to take her up on the offer. But, just as with Jake, she didn't want the woman trudging up and down two flights of stairs for no good reason. While spry for her age, Mary Ann had gone through at least one knee-replacement surgery. And besides, now that Darla had allowed herself more time to consider all possibilities, the only reasonable explanation was that Hamlet had been the culprit after all.

"Mary Ann, you're a champ. I appreciate your offer, but it's not necessary," she assured the other woman. "I think you're right, and Hamlet was just looking for some attention. Detective Reese should be stopping by to see Jake later, so I'll ask if he thinks there's any cause for alarm."

"That's a sensible idea, Darla," Mary Ann said in an approving tone. "But I'll keep my eyes open, anyway, and you can call me if anything else strange happens."

They exchanged a few final pleasantries, and then Darla hung up to find Hamlet back among the books. This time, with one large paw, he was methodically knocking the carefully arranged books, one at a time, onto the floor. Each landed with a small thud atop the previous into what was becoming a new pile. This stack, however, had a distinctly haphazard appearance to it.

"Enough with the books, Hamlet," she sternly told him, setting down her phone to shoo him away. The entire situation was making her brain hurt. Better to hurry and reshelve the volumes, and put an end to the strange incident.

But first, she had to deal with Marnie.

Darla marched down the two flights of stairs with no clear plan in mind for confronting the woman. In fact, she couldn't say exactly why she was so outraged by the woman's presence there at the Valerie shrine. She'd never seen anything in Emily Post's column about it being bad manners to hang around an accident site where you were the one responsible for the victim's death. And there was nothing wrong about exercising one's First Amendment rights in a public setting, no matter that said person's opinions fell somewhere between outright mean and bat-pooh crazy. Technically speaking, since she couldn't claim aggrieved relative status, it wasn't even Darla's business what the woman did.

Maybe it was simply the figurative bad taste that Marnie's original, caps-filled letter had left in Darla's mouth that made her want to speak her piece to the woman.

By the time she reached the sidewalk, the two teens who Marnie had been lecturing had escaped. The woman had buttonholed another victim, however: this one, a boy who looked no more than fourteen. As Darla drew closer, she could see that despite his somewhat threatening appearance—lots of black leather, black denim, and various bits of chain and metal, including what adorned his ears and nose—he appeared on the verge of tears as he listened to her spiel.

"Now, you do know that the Lord Jesus Christ smites those who read Valerie Baylor's books instead of his word," Darla overheard her declare. "Much as I hate speaking ill of the dead, I must tell you that she is already suffering the agonies of hellfire for polluting young minds with her blasphemous writings. If you don't want to join her in Satan's domain when you die, you must reject her teachings and accept Jesus as your Lord and Savior. Do you understand me, son?"

Her soft, twangy accent somehow made the callous words seem even harsher. The boy was attempting to back away from her, but he'd maneuvered himself up against a stoop, leaving him no choice but to stand there. For, despite the fact he'd been polluted with blasphemy, he also appeared too polite to simply push past Marnie and make his escape that way.

Darla's redhead temper—the one she kept in check ninety-nine percent of the time—flared to volcanic life. If there was one thing she despised, it was a bully . . . male or female.

"Back off, Marnie," she said in a stern voice as she approached. To the youth, she went on in a kinder tone, "It's all right, I'll take care of her."

With a grateful nod, the boy skittered past them and ran down the street, chains jangling. Marnie, meanwhile, whipped about to face Darla.

"How dare you interrupt me in doing the Lord's work?" she demanded, outrage tingeing her cheeks and lips scarlet, so that she looked like she'd dipped into Mavis's makeup kit. Wide blue eyes narrowing, she leaned closer. "I was opening that boy's mind to the truth. Why, look at this," she cried with a gesture toward the flowered tribute. "They might as well be worshipping at the feet of a golden calf!"

She had a point, Darla thought with an inner snort as she surveyed the burgeoning mound of flowers; still, that didn't excuse the woman's outrageous behavior. Striving for a bit of calm, she went on, "I know you and your church don't approve of Valerie Baylor's books, but that doesn't give you the right to censor what other people read. And you certainly have no right to bully minor children into submission. Why, I bet you've never even read one of her books."

"Certainly not! Do you think I would pollute my own mind like that? And as for your vile accusations"—Marnie gave her a chill look, shaking her handful of tracts in Darla's direction as if they had the power to ward off evil—"I'm not censoring and bullying anyone. I'm merely encouraging people— especially young people—to reject the Devil's lies and live a righteous life. And I won't beg your forgiveness for my actions."

"It's not my forgiveness you need," Darla snapped, losing her grip on her temper again. "It's Valerie Baylor's grieving family you'd better be begging forgiveness from."

As soon as the words left her mouth, Darla regretted them, for Marnie's flawless face crumpled, and her lips began to quaver.

"Don't you know that's all I think about, gaining their forgiveness?" she softly wailed, tears welling in those blue eyes. "Why, everywhere I look, all I see is that poor woman leaping out in front of the van, and there's nothing I can do to keep from hitting her. And I have to live with that for the rest of my life, Darla."

She was weeping outright now as she went on, "Our Lord said to hate the sin and love the sinner, and so I did love Valerie Baylor. And that's why even though the police said it wasn't my fault, it pains me beyond belief to know that I'm the one who sent her to hell before she had a chance to find salvation in him."

Darla, who had begun to feel lower than worm poop for

making Marnie cry, raised her brows at this last declaration. There was no winning with this woman . . . not now, not ever.

"Look, Marnie," she said with a sigh, "this has been an awful few days, and your being here on the street isn't doing anyone any good. The signing was a flop, and Valerie Baylor is dead, so mission accomplished. Why don't you and the rest of the congregation go back home to Dallas and find another cause?"

Marnie sniffled delicately into a handkerchief that she'd pulled from the sleeve of her jacket. "I would be happy as a clam to leave this Sodom," she declared in a wavering if defiant tone, "but unfortunately, we can't right now. The van needs repairs before we can drive it again. My fellow congregants and I will have to wait until the church can raise the cash and wire it to us."

"Just how much money do you need?"

"The repair shop said a thousand dollars should cover it," Marnie replied, still snuffling, "but it might as well be a million dollars. I fear we are doomed to remain here a long while."

Darla sighed more deeply this time, mentally weighing guilt and peace of mind against Christian charity and principle. Before she could stop herself, she heard herself saying, "I can lend you the money, Marnie, and you can repay me whenever your church raises the funds. I just need your promise that you'll stay away from the store and these kids, and go back to Dallas as soon as your van is roadworthy."

"Do you really mean that? You'd lend us the money?" Marnie looked up from her handkerchief, eyes wide. "Why, you don't really even know me from Adam, and yet you'd do that for me, Darla . . . especially, after all that's happened?"

At her reluctant nod, the woman smiled brightly and flung her arms about Darla in an enthusiastic hug. "You literally are the answer to my prayers," she cried. "I spent most of last night on my knees asking the Lord to intercede. And here you are."

"Yes, here I am," Darla agreed as she awkwardly disentangled herself from the woman's grasp and took a step back. Managing a smile in return, she added, "Just call me the First Bank and Trust of Darla."

Already, she was beginning to regret this impulse. For the moment, however, bankrolling a get-the-hell-out-of-Dodge fund for Marnie seemed the lesser of any evils that might befall the greater Brooklyn area should the church group keep hanging around town. Thanks to various of Great-Aunt Dee's smaller bank accounts that Darla had inherited, she could spare the money. And if the church didn't repay her, well, she'd make Marnie send her a receipt and call it a charitable deduction.

Aloud, however, she simply said, "Wait right here, and I'll be back in a minute with a check."

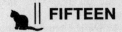 **FIFTEEN**

WITH THE MARNIE SITUATION SETTLED—OR SO DARLA hoped!—she spent the next hour or so returning the displaced books to their proper places. Of course, being the avid reader that she was, she couldn't resist flipping through a few of her favorite novels, stopping outright more than once to sit cross-legged on the floor to read a chapter or two. Only when she found herself weeping for probably the hundredth time over Beth's death scene in the battered copy of *Little Women* that her grandmother had given her as a child did she take herself firmly in hand. She was due back downstairs at Jake's for pizza at six o'clock, which was fast approaching.

She finished with the books and spent the rest of the time doing weekend household chores. Once, she gave way to morbid curiosity and flipped on the cable news station to see if there were any updates on Valerie Baylor's death. A brief segment regurgitated that morning's broadcast and included the news that no charges were being filed against the Lord's Blessing Church or its driver, Marnie Jennings.

The newscaster also mentioned that private services would be held this coming Thursday. Remembering Hillary Gables's promise to try to finagle an invite for her to the exclusive service,

Darla made a mental note to check with the agent the next morning.

When six o'clock rolled around, she left Hamlet with his kibble and headed downstairs. Jake greeted her at the door, wiping a smear of tomato sauce from her chin as she ushered Darla inside.

"Sorry, snacking on some breadsticks and marina. And watch out, Reese went a bit overboard on the food," Jake explained, gesturing her to take a seat.

Overboard was an understatement, Darla thought with a grin. In addition to the aforementioned breadsticks, the table held an immense sausage and black olive pizza (a couple of slices already missing), a heaping plate of wings, a six-pack of imported beer (also missing a couple), and a salad—that last presumably to counteract the calorie-fest that was the rest of the meal.

Reese sat in one of the matching chrome chairs doing the Henry the Eighth routine, a wing in one hand and a slice of pizza in the other. She'd caught him in midchew, so he limited himself to a nod as Darla plopped into one of the other chairs.

"Better hurry if you want anything, kid," Jake warned, serving herself salad and then passing the bowl to Darla. "A couple more minutes, and Reese will finish everything that's not nailed down."

"Yeah, you know, but at least I'll work it off in the gym tonight," he defended himself in a muffled voice as he swallowed. Giving her an evil grin, he added, "Which is more than I can say for some people. I think you've packed on a couple of extra pounds since I last saw—"

His comment was cut short as the remainder of Jake's breadstick flew across the table to bounce off his forehead. But her tone was amiable as she said, "That's right, pick on the crippled lady. But you know what they say: old age and treachery beats youth and skill every time. You and me ever tangle, you better put your money on me."

"I know I will," Darla agreed in solidarity as she dug into her lettuce. While they ate, Reese gave a more detailed account of his interview of Janie. It seemed that, after waiving her rights, she had been eager to tell her story. According to Reese, she'd grown defensive only when he'd pointed out that such a stunt, if actually sanctioned by the publisher, would not have entailed anonymous Internet advertising and cloak-and-dagger payment. When Reese had pressed her on the issue, she had finally admitted that she'd had her own suspicions, but that she needed the money for school.

"Ahem," Darla interrupted him, putting aside her fork. "Speaking of cloak-and-dagger, I understand you put me on the suspect list for Janie's mysterious Scarf Lady. Something about a southern accent?"

She gave those last words her best Texas drawl by way of emphasis, drawing a grin from Jake. Reese merely shrugged, but his expression was sheepish as he said, "So sue me, it's my job. I gotta look at everyone, and you fit the bill. Accent, connection to Valerie Baylor. You would have been a shoe-in, except for that red hair. No way the girl could have missed that in her description of the suspect."

This time, it was Darla who hurled the breadstick.

Reese was quicker this time out, catching it in midair and then taking a large chomp out of it. "Anyhow, we're still looking for whoever hired her," he said as he chewed. "One of our IT guys is backtracking the email address for me. And we'll be interviewing people who Janie says can corroborate her claim that she was long gone before Ms. Baylor ended up in the street."

"But why leave the apology card at the shrine," Darla wanted to know between nibbles of the chicken wing she'd moved onto, "if she wasn't the one who pushed Valerie off the curb?"

"Apparently, she felt like she'd enticed Ms. Baylor out into the street with her protest, and that none of this would have happened if she hadn't been outside marching around."

"But what about that whole pushed-versus-fell thing?" Jake chimed in. "The witness statements were pretty iffy, and your YouTube clip didn't exactly resolve the question. If it was a push, and your girl didn't do it, you're gonna have to line up some more suspects."

"Yeah, thanks for pointing that out, Detective Martelli. I might not be an old warhorse like you, but I know how to do my job."

"Just sayin'," Jake countered with a shrug, ignoring the age jibe. "By the way, I finally called Roy in Traffic this afternoon about the Shrine That Took Over Crawford Avenue. It was bad enough today with all the rubberneckers, but tomorrow's rush hour is gonna be a beast. He said he'd send someone out for a couple of hours during peak drive time to keep things moving."

Darla slid a piece of pizza onto her plate while Jake and Reese continued debating the merits of tax dollars being spent to accommodate public nuisances like the shrine. Once she'd finished off her slice, she waited for a lull in the conversation to announce, "Oh, I almost forgot. Something peculiar happened after we got back from chasing down Janie."

She went on to describe how she'd found Hamlet and the books, and how she had first thought an intruder had been responsible for the neatly stacked piles of volumes. Feeling somewhat proud, she detailed how she'd searched the apartment and then checked in with Mary Ann before finally concluding that Hamlet had been the culprit after all. The only thing she left out was Mary Ann's poltergeist joke. She didn't need Jake and Reese to think she was losing it.

Even before she had finished her story, however, both Jake and Reese rounded on her with equal sternness.

"Why didn't you call me?"

"Why didn't you call Jake?"

Jake, in particular, appeared upset, pushing back from the table and giving Darla a dark look. "Rule number one, kid. You come home and it looks like someone's broken into your place, you get your butt right out again and call 9-1-1—or me—but you don't play cop. Better safe than sorry applies in spades here."

"But it wasn't a break-in after all," Darla defended herself.

Jake shook her head. "This time, maybe not. But if it really had been a B and E, and you'd found the perp hiding in the back room, we might have had two dead bodies in two days. And for the record, just because Hamlet wasn't raising hell wouldn't necessarily mean that the bad guy took off. It could have been someone he knew, and that person could have still been there."

Darla hadn't considered that last. Nodding soberly, she held up both hands in surrender.

"Okay, I get it. Bad decision. I promise next time Hamlet strikes that I'll drag Jake up to see his handiwork."

She paused for a deep breath. One revelation down and another to go. Might as well get it all out into the open.

"Oh, and there's a Part Two to what happened this afternoon after y'all left," she added in a bright tone. "While I was talking to Mary Ann, she mentioned seeing a woman mixing with Valerie's fans. It turned out to be the van driver, Marnie Jennings, handing out Bible tracts to the goth kids and scaring the bejeebers out of them with her lectures on how Valerie Baylor is burning in hell right now."

The announcement had just about the effect that she anticipated. Reese choked on his beer, while Jake missed her mouth completely with her pizza slice and dumped half the toppings into her lap.

"That's pretty damn cold," Reese said with a shake of his head when he could speak again. "You run over someone and kill them, and then hang out at the accident scene talking smack like that? She's lucky those kids didn't take her apart."

"Yeah, well, I doubt she was running around with a name tag on," Jake countered, muttering a few choice words as she scrubbed tomato sauce off her jeans. "Now, don't tell me, Darla . . . while I was sitting all snug and clueless down here, you went outside and had a chat with her, didn't you?"

"I was only out there a few minutes. I rescued some boy she was trying to save, basically told her what a jerk she was, and loaned her a thousand dollars so she could fix her van and leave town."

She mumbled that last in a rush, but Jake didn't miss a word. She shoved her chair back from the table and stared at Darla.

"You loaned her a grand, just like that? What, so you two are BFF's now?"

"I wasn't doing it to be nice," came Darla's defensive reply. "She and her friends were going to be stuck here until her church could raise the money for the van repairs. I was just trying to get her out of town before anything else happened."

"Like running over one of the most famous authors of the decade?" was Jake's ironic response. Reese's reply, however, was even more stinging.

"Hate to tell you this, but someone might think you were paying off this Marnie to leave town. A little hint, Darla: it just doesn't look good, handing over that kind of cash after an incident like this."

"It was a personal check," she countered. "And why would I need to pay her off?"

Reese merely quirked a brow, but it was enough for Darla to realize just where his thoughts were headed. Her redhead's temper flared from zero to volcanic as she leaped from her chair and stared him down.

"Oh my God, don't tell me you think Marnie and I were in cahoots, that we planned to kill Valerie Baylor together!"

She shot a look at Jake, who promptly raised her hands as if to ward off a similar accusation.

"Calm down, kid, I know you're in the clear," Jake hurried to assure her. Turning a stern look on Reese, she added, "And Mr. Detective over here does, too. But as for Princess Wackaloon . . ."

She trailed off with a shrug and then added, "Yeah, yeah . . . I know it was an accident, but I have a sneaky feeling your buddy Marnie isn't as sorry as she acts."

"Now, that's not fair, Jake. In her own narrow-minded way, she really *is* devastated by what happened," Darla shot back, a bit surprised to find herself taking Marnie's side. No doubt it was one of those reflexive support-your-homegirl things.

Jake must have picked up on that vibe.

"Jeez, kid, just because she knows your sister doesn't mean you owe her a damn thing. Have you forgotten that letter she sent, trying to blackmail you into cancelling the Valerie Baylor autographing?"

"Letter?" Reese interjected before Darla could answer. His gaze whipped between her and Jake. "What letter? And what the hell did Jake mean about the Jennings woman knowing your sister?"

Jake raised her brows. "You didn't mention any of this to Reese when you gave your statement?"

"I guess it kind of slipped my mind?"

Still offended by Reese's earlier unspoken accusation, Darla gave him a defiant look. When her questioning tone didn't buy her a pass from either of them, she went on, "All right, I was tired, and I figured the cop handling things outside would share with Reese. It didn't seem that important anymore, especially once they decided not to charge Marnie with anything."

"Yeah, but if I'd known that little tidbit about a threatening letter, we might have taken another look at the woman. If nothing else, I would have put her in a lineup with a bunch of scarf-wearing women for Janie to look at. So, do you still have it?"

By now, Darla had regained control of her temper. Reese was a cop, she reminded herself, and part of the job was asking unpopular questions. And she was pretty sure he had long since crossed her off any list of suspects.

Pretty sure.

"It's upstairs," she answered. "If you want, after we finish eating, you can come up and take a look, and I'll tell you the whole story. So, Jake," she added in a hopeful tone, "I don't suppose you have some wine to go with this pizza? I'm not feeling much like beer."

"Right, change the subject," the woman muttered, but she obligingly found a bottle of decent white chilling in her refrigerator—not exactly what Darla would have chosen to pair with marinara, but it would do. She was hardly in a position to complain.

To her relief, Reese let the matter of the letter slide while they finished supper, though the occasional stern look he shot her over the course of the meal told her he wasn't about to let her off easily. It was a little after eight when Darla slid back her chair and said, "I'm going to call it an early night, since I'll be opening up tomorrow as usual. Reese, if you want to see that letter, you'd better come up with me now."

"Sure, let's go," he agreed, polishing off his beer and getting to his feet.

Darla rose a bit more carefully, mindful of the two glasses of wine she had downed. She should have just run upstairs earlier and brought the letter down to him, but she had to admit that after that afternoon's fright, she wasn't looking forward to entering the apartment alone. And, whatever his shortcomings as a dinner companion, Reese definitely was tough enough to best any intruder, human or supernatural.

"You sure you don't need help cleaning up?" she asked Jake as she surveyed the aftermath of their evening's gluttony.

Jake waved her off. "I'll send the leftovers home with Reese, and a trash bag will take care of the rest. Now, go, before Hamlet sends out the search party."

They went. The cool night air outside Jake's apartment did a little to dispel the fuzziness that seemed to have gripped her brain, for which Darla was grateful. Last thing she needed was to be off her guard around Reese. Deliberately keeping a bit of distance between them, she hurried up her own concrete steps, glad she'd remembered to turn on the small light that illuminated the door. She paused there, however, to reflexively glance back in the direction of the Valerie shrine.

The sidewalk tribute hunkered in the dark like an immense petalled caterpillar, stretching the length of one brownstone. Someone had lit the dozens of candles that had been left among the flowers, and their flickering golden light seemed to give movement to the mound. For an instant, she could swear that a caped female figure stood in the shadows among the flowers, watching her.

She shivered despite herself.

"Chilly," she explained aloud to Reese as she dug into her pocket for the key, though in fact the wine had warmed her sufficiently that she didn't need a coat.

Reese, snug in his leather motorcycle jacket, merely shrugged. He, too, appeared taken by the sight of the shrine.

"Looks like the votive candles at church," he remarked as he joined her. "Except these days, the real candles have been replaced with those electric ones. Fire codes, you know. It's not the same."

"Kind of takes away some of the mystery," Darla agreed and unlocked the front door. Barely had she opened it, however, when Reese put out a restraining arm.

"No way you're going up first," he declared, and she saw from his expression he was serious. "I know you told Jake you're sure Hamlet caused that little problem in your apartment this afternoon, but I'm pretty good at reading people. You don't believe it yourself, do you?"

Darla started to protest, and then shook her head. "Yes . . . no . . . maybe?" she answered, trying to smile but not doing much of a job of it. "I mean, I've seen him pull books off a shelf, but there's no way a cat could stack them on top of each other so neatly. It had to be a person . . . or like Mary Ann said, a poltergeist. She was kidding, of course, but that's as good as any theory I've come up with so far."

"Poltergeist?" Reese echoed with a snort that promptly made her regret mentioning that conversation. "I saw the movie . . . scared the crap out of me when I was a kid. But if it will make you feel better, I've seen a lot of strange things in my fifteen years as a cop, and ghosts ain't one of them."

He started up the steps, Darla behind him. It was obvious from the view she had that his gym workouts were doing the job, she thought with an inner grin of appreciation. Though, to be honest, she could tell that the past few months of marching up and down two flights a couple of times a day had helped in the posterior area for her as well. But recalling the way she'd been outrun that morning, she knew she should still consider adding wind sprints to her workout routine.

When they reached the top landing, Reese stepped aside long enough for her to unlock that door before again taking the lead. "Stay out here in the hall," he said in a low tone, "and I'll give you the all clear once I've had a look."

Though Darla felt certain that no one had broken in during the past few hours, she found herself holding her breath in nervous anticipation as he slowly turned the knob and inched open the door. The faint light from the single lamp she'd left burning in the living room threw a pale white ribbon onto the faded cabbage-rose pattern of the landing. So far as she could tell, all was silent inside. Reese signaled her to wait, and then pushed the door open the rest of the way.

"A-a-a-i-i-i-e-e-e!"

A drawn out, ungodly shriek split the silence. The singular sound was followed by a flash of black and a thud that collided squarely with Reese's chest.

The detective let loose with a few pithy epithets that included the FCC top seven plus several that Darla couldn't recall previously hearing. She didn't have time to be offended, however—she was too busy trying not to burst out laughing. Reese, meanwhile, made a hasty retreat back into the hall and slammed the door closed again.

He stared down at his battered leather jacket, which now sported four distinct claw marks angled from shoulder to opposite hip. Shaking his head, he said, "I guess we have our answer. Your buddy Hamlet's not going to let any intruders into your place."

That did it for Darla. Whether it was the wine, or the stress of the past days' events, or simply the look of disbelief on Reese's face, she lost it. With an outright howl of hilarity, she collapsed onto the carpet and laughed herself silly.

It was a good two minutes before she had herself sufficiently in hand again to be able to stand. The detective, meanwhile, was surveying her with a sour look. "Guess I provided the entertainment tonight, huh?"

"Sorry," she said, trying for contrite but not quite making it. "He must still be mad at you from this afternoon. But that doesn't excuse the ninja strike. I'll be glad to pay for the damages to your jacket."

"Not necessary . . . it's been through the wars already. A couple of cat scratches won't do anything, except get me some ribbing from the guys. You wanna try it again?"

"I'll lead," she agreed. "I think if anyone was inside, we'd have seen the body lying right inside the door, with Hamlet crouched over it."

Feeling much lighter in spirit than she had in some hours, Darla reopened the door and stuck her head around its edge. "Hamlet, it's me," she called. "Lay off the attack mode, okay?"

She opened the door the rest of the way and walked in, Reese right behind her, using her as a shield. This time, their entry was uneventful. Hamlet lounged atop his usual spot on the horsehair couch. He yawned and flicked a cool green look in their direction, but otherwise it was as if the earlier ambush had never happened.

Reese made the obligatory search while Darla waited near the door. He rejoined her a few minutes later to give the all clear. "No sign of anyone. Now, first things first. Do you want to show me that whole book thing from this afternoon?"

Darla gave him the rundown again, pointing out which shelves had been emptied and where the books had been piled. He studied the scene with a thoughtful look. "I don't suppose you took any pictures of the stacks?"

"No. I even had my phone in my hand, but I guess I was too rattled by how strange it was to even think of that," she admitted. "But if it happens again, you can bet I'll do video, pictures, grid drawings . . . the whole nine yards." Then, seeing something in his expression, she asked in some concern, "Do you think there really was someone in my apartment?"

"With all the craziness from Ms. Baylor's fans, it's not impossible that there might be some loony kid running around playing games. You have to admit some of the ones we saw the other night were, you know . . . odd."

Remembering Robert and Sunny, Darla replied, "Some of them are pretty intense, sure, but most of them seem like really good kids."

"Yeah, but until we figure out this whole accident thing, I don't want to discount any possibilities."

He hesitated, and then added, "I know why you didn't call Jake. She's a tough broad, but that bullet did more damage than she'll ever admit to any of us. But, believe me, it would hurt her a whole lot more to know something happened to you because you were being thoughtful. So the next time you have intruders or poltergeists or whatever, do me a favor and call her."

"I will. I guess you want to see the letter now?"

At his nod, she went over to her desk and pulled it from the top drawer. She handed it over and gave a quick explanation of Marnie's tenuous connection to her sister, though emphasizing she herself had never before met the woman. After asking a few clarifying questions, Reese studied the envelope a moment before carefully extracting out the single sheet and reading it in silence.

"It's a bit over-the-top," was his assessment a few moments later, "but as far as threats go, it's pretty tame. And it was directed at you, not Ms. Baylor. Even so, I'd like to hang on to this for a while if you don't mind."

"It's all yours." Then, with a pointed look at her watch, she said, "I appreciate the personal apartment sweep and all, but I'd better throw you out now so I can get a few things done before I go to bed."

"Yeah, yeah, I've been thrown out of worse places."

He was grinning, however, as he trotted out the cliché.

Darla grinned back and decided that, even if he'd been a jerk about trying to make her look like a suspect earlier, she really did like the guy.

Just not in that way.

And where did that *come from?* she wondered in embarrassment, hoping he hadn't noticed the sudden blush that warmed her cheeks. Deliberately, she shoved aside the thought. Unfortunately, said thought sneaked right back in after she'd walked him back down the two flights of stairs to the main door, and he paused there with one broad shoulder propping it open. Faint alarm bells went off in her brain.

"You know, there's something I've been wanting to ask you all day," he announced with an intent look at her, causing the bells to ring more loudly.

She nodded uncertainly, praying he wasn't about to ask her for a date or make some other unwanted declaration. Dealing with that situation would be too uncomfortable, especially considering he was a good friend of Jake. Damn it, where was Hamlet when she needed him?

The detective paused for a moment, as if weighing his options, and Darla felt herself tense. Finally, just as she was prepared to give him the literal heave-ho onto the stoop, good manners be damned, he blurted, "Who in the hell gives a sweet Mercedes a name like Maybelle?"

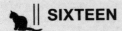 **SIXTEEN**

"AS OF EIGHT FORTY-FIVE THIS MORNING, THE BIDDING WAS at eight hundred seventy-nine dollars for my first autographed Valerie Baylor book."

His tone satisfied, James gave a brisk nod and straightened his vest. "I suspect the bids have reached one thousand dollars by now," he went on. "I have made this a twenty-four-hour auction to heighten the interest. I shall post another book at the end of the week to take advantage of those who missed out on the first offering and are regretting their timidity in bidding. I predict that second auction will be even more profitable."

Darla shot him a wry look. "Well, good for your retirement fund. I have to admit, we did pretty well here yesterday, especially since we were technically closed. Maybe I should have jacked up our prices, too."

She gave him a quick rundown of yesterday's impromptu sales. "I felt like I was running a speakeasy," she added with a sigh. "Let's just hope that we don't see a backlash today, with everyone staying away in droves."

So saying, Darla flipped the sign to "Open" and unlocked the front door of the shop. Much to her surprise, she had managed a full night's sleep last night, with her dreams undisturbed by authors, poltergeists, or cops. She didn't wake until almost seven, when Hamlet commenced with his usual hurry-up-and-feed-the-poor-starving-kitty routine.

Feeling masochistic, she had flipped on the television news for a Valerie update while she pulled on the day's work outfit of a pale green sweater set and a knee-length denim skirt. The author's untimely death still rated a periodic ten-second crawl along the bottom of the screen, but other more pressing world events had knocked it off the main broadcast rotation. A look out her front window had shown the Valerie shrine still intact, but seeming to have reached maturity. All but a few of the largest candles had long since sputtered into misshapen wax puddles, and the bloom was definitely off the blossoms.

Now, she took another look. The tribute remained an impressive if faded sight. A few hardcore Valerie fans had already returned to set up mute vigil on the sidewalk in defiance of truancy laws . . . and, hopefully, not as a precursor to Sunny and Robert's proposed boycott. And, on the bright side, the television news crews had seemingly lost interest in the story, for she'd not seen any more reporters stopping off to shoot a bit of video.

She glanced down to see that a fresh bundle of the local free paper lay on the stoop, and she carried the stack inside to set by the register. At least this newspaper didn't have headlines about Valerie Baylor's death, she thought in relief. But she was pretty sure the story would be different when the distributor brought this week's allocation of news and gossip magazines. Chances were those publications would have pages dedicated to the story. She only hoped that she and the store could continue to stay out of the limelight. She'd managed so far to avoid the press, but her luck wouldn't hold forever.

While James worked the most recent rare-book orders, Darla reconciled a few invoices while glancing occasionally toward the door. The bell remained disconcertingly silent, however. When it finally jingled around noon, both she and James gazed up with anticipation, only to let loose with a collective sigh of disappointment.

"Uh, hey, Jake," Darla managed.

James gave a formal nod and echoed, "Ms. Martelli."

"Wow, back down on that enthusiastic greeting," the woman replied with a tired grin. Glancing around the otherwise empty shop, she added in commiseration, "Slow day, huh."

"Yeah, they're beating down the doors not to get in," Darla replied. "We got the hard-core Valerie fans yesterday, so I figured today it would be the regulars and probably a few ghouls who'd want to see the store where she did her last signing. But, nada . . . zip."

"Maybe they thought you'd be closed for the day," Jake suggested, plopping down on her favorite beanbag chair in the children's section. "Don't worry, kid, I'm sure business will pick up tomorrow. So, anyone feel like having lunch delivered?"

James called out for soup and salads, and they made a small party of it in the tiny courtyard outside, leaving the door open so Darla could listen for the front bell. While they ate, the retired professor regaled Jake and Darla with stories of deceased authors from the past two centuries whose books appreciated significantly after their unexpected demise.

The fact they were holding this conversation in one of the spots where Valerie Baylor had spent some of her final moments was not lost on any of them.

"And then, as far as twentieth-century writers go, you have Hunter S. Thompson," James said once he'd exhausted writers of the 1800s. "And, more recently, you might recall an interest in Michael Crichton, though the value was sentimental rather than literary. Of course, there is always Salinger. He never signed many books to begin with, and so the pool for collectors has always been limited. The occasional tome turning up with his reputed signature always brings a frenzy of interest among serious bidders."

While Jake nodded in interest—genuine or feigned, Darla was not sure—he continued, "With Ms. Baylor, she had just begun her tour for this book, and so had signed only a few copies to this point. Once again, we are talking scarcity. For the books I am auctioning, I am providing a framed print of the photographs that I took, as well as our store certificate signed by me, to guarantee authenticity. Of course, since Ms. Baylor is not a literary figure in the classic sense, the value for her signed works will drop appreciably once the grief factor dissipates. But until then, I will take my profit where I can."

With a look over at Darla, he added, "I think it would appear, shall we say, inappropriate for Pettistone's Fine Books to have a presence on a public auction site; however, I intend to send private messages to some of our more avid collectors of popular fiction to gauge interest in our signed store copies."

"Wouldn't want to be inappropriate, now," Jake agreed with a grin, which broadened as she turned to Darla. "Speaking of which, Reese wasn't upstairs very long last night. Here I all but gift wrap this good-looking hunk of a man for you and send him up to your place, and you don't take advantage of the situation?"

"Hey, just being polite," Darla replied, trying not to blush. "I figured he might be off-limits, since you and he are so tight."

"Not a chance. You'll never catch me on the cougar prowl," she replied, doing a little mock claw swipe. "Don't get me wrong, I don't mind looking at cute young things, but when it comes down to it, I like my men a bit more seasoned. But the two of you would make a cute couple, and he could use a change from his usual type."

"Really, Jake, I trust you are not pimping out your friends to my employer, or vice versa," James interjected in a disapproving tone.

The woman was not to be squelched.

"Don't be such a killjoy, James," she shot back, turning the grin on him. "Darla's a big girl. She can tell me to back off if she wants."

"Okay, back off," Darla agreed, but she said it with a smile, even as she wondered what Reese's usual type was. Probably barely legal, with that whole Jersey Shore look going on. "Reese is a nice guy, but I can't see him as anything but a friend. Especially while we still have this whole Valerie mess hanging over our heads."

Her smile faded at that last, and she abruptly stood to peer into the store in case a customer had managed to slip in without triggering the bells. It was still empty, except for Hamlet. He padded past the open doorway, tail waving in a carefree manner. Apparently, he enjoyed having the place to himself.

"It's after one o'clock," she proclaimed, looking at her watch, "and we haven't had a single customer. James, why don't you go on home? I'll pay you for the whole shift, of course."

"If you insist. I *am* rather anxious to check the status of my auction."

"I insist. I'll hang out here a bit longer and then shut down for the day. Maybe business tomorrow will be better."

"I am certain it shall be. And I will make sure to send out those emails of inquiry from home. Good afternoon, ladies," he finished with a formal nod, and headed back into the store. A few moments later, jingling bells announced his exit.

Darla sat back with a sigh and raked her hands through her wavy auburn hair, which she'd let hang loose this day. "I'll call Lizzie and tell her not to bother coming in after class this afternoon. Maybe she can do some social networking on our behalf. And I'd better have her post a message of condolence on our website, too."

"Good idea, kid. Don't worry, the customers will be back."

She stood and helped Darla gather the remains of their lunch; then, once the cleanup was completed, Jake too headed for the door. "I'll let you know if I hear anything new from Reese," she promised. "Now go home and have a relaxing afternoon."

As if, Darla wryly thought while the sound of jingling bells followed her friend out. She'd probably spend all afternoon with her nose pressed to the window watching for a return of Marnie, or else sit glued to the cable news channels waiting for segments on the whole Valerie fiasco. With the funeral on Thursday, the media vultures would be hovering again. Which reminded her . . .

Grabbing up the store Rolodex, she flipped through until she found Hillary Gables's phone number. Surprisingly, she reached the agent at her office on the first try.

"You can imagine what it's been like here," the woman told her after they exchanged pleasantries. Her sharp New York City demeanor, punctuated by a few sniffles, seemed to slice through the phone lines as she went on, "The tour had just begun, and we had radio and television spots booked. And, even worse, we don't have another manuscript from her.

Her contract allows two years between books, so her next one wasn't due for a couple of months. I'm afraid this is the end of the line, unless we can ghost out the book to someone else to finish."

She paused, and Darla heard a small chuckle on the other end. "Ghost out . . . kind of appropriate, when you think about it," she added, sounding far more chipper about the entire situation than expected.

Darla simply said in return, "You told me the service for Valerie would be Thursday. Will you still be able to get me in to pay my respects?"

"Sure, why not? But, remember what I said. Don't tell people who you are if you can avoid it. Some of the relatives might hold a grudge. Know what I mean?"

Darla agreed that she did. Satisfied, Hillary gave her the location of the church in Southampton, adding, "Be there by two. Your name will be on the list, but I'll keep an eye out for you in case security doesn't want to let you in. Oh, and dress up. It's not Brooklyn out there. The Hamptons might go casual for everyday, but make it a social affair like a funeral, and they'll dress for it like it's the red carpet."

Darla managed not to make a snide retort to that last. Instead, she thanked the agent and rang off, wondering now if attending the funeral would be a mistake. Hillary might be right, in that Valerie's family could well be blaming her for what happened.

She wondered, too, if Marnie and her fellow congregants would somehow find their way to the church with their protest signs on Thursday. Chances were the van wouldn't yet be repaired, meaning they'd have plenty of spare time on their hands for their demonstration. But at least if they were picketing there, that meant they wouldn't be marching in front of her store. Despite Marnie's promise, Darla wouldn't put it past the woman to make at least a token protest at Pettistone's before she left town, if only to satisfy the tax man that she and her associates had indeed been traveling on church business.

Darla sighed and then slowly spun around, surveying her small kingdom of books. She hadn't realized until now just how much this store had come to mean to her. Before, it had been strictly business, working as a matter of duty and pride to keep her fiscal head well above water in these challenging economic times. After all, she'd been handpicked to carry on this piece of the Pettistone legacy. Great-Aunt Dee could have willed her literary child to any one of twenty other relatives. No way was Darla not going to come up to Pettistone snuff.

Good intentions, however, were not enough. Between the online bookselling behemoths undercutting the little guys, and e-books swooping in to take their surprising share of the market, it was getting harder and harder for brick-and-mortar places to compete. Every day, it seemed, she read in the trades about another well-established bookstore that had slipped into bankruptcy. Keeping a positive attitude after each such doleful announcement, she continually told herself it wouldn't happen to her.

But if today was a harbinger of things to come, she might be the next in line to be washed away by that red-ink tide.

And then what in the heck would she do?

"No sense borrowing trouble," she muttered, reflexively channeling her mother, who was prone to spout such well-worn chestnuts. She had a flexible business plan, and so long as she stuck to it, she should be able to weather the unfavorable economic storm. And if not, maybe she'd simply have to ditch the books and reopen as a coffee shop or a New Age boutique.

Her true dilemma for the moment would be deciding what a good old Texas gal should wear to a filthy rich New York author's funeral.

"DAMN IT, I WAS AFRAID YOU'D ANSWER."

Awakened as she'd been from a sound sleep, it took Darla a few moments to realize that the soft voice on the other end of the phone was Jake's. Alarmed, she grabbed up her bedside clock to check the time.

Five after two in the a.m. Like her dad always told her, nothing good ever happened after midnight. Reflexively, she dropped her own voice to a whisper and demanded, "What's wrong?"

"Footsteps," was Jake's succinct answer. "It's that same

sound of someone walking around in the store again. I'm headed up to take a look."

Not again!

Tracking down possible intruders in the dead of night was the last thing Darla wanted to do after all that had happened. Unfortunately, her sense of responsibility kicked in right on schedule, and she heard herself saying, "I'll go in through the side door. I'll be down as soon as I throw on a robe."

"The hell you will. We've had this discussion before. You can wait downstairs in the hall if you want, but don't you dare set foot inside the store until I open the door for you."

This time, it was Jake's phone that went dead before Darla could protest. She set down the receiver and flipped on the light, and then grabbed her robe. To be honest, she was relieved that Jake had insisted she stay out. Sooner or later, they were going to catch whoever—or whatever—was stomping around the store after hours.

Just to be sure, she took a quick look around the apartment for Hamlet, finding him in his lounging spot in front of the refrigerator. He yawned and blinked in irritation as she flipped on the kitchen light, a pretty good indication that he wasn't the one responsible for the commotion Jake had heard.

This left two possible explanations. Either there was an intruder in the shop, or else Great-Aunt Dee had returned from the Beyond to do an inventory check.

Oh, and there was a third option, she reminded herself. Maybe the ghost of Valerie Baylor had decided to come back and finish her interrupted autographing event.

"Ridiculous!" she protested aloud, the vehemence in her tone drawing an offended meow from the cat.

She tugged on her robe with more force than necessary, angry at herself that such thoughts had even crossed her mind. Surely it was only because she was stressed and had been torn out of a sound sleep that her overtaxed brain had conjured up such far-fetched explanations. Though, in a way, the haunting thing was preferable to having someone continually breaking into the bookstore for some unknown purpose!

She snatched up her keys and hurried out the door. The light from the replica Tiffany lamp on the small table near her front door put out just enough of a golden glow to light her way down. She took the stairs as quickly and quietly as she could in her bare feet, reaching the foyer in record time.

The sight of a shadowy figure looming beyond the frosted glass of the hallway's outer door made her gasp. In the next instant, she heard the soft scrape of a key in the lock and realized from the silhouette's shape that the intruder was Jake. Doubtless the ex-cop had decided to try a different tactic and sneak in the side door, rather than come in with figurative guns blazing through the front.

Maybe it was time to hang a nice opaque curtain behind the glass, Darla fleetingly thought, realizing that the lamp that had brightened the stairwell also illuminated the foyer sufficiently so that someone outside the hazy glass door could see her shadow, too.

Making a mental note to check in with Mary Ann for something suitably vintage in window coverings, Darla hurried to let her friend in.

Jake, unlit flashlight in hand, gave her a look of annoyed resignation as she stepped inside and then moved to the other door. The panel light at the jamb still flashed red, meaning that no one had turned off the alarm. Jake frowned and then punched in the code, bringing it back to green status.

"I'm going in," she whispered. "Wait out here for me, and don't you dare come in until I give the all clear."

Darla waited until Jake was safely inside and then pressed a cautious ear to the door. She stood there listening for several moments, hearing no movement through the paneled wood. Soon enough, her nervousness blossomed into concern. How long had it been since Jake had gone in? Five minutes, perhaps? Surely time enough to sweep through the store and see if anyone was inside. So where was she?

By way of answer, the door abruptly opened inward with Darla still pressed against it.

She gasped and stumbled into the store, catching her balance with Jake's help. All the store lights were on, and she squinted against the sudden brightness for a moment. When her eyes adjusted, she saw Jake standing before her, expression one of extreme disgust.

"Not a damn thing," the woman groused, slapping her flashlight against her palm in obvious irritation. "I thought I saw a shadow on the stairs, and I could have sworn I heard more footsteps, but when I ran up to the second floor, there wasn't anyone there. I searched every square inch of the place. Twice. And, nada."

Then, as Darla stared at her, wide-eyed, Jake's anger fizzled.

"Oh God, listen to me. If someone was telling me this same story, I'd be looking at them like they were crazy, too," she said with a deprecating little laugh. "I swear, I truly did hear someone in here. You believe me, don't you?"

"I believe you, Jake," Darla assured her. "Maybe there really is a poltergeist, like Mary Ann said."

"Don't even go there," Jake countered. "I've lived in apartment buildings all of my life, and believe me, I know what someone walking on the floor above you sounds like. This isn't one of those Valerie Baylor books, and those weren't little ghost-y footsteps."

"Okay, scratch the poltergeist. But maybe it's time I get a security camera installed."

The idea had just come to her, and she couldn't help but think it was the only solution to the problem. Jake obviously agreed, for she gave a vigorous nod.

"Good idea, kid. I know a guy named Ted who's in the security business. I'll call him for you tomorrow and see what kind of deal he can cut you on some cameras. I think that's the only way we're ever going to put this one to bed. Speaking of which, I guess we both might as well head back to ours."

"Sure. Thanks for checking things out. I'll see you tomorrow morning."

She let Jake out the front and locked the door after her before setting the alarm and leaving through the side door, as usual. Her mood was thoughtful as she made her way back upstairs. Hamlet was waiting for her inside the front door, having apparently decided that the middle of the night was as good a time as any for a little snack.

She topped his kibble with some fresh but passed on anything for herself. Instead, she settled at her desk and turned on her computer. She hesitated a moment once she'd brought up the search engine; then, feeling only a bit foolish, she typed in the word "poltergeist."

Instantly, the results popped up—well over five million results. Staggered, she sat back in her chair. Talk about information overload! Cautiously at first, and then more rapidly, she began to click on the links, skimming the pages.

"Well, Hamlet," she told him after half an hour of reading, "all the so-called experts say that if I have poltergeist activity, it should stop as quickly as it started, and shouldn't last more than a few months. On the other hand, if it's a ghost hanging out in the building, I'm pretty well stuck with it unless I get one of those paranormal teams in to run it off. They also say that there can be plenty of non-supernatural explanations, like high electromagnetic frequencies, mold, and animal infestations. So what do you think? Do we bring in a team, or tough it out on our own with a security camera?"

Hamlet apparently had no opinion on the subject, for he looked up from where he'd settled on the couch, gave her a cold green stare, and then went back to napping.

Darla snorted and started to shut down the computer again, when another unsettling thought occurred to her. Jake had seemed more than a little upset at the idea that she could have imagined the sounds, or that Darla might have thought she had. Maybe the ex-cop had encountered some similar situation during her career that made her sensitive to the likes of ghosts and mysterious footsteps in the night.

Fingers on the keyboard, she hesitated. Then, feeling equal parts determined and unaccountably guilty, she typed her friend's name into the search engine.

By inputting all variations she could think of, Darla found herself with several pages of entries about Jake. Some were but a sentence or two mention. Jake had been on the building committee at Mary Queen of Peace Catholic Church five years earlier and had taken part in a fund-raiser for the Big Sisters. Others were police accounts where she'd been the arresting officer. Nothing, however, about ghosts.

Finally, Darla found a news story recounting the circumstances of the shooting that had led to Jake's retirement from the force. She clicked on the link and read with interest. The report was straightforward and echoed the story she had pieced together herself via offhand mentions from Jake.

Authorities are charging the man who shot at a New York City police officer this morning with attempted capital murder. Martin Edward Rose, 52, remains at City Medical Center in good condition after he and the officer exchanged gunfire Tuesday morning in the 300 block of West Olive Street.

Police officials say Rose allegedly fired first, wounding Detective Jacqueline Martelli, a 20-year police veteran. Despite a bullet to the upper thigh, she was able to fire back, hitting him in the torso. Other patrol officers arriving on the scene pulled Martelli to safety and subdued her shooter. Both were taken to the hospital.

Martelli was attempting to arrest Rose on a previous charge of aggravated assault with a deadly weapon. Her condition was upgraded this morning from critical to serious, and she is expected to recover.

A follow-on story from the day after reported that the suspect had been released from the hospital and subsequently denied bail on all charges, while mentioning that Jake's condition was now "good" and that she would be released in a few days. *No alarm bells in any of that,* Darla thought in relief. She had been afraid she might find something untoward, like, *Crazed police officer claims to have shot undead suspect.*

"See, Hamlet," she exclaimed, glancing over her shoulder at the cat. "You were worried for no good reason."

But barely had the words left her lips when she noticed at the bottom of the screen a link to a story dated a few weeks after the shooting. Jake's name was highlighted as a keyword, and the stark headline said it all.

POLICE OFFICER ON DISABILITY LEAVE
CHARGED WITH ATTEMPTED MURDER

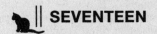 || **SEVENTEEN**

"HOW ABOUT THIS ONE, DEAR?"

Mary Ann held up a length of gold fabric with a faint stripe pattern that gave it a vintage tone-on-tone look. When Darla admired it and ventured aloud that it resembled organza, the old woman smiled and shook her head.

"Very similar, yes, but this is called grenadine," she explained. "It was considered a dress fabric as far back as the eighteenth century, but it fell out of favor right about World War I. Of course, everything old is eventually new again, and it was reborn sometime in the 1920s as a curtain fabric. If you look at old dry goods catalogues from the 1930s through the 1950s, you'll see listings for just that—curtain grenadine. I think this example would look lovely in your foyer."

"I'll take it," Darla agreed, stifling a yawn as she handed over her credit card.

Since Wednesdays were James's day off, she had left the bookstore in Lizzie's care this morning while she did a little shopping at Bygone Days Antiques. After last night, her primary motivation had been to find something to cover the glass door leading up to her apartment. But it had also been a handy excuse for her to take another look at The Hat.

For it had occurred to her that a vintage picture hat would be the ideal thing to wear to a celebrity funeral. She already had a decent black dress, so it didn't make sense to buy a new one just to impress people she'd never again see after tomorrow. Splurging on some one-of-a-kind headgear, however, seemed a perfectly justifiable expense.

"Do you have a curtain rod to hang the fabric?" Mary Ann asked, breaking in on her thoughts. "If not, we have some reproduction hardware that would be quite appropriate for the era. And, I'm sure Brother wouldn't mind popping over to install it for you, free of charge."

Darla smiled. The old woman definitely had mastered the art of the up-sell. Maybe she should ask her if she wanted a few paid hours at the bookstore . . . that was, assuming things ever got back to normal.

Her smile faded. So far that morning, the only person besides her and Lizzie to set foot inside the store had been a reporter from a tabloid magazine looking for a new angle on Valerie Baylor's tragic death. Feeling certain that if she didn't provide a few pithy quotes, the reporter would make up his own, she'd agreed to a brief interview.

Much to Darla's dismay, Lizzie had been eager to get in on the act and spin her own dramatic take on events. As she'd launched into her version for the reporter's benefit, however, Hamlet had leaped on the counter and knocked over a display of bookmarks. In the confusion to recover the scattered inventory, Darla had managed to escort the reporter out the door before Lizzie realized in disappointment that he'd gone.

And, after waiting a few minutes to make sure the reporter wouldn't return, Darla had retrieved a bit of chicken breast from the salad she'd brought for lunch, and given it to Hamlet as a reward.

Now, she nodded her approval of a curtain rod.

"Why don't you pick out something for me and add it to the bill? And you can tell Mr. Plinski to stop by anytime it's convenient for him to do the install."

"Wonderful! I have one in mind that is eye-catching without being terribly ostentatious, and it's reasonably priced, to boot," she replied, carefully refolding the vintage curtain. "And

I'll make sure Brother takes care of this today. Now, is there anything else for you, my dear?"

"Well . . ."

Darla walked over to the mannequin that still sported the black picture hat with its drape of black veiling. Examining it more closely, she saw that the satin ribbon around its crown was a soft shade of dove gray, and that a matching gray satin rose was pinned to it.

"I know I really shouldn't," she began, only to have Mary Ann cut her short.

"Of course you should, dear," she exclaimed, lifting the hat from the painted head and placing it at a rakish angle atop Darla's red waves.

"It's good to treat oneself on occasion," she went on as she adjusted the veil down over her chin. "After all, you never know if a particular day will be your last. Oh dear."

Mary Ann stepped back, looking abashed at her unfortunate observation, and Darla smiled. "Actually, I was thinking of wearing it to Valerie Baylor's funeral tomorrow. It seems appropriate."

The woman nodded and held up a silver-framed hand mirror so Darla could admire her reflection. "It looks lovely on you, and I think quite somber enough for the occasion without looking too funereal. And suppose I give you a little discount, just so you don't feel guilty about indulging yourself?"

They concluded the transaction, and Darla walked out feeling quite stylish in her new purchase. When she entered the bookstore, however, Lizzie surveyed her with something less than approval. Jake had stopped by in Darla's absence, and she also stared in dismay at Darla's approach.

Darla didn't blame them. After all, she was dressed for work in brown slacks and a bulky café au lait sweater that blunted the frothy feminine effect of the hat, not to mention that it worked off a whole other color palette.

"Uh, nice chapeau, kid, but lose the outfit," was Jake's blunt assessment.

Lizzie shook her head and looked pained. "Oh, Darla, please tell us you haven't been wandering around town dressed like that."

"Don't worry," Darla replied as she carefully folded back the black veil and removed the hat. "I bought this over at Mary Ann's while I was shopping for a curtain. I thought I'd wear it to Valerie Baylor's service tomorrow."

"Oh, then that's okay," was Lizzie's response. "And then next year, you can wear it to the Kentucky Derby." She pantomimed sipping from a glass while fanning herself with her free hand. Then, lapsing in what Darla assumed was an imitation of her Texas accent, the woman exclaimed, "Whah, yes, Ah would like another mint julep. They're so refreshin'."

Jake chuckled appreciatively, while Darla rolled her eyes. It had been an ongoing mission ever since she moved to New York to educate the natives that not all southerners talked alike, and that not all native-born Texans shared a common accent. Unfortunately, said mission was usually greeted by blank looks, particularly from those who were certain they could imitate Darla's twang. And since she'd tried and failed with Lizzie several times already on this subject, she decided to let it slide.

Instead, reaching beneath the counter for tissue paper and an oversized plastic bag in which to temporarily store her hat, she said, "Don't forget, Lizzie, I'll be gone most of the day tomorrow. Can you and James get along without me?"

She meant, as in *play nicely together*, but Lizzie chose to take the other meaning.

"If tomorrow's anything like today, there's probably no point for me to come in at all," she said with a sigh. "So far, the only one to come in besides Jake was that reporter."

Jake, of course, wanted to hear that story, which Lizzie told with great relish, even as she bemoaned the fact that the reporter had left before she could share her version of the night's events.

"You know, I think Hamlet knocked over those bookmarks on purpose, just to spoil my interview," she said with a pout in the feline's direction. Hamlet, who was sprawled now at his favorite sunny spot near the door, merely flicked a whisker but didn't deign to otherwise acknowledge the accusation.

Darla had finished packing up her hat by now. She sidestepped the subject of the interview lest it occurred to Lizzie that it had been she who'd shooed out the reporter, rather than he who had escaped while Lizzie was distracted. Instead, she agreed. "If you don't mind taking the day without pay, go ahead and stay home. If we're lucky, the worst of it will have blown over by next week, and things will be back to normal again."

"Do you want I should tag along to the memorial service with you tomorrow?" Jake chimed in.

"No! That is, they won't let you in. Hillary said the list will be checked, and your name has to be on it."

Her reply was more abrupt than she'd intended, and Jake gave her a questioning look. Darla shifted a little under the scrutiny, aware that her view of Jake had taken a slightly different tilt since she'd gone poking about the Internet last night.

Unfortunately, the story about the second shooting that Jake had been involved in had been frustratingly vague despite its incriminating tone. Short as it had been, Darla had memorized it in a couple of readings.

An NYPD detective recently wounded in a high-profile shooting incident has been involved in yet another shooting controversy. Detective Jacqueline Martelli, a 20-year veteran, was charged yesterday with shooting and seriously injuring an alleged mugger in a local parking garage. The officer remains on paid leave pending an internal investigation. No charges have been filed as yet against the shooting victim.

Once she'd gotten over the original shock of finding that bit of intelligence, Darla had spent another good hour trolling the Internet for additional information. Despite her best efforts, however, she could find no more references to the incident. Finally, bleary-eyed, she'd crawled back to bed wondering how she would approach her friend with this new knowledge. Two shootings by one police detective in just a few weeks seemed extreme, even in Brooklyn.

"I can always wait down the street somewhere until it's over with," she heard Jake reply, the words dragging Darla back into the moment. "Besides, I'd kind of like to get a look at the guest list, if you know what I mean."

"You mean, investigate?" Darla shot her a look, momentarily forgetting her other concerns. "Do you think whoever hired Janie might be at the funeral?"

"You never know, kid. Anyhow, I told Reese I'd see if I couldn't tag along."

"I suppose I could tell anyone who asked that you're my driver," Darla agreed, hurrying to add, at the covetous look in the woman's eyes, "not that you get to drive Maybelle . . . at least, not until we're almost there."

And the long car ride might make for an ideal opportunity for her to question Jake about the whole shooting thing. Of course, that tactic could also backfire on her. If there was more to the story than what the news articles had indicated, Darla might find herself stuck in a car for a very long time with a very p.o.'d ex-cop.

"Wait," Lizzie broke in, her tone excited, "maybe I can go, too, since you gave me the day off—"

"No!" Darla and Jake chorused, rounding on the woman at the same time. Darla tempered their response with the reminder, "This isn't a social event, it's business. I'm representing Pettistone's Fine Books. And like I told Jake, there's a list."

Lizzie sniffed, not to be mollified. "Fine, I know when I'm not wanted. I think I'll go unpack some more books. And, just for the record, I think that hat is ridiculous."

She took off for the storeroom, with Darla unsure whether to laugh or be annoyed. Jake gave her an encouraging nod. "Ignore her, kid. I think your hat is kick-ass. If you don't wear it tomorrow, I will."

The mental picture of Jake the Amazon decked out in that sort of frippery tilted Darla back toward amusement, and she smiled. "The hat's mine," she said with a shake of her head, "but tell you what. Do a good job of giving me directions to the church tomorrow, and I might even let you drive back."

"Deal. Oh, and by the way, I made that call for you. Ted the security guy can come by today if you want. I'll give you the number so you can make the arrangements with him."

The front door bell jangled just then, and two customers came into the store. Sending up a silent *thank you* to the literature gods, Darla told Jake to write down the number and then rushed over to help her first customers in days. By the time she had loaded them up with half a dozen books each and explained about the increasingly forlorn-looking flower memorial down the block, Jake had gone and a still-pouting Lizzie had run off on lunch break.

Darla took the opportunity to put in a quick call to James at his home to warn him about the security system that would likely be in place by the time he arrived in the morning. She opted against telling him about the late-night footsteps that Jake had been hearing—no need to drag James into that other melodrama. Rather, she used the confusion surrounding the autographing and its ghastly aftermath as the reason for the additional safety measures.

He agreed that the cameras were a good idea.

"Given the fact that many of our first-edition books are quite valuable, it would seem prudent to protect that investment," he opined. "And, as you said, if we are ever faced with a similar, ahem, situation as we had with Valerie Baylor . . ."

He trailed off, leaving unsaid what they both knew. Darla fleetingly wondered if she should take the opportunity to also ask him about the news stories that she'd found on the Internet the previous night. The question was, would he speak freely to her concerning Jake?

Not that she didn't trust James implicitly. Between her aunt's provisions for the man in her will, and the lawyer's glowing assessment of the former professor, Darla felt confident that James had no ulterior motives or shady past that would come back to bite her. But he had known Jake for far longer, and his loyalties might lie with her.

Deciding there was no need for the moment to put her store manager to the test, she rang off and then went to call Ted.

The security man arrived a couple of hours later, dragging an oversized case on wheels behind him. A blond bulldog of a man, Ted had a tendency to punctuate his conversation with mock shots from finger pistols.

"I know you're in a hurry to get it done today, ma'am, so here's the plan."

Pow, pow.

"If it's okay by you," he went on, "I'm gonna get it all set up this afternoon and come back tomorrow to hide the wires all nice and neat."

It was okay by her, Darla assured him. Grinning, Ted blew

imaginary gun smoke from the tips of his forefingers and then dragged his case to the back.

The rest of the afternoon proceeded with no particular drama. And, much to Darla's relief, customers began to trickle in as well. It was not quite at the usual pace, but the earlier drought seemed to have ended. For his part, Hamlet spent the afternoon sulking high above the action. His self-imposed exile had come after he attempted a stealth attack on Ted. That assault had backfired, however, when the man calmly pulled out a can of compressed air from his case and puffed it in the cat's general direction.

The resulting hiss from the can, which sounded like an even larger, more obnoxious feline than the one doing the stalking, had sent Hamlet scrambling for cover in a most undignified fashion. Safely ensconced among the various flavors of *Soup* books, he had alternated between napping and sending Ted the green stink eye. Darla had received her share of nasty cat looks, too, even though she had been careful not to laugh at his comeuppance. Obviously, Hamlet was aware that she'd authorized Ted's presence in the shop, and he made sure that Darla knew it.

Lizzie had proved almost as great a distraction as Hamlet, announcing her own technological expertise and offering to help Ted out. Rather than using the spray can on her, however, Ted had distracted her with a manual the size of an old Sears catalogue that he asked her to review in case he needed help later. As Lizzie staggered off self-importantly under the burden, he and Darla had exchanged glances. Ted mouthed a single *pow* as he triumphantly shot off one of his finger pistols, causing Darla to swallow back a laugh lest the woman hear it and realize she'd been had.

Ted proved as good as his word. A little before six, he called the three of them—Jake had rejoined them by that point—over to the store's computer to demonstrate the equipment.

"What you got here is my custom EZ-Does-It kit," he explained proudly. "You got your six cameras: two down here, two upstairs, and one each outside at the front door and back. The outside ones and one of the cameras on each floor are your night vision."

At Darla's nod, he went on, "The other two, they're your standard-resolution indoor dome cameras. They're hooked directly into your computer system so you can watch and record right there on your PC. If you've got another computer upstairs in the apartment, you can log into this system from there. There's even a microphone to the audio input on your computer if you want to listen to what's going on."

He shot a look at Jake and then clarified to Darla, "Of course, it's illegal for you to record anything unless the other person knows he's being recorded. I'll leave you some stickers you can slap on your front windows to let people know they're under audio and video surveillance."

He pulled up the monitoring screen, which was divided into six sections, each a bird's-eye view from one of the cameras. He spent another half hour showing them how to switch to a single channel, zoom in live, and review previously recorded images.

"Now, the way you got this place divided up with all this shelving, we still got a couple of blind spots on both floors," he reminded Darla. "But, hey, I can always expand the system if you want, bring in another camera or two."

"No, this looks wonderful," Darla exclaimed, feeling like a combination spy and casino security guard as she stared at the small picture of the four of them gathered near the register. Funny what was visible from up above. She'd never noticed until now that Jake had more than a few gray hairs among the black curls. Neither had she realized until this moment that her own hastily plaited French braid was decidedly off-kilter.

Putting a self-conscious hand to the offending hairstyle, she asked Ted, "I don't suppose you have a dummies' version of the manual to go with all this?"

He grinned. "Don't worry, there's a one-page checklist at the front of the binder. That's all you should actually need. You have any problems, though, you call old Ted for help."

Right on cue, the finger pistols went off. She thanked Ted, choked a little at his invoice—"Just pay me tomorrow, when I finish the wiring"—and then showed the man out.

After locking the door behind him, she returned to the counter to find Jake and Lizzie focused on the live-action shot being broadcast from outside the front door, where Ted stood at the curb, alternately hiking up his trousers and adjusting the resulting wedgie. He repeated the gesture several times, while a grinning Jake zoomed in and out.

"Big Sister is watching," she said with a chortle.

Then, catching Darla's disapproving look, she said a bit defensively, "Oh, come on, everyone is a voyeur at heart. And it's not like old Ted didn't know he'd be on camera standing right in front of the steps like that. He probably did all that on purpose, just to see if we were watching."

"Well . . ." Darla allowed herself a reluctant smile. "You're probably right," she finally agreed. "But keep in mind I'm spending the big bucks for these cameras for security reasons, and not for our personal entertainment."

Unless, of course, the cameras caught a poltergeist, in which case she planned to post that video online and wait for it to go viral!

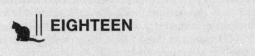 **EIGHTEEN**

"SO DID YOU CATCH ANYTHING ON CAMERA LAST NIGHT?"
Jake had come knocking at the shop's front door that next morning a few minutes before ten. Darla had let her in, and then gone back to finish her opening routine. Now, having given the new security system a quick look—the program allowed her to fast-forward through hours of tape in a matter of minutes—she gestured toward the screen with its compound eye of a store view.

"It all looked pretty quiet. I assume you didn't hear any footsteps after midnight again?"

"Not a step," Jake replied. "And I assume Hamlet didn't build any more book towers?"

"He was still sulking about Ted getting one over on him yesterday, so he stayed pretty well behaved all night long."

Before she could say more, another tap at the door sounded. It was James, coffee thermos in hand, ready to start his shift.

"Good morning," he greeted her, and then gave an approving nod. "I heard about the hat from Jake. I am glad to see you found an appropriate outfit to go with it. I predict you will be the hit of the memorial service."

"That wasn't exactly my intent, but thank you," Darla said a bit sourly as she flipped the sign to "Open."

She was dressed for the memorial service in a basic black wrap dress, which had already seen funeral duty a time or two since its purchase. She'd dragged it from the back of her closet last night, along with a lacy black shawl that she'd tossed over one shoulder. With her cape of auburn hair twisted into a neat bun at the nape of her neck and the hat pinned on at a casual angle, she had been pleasantly surprised at the stylish results. Of course, it was the hat that made the difference. Maybe she'd been missing something all these years, limiting her headgear to ball caps and those knit toboggan thingies, she now told herself as she bagged it up again for the car ride.

Jake ostentatiously cleared her throat. "Hey, what about me?" she demanded. "And here I have that whole Kato vibe going."

Darla grinned at her friend. In her black pantsuit with a tightly cinched jacket waist, and her curly hair neatly tucked under a driver's cap, Jake *did* rather resemble the Green Hornet's sidekick . . . except, of course, that she was female, Caucasian, and a good six inches taller than the late Bruce Lee.

"I think you look like you could kick some serious butt," she told the ex-cop. To James, she added, "Thanks for running the place alone for a few hours. Since you'll be stuck here for lunch, feel free to have the deli deliver you something, and tell them put it on my charge card."

"I shall do so. And I expect a full report upon your return."

She and Jake had started for the door, when the other woman paused. "Since I'll be sitting around for a while, you think I can borrow something to read?"

"Sure." Darla smiled and reached for a book off the stack of *Haunted High* novels and handed it over. "This seems appropriate."

Jake took it and smiled a little, too, as she tucked it into the big hobo bag she carried. "Guess I should go ahead and read it, since the whole rest of the world already has."

They walked to the garage in near silence. For once, Darla didn't even make her usual half-serious protests about having to hoof it everywhere. Instead, she mulled over how best to approach the matter of the shootings with Jake. By the time she'd retrieved Maybelle from her slot and driven down the ramp to pick up her friend, she had decided that a direct approach was the best.

Jake, however, beat her to it.

"Okay, kid, spill it," the woman demanded once she'd buckled herself in and they pulled out from the garage. "You've been acting odd ever since yesterday and something tells me it's not because you're eaten up with grief over Valerie Baylor."

"You're right."

Darla glanced Jake's way. The woman had pulled out her mirrored sunglasses and slid them into place, so that Darla couldn't read her eyes. Which, in a way, made it easier. Taking a deep breath, she blurted, "What's the story behind you shooting that guy in the parking garage?"

"What guy?" Jake swiveled around in her seat for a swift look back at where they'd just left. "What in the hell are you talking about, kid? I don't even have my service revolver on me."

Then Darla saw realization dawn on the woman's face before her features hardened into an unreadable expression beneath the mirrored lenses. "Oh, yeah, the parking garage. So, where did you hear that story? Was James talking out of school?"

"No, he didn't say a word. I searched your name on the Internet and found an article mentioning it."

"You Googled me?"

Jake's voice hit a high pitch that Darla had never heard out of her before. "What in the hell did you do that for? Who do you think I am, some loser you met on an online dating site?"

They had stopped for a red light. A bit defensively, Darla turned to meet her gaze.

"Okay, maybe it was a crappy thing to do," she admitted, "but I was getting concerned that you kept hearing footsteps in the night, and we never found anyone in the store. So I went online. I started by looking up poltergeists, and it ended with looking up you. I found the article about how you got shot trying to arrest a suspect. It all seemed pretty straightforward, and I decided I was worried for nothing. And then I stumbled across that story about the guy in the garage."

Jake began to sputter in outrage, but Darla held her ground.

"I mean, I thought we were gun-happy in Texas, but finding out about your shooting two guys in two months was kind of scary."

Before Jake could respond, a car behind them blared its horn. Darla looked up to see the light had changed back to green. She threw Maybelle into gear and hit the gas, wishing she could leave behind this awkward conversation as well.

If only Jake had let her ease into the subject instead of forcing her to leap right in, she thought in annoyance, her grip on the steering wheel tightening. Maybe she should swing back around and drop Jake back at the building, because it looked like her fear of spending the day stuck in the same car with an angry ex-cop was justified.

When she glanced over at Jake again, however, she was surprised to see that the woman was smiling. To be sure, her expression held more than a note of irony, but it was better than the outrage Darla had expected.

"Okay, kid, why don't we clear the air a little?"

"Works for me," Darla agreed in relief, deciding she could risk continuing toward the expressway, as planned, rather than turning back around and heading home again. That was, assuming that the shooting story could be explained away in a rational fashion.

She looked over again in time to see Jake's smile slip just a little.

"Now, as far as the guy in the garage, your news story was right, to a point," she began. "I did shoot him, but the bastard damn well deserved it. No, no, not this lane . . . move over to the left!" she loudly interrupted herself and made wild gestures as a four-door whose main color was primer abruptly swerved into their lane. Darla hit the horn but held her ground—years of negotiating Dallas rush hours had prepped her for New York City driving—and reclaimed her spot.

Crisis averted, Jake went on in a milder tone, "It happened just a few days after I'd been discharged from the hospital. Ma had driven all the way up from Florida to stay with me until I could get around on my own. So here we were in this parking garage, trying to find where she'd left her car—me in a wheelchair, and my seventy-year-old mother pushing me. And then some punk leaps out from behind a van waving a knife and demanding our money."

Darla gasped as Jake continued, "Of course, being the good Jersey girl she is, Ma wasn't going to take crap off of anyone. So before I could say anything, she jumps in front of the wheelchair and yells at the guy, *You stay the hell away from my little girl.*"

Jake's smile grew grimmer. "Then he starts cursing at her and acting like he's going to cut her, and she's yelling at him that he'd better pray his mother doesn't find out what he's doing. Meanwhile, I'm stuck in my wheelchair yelling at Ma to get behind me, and yelling at the punk to put down his knife because he's under arrest, and neither one is listening to me. So, I pulled out my piece, grabbed Ma and dragged her into my lap, and then blew off the punk's little toe, more to shut him up than anything else."

"Wow," was Darla's succinct reply, torn as she was between amazement and admiration. She made another quick lane change, catching a look at Jake's coolly satisfied expression in the process. Clearly, the Martelli women as a group were not to be messed with, particularly if one wanted to keep all one's digits.

Jake merely shrugged.

"The perp tried to run off, but he didn't get far," she continued. "The patrol officer who responded followed a nice little blood trail and found him one level down, crying behind a Delta Eighty-Eight and holding what was left of his tootsies. I found out later on that he had a rap sheet that stretched from here to next year . . . and, that he was suspected of attacking two other elderly people in two different parking garages that same week. One of the old guys didn't make it, and the other one was laid up in the hospital for a month. Anyhow, the shooting was ruled justified, and Toeless Joe ended up sentenced to life. Guess the papers forgot to report that part."

"Wow," Darla repeated, a bit inadequately. "He's lucky you didn't hit him somewhere more vital."

"Actually, I was aiming for his crotch. Ma jerked my arm at the last minute and knocked my aim off."

They drove in silence for the next few minutes, with Darla feeling slightly lower than worm footprints over the whole situation. She should have known that Jake was just what she appeared to be, and all the drama was in her own head. She glanced Jake's way again and in a meek tone said, "Sorry."

"Yeah, well, next time you think I've turned into some sort of deranged ex-cop with a vendetta, how about you ask me about it first?"

She said it without rancor, however. Darla felt her earlier uneasiness lighten, while her death grip on the steering wheel loosened.

"And if it makes you feel any better," Jake added, "when I found out you were the one inheriting Dee's estate, I went ahead and had an old friend of mine in Records run your name, just to make sure you were legit."

When Darla did a little sputtering of her own, Jake grinned.

"Kinda pinches, that shoe on the other foot, eh? But we all decided that you were about the most boring person we've ever run, so I was pretty sure that Dee knew what she was doing. Now, you wanna call it even, and we'll move on?"

"Even," Darla agreed with a smile and no little sense of relief.

They drove on for a while, then Jake announced, "Okay, that's out of the way, let's plan how we're going to handle this funeral. I know the reason you're going is to pay your respects, but you might as well take advantage of the opportunity. It might sound like a cliché, but you'd be surprised at how often killers show up at their victims' funerals."

Then, when Darla shot her an alarmed look—*killer?*—Jake gave a wry shrug.

"I'm not saying that I think Valerie was murdered, but let's cover all the bases. Look around, see who's there, and listen to the gossip. You never know, someone might fling themselves on Valerie's coffin and admit to doing the deed."

They stopped for a brief lunch once they got out of the city; then, switching places so that Jake was driving and Darla was sitting in the back, they hit the road again.

It was a quarter to two when they pulled up in front of the Episcopal church: an elegant, white-stoned edifice complete with bell tower and cross, and set well back from the road in the midst of a manicured green lawn. A curved drive led from the street to a small parking lot along one side of the building. Darla could see a sleek black hearse and two limousines idling under the distant portico, but further vehicles were blocked from joining them by a row of oversized orange cones.

All this meant that the mourners had to hike the distance from curb to church. Shiny new Jaguars, Bentleys, Porsches, and BMWs made up most of the vehicles discharging passengers there at the gated front walk, though Darla also noticed a couple of Rolls-Royces purring past. She saw, as well, that a large wooden podium manned by half a dozen crisply uniformed young men had been set up along the curb. As each new group of mourners piled out, their respective drivers were pointed toward a nearby lot where they could await their employers' return. For those mourners slightly lower down the food chain—meaning they had driven themselves—one of those youths promptly leaped behind the wheel of the empty car and drove it off to a second location.

"Valet parking at a funeral," Darla murmured in amazement, wondering if one was supposed to tip in such circumstances and feeling slightly smug that she had a driver of her own.

Jake grinned. "That's the Hamptons for you."

Darla pinned on her oversized hat again as Jake pulled into line with the rest and waited their turn. She noticed a couple of local police cars prowling the winding road, no doubt dispatched to hustle away any paparazzi, fans, or Lord's Blessing Church protesters who might have learned the location of the service. For the moment, however, it appeared that the destination remained a secret. The only black garb she spied was the fashionable funeral attire worn by the parade of wealthy guests.

As they reached the valet stand, a young man rushed to Darla's side to open her door.

"Enjoy hobbing with the nobs, kid," Jake told her as she climbed out. "And if you see anyone there you think I should meet"—she pulled her glasses down to her nose and waggled her brows meaningfully—"send me a text."

Darla adjusted her veil so that it caught on her chin and draped the shawl over her shoulders before starting down the walk toward the church. Ahead of her, a sixtyish man in a black suit was escorting a paper-thin blonde less than half his age who could have been a model. Darla was pleased to see that the young woman wore a black wrap dress similar to Darla's own, though hers had a stand-up white collar and was hemmed a good foot shorter than Darla's knee-length outfit. She suspected, however, that the model's dress was also worth twenty times the cost of Darla's sensible knit, which she had found on sale for less than a hundred dollars.

Her feet in the unaccustomed heels had already begun to ache by the time she reached the broad marble staircase leading up to the church's pair of arched wooden doors. She thought longingly of the running shoes she'd left behind in the car, but she knew too well that the fashion of pairing that footwear with formal wear had gone out with the eighties.

Several other guests already were gathered, waiting to enter. The promised security was there, too: two beefy, black-suited men situated on either side of the massive entry. Darla didn't need a second look to recognize one of them. Everest stood with a clipboard in hand as he marked off the names of each arrival.

"Ms. Pettistone," Everest greeted her with professional pleasure when it was her turn to give her name. "It's good to see you again, ma'am, despite the circumstances. Let me see if you're on the list."

Frowning, he scanned his clipboard and then shook his head. "John," he called to his cohort, "check to see if Ms. Pettistone is on your list."

The other man obediently scrutinized his paper before shaking his head as well. "She's not on it."

"I'm not?" Darla stared at Everest in consternation, feeling herself blush behind her veil. She'd never in her life gate-crashed an event, but now it appeared she was on the verge of doing just that. "I don't understand. Hillary Gables promised that she would add my name."

"I'm sure she did, Ms. Pettistone," came Everest's diplomatic reply.

Unspoken were the words, *Yeah, that's what they all say, lady.*

Her blush deepening, she went on, "Seriously, Everest, I talked to Hillary not two days ago. She's the one who gave me directions. She even said she'd look out for me just in case there was a problem. Maybe I can pop into the church and find her so she can come back out and vouch for me?"

Everest shook his head, his diamond earring sparkling in the afternoon sun.

"I'm afraid I can't do that, ma'am. If it was just me, I'd let you right in, but I have orders from the family to stick to the list. I hope you understand."

"How about if I wait here in case Hillary notices I'm not inside and comes looking for me?" Darla persisted, biting back the few choice words for the agent that threatened. How could Hillary let her come all the way out here from Brooklyn, only to forget to put her on the list? And how was she supposed to do the look-and-listen routine that Jake had assigned her if she couldn't even get past the door?

The bodyguard glanced at the Rolex on one beefy wrist and then nodded. "I suppose it wouldn't hurt if you stood here for a few minutes, at least until the service starts. But I do ask that you step aside so that the other guests can pass by."

"Sure."

Darla stepped aside and pretended she had come out of the church for a breath of fresh air. If not for the circumstances, she might have enjoyed the wait. The afternoon breeze coming off the Atlantic Ocean was just cool enough to offset the sun, and she was in the center of more greenery than she'd seen since she moved to Brooklyn. A veritable meadow stretched before her, the meticulously manicured lawn as carefully maintained as any golf course. Across the distant street, she could see where all the valet cars were parked. They appeared arranged in order of retail value, with the Rollses up front, and the other cars behind.

As for the guests, their numbers at the door had increased dramatically. Darla recognized a couple of B-list film stars and even one controversial radio personality among them, as well as several faces from the publishing industry that she had seen in various trade magazines. She glanced at her non-Rolex and saw it was but a couple of minutes to two. Was one always fashionably late, even to a funeral, in the world of the rich?

As unobtrusively as she could, she pulled out her phone and texted Jake. *Not on list, Security won't let me in. What 2 do?*

A reply popped up almost immediately: *Sneak in with someone else?*

Can't, she typed back. *Hat's 2 big.*

Lose it!!!!!

Darla glanced around. The crowd at the door was growing, so that it looked more like the line outside a popular club than a gathering of mourners. John and Everest were busy going over their lists, and someone had finally propped open the immense arched doors to better accommodate the flow. She looked around one last time for Hillary but didn't see her. *It's now or never*, she told herself.

As casually as she could, she reached up hands that suddenly were trembling and unpinned her hat. Tucking the lavish headwear beneath her arm, she pulled up her shawl like a mantilla. Now, it covered her red hair and draped over her shoulders, concealing the hat as well. The result harkened back to the old-school Catholic-lady look she remembered from her childhood, but it would serve to disguise her, at least until she got inside the church. What she needed to do was find someone—preferably male, older, and very nearsighted—who'd already been checked off the list. Then she could latch onto him and slip past the door right under Everest's nose.

With a bit of genteel shoving, she made her way into the center of the crowd. Directly ahead of her was a man who, at least from the back, looked like a perfect candidate to serve as her shield. He was tall and thin and dressed in the requisite black, so that his shock of white hair appeared even whiter. Best of all, he appeared to be alone.

She pressed in closer behind him, keeping her head tilted downward so that the shawl concealed her face from either side. Not satisfied with that, she hunched her shoulders and sank into herself a little, hoping to present a more convincing silhouette that might pass for the old fellow's wife. He had reached the front of the line now, and she could feel her heart pounding with nervous anticipation as she crowded closer still to him.

Despite herself, she jumped as she heard Everest's familiar rumble. "My apologies, sir, you shouldn't have stood in line out here. Please, step right in."

She took this as her cue and reached forward to grasp the

man by one thin but surprisingly sinewy arm. "Let's go inside, dear," she said before he could protest. Using him as a veritable human screen in front of her, she hustled the unresisting man past the bodyguard and into the church's dim foyer.

She expected to feel Everest's beefy hand closing over her shoulder at any instant, but a glance back showed that he was already distracted by the next person in line. Her subterfuge had worked! Now, all that was left to do was unload the old geezer and find a seat for herself in the main sanctuary.

"I hope you'll forgive me," she began, letting go of his sleeve so she could put her hat back on and resettle her shawl back on her shoulders where it belonged. "I've been waiting for Hillary Gables and she seems to have been delayed, so I'm afraid I took advantage and slipped past security with you."

"I quite understand. Ms. Gables is not the most . . . dependable of people."

The voice was far younger than she'd expected, and she glanced up in surprise. He had turned now to look at her, and she saw that he was not an old man after all. He was gauntly handsome and likely no older than she. It was the hair that had fooled her, hair that was preternaturally white-blond. But more odd was the fact that something about him—perhaps it was his pale blue eyes—seemed vaguely familiar.

"I'm sorry, have we met?" she asked, putting out her hand. "I'm Darla Pettistone. I knew Valerie, uh, professionally. Were you a friend of hers?"

He gave her a faint smile, and the first thing that struck her was that his smooth forehead did not reflect that change in expression. The second thing she noticed as he lightly clasped her hand was that he wore a heavy gold puzzle ring on one long finger.

"I'm Morris Vickson," she heard him say. "Valerie's brother. Her twin brother."

Darla stared at him for a long moment through her veil, even as she murmured the appropriate words of sympathy. All the while, however, one thought was swirling through her mind, a realization at once unbelievable and patently obvious. There was no question about it—Valerie's brother Morris was, in reality . . . Mavis!

NINETEEN

IF THIS PARTICULAR MEMORIAL SERVICE HAD BEEN A scene in one of Valerie Baylor's books, the woman in the coffin would have suddenly opened her dead blue eyes wide as Darla stared down at her. No one else in the church would have noticed, of course, nor would they have seen the woman grasp her wrist in unrelenting cold fingers or heard the words meant only for Darla's ears.

We fooled you all, Mavis and I, didn't we?

Darla abruptly drew back from the casket, that fleeting lapse into imagination a bit too real for comfort. But Valerie's eyes with their dusting of taupe shadow remained closed, and her slim hands remained demurely crossed just above her waist. What appeared to be the same red fountain pen as in her poster was tucked between her fingers, as if she'd drifted to sleep while dashing off a page of her latest manuscript. Minus the scorn, and with coral lipstick rather than the typical slash of red, she looked softer and far more pensive in death than Darla remembered her.

Indeed, for the first time, she actually felt more than the obligatory polite regret for the woman's passing.

She hadn't intended to go up to the front for the ritual up-close-and-personal look. In fact, she was surprised to even see the open casket in church, since James had told her that it wasn't a typical practice for this denomination. Besides, she'd already seen Valerie lying dead in the street, and that image would be with her for some time. But Morris had politely insisted on walking her up to the line of mourners who were paying their respects at the open casket, so she'd not had a choice in the matter.

Now, feeling self-conscious, she turned to make a quick retreat. Valerie had rated a full house, and with all the black in evidence Darla was reminded of the ill-fated book signing. She spied an open seat near the back of the church and headed toward it, grateful for the small concealment provided by her hat and veil. Not that she'd technically done anything wrong, she assured herself. Hillary had said she was invited, and it was hardly her fault that the woman had not bothered to update the list.

She passed by the front row, where Valerie's family were sitting. A tiny woman in her sixties with dyed black hair and sharp features sat between Morris and a nattily dressed gentleman about her same age. Darla swiftly identified the older couple as Valerie and Morris's parents. The man had that same Thin White Duke look going on as his son, while the woman bore a striking resemblance to the dead author. The rest of the pew and the one behind it held what were presumably various aunts, uncles, and cousins, each face reflecting genteel sorrow.

A few rows back, she finally spied the agent. Hillary Gables had pinned back her hair into one of those eyebrow-lifting buns on top of her head and wore a black skirted suit with a white blouse. As Darla watched, Hillary dabbed at her eyes and nose with a tissue, the gesture of courteous grief. She didn't notice Darla, perhaps because she had leaned in the opposite direction to whisper into the ear of a man old enough to have been her grandfather.

Except Darla was pretty certain that no decent grandfather allowed his granddaughter's hands to linger where Hillary was letting them wander.

Darla didn't see Koji anywhere. Apparently, the publicist hadn't made the cut, either. Or maybe he had, Darla wryly thought, and right now he was pounding the pavement look-

ing for a new job instead of—as Jake had put it—hobbing
with the nobs.

It was with relief that she finally slipped into a seat. On her
right was a thirty-something man large enough to be a line-
backer for a major league team, and judging by the abundance
of diamond jewelry on his hands and earlobes, likely was. On
her other side was a woman in her eighties who had bucked
the black trend by wearing what appeared to be a vintage
Chanel suit in deep forest green. Balanced on her spindly
knees was a purse that Darla recognized from a recent newspaper article on fashion as retailing for four figures. Both
pew-mates gave her polite nods as she settled in, but Darla
could feel their mutual if unspoken question: *How did* she *get
in here?*

As unobtrusively as she could, Darla pulled her cell phone
out of her bag and typed out a quick text to Jake.

Snuck in with VB's bro. Ur not going 2 believe who he is!

Darla hit send; then, as she tried to think the best way to
explain the situation in text speak—*Mavis = Morris = Val's
bro*?—a sharp poke in her side made her gasp. The poker was
the elderly woman beside her, who'd apparently noticed her
etiquette transgression of texting in church and did not approve.
As Darla rubbed her bruised ribs and contemplated battery
charges, the woman pierced her with a condemning look and
gave an audible *tsk*.

Darla gave her an equally condemning look in return. "I
beg your pardon, I'm a surgeon," she lied in a stern stage
whisper. "I have to check in with the hospital. I've got a trans-
plant patient waiting on me."

The old woman appeared mollified by this explanation, for
her sour expression thawed slightly. Satisfied she had gained
herself a bit of credibility, Darla settled back in the hard
wooden pew and put her phone away without sending another
message. She still needed time, herself, to wrap her brain
around the apparent fact that Mavis the makeup artist and
Morris the grieving brother were one and the same person.

What took her aback more than anything else was the fact
that his introduction of himself had been straightforward, with
no indication that they'd met before. Thus good manners, if nothing else, kept her from blurting out that she definitely recalled

him—or, at least, Mavis—from that unfortunate event. But surely he remembered her from the bookstore, especially since she had given him her name. She'd expected a wink or a knowing smile. Instead, he'd acted as if they were strangers meeting for the first time.

Or were they?

Now that a few minutes had passed, doubts began to assail her. She was certain she hadn't been mistaken the night of the signing when she realized that Mavis—for all her flawless makeup and fashionable dress—was actually a male in women's clothing. Of course, no one else had made mention of their suspicions that Mavis was something other than what she appeared to be, though that might simply have been good manners on their part. But to tell the truth, so artful had his Mavis persona been, she might never have made the connection had she not recognized his ring.

But she had to be right. The baritone voice she remembered from that night, so similar to Morris's, was proof enough, while the large hands were another giveaway. And surely she wasn't imagining now the striking resemblance between the Botoxed-looking Mavis and the equally smooth-faced Morris.

While she struggled with those questions, the last of the mourners passed the casket. Now, two of the funeral-home staff closed the lid and draped a white cloth over it. Darla felt relieved that Valerie was safely tucked away and not likely to rise from the dead anytime soon.

A young, movie-handsome clergyman in full vestments took the lectern. The reverend was a trained orator, and the sprightly organist who played between the formal prayers could have sold out a concert hall. Even churchgoing was an event in the Hamptons, Darla decided as she joined the rest of the mourners in gustily singing along with those hymns she knew.

At the conclusion of the formal service, the reverend spoke for a few solemn moments on the brief life of Valerie Vickson Baylor. Then he relinquished the lectern to the same older man whom Darla had noticed heading into the church with his impossibly thin consort. She was surprised when he introduced himself as Howard T. Pinter, owner and publisher-in-chief of Ibizan Books.

"We discovered Valerie Baylor," he proclaimed in suitably doleful tones as he took a pair of reading glasses from his breast pocket, "and she, in turn, brought glory to Ibizan Books."

Unfolding a paper he pulled from a second pocket, he went on in this vein for some moments. Then Pinter beckoned forward from the pews a small parade of men and women who expounded for exactly three minutes each—Darla began timing them after the first two—on Valerie's life. She listened intently at first, hoping to hear something that Jake or Reese might deem important. By the fourth fulsome speaker, however, she knew that no scandals would erupt from this admiring crowd. And so she let her thoughts drift back to Valerie's brother, and the other unexpected revelation that had come of their momentary encounter.

Twins, Morris had said.

After the first shock, she could easily see the familial resemblance between him and the dead author. And knowing what she did about Morris's alter ego, she found herself wondering just what had been the relationship between Morris-as-Mavis and his/her sister. Valerie obviously knew of her twin's proclivity for dressing as a woman. The fact she kept Mavis as part of her entourage could mean that Valerie accepted, perhaps even approved, of Morris's other life. On the other hand, she had seemed to treat Mavis with barely concealed contempt, while Mavis hadn't seemed to harbor much affection for her in return. But Darla could not forget the obvious shock and grief that Mavis had displayed when learning of Valerie's death.

Perhaps there had been genuine love after all. Or maybe Morris's acting abilities went beyond a talent for female impersonation.

Abruptly, Darla's thoughts began to take a darker turn. When it came down to it, no one had been fully accounted for during the thirty or so critical minutes before Valerie's death. Was it possible that Morris might have been the same hooded figure who had struggled with Valerie outside that final time? Could he have been the one present when she'd taken her tumble into traffic . . . perhaps had even pushed her himself?

The notion grabbed hold of her and wouldn't let go, even as she reminded herself that the incident had not been ruled anything other than an accident. But why would Jake have told her to keep her eyes open, she wondered, if she and Reese didn't think something was suspicious about the situation?

For it all makes terrible sense, she realized. Hadn't she read somewhere that when a person was murdered, it was most likely that his killer had been a close acquaintance rather than a stranger? But what would have been Morris's motive to murder his sister?

Money? But the family was already well-off. *Jealousy over her fame?* Given his double life, surely fame was the last thing that Morris would want. Or maybe it was something more basic? Had Valerie threatened to expose Mavis as Morris's alter ego, and he had taken desperate measures to keep his secret safe?

And yet, except for the one lapse during the signing where Mavis had let loose with a rude descriptive, Valerie's twin had appeared a mild and polite person, even reserved. Somehow, she didn't see in him the strong emotion it would take to commit such an act.

So caught up was she in her speculations that she almost missed it when Morris himself abruptly rose from his pew. Looking elegant in his well-tailored black suit, he moved with languid grace as he made his way to the lectern.

"He's such a handsome gentleman," the old woman next to Darla muttered, apparently forgetting her earlier disapproval with this opportunity for gossip.

She leaned close enough that Darla got a whiff of rose-scented cologne tinged with body odor. "It's a shame he hasn't married yet, but then he's always been so shy, and always so devoted to his sister. Why, he never even moved out of his parents' home, not even after poor Valerie ran off to a state university, of all things. And she then married that upstart from California. New money, you know," she added in a stage-whispered aside. "But with his sister gone, maybe now . . ."

She trailed off meaningfully.

Realizing some response was expected of her, Darla managed a noncommittal smile and a little shrug, even as she tried to puzzle out said meaning. Was the woman implying that Morris had had an unhealthy attachment to Valerie, or was she trying to say that Valerie had somehow held her brother back?

Morris's eulogy turned out to be almost startlingly brief. He bowed his head and stood in silence behind the lectern for several moments, long enough that people began to shift uncomfortably in their seats and glance at one another. Watching him, Darla found herself playing psychiatrist, wondering if he suffered from some sort of social anxiety or phobia. Maybe that was the reason for his Mavis persona, a way that he could hide in plain sight, so to speak. Finally, he lifted his head and spoke.

"As you might guess, this has all been a terrible shock for our family. I think I can safely say that I knew my twin sister better than any one of you, and that I am lost now without her. We spent our first nine months with our arms wrapped around each other, and for the first time in my life, my arms are now empty."

With that stark yet oddly emotionless proclamation, Morris left the lectern and started back toward the family pew. He stopped to accept hugs from several people who were seated nearby before once more resuming his own place between his parents. Darla noted from her vantage point that he did not actually return any of those physical gestures—nor did he ever look back toward the closed casket that held his twin.

A few minutes later, the service was over. Darla rose with the rest of the mourners to watch as the pallbearers rolled Valerie's casket toward the door and the hearse that waited outside. The graveside service would be for family only. So how could she contrive to meet with Morris again and see if she could get answers to any of her suspicions? She needed more than just the revelation that Morris and Mavis were one and the same to convince Jake and Reese that she might have stumbled across a viable suspect in Valerie's death.

Not your job, Nancy Drew, she could almost hear Jake saying. She tried to think of a retort to that argument but came up empty. Fine. She'd tell Jake what she learned and let the woman pass on that info to Reese to do with as he would. Her work here was done.

Besides which, she realized, she didn't want him to have had anything to do with his sister's death. She liked Morris . . . *and* Mavis.

That burden lifted from her, she turned her attention to

getting out of there, impatient as she was now to drop the whole thing into Jake's lap. Valerie's family was gathered just outside the church to receive condolences. She ran that gauntlet of grief as swiftly as she could without looking rude. Plucking every clichéd phrase she could find from her mental file of appropriate things to say to the bereaved, she shook hands and exchanged air kisses with a dozen people who had no clue who she was but were content to accept her kind words. Finally, she came to Morris.

"A lovely service," she told him as she clasped his hand. "I'm afraid I knew Valerie just a short time, but she made quite an impression. She will be missed."

"Yes, Valerie had a talent for making . . . impressions," he replied with a dry little smile. "I've been particularly touched by the outpouring from her fans. We've received letters from all over the world from people hoping that she left behind a few more manuscripts."

"Did she?" Darla asked, genuinely curious.

She knew that most writers were usually well into completing their next manuscript by the time the most recent book hit the shelves. And though Hillary had claimed there wasn't another one, maybe she simply didn't know what Valerie had been working on when she died.

Morris, meanwhile, gave a noncommittal shrug. "I suppose we'll find that out when I sort through her papers."

"Oh, of course."

She hesitated, choosing her words carefully.

"I'm not sure if you know this," she went on, "but I'm the owner of the bookstore where Valerie held her last signing. All of our employees were devastated by what happened, and we're hoping to donate some of our profits from her books to a literacy cause in her name."

Darla had come up with the idea on the spur of the moment, but she found herself liking it. She'd let James handle the details. Emboldened, she continued, "We took several pictures of the event before . . . well, you know. If you give me your email address, I would be happy to send you copies of them."

"That would be lovely," he replied and reached inside his jacket.

Pulling out a business card and a pen, he scribbled

something on the back and then handed the card to her. "Send the pictures there, if you don't mind."

She tucked the card in her purse. With an appropriately subdued nod, she replied, "I'll be in touch. It was a pleasure to meet you, Mr. Vickson. I'm only sorry it was under such tragic circumstances."

They exchanged a final polite handshake, and then Darla started down the steps. Everest was standing below at the walk, his expression distinctly disapproving as he caught sight of her. She met his gaze and gave an apologetic shrug as she drew even with him.

"I never did find Hillary, but Mr. Vickson kindly escorted me in," she told him, neglecting to mention that the escort had been entirely involuntary.

Everest, however, seemingly read between the lines, for his scowl deepened. "I expected better of you, Ms. Pettistone. I trust when we get to the cemetery that I won't find you in the back of the hearse with the casket."

"No fear of that," she declared with a shiver that wasn't feigned. "Good-bye, Everest."

She headed down the walk and reached for her phone to dial Jake. A crowd had gathered around the valet stand. With luck, Jake in her role as driver could could bypass the line and beat the crowd. Given what she had learned about Morris, she was liable to explode if she couldn't share this bit of intelligence in the next few moments!

"So what the hell was that message about Valerie's brother?" the woman demanded as she answered Darla's call, sounding equally as eager to hear the news. "I tried texting you back, but I guess you'd shut off your phone already."

"Can't tell you now," Darla replied with a look around. "Too many people. Just hurry and get over here."

"Don't worry, I bribed the valet directing the self-parking with that copy of Valerie's book you gave me, so he put me in a nice spot right up front with the Rollses. I'm pulling out of the lot now."

By the time Darla reached the curb, the Mercedes had nosed to the front of the line and was waiting for her. As she made her way through the knot of other guests awaiting their rides, she almost stumbled into Hillary Gables. The woman was clutching her ersatz grandfather's arm as they stood on the sidewalk with the rest.

Darla gave the agent a bright smile through her veil.

"Hello, Hillary. Lovely service, wasn't it? But I almost missed the entire thing. It seems my name wasn't on the list."

"Oh, yes, Darla." Hillary returned her smile with a blank look, eyes unblinking behind her glasses. "I didn't recognize you at first. So sorry about the list. You know how it goes."

"Of course. I'd love to chat more and meet your grandfather, but as you can see my car is waiting. Maybe next time."

With a wink and an even bigger smile for the old man, Darla turned on her heel. Before the valet could open the door, she'd climbed into the front passenger seat of the Mercedes. Jake, still in her driver's outfit, glanced over at her as she buckled herself in.

"Let's get a few blocks down the road," the older woman said as she accelerated, "and we can switch places. In the meantime, spill. What's up with the brother?"

"Give me a sec," Darla replied as she kicked off her heels with a sigh and unpinned her hat, carefully setting it in the backseat. Then, feeling rather like the gossipy old woman who'd been sitting beside her in the church, she burst out, "Mavis is Valerie's brother."

"Uh, would you like to elaborate?"

By then, they'd reached a spot where Jake could stop the Mercedes. She slid over to the passenger side while Darla hopped out. After a quick look around for oncoming traffic, she tiptoed barefooted around the car and took her place behind the wheel. As they started off again, she began relating the events of the past hour, building up to the point where she'd learned about Morris.

"So Mavis, Valerie's assistant, is actually Morris, Valerie's twin brother," Jake mused. "I assume some of them must have guessed she was a man, but I wonder if any of the rest of her entourage had any idea about the family relationship. That does open the possibilities a bit. But obviously, just because the guy is a cross-dresser doesn't mean he killed his sister. That kind of stuff is for the movies."

"So you don't think Morris is any kind of suspect?"

"Never say never. For the moment, the only real question I

have is whether he gave Reese his real name when he made his statement the night of the accident. If Mavis—or, rather, Morris—lied, that could be problematic. He might get charged with obstruction. At the very least, they'll probably drag his butt back in for more questioning."

"And if he told Reese the truth?"

"Then that's that, unless we learn something else that puts him on a suspect list." Jake paused, her expression thoughtful. "Of course, there's nothing to stop you and me from scheduling a little gossip-fest with old Morrie. Since you two are best buddies now, do you think you can get her . . . him . . . back to the store for a little chat?"

"I told him about the pictures we took at the autographing, and he gave me his contact info so I can email them to him. Maybe I can tell him that I also found something at the store that might belong to Valerie. I'll say that I'd prefer not to mail it and ask him if he can swing by to pick it up."

"Good idea, but what could she have left behind? Remember, Reese had all her things couriered over already."

"Maybe a vintage cigarette lighter?" Darla suggested, wrinkling her nose a little at the scent of smoke that clung to her friend. No doubt Jake had indulged in a cigarette or two while she waited. Even though she knew Jake would never smoke in her car, Maybelle still would need an airing out to be rid of the lingering odor.

The other woman nodded in approval.

"You could say you found a fancy lighter in the courtyard and thought it might be hers. But, of course, you wouldn't want to mail it to him without knowing for sure, in case it belonged to a customer, instead. You could borrow some gaudy antique thing from Mary Ann's shop to show him. While he's there, we'll chat him up for a while and see if he spills any secrets. But don't get your hopes up, Nancy. Chances are the only secret Morris is hiding is that whole Mavis shtick."

"It's a plan," Darla agreed. "Now, what about you? Any good gossip from your fellow chauffeurs?"

Jake snorted. "I learned about one ballplayer's drug problem, found out a former child actress turned rock star is a closeted lesbian, and that two major players in the financial world brought their mistresses and not their wives to this little shindig. And those are the boring parts. But nothing about Valerie Baylor."

They chatted more about the service and the fact that Hillary apparently—and deliberately—had left Darla off the guest list. But it wasn't until they reached the garage again and had started out on foot toward the brownstone that Darla dug into her purse for the gold-embossed business card that Morris had given her.

She studied it more closely while Jake trailed a few steps behind her to indulge in a quick smoke. The title CEO was printed after his name, and "Morris Vickson Enterprises" was his company's name, with no other clue as to the nature of said business. Since he apparently had time to accompany his sister while dressed as Mavis, did he actually do anything as CEO? His money might come solely from his parents, meaning he was living off their largesse with corporate title and company nothing more than a polite fiction.

Unless it was Mavis, not Morris, who was the money-maker?

Darla frowned, considering that possibility. She wondered if, in his Mavis guise, he had any other clients besides his sister . . . wondered, too, how much money a professional makeup artist could bring in. Maybe he hired out Mavis through his company? Doubtless any number of positions existed in New York City's fashion and television and theater worlds for a talented makeup artist. He might well be bringing in a decent paycheck.

Oddly enough for someone who hailed from the Hamptons, the address listed on the card was in Brooklyn, though she didn't recognize the street name. But that was not what made her stop in midstep and catch her breath.

She had flipped over the card to read the email address that Morris had scribbled on the back. "Jake," she said as her friend halted beside her in concern, "Reese still has that lipstick note that Hamlet found, right?"

"Yeah. Why?"

Darla took a deep breath. "I think I know now who wrote it."

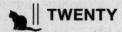 **TWENTY**

"LET ME GET THIS STRAIGHT, DARLA. YOU SNUCK INTO A private memorial service hoping to get the dirt on someone?"

Reese's tone was disapproving, and his words were all too familiar. In fact, it was a virtual repeat of the conversation she'd had with him a few days earlier regarding the Lone Protester. Given the fact she had been proven correct then—and, it would seem, now—Darla met the detective's disapproving look with equanimity.

They were downstairs in Jake's basement apartment, in the middle of polishing off a hasty supper of spaghetti that Jake had put together. "Ma whips up a huge batch of sauce and meatballs anytime she visits. I freeze it for emergencies like this," she had explained with a grin when Darla marveled at the speed with which she had managed a homemade meal.

With afternoon traffic, their return from the Hamptons had been longer than the trip out. Once they arrived back at the brownstone following Valerie Baylor's posh memorial, Jake had put in the call to Reese to stop by on his dinner break. Darla, meanwhile, had made a quick stop to check on things at her own store before make a beeline for Bygone Days Antiques.

"No time to talk, Mary Ann," she breathlessly had told the

old woman. "I need to see if you have something old and expensive in the way of a cigarette lighter." A few moments later, as Mary Ann brought out a few possibilities for her to examine, she added with an apologetic wince, "But I don't actually want to buy anything. I just need to borrow one for a day . . . police business, you know."

"So long as you bring it back undamaged, you are welcome to take any one of them," the old woman agreed with a smile. "But I will expect a full explanation later, my dear, or else I will perish of curiosity."

Then, with a quick look over her shoulder to the back of the shop, Mary Ann had added in a conspiratorial whisper, "We just won't mention this to Brother. Now, which do you prefer, the green enamel with silver, or the gold with the embossed swan?"

Since Jake had proved equally successful in her mission to persuade Reese to stop by, enticing him with the twin draws of home-cooked food and some potentially interesting information regarding Valerie Baylor, their plan had seemed to be falling right into place. Then Darla scored the final point. After running upstairs to feed Hamlet and change from her funeral garb into jeans and a sweater, she had taken a deep breath and with shaking fingers, dialed Morris's number.

She had been surprised when he actually answered the phone, even though she'd been pretty sure that, in the Hamptons, the neighbors did *not* all gather together after a funeral to share a covered-dish sit-down. But perhaps he would have lingered at the gravesite. Her plan had been to leave a message and hope for a return call, so she had been taken off guard when he picked up almost immediately.

Morris's tone had been polite if puzzled by her unexpected call so soon after the funeral, until she mentioned the expensive cigarette lighter she supposedly had found. When she suggested that he stop by to identify it as Valerie's, silence had met her words. She had feared for a few uncomfortable moments that she had crossed a line of some sort. Then, to her relief, he responded in the affirmative to her invitation.

"I don't often go out," he explained, "but perhaps I can manage, since this has to do with my sister. Would one o'clock tomorrow be convenient?"

With the plan in place, the three of them—Darla, Reese, and Jake—now were gathered for what Darla privately called a war conference and what she suspected Reese thought of as an annoyance wrapped inside a darned good meal.

She had waited until they had made significant dents in their respective overflowing plates before launching into an account of the day's events. But she had barely begun her explanation when Reese stopped her with his words of disapproval.

Now, she reminded him, "I was supposed to be on the guest list for the memorial service. It's not like I bribed someone to find out where it was being held. Hillary Gables gave me the directions herself. So why don't you quit acting like Miss Manners and let me tell you the rest?"

While Reese went back to shoveling in spaghetti, Darla went on to explain her shock at realizing that Morris was actually Mavis. She waited for Reese's reaction to that, only to realize when none was forthcoming that, as Jake had suggested, he must have known this already.

"Yeah, your buddy Morris gave me his real name and address when I took his statement," the detective confirmed, grinning a little at her disappointment. "He did leave out the part about being Valerie Baylor's brother, though, which is suspicious, but not really enough to make the case active again. Still, score one for you, Red . . . er, Darla."

She bristled a bit at that last but let it pass, going on instead to recount Morris's strangely brief eulogy. She wrapped up by asking, "Besides the YouTube video and some conflicting witness statements, the only other potential evidence you have is the lipstick note that Hamlet found. Correct?"

He gave a noncommittal shrug. "The key word is actually *had*. In case you missed the memo, Ms. Baylor's death was ruled an accident, and there wasn't sufficient evidence or eyewitness testimony to keep the case open beyond that."

"What would you say if I had another sample of handwriting that matches it, and the writing just happens to belong to one Morris Vickson, aka Mavis?"

Darla tossed Morris's business card—carefully sealed now in a plastic zip-top bag—onto the table, her smile as triumphant as if she were throwing down a winning poker hand.

The three of them stared at the back of the card where Morris had scribbled his personal email address. The resemblance between the two samples was unmistakable . . . at least, in Darla's opinion.

She was gratified when Reese picked up the bag and studied the card inside more closely. "Yeah, it's similar," he conceded. "I suppose I could get one of the handwriting guys to take a look. But I have to warn you this is still pretty slim as far as evidence goes, even if it turns out that the same person wrote both. The note wasn't exactly a smoking gun or a confession, and I can't see this"—he flapped the business card—"being enough to open the case again."

"And that's why we're luring Morris to the store to see if he'll squeal," Darla proclaimed, hoping her cop-speak wasn't too dated.

Reese rolled his eyes and looked over at Jake. "*We?* Are you part of this, Martelli?" he asked with a sigh.

Jake's answering smile was a touch sheepish. "Yeah, well, I figured it wouldn't hurt to do a little of the dirty work for you," she admitted and went on to explain their plan about the cigarette lighter.

When she finished, Darla hurriedly added, "I called Morris right before I came down here. He said he'll come by the shop tomorrow around one to take a look at what we have." Then, exchanging hopeful glances with Jake, she waited for Reese's response.

The detective wiped his mouth a final time and leaned back with a sigh that had nothing to do with the meal he'd just finished.

"Technically, I should tell you to call off this little meeting. Case is closed, what you're planning to do borders on harassment, et cetera, et cetera. So let's pretend I didn't hear this plan of yours, and you let me know later if anything comes of your face-to-face, okay? But now, if you'll excuse me, I gotta get back to the precinct."

Jake rose with him and walked Reese out while Darla took the opportunity to snag her third piece of garlic bread.

"So, are we crazy, or what?" she asked when Jake returned.

Jake shook her frizzy head. "Probably what," was her wryly cheerful assessment. She reached for the uncorked bottle of red that had been breathing on the table. Since Reese had still been on the clock, she and Darla had politely refrained from drinking with their meals. Now, however, Jake refilled their empty water glasses with a healthy pour of wine.

"Grab your glass and let's sit outside," she suggested. "Who knows, maybe we can get one of those kids hanging out there by the shrine to channel Valerie for us. That would save us the trouble of grilling her brother tomorrow."

Remembering her final look at Valerie in her casket, and the fanciful thoughts that had accompanied the viewing, Darla shivered a little even as she managed a laugh.

"Thanks, but I'll pass on the séance and stick with good old Morris," she said as she grabbed up her glass and stood. "Besides, I don't have a choice. Mary Ann will be disappointed if I don't bring back a dramatic story when I return the cigarette lighter to her."

"CERTAINLY, IT'S AN INTERESTING PIECE," MORRIS VICKSON OPINED AS he examined the sterling silver and green enamel cigarette lighter that Darla had handed him. "It has an art deco look to it, don't you think? I'm no smoker, but I fancy myself something of an expert when it comes to vintage silver."

"Mary Ann said it dated from the thirties," she agreed. When the man gave her a questioning look, she hurried to explain, "She and her brother own the antique store next door. I had her take a look at it."

"Ah," Morris said with a nod as he handed back the lighter. "I'm not surprised you thought it might belong to Valerie," he went on, "but I'm afraid I don't recognize it. She did own a fancy lighter or two that people had given her as gifts, but this wasn't one of them. Besides, she had a practical streak. For everyday she used those cheap plastic throwaways."

"Oh dear, then it must have been a customer who left it," Darla said as she tucked the lighter in the drawer beneath the register. "I'll just hold it here until someone comes looking for it."

Morris's arrival had been timed perfectly, Darla thought in satisfaction. With it being Lizzie's day off, she had only James to contend with. Fortunately, his usual lunch hour coincided with the appointment time Morris had given her, so only she and Jake were in the store with the late author's brother.

With a glance now at Jake, who was casually thumbing through a bestseller at the counter, she told him, "I'm so sorry I brought you here on a wild-goose chase, Mr. Vickson. But Mary Ann said the lighter might be worth a couple of hundred dollars, so I couldn't just mail it off to you without knowing for sure it really was your sister's."

She felt a sting of guilt at this litany of small lies. No matter what role, if any, Morris had played in his sister's death, returning here to the store surely had to have been difficult for him. But if he were distressed, he hid it well under a gracious manner.

"I completely understand, Ms. Pettistone, and I hope you find its proper owner. Oh, and I do thank you for the photos. That was thoughtful of you, to make prints as well."

He gathered up the neat stack by the register. Once Darla had confirmed that Morris would be stopping by that afternoon, she'd put in a second call to James asking him to print out some of the photos he had taken at the autographing and then bring them to work with him.

James had complied. And, being James, he first had cropped and touched up each picture to its best advantage and then printed them on expensive photo paper. He had even included a disk of the files in case Morris cared to upload the pictures to his own computer. Now, as Darla watched, the man thumbed through the copies.

He paused at one that showed Mavis applying a dusting of powder to Valerie's face. While a candid shot, the scene as James had cropped it had an artistic look to it, with both figures in profile. The resemblance between the two was so obvious now, Darla wondered how she could've missed it.

With a sigh, Morris let the pictures slip back to the counter.

"You know," he said in a thoughtful tone, "this is all still so fresh. Every morning since she died, I go through this strange sort of countdown. I wake up and tell myself, *Just a day ago, my sister was still alive . . . just two days ago, my sister was still alive . . . just three days ago, my sister was still alive.*"

2

4 ALI BRANDON

He paused and shook his head.

"Two more days, and the countdown will change. It will be, *My sister died a week ago . . . my sister died two weeks ago . . . my sister died three weeks ago.* Then it will change to months, and then it will move on to years. At what point, Ms. Pettistone, do you think I'll finally stop counting?"

"Probably never," Darla replied, sympathetic tears unexpectedly filling her eyes.

She had done much the same thing as a teenager, when a beloved cousin of hers had died, too young, in a car accident. For weeks afterward, she had mentally checked off each day on her personal cosmic calendar as one more day without Amanda being there for her to write to or call. Even now, she sometimes still went through that mental litany, marveling as she did so at just how much time had passed.

She hurried to add, "But after a while, it won't be every day, and in time it won't hurt quite as much."

"Do you think so?"

Smiling a little, he gathered the photos again and slid them back into their envelope, tucking the packet into his messenger bag. "Please thank your manager for me. My parents and I will enjoy having these pictures."

"I'll gladly tell him, but please don't feel you must leave right away," Darla insisted, hoping no desperation had seeped into her tone.

The conversation had wound down far more quickly than she had hoped. She reminded herself that this should not have surprised her—not if her previous guess that he did, indeed, suffer from social anxiety was correct. Somehow, though, she needed to keep him there and talking.

"James took a late lunch," she went on, "but he will be back any minute if you would care to thank him yourself. And I've just made a pot of fresh coffee if you'd like a cup while you browse the shop for a bit."

Too late, she realized she had forgotten the nearby stack of *Haunted High* books. She saw the pained look on Morris's face as he caught a glimpse of the books, and she mentally kicked herself. So much for browsing.

She threw a helpless look at Jake, who gave a small shrug. Short of tackling the man and insisting that he indulge in chitchat, there wasn't much either of them could do. But before they had to resort to such drastic measures, the bells on the front door jingled. The door opened to admit a small pigtailed figure wearing round black glasses and a blue plaid school uniform, and carrying a pink backpack.

"Callie!" Darla exclaimed in pleasure, gesturing the girl in. "I was hoping you would stop by. But what are you doing here in the middle of a school day?"

"Today was a half day," the girl explained with a precise nod, "so my mother let me go shopping with her. She's in the bath store down the block. She let me come in here by myself because I told her you had a book for me."

"Why yes, I do."

Darla reached under the register and pulled out one of the autographed copies of *Ghost of a Chance*. "I saved this one for you, just like I promised."

"Wow." Callie took the book in both hands and stared at it in awe. "I can't believe I have a signed copy!"

Shifting the treasured tome so that she hugged it with one arm, she dug with her free hand into her uniform pocket. "My mom gave me money to pay for it," she explained and held out two crumpled twenties.

Darla smiled and shook her head. Out of the corner of her eye, she saw Morris taking advantage of her distraction to start toward the door. "Tell your mom that the book is my gift to you for being such a good customer."

A desperate idea occurred to her. Gesturing toward Morris, she went on loudly, "And I have another surprise for you, Callie. This gentleman is Mr. Morris Vickson. He's Valerie Baylor's twin brother, and he stopped by for a visit."

The announcement stopped Morris in his tracks, and he glanced at the young girl with polite uncertainty. Darla pressed her advantage, telling him, "This is Callie. She's one of your sister's biggest fans."

"I'm very pleased to meet you, young lady," Morris said with a hesitant smile, putting out a hand adorned with the familiar puzzle ring.

Despite her youth, Callie knew the routine, for she smiled and took his hand in return. Her tone polite, she said, "Nice to meet you, sir. I'm very sorry about your sister. She was a wonderful writer. When I grow up, I want to write books just like her."

"Well, all good writers start out as good readers," he assured her. Then he frowned, his expression considering. "Tell me, Callie, what did you think when Lani learned the secret of the Janitor's closet in the second book?"

"You mean how the closet was actually a mysterious portal to h-e-l-l?"

When Morris nodded, the girl gave an exaggerated shiver. "That was pretty darn scary. I had to keep the light on all night after I read that. But that's okay. I think it would have been dumb if Lani didn't check out the closet once she found out about those kids disappearing."

"And what did you think of the Janitor?" Morris wanted to know.

Darla had thought that the Janitor—by day a mild old man with a lisp and a kind smile, and by night a malevolent demon with sharp teeth and pupil-less eyes—was one of the creepiest characters she'd ever read. She, too, was curious to hear Callie's take on the character.

The girl shrugged. "I thought he was pretty mean, at first, but later on I decided he was more sad than scary. I kind of felt sorry for him, even though he tried to kill Lani's best friend. And I was kind of mad when the ghost gang destroyed him with a séance at the end of *School Spirit*."

"Then I think you'll find the third book quite interesting," Morris assured her. "Not that I will reveal any secrets, of course. You'll have to read all that for yourself."

"Ooh, I bet that means the Janitor comes back!" Callie exclaimed, jumping up and down with excitement.

Then she halted in midhop, and her smile faded. It was replaced by a look of confusion, and an instant later, by realization.

"Wait," she declared, taking a step back and staring hard at him. "I know who you are." Her eyes behind her round glasses narrowed. "You're one of the ladies who came to the autographing with Ms. Baylor."

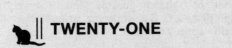

TWENTY-ONE

FROM THE MOUTH AND SHARP EYES OF BABES, DARLA thought in astonishment as Callie made this pronouncement. As for Morris, he stood staring at the girl as if he'd been poleaxed.

Composing herself, Darla guilelessly told her, "Why, Callie, surely you can see that Mr. Vickson is a gentleman, and not a lady. I'm afraid you're mistaken, honey."

"I'm not."

Callie's rosebud lips formed a small stubborn line as she studied Morris even more closely. "You had on a dress and your hair was long, but it was you. You were the makeup lady. I saw you get out of the limo, and then I saw you putting lipstick on Ms. Baylor while I was waiting in line here in the store."

Setting her book on the counter, she reached into her backpack. She fished out her phone and pressed a few buttons.

"See, I even took your picture. It looks just like you," she proclaimed and held up the phone so that both he and Darla could see the image there.

Darla glimpsed a thin blonde frozen in midgesture as she wielded a bright red lipstick. She didn't require a closer look to know the figure was Mavis. Morris's suddenly stricken face was all she needed to see.

His lips moved, but he couldn't seem to summon a protest beyond a bit of sputtering. Jake, meanwhile, had set down the book she had been pretending to read and was watching him with cool calculation. Darla knew she should say something, but what? Admit she'd already guessed Morris's secret, or once more feign disbelief? But while she struggled for the right words, Callie again stepped in.

"Don't worry, I don't think you tried to fool me on purpose. And it's okay if you like pretending to be a lady sometimes," the girl reassured him. "My mom says that so long as people don't hurt anyone, what they do in private is none of our business. So I promise I won't tell anyone that you're really the makeup lady."

She returned her phone to her pack and grabbed up her book again.

"I have to go now, but thanks a lot for the book," she told Darla. "I'm going to start reading it the minute I get home, and I won't stop until I'm done, even if it's after my bedtime. Boy, I sure hope the Janitor is back!"

Callie paused at the door for a final wave at all of them and then skipped out hugging the hardcover to her chest. As the bells jingled her exit, Darla and Jake turned as one toward Morris.

The composure had begun to return to his face, and his tone was cool again as he said, "Cute kid, but she was obviously having a little joke at my expense. Now, if you'll excuse me—"

Jake, however, was not to be dissuaded. "Anything you'd like to tell us, Morris . . . or should I say, Mavis?" she asked, subtly positioning herself so that she stood between him and the door.

He blinked. "And who are you? I don't believe we've been introduced."

"That's Jake Martelli," Darla broke in. "She's a friend of mine, and she happens to be in charge of security here. You probably saw her at the autographing. She's an ex-cop."

"Ah . . . 'ex' being the germane word here," Morris replied, seemingly in control once more. "That being the case, you no doubt realize that you have no right to question me, Ms. Martelli. And you certainly have no authority to detain me, so please step aside."

"There's something you might not know regarding your sister's death," Jake countered, holding her ground. "We found an odd note here in the store that apparently was written during the event. We think that message might have been used to lure Valerie Baylor outside the store that night. Funny, though, that the note was written in lipstick the same color as what Mavis was using on Valerie. Even more interesting, the handwriting on it appears identical to the sample we have of your writing from the business card you gave to Darla."

Morris gave a hollow little laugh. "Oh, come on. You can't expect to compare lipstick with ink and claim a match."

"Maybe not," Darla interjected, "but what about your puzzle ring? Mavis had on the identical ring the night of the autographing, even down to wearing it on the same finger as you wear yours."

"Coincidence." His tone took on a hard edge, while his normally emotionless face hinted at anger. "Not that I owe either of you an explanation," he clipped out, "but the puzzle ring was a gift from my sister. Perhaps she gave both of us the same ring."

He paused and reached into his jacket pocket, pulling out a slim cell phone. "Now, do I need to call my attorney and tell him that I'm being harassed, or will you let me leave?"

Jake exchanged another glance with Darla and then took a step to the side. "Of course, Mr. Vickson. Our apologies for holding you up."

Darla, meanwhile, frantically searched her mind for something clever to keep Morris there a few minutes longer. But nothing brilliant came to her, and she realized in resignation that they had blown whatever chance they'd had to gain a confession from the man.

Hamlet, however, apparently had a few ideas of his own.

Darla had left him peacefully sleeping upstairs. Yet now, a sharp meow abruptly announced the feline's presence in the shop.

As Darla watched, he leaped up onto the counter and ran its length, and then sprang off again like an Olympic gymnast performing a vault. With execution worthy of a perfect ten, he made a graceful four-point landing on the floor right in front of Morris.

Darla gasped, fearing a sudden swipe of paws or gnashing of fangs that would shred clothes and flesh alike. That definitely would rate a call from Morris to his attorney, she thought in dread. But to her surprise, Hamlet pulled a trick she had never before seen.

Rearing up on his haunches, he stood with his paws neatly tucked against his chest and his green eyes wide, looking like a begging pup. Then, just to underscore this scene of extreme cuteness, he cocked his head and gave a series of soft little chirps designed to melt the heart of even the staunchest cat hater.

Morris did not fall into that category. In fact, Darla recalled Valerie announcing how Mavis adored cats . . . which meant, by extension, that Morris must be an ailurophile as well. So she wasn't surprised when this endearing feline tableau drew a genuine smile from the man.

"You must be Hamlet," Morris said, pausing to reach down and scratch the cat behind one ear. "What a clever boy. You certainly are the handsome fellow, aren't you?"

"He certainly is," Darla agreed with a small triumphant smile. "But if you've never been in my shop before, how did you know that the cat's name is Hamlet?"

Morris straightened and stared from Hamlet to Darla and back again, and then gave a helpless shrug.

"I–I'm sure someone told me," he managed and started for the door again.

Jake called after him, "I doubt Hamlet's name came up during the memorial service, but Mavis knew it."

Morris didn't look back.

Jake went on, "Mavis heard all about Darla's cat from Valerie. So why don't you come clean, Morris? Just because your sister's death was ruled an accident doesn't mean the investigation can't be reopened if some new evidence shows up. And all these various handwriting samples floating around are adding up to something interesting. If you don't talk to me and Darla now, you'll just have to talk to the police later."

"Then I'll talk to the police. Good day," he exclaimed and walked out the door.

Jake waited until the sound of jingling bells faded before turning again to Darla.

"That went well," she observed with a snort of disgust. "Hell, Hamlet was the only one who had a handle on things. I have to admit, that was some clever work on his part."

"It was, wasn't it?" Darla agreed, beaming down in approval at the cat.

He had abandoned the balancing act and now lay flopped with careless abandon on one side. Hearing Darla's words directed at him, he promptly rolled into a sitting position and flung one leg over his shoulder in his patented kiss-mine position. For once, though, Darla didn't mind the insult. The fact he'd vindicated her theory was enough for her.

Then she sighed. "I guess I was hoping he'd confess to something, but all we've done is tick him off. I don't think we're going to get any more information out of Morris, are we?"

Her friend gave a grudging shake of her head. "Even with the ring and the cat and the pictures, you've pretty much got bupkes." Then she stopped short and slapped her forehead with her palm.

"The pictures! If Callie was taking pictures here in the store during the autographing, maybe she got something useful. Where did she say she was meeting her mom?"

"Probably Great Scentsations," Darla replied. "You've seen it. It's that new bath and body-lotion place down the block that just opened a couple of weeks ago where the old grocery used to be."

"Then what are we waiting for?"

"James. I can't just run off and leave the store until he comes back."

Fortunately, James chose that moment to walk in, juggling a Cobb salad and an offsetting chocolate shake. He gave a crisp nod and greeted them. "Ladies."

"Thank goodness you're back! We've got to leave for a few minutes," Darla exclaimed as Jake grabbed her arm and dragged her to the front door. "Keep an eye on things, would you?"

Leaving an astonished James to stare after them, they rushed outside and down the steps.

"What are you going to do if we find Callie there?" Darla asked as they race-walked their way toward the bath shop. "You can't just commandeer her cell phone, you know."

"Hey, I'm leaving that part up to you, kid. You're the queen of customer service. You can charm the mom and get permission for me."

A glorious waft of floral perfume—gardenia, Darla decided—gently assailed them as they entered Great Scentsations. Another time, she would have enjoyed the chance to wander the aisles with all manner of soaps and lotions and candles displayed with a lacy Victorian flair. She'd met the owners—a stylish middle-aged woman and her twenty-something daughter—in passing, but this was her first chance to visit their store. Unfortunately, now was not the time, either. Her only concern at the moment was for a different mother-daughter team.

"Look, Mom, it's the lady from the bookstore," Callie piped up.

The girl and her mother stood beside a tiny pink-velvet-draped table where colorfully boxed soaps were arranged on end in a spiral pattern, much like dominoes set to topple. In fact, the first few boxes lay facedown, as if the display had begun its tumble. Darla fleetingly wondered how many times a mischievous customer had succumbed to temptation and jostled the first of the remaining standing soaps just to see the resulting chain reaction. From the way Callie stood with hands deliberately clenched behind her back, it was apparent that she was trying to resist that very temptation.

Making a mental note to try a cute display like that back in her own shop, Darla zeroed in on the pair, Jake on her heels.

"Hi, Callie and Mrs., um, Callie's mom," she said with a bright smile, extending her hand. "We've never formally met, but I'm Darla Pettistone from the bookstore. And this is my friend, Jake Martelli."

"Sure, sure," Callie's mom replied with a small smile, pushing up her sliding glasses with one hand and shaking with the other. "That was real nice of you, giving Callie the book. She loves that Valerie Baylor."

"That's why I'm here. We're planning a, um, memorial display at the store," Darla improvised. "I know Callie had some pictures from the event, and I thought maybe she could share a few of them."

"I dunno . . . that's up to Callie."

Callie met her mother's questioning look and gave an eager nod. Then, turning back to Darla, she exclaimed, "I took lots of pictures. Do you want to look at all of them?"

"Of course, honey." Darla exchanged a pleased look with Jake. "If you don't mind, we can see them right now."

The two women crowded around the girl as she dug her phone out of her backpack and once more brought up her pictures on the tiny screen. The first couple of dozen had been taken outside the store before the autographing started. It was all Darla could do to control her eagerness as the girl took her time, commenting on each picture. From Jake's expression, she could see her friend was equally impatient. Finally, however, one image flashed on screen that Darla promptly recognized as taken inside the store.

"There's that big bouncer guy," Callie said, referring to a close-up of the back of Everest's shaved head. "He was kinda scary. And this is the nice old lady at the cash register," she went on, displaying a picture of Mary Ann holding a fistful of cash.

"Oh, and this is the one I took of Susanna's butt," she said with a giggle, though she promptly sobered when her mother shot her a disapproving look before she picked up her wicker shopping basket and went to the counter to pay.

"Guess I'd better delete that one. Oops, and this one, too," she added with a guilty look at Darla. She hit "Erase" and "Yes," but not before Darla glimpsed a blurry shot of her own hindquarters filling the screen.

Ignoring Jake's snort of amusement, Darla wryly answered, "Yes, I don't think we want that one for the memorial. Do you have any pictures of Ms. Baylor and her friends?"

"Sure!"

Callie scrolled through a few more. Now Jake was staring intently at the small images that flashed past. She halted Callie when one picture popped up showing Mavis in the background walking up the stairs to the second floor. The next picture captured only a glimpse of that same staircase, but Darla could make out a hooded, black-caped figure walking back down the steps again.

She and Jake exchanged glances. Apparently, Lizzie had been truthful in her claim that she'd seen Mavis sneak upstairs and then come back down costumed like the rest of them.

"Wait," Jake said as Callie flashed onto the next view. "It looks like Valerie and Mavis and Hillary and Lizzie are all here in their capes. Okay, go to the next one."

The girl obliged. This picture apparently was taken a few moments later, but the caped figures that were the focus of Jake's scrutiny now were down to three. From the small size and angle of the picture, Darla couldn't tell which of the four was missing. In the next shot, a second figure was gone . . . and in the one after, a third was gone. Once again, given the size and the angle, Darla couldn't tell who remained in the scene. Whether any or all of them had left out the back of the store was also impossible to say.

"Hang on," Jake repeated, her tone more urgent this time. "Go back one picture, Callie."

She studied the shot more closely, but Darla couldn't tell what exactly had caught her attention. Finally, Jake asked the girl, "Could you maybe email these last five pictures you showed us to Ms. Pettistone?"

"Okay," Callie agreed while Darla dug into her pocket for a crumpled business card with her email address on it. Fingers flying, the girl sent off each picture and then gazed up at Jake. "You're the lady who was out on the street with Mr. Reese, weren't you?" Callie sighed. "I wish you could have kept Ms. Baylor from falling in front of that van."

"Yeah, kid, me too," Jake answered, her expression grim. "Say, do you think I can get you to save all your pictures from inside the store for a while in case Mr. Reese would like to see them?"

"Mr. Reese is a policeman, isn't he?"

When Jake nodded, the girl gave her a narrow look from behind her glasses and declared, "I think something sneaky's going on, and that's why you wanted to see my pictures. It's not for the store."

Then, before Jake could reply, Callie's eyes widened in

fear. "Did someone hurt Ms. Baylor on purpose? Maybe there really is a Janitor in real life, and he got her. Maybe he's there in my pictures, too!"

"No, no," Darla hurried to reassure her as the girl stared at her phone in horror. "Ms. Jake used to be a police officer, so she likes to look for bad guys everywhere. It's like a hobby for her. Don't worry, the Janitor is only in the *Haunted High* books. Besides," she added with a comforting smile, "even if he were real, Mr. Reese is still tough enough to beat him up. You believe me, don't you?"

"Yeah, I guess." Callie's tone was small and sounded unconvinced, but she managed a smile. "I have to go now, okay?"

She didn't wait for Darla's answer but rushed over to the register where her mother was standing. The woman gave Darla and Jake a friendly smile as she and Callie walked past. "Nice meeting you ladies. Say good-bye, Callie."

"Bye," the girl obediently replied, though she clutched her mother's arm and turned her face into her shoulder as they walked out the door.

"Score another one for our team," Darla muttered, shaking her head as the door closed after the mother-daughter duo. "Now the poor kid is going to need therapy."

"She'll be fine," Jake absently replied, her gaze moving about the store. Fixing on one of the displays, she added, "Why don't you go on back to the store and download those pictures? I want to pick up a couple of things here, first."

"Sure," Darla agreed, trying not to show her surprise. Jake was the last one she'd expect to shop there among the frills and perfume. Leaving her friend to browse, she headed back to the bookstore. She found James busy helping two fashionably dressed older gentlemen who had brought to the register a small stack of travel essays and guides.

"Enjoy your trip to Rome," he said as he bagged the last volume. "And don't forget to try that café near the Vatican that I told you about."

"We'll make sure to stop there," the shorter of the two replied with a fond look at his mustachioed companion. "We've been planning this trip for ages, and we intend to sightsee and eat ourselves into oblivion."

Darla waited until the smiling pair had left before addressing James. "Sorry to leave you like that," she said. "Jake was following up on a lead."

"You mean regarding Ms. Baylor's unfortunate demise?"

"Well, yes."

She'd kept her conversations with Jake and Reese confidential, but it occurred to her that James might also have some insight into the matter. "You know those pictures you printed for me? I don't suppose you took any others once the autographing started, did you?"

"Unfortunately, no. I was busier than the proverbial lower-extremity amputee participating in a posterior-kicking competition."

He paused and gave Darla a keen look. "You and Ms. Martelli have been carrying on about something for the past week. Should I assume that there is more to the accident than we have been told?"

"I think that's the problem, James. We're not certain it was an accident."

She hesitated. Surely there was no reason she couldn't let him in on their suspicions. James had been there that night and had the same passing acquaintance with all the major players she did—more, in some cases, like Lizzie.

She gave him a brief recap of what little they'd gleaned. Then, casually, she asked, "By the way, did you notice anything unusual about Valerie's makeup artist, Mavis, the night of the signing?"

"You mean other than the fact that *she* was a *he*? Though, in fairness, he did carry off the masquerade rather well, do you not agree?"

Darla looked at him in surprise, even as she reminded herself that very little got past the former professor. James, meanwhile, frowned as he considered the matter.

"Mavis and Ms. Baylor did exchange a few confidences during the event," he finally said, "but nothing about their conversation appeared alarming. Should I assume that this makeup artist might be under suspicion?"

"I'm not sure 'suspicion' is the right word," she conceded, "but remember how you printed off those pictures for me to give to Valerie's brother, Morris? It happens that Valerie and

Morris were fraternal twins. And it turns out Morris has an even closer relationship to Mavis than that."

She gave James a significant look, waiting for him to pick up the hint. When he merely looked at her expectantly, she clarified, "Morris and Mavis are one and the same."

"Indeed?" James raised both brows. "I must admit, I was not expecting that. Intriguing family dynamic."

Before Darla could continue her story, one of their regulars walked in to pick up a special order. Leaving further conversation for later, she left James to wait on the woman and went to the computer to check her email.

Along with the usual store-related correspondence and a few personal messages, she found the pictures from Callie. She immediately saved them to the hard drive and was in the process of pulling up the first when she heard the door jingle again.

Jake entered, carrying a tiny, pink-lace printed bag that starkly contrasted with her uniform of boots, black jeans, and black sweater. She seemed unaware of the incongruity, however, as she hurried over to join Darla at the computer.

"Did you get the photos?"

"Yep. Just looking at them now."

On a full-sized monitor, the figures were grainy, but far easier to distinguish. Even better, Callie had had a surprisingly clear view of the action from her vantage point, which included the autographing table and the back door leading to the courtyard.

In the first photo, Valerie was seated at the table, visible behind a line of fans wearing similar capes to hers. Her own hood, however, was draped over her shoulders, her dark hair spilling in a heavy waterfall down her back. The figure directly behind her appeared to be Lizzie, for a bit of brown bob peeked out one edge of her hood. Hillary stood to one side, distinguished by the glint of her glasses. The fourth figure had to be Mavis, though the hood made it difficult to tell for certain.

Scrolling through the series a second time, Darla was now able to pick out who was missing from each subsequent shot. First, Valerie vanished, then Lizzie. In the third shot, Hillary was gone, presumably leaving only Mavis remaining. But it was the fourth shot that held Jake's attention.

"Zoom in," she commanded. "Now, scroll over to the right. Okay, zoom again. Again. To the right again, and zoom one more time."

What filled the screen now was a blur of black, the images so pixilated that the details were fuzzy. But Jake was smiling in satisfaction.

"Look," she said and pointed to what appeared to be Mavis moving toward the back of the store. "See his—her—hand? She's holding something white with streaks of red on it. Morris has the lipstick note."

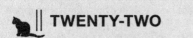

TWENTY-TWO

DARLA STARED AT THE INCRIMINATING SHOT FOR A LONG moment and then met Jake's triumphant gaze. "It does look like the note," she agreed, "but that still doesn't tell us if Mavis—or, rather, Morris—only received it, or if he was the one who wrote it. And there's something else."

She reached under the register for her purse. Just as with the lipstick letter, she had thought that Reese might confiscate Morris's business card as possible evidence, so she had scanned it and stuck the copy into her purse for safekeeping. Now, she retrieved that folded page and set it on the counter, and then pulled out one of the autographed copies of *Ghost of a Chance* she'd hidden away. Setting the book beside the note, she flipped it open to the title page where Valerie Baylor had signed it.

"I thought about this when Morris pointed out that it was hard to match lipstick to ink. We all agreed that the lipstick writing looks a lot like the writing on the back of Morris's business card . . . but doesn't it look a lot like Valerie's hand-writing, too?"

Jake took a look at the similar sharp pen strokes and then muttered a choice expletive. "I see your point," she conceded. Feeling a bit odd to suddenly be arguing the opposite point, Darla went on, "And aren't we forgetting that little thing called a motive? Why would he kill his own sister?"

"Sibling rivalry . . . he got tired of her snide comments . . . she threatened to reveal his secret hobby of cross-dressing," Jake said, ticking off the possibilities on one hand . . . the same possibilities that previously had occurred to Darla. "Maybe Valerie did something that finally sent him over the edge after years of putting up with her bull, and he snapped."

"Ahem."

The sound made them both jump. James had come up behind them and now stood there shaking his head.

"Really, Jake, I realize you are bored with your forced retirement, but you should know better than to jump on Darla's bandwagon and try to make a murder out of a molehill," he said, his expression disapproving.

When Jake opened her mouth to protest, he raised a silencing hand and went on, "And both of you should keep in mind that your would-be suspect and his supposed victim were fraternal twins. I have done a bit of research into the psychology of siblings, and I can assure you it would be almost unheard of for one twin to deliberately kill the other. The symbiotic relationship between fraternals is almost as close as that of identical twins. When one of the pair dies, the other is left feeling half a person. Indeed, the research on surviving twins and their stages of grief makes for interesting—"

"Thanks, cowboy." Jake cut him short with a sour look. "Here, I had just joined Team Darla, and now you're shooting holes in my theory."

James raised a brow and, indulging in a rare bit of whimsy, blew imaginary gun smoke from his finger pistols a la Ted the security guy.

"Call me Sheriff James. But now, if you will excuse me, I have a few special orders to finish up before day's end."

He left the two of them staring at the picture on the monitor. Darla was the first to break their mutual silence.

"We might be trying too hard, but to quote Callie, I still think there's something sneaky going on with Morris," she said in a determined tone.

Jake shrugged. "Yeah, but much as it pains me to admit it, James is right. Sneaky doesn't equal motive or evidence."

"So what you're really saying is that we've hit a dead end."

"No, I'm saying that we need to step back and see if we've missed anything. Because Professor James *was* wrong about one thing: swapping theories with you has nothing to do with me being bored."

Jake's tone took on a hard edge. "No matter how it happened, your author ended up dead on my watch. If Valerie was deliberately pushed, no way am I letting the person responsible get away with it. Even bitches deserve justice."

"Sounds like a T-shirt slogan," was Darla's wry reply.

Before Jake could comment, her cell phone went off, the ring tone sounding suspiciously to Darla like the first notes of that old Bee Gee's song from *Saturday Night Fever*. She wasn't too surprised when the other woman announced, "It's Reese," before taking the call.

Jake's end of the conversation was maddeningly cryptic. Certain it had to do with the Valerie Baylor situation, Darla waited impatiently for her to hang up and share whatever news she'd learned from the detective.

Jake, however, wasn't doing any sharing.

"Sorry, kid, I need to help Reese out with something," she said as she ended the call. Heading toward the door, she called back over her shoulder, "Do me a favor and forward me those pictures when you get a chance, okay?"

"Sure," she agreed, trying not to let curiosity consume her over whatever "something" it was that Reese needed. She'd simply have to go on the assumption that, if she needed to know, Jake would make sure that she did.

James was taking care of the customer who'd just stopped in, so Darla took the opportunity to scan through the photos one more time before sending them to Jake's email address.

The photo she kept returning to was the one where the four caped figures stood in close proximity to each other. It was interesting, she thought, how such a simple garment gave such anonymity to such a varied group. Even knowing who they were, she had to look closely to distinguish them from each other—all of which demonstrated that a disguise didn't need to be elaborate to be effective. Hadn't the Scarf Lady who'd hired Janie made do with only a pair of oversized sunglasses and a length of cloth around her head, when even Callie had recognized Morris underneath the elaborate masquerade that was Mavis?

Mavis!

A thought occurred to Darla as she stared again at the picture on the computer screen. Had they overlooked another, perhaps even more obvious possibility? Could Janie's Scarf Lady actually have been Morris? Had Valerie's own brother planned an entire secret campaign against her . . . which might or might not have culminated in his deliberately throwing her in front of the Lord's Blessing Church's van?

The more she thought about it, the more likely her theory seemed. But given that she'd not been able to get any sort of admission from Morris regarding his Mavis alter ego, it seemed unlikely he would spontaneously confess to the Scarf Lady masquerade should she confront him with that accusation. But perhaps she could try a more subtle tactic.

According to Reese, Janie's contact with her mysterious employer had initially been via email. Doubtless, whoever had contacted her would have used one of those free email address services to hide her—or his!—identity. From what Reese had indicated, however, he'd passed on that address to the police department's IT group, which could then backtrack it to its true owner. But would the police even bother to pursue that lead now?

Nothing was stopping her from doing a bit of cybersleuthing herself, she decided.

She gave a thoughtful frown. A cleverly worded email to the Scarf Lady's address might prompt its owner to inadvertently reveal his or her identity. Unfortunately, she had no idea where Janie had sent her messages.

She shut down the computer's photo viewer and took another look at the page with Morris's email address. It was straightforward: Morris@VicksonEnterprises.com. No guesswork there, she wryly thought. Had that been the address Janie supplied to Reese in her statement, Morris might well have been behind bars by now. And since she doubted Reese would share what he likely considered to be confidential police information, what she needed was to find the ad that Janie had answered and get the poster's email address that way.

Her frown deepened. Jake had said that the Lone Protester

had found her so-called performance-art job by trolling
TheEverythingList. If she was lucky—or the poster had been
careless—perhaps the ad was still there. Mentally crossing
her fingers, Darla swiftly logged onto the site and plugged in
a few keywords to search.

"Valerie Baylor" didn't do it . . . nor did "book signing" or
even "performance art." She was about to give it up, assuming
the unknown poster had taken down the ad already, when as a
last resort she finally typed in the word "protester." To her
surprise, an ad popped up titled "Professional Protester." That
had to be it!

Professional protester needed for worthwhile cause. Must
be willing to picket popular literary figure while dressed in
costume. $50 per appearance, one week only. Email to
prettywoman-ny@theeverythinglist.com.

Darla rolled her eyes. *You would think Mavis would be
more subtle*, she told herself, even as a small thrill of anticipation swept her. It looked like her theory was about to be
proven correct. Now, all she had to do was send a message to
that address and see if Mavis—or, rather, Morris—replied.

She thought a moment, and then swiftly typed, *Sorry that
our last conversation ended on an unpleasant note. Please let
me know if there's anything I can do for you. Darla.*

She hit "Send" before she could change her mind. As the
email vanished off the screen, she stepped back from the computer and let her breath out in a whoosh. *Just doing a little
trolling, as they say back home*, she told herself, hoping she
didn't regret this spontaneous attempt at undercover work.
Her email address had the Pettistone's Fine Books web address
in it, which along with her signature file made it obvious that
she was the sender. With luck, that blatant announcement as to
her identity would give the impression that she simply was
making casual contact in her role as store owner.

She stared at the screen for a few moments, waiting to see
if a reply would pop up. None did. Darla shook her head. She
couldn't stand there for the rest of the afternoon hoping for a
return message. Despite the customer slowdown, there was
still work to be done around the store.

"Like right now," she muttered at the now-familiar clatter of a book hitting the floor. Hamlet, at it again!

"I'll take care of it," she called to James, who nodded back from his perch on the ladder where he was pulling down some overstock to fill a few gaps in the inventory.

She stalked back to the classics shelf, which seemed to be the feline's current choice of playground. At least this time, he had limited himself to a single volume instead of half a dozen. Even so, she shot him an annoyed look and threatened, "If you keep this up, I'm going to trot your furry butt down to the vet and get you declawed."

Not at all dismayed by her ire—no way would she do that, and he knew it—Hamlet sat boldly in the middle of the aisle beside his latest literary victim. Maybe she should get some of that canned air like Ted had used and try a little aversion therapy with him. Snag a book, and hear a nasty hiss. To be quite honest, however, his mischief was far less destructive than that of some of her customers.

Particularly the children.

She still shuddered at the memory of finding a half-eaten lollipop stuck between the pages of one of her most expensive art books a few weeks earlier. She'd had to mark it down to half price and put it on the "hurt book" table. There it still sat along with other vandalized volumes, including a popular bestseller where some high-minded customer had thoughtfully used a black marker to obliterate all references to male and female anatomy.

"All right, Hamlet. What say we give this little game a break until tomorrow," she declared as she bent to retrieve the volume.

A glimpse at the title gave her momentary pause.

"So you like Russian literature, do you?" she asked with a quirk of a brow as she read the title, *Crime and Punishment*. Giving him a stern look, she added, "Or are you trying to tell me something?"

The feline did not bother to respond to either question. Instead, with a dismissive flick of his whiskers, he turned tail and headed for the stairway leading to the second floor. Darla watched him go and then returned her attention to the book she held. Coincidence, or . . .

"Coincidence," she firmly said and returned the volume to its spot.

She checked her email twice more during the course of the afternoon, only to find each time that "prettywoman-ny" had made no reply to her earlier message. But at least she had tried, which she suspected was more than the police IT department had done.

It was closing time, and James had already left for the day when she pulled up her store email one final time. And there, sandwiched among a few end-of-day announcements from various publishers and distributors, she saw it: a return email from prettywoman-ny.

Success! came her first triumphant thought, followed immediately by a wave of nervousness. She had found the Scarf Lady . . . now, what was she going to do about it?

"How about opening the email?" she muttered aloud after several moments spent simply staring at the sealed envelope icon with its "re: follow-up to our conversation" subject line. She took a deep breath and then clicked.

Darla had been prepared to read anything in that return message—anything, that is, except for the few brief sentences that popped up on her screen and hit her like a figurative punch. Disbelief swept her, and she reread them a second time, and a third. But multiple perusals didn't change what the message said.

That's ok, I forgive you. So, was business any better today? I still plan to come in tomorrow unless you want to pay me to stay home, ha ha. See you tomorrow. Lizzie. P.S. How did you get this email address?

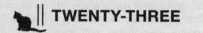 **TWENTY-THREE**

MR. CATS-CAN-BE-VANDALS-TOO WAS BACK IN THE CLAS-
sics area doing his book snagging thing. But unlike the previous times, this morning Darla actually had caught the wily
feline in the act as she'd slipped in the side door. Her victory
was a hollow one, however, distraught as she had been since
the previous night over more important concerns. Namely, that
her very own employee, Lizzie, was in actuality the same
Scarf Lady who had masterminded the Lone Protester's campaign against Valerie Baylor.

She had stared at the incriminating email for a good quarter of an hour before snatching up the phone and calling Jake.
After explaining how she'd managed to uncover the same
email address that Janie already had supplied Reese, Darla
reminded Jake that Lizzie fancied herself a fair mimic when
it came to southern accents.

"It all fits, Jake. Lizzie has to be the Scarf Lady. What do
we do about it?" she had asked in true dismay.

The ex-cop had given her swift instructions not to do anything about the message until Reese had been informed. A bit
later, after Darla had closed the shop and numbly made her way
back to her apartment, Jake had phoned her back and outlined
their plan for this morning. She'd also revealed something

more; that, just that afternoon, someone in the precinct's IT group with a bit of spare time finally had traced that same email address back to Lizzie. That had been what Reese's earlier call to her had been about, Jake had explained.

Darla had considered berating Jake about not telling her right off the day before that the police knew the email belonged to Lizzie, but then thought better of it. Doubtless Reese had asked Jake to keep the matter confidential, and she'd simply complied.

Darla sighed now as she considered her own responsibilities as Lizzie's employer. She didn't relish what was to come when the woman arrived in another half hour to start her shift. Cliché as it seemed, it was true that you never truly knew what a person was capable of doing, until they up and did it. Still, she had never expected that, one day, someone of her acquaintance might turn out to be a cold-blooded killer.

"Might be," she reminded herself. "The two things might not even be connected."

To distract herself, she began picking up the volumes that Hamlet had pulled down from the classics shelves, idly lecturing him when she noticed one of the volumes was one of the more sensational biographies of the Roman emperor Caligula.

"Much too gory reading for a cat, and half the claims aren't even historically proven," she declared. Firmly closing it, she put that book back on the shelf and picked up a second one.

"The Adventures of Huckleberry Finn," she said and nodded her approval. Glancing at the page where it was open, she went on, "Here's a bit of wholesome reading for you. Huck and Jim are on the run. And see, this is the chapter where Huck disguises himself like a—"

She looked up from the page she was reading to see the cat in midyawn. With a frown at him, she snapped the book shut again and stuck it on the shelf. "I try to give you a little culture, and you act bored. But you're right, we don't have time for this now. Jake and Reese will be here any minute."

Barely had she said the words when a knock sounded. Grabbing up the last of the books from the floor, she left them on the counter by the register and hurried to the front door. Through the hazy glass, she could see the detective and Jake standing on the stoop. Since it wasn't yet ten, the door was still locked and the sign still proclaimed that the store was closed.

"We'll wait off to the side and out of sight," Reese said without preamble once she'd opened the door and he and Jake had slipped past her. As she shut the door after them, he added, "We don't want to tip our hand until she's safely inside. I don't feel like another sprint, if you know what I mean."

"Did you call her last night and make sure she was coming in?" Jake wanted to know as they walked toward the register.

Darla nodded, and glanced at the clock on the far wall. *Nine forty-five.* "I told her exactly what you said. She promised to be here on time."

"You don't have to stick around," Reese said, taking note of her distress. "All I want to do is question her at this point. Even if she was the one who placed the ad that Janie answered, technically she didn't do anything illegal. I won't arrest her unless there's reason to believe she was the one who pushed your author in front of that van."

"Thanks, but I'm not going anywhere until I know what her involvement was in all this."

Darla grabbed up the books she'd set on the counter and marched over to the classics shelf again, needing to channel her nervousness in movement. Soon enough, she'd know the truth about what happened to Valerie Baylor . . . or, at least, have a better idea of what had set the tragedy into motion.

It was five minutes before the hour when the bells on the front door jingled, the usually pleasant tinkle sounding ominous under the circumstances. Darla wiped her sweat-dampened hands on her denim skirt and started toward the front. Reese and Jake had taken up position on the other side of the register, so that they were partially blocked from view. The deception would need to last only a few moments, just long enough for their suspect to move clear of the doorway.

"Hi, Darla," Lizzie greeted her, closing the door behind her with another chiming of the bells. The smile she turned on Darla was bright, if a trifle crooked as a result of her careless application of pink lipstick.

Juggling her usual oversized tote bag with the ever-present manuscript-in-process bulging from its top, she slipped out of her beige cardigan to reveal sensible brown slacks and a pink blouse printed with tutu-wearing brown poodles. She glanced about the store, her smile brightening as she noticed Jake and Reese. They had left their posts and quietly circled around back of Lizzie. The move reminded Darla of one of those *National Geographic* specials, where the lions cut a weak gazelle from the rest of the herd.

Except in this case, the gazelle was a plump middle-aged woman who was unknowingly turning a friendly look on her lions.

"Oh! Hi, Jake, Detective Reese. I didn't expect to find you here again," she said, not sounding particularly guilty of anything . . . at least, not to Darla's ears. "I saw that big pile of flowers was still out on the sidewalk. I guess you're here to keep an eye on things, with all those kids and those crazy protesters coming around, right?"

"Actually, Ms. Cavanaugh," Reese replied, "I'm here to ask you a few questions about one of those protesters. Maybe you'd like to take a seat."

He gestured her toward one of the chairs reserved for browsing customers. Lizzie glanced from him to the chair, and then back to him again. Her expression tightened, while a faint air of defensiveness emanated from her as she crossed her arms over her chest. "Questions?" she echoed. "I can answer them standing up. What do you want to know?"

"It's about that protester with the sign who was hanging around the Valerie Baylor autographing . . . except, she wasn't protesting because she believed in a cause. It seems someone paid the girl to stand there and hold her sign."

He reached into his jacket and pulled out a folded page.

"She claims she answered an ad on TheEverythingList— you know, one of those online classified services. We checked it out and found the ad in question. I've printed it out."

He paused and held out the paper. "Would you mind taking a look and telling me if you recognize the email address on it?"

Lizzie reached out a reluctant hand, as if he were proffering a rattlesnake instead of a single sheet of twenty-pound bond. She took a look, barely long enough to read the few lines, and then thrust it back at him, her manner one of defiance now.

"No, no, I don't recognize it."

"You might want to rethink that answer, ma'am. Your employer"—he glanced at Darla—"says that she sent a message to that same email address, and you replied. And my department traced it back to your home address."

The belligerence seeped from the woman like a bicycle tire going flat. She let her bag and sweater drop to the floor while she turned a pleading look on Darla. "I tried to tell you before what Val did to me. Back in college, she stole my first manuscript—the one about the girl who goes to the police academy and then arrests her ex-fiancé—and she published it as hers."

"The Lady Cop and the Collar," Jake exclaimed with a snap of her fingers, causing Darla and Reese to stare at her in surprise. "I read that one. You mean to say it was really *your* book and not Valerie Baylor's?"

Lizzie nodded, seemingly intent on reviving her previous air of bravado. "She stole it . . . I mean, literally stole my manuscript out of my bag one night after class," she explained, sniffling. "I had it packed up in a Bloomingdale's box, ready to mail it out the next day. Valerie suggested we all stop for a drink after class to celebrate, but she left before I did. I didn't even know the manuscript was gone until I went to pay my tab. Everyone told me it must have been someone in the club who thought there was something valuable in the Bloomie's box, but I knew the truth. I should have been the famous author, not that—that thief. So I called her on it. What's wrong with that?"

"What's wrong," Jake went on in a firm yet sympathetic tone, "is that Valerie Baylor is dead, and we have what might be video evidence showing someone shoved her off the sidewalk and into the van's path. And, unfortunately, you had the motive and the opportunity to do it."

"But I didn't!" Lizzie wailed, bravado forgotten as tears pooled in her brown eyes. "I wouldn't murder anyone. What about that girl I paid? How do you know she didn't push Valerie just because?"

"Reese has spoken to her already, and he has cab company

records and statements from witnesses that put her away from the scene before the accident."

"But I was inside the store the whole time during the autographing. Darla, you saw me helping James. Tell them I was here in the store when Valerie was killed! Tell them I wouldn't have shoved her," she pleaded.

Darla didn't hesitate. "Of course you couldn't kill anyone, Lizzie. I don't believe that for a moment."

And she didn't. True, she'd known Lizzie for only a few months and had often found her prone to melodrama, but she had never seen any indication of malice in the woman. But could she say with any certainty that Lizzie had never left the store?

Now, she did pause. She herself had been in and out several times during the event, and with the glut of black capes it had been difficult to distinguish anyone. And during the time that Valerie had vanished on her supposed smoke break, she had noticed that a few other people had been missing as well. Had Lizzie been one of them? She simply couldn't recall.

"I'm sorry, Lizzie," she finally answered, feeling equally as deflated as her employee, "but if I had to testify in a court of law, I couldn't say with one hundred percent certainty that you were inside when Valerie Baylor was hit."

The other woman's features crumpled, and she bent her head, shoulders shaking. Silent tears trickled down her cheeks, catching in the gently swaying edges of her sleek brown bob. Staring at her, Darla felt like weeping, too. She turned to Reese.

"Are you going to arrest her?" she asked, choking a little over the words.

"I'd like to take her down to the station for questioning. Ms. Cavanaugh, will you come with me?"

Lizzie gave a soft wail by way of response but nodded. Darla hurried over to the counter and pulled a business card out from her Rolodex, and then rushed back to where Lizzie stood.

"This is the number for a criminal attorney who was a friend of Great-Aunt Dee," she said, pressing the card into the woman's limp hand. "If you don't want to answer the cops' questions, tell them you have a right to ask for a lawyer, and then call him."

"Don't worry, Darla," came Reese's dry response from behind her.

She turned to see him hanging up his cell phone. He added, "I don't know how they do it back in Texas, but here we're pretty good about reading people their rights and all that official stuff. Right now, this is all informal, and Lizzie is coming in of her own free will. If for some reason we get beyond that point, and she decides she needs an attorney, she'll get one."

"Oh, right," she mumbled, having forgotten for a moment that he was one of the cops in question. She gave the woman a quick hug and stepped back to let Reese take her by the arm.

His expression had morphed back into the same neutral mask he'd worn while acting as security for the autographing. His grip on Lizzie, however, was firm, and Darla recalled his comments about not wanting to take part in another sprint. He nodded in her direction.

"I put a call in for a car. Take a look outside and see if it's here yet."

Darla did as instructed. Sure enough, a patrol car had pulled up to the curb, and the officer already had the rear passenger door open to the sidewalk.

"It's here," she said with a nod and opened the shop door.

Jake had already grabbed up Lizzie's abandoned cardigan and purse, tucking the former into the latter before hanging the bag from the woman's free shoulder. Reese walked her toward the front.

And so the lion captures his prey, Darla told herself, though the realization brought dismay rather than satisfaction. Lizzie kept her gaze downcast, not acknowledging her as the pair passed by and then started down the steps. She waited until Reese had safely loaded the woman into the backseat and then climbed in up front beside the officer. Then, with a sigh, she shut the door and turned to Jake.

"I still can't believe it. Do you really think that Lizzie could shove Valerie Baylor into traffic like that?"

"She admitted to placing the ad, and she disguised herself so that Janie wouldn't recognize her," Jake reminded her.

"That's a lot of trouble to go to, if all she wanted to do was prove a point."

"But murder!?"

Darla sank into Jake's favorite beanbag chair and shook her head. "As far as the protester, I guess that makes sense. I'm sure she was afraid I'd fire her if she went out and held up the signs herself."

"And would you have?"

"No . . . yes . . . maybe," she replied in frustration, realizing as she did so that she was echoing her words to Reese about her little poltergeist problem. "All I know is that I have to fire her now, damn it."

"Listen, Darla," Jake told her, "I've seen people kill other people over a five-dollar bet. I once arrested a guy who stabbed his wife to death because his steak wasn't cooked right. They didn't plan to do it—at least, that's what they all swore—but their victims were dead, all the same. Something about impulse control . . . some people just don't have it."

Darla frowned, trying to recall if she'd ever seen Lizzie lash out at anyone but unable to think of an example. On the other hand, Lizzie had been married to a womanizing control freak for twenty years. No doubt she harbored resentment on that front. And Darla had seen her flash of anger the day of the ill-fated autographing as they'd watched the Lone Protester doing her thing . . . which had turned out to be Lizzie's thing. Given all that, was it possible that she had impulsively taken revenge on her former college classmate when the opportunity presented itself?

The front door jangled again, and Darla realized in dismay that she'd forgotten to relock it. A customer finally had decided to stop by, with her in no mood to play ye olde shopkeeper. But it wasn't a customer after all, she saw as she struggled out of the beanbag's squishy embrace. It was Mary Ann.

The elderly woman rushed toward her, her maroon shirt-dress flapping about her bony knees. "Thank God you're here, Darla," she gasped. "I happened to glance out my window and saw Lizzie being put into a police car by that nice Detective Reese. Why, it looked like the poor girl was under arrest!"

"She's just going into the station to answer a few questions," Jake assured her before Darla could reply. "I'm sure she'll be home again in a couple of hours."

"Questions?" Mary Ann echoed, eyes wide. "Oh my gracious, surely this doesn't have anything to do with that terrible accident the other night, does it?"

"We might as well tell her," Darla said before Jake could toss out another evasive answer. "It turns out that Lizzie was the one who orchestrated having that girl holding up the signs and protesting Valerie Baylor's appearance here. Now the police are trying to figure out if she's also the one who shoved Valerie in front of the van."

"Oh my gracious!"

Mary Ann clutched the bodice of her dress in the clichéd be-still-my-heart gesture that Darla had always associated with old ladies in television melodramas. Mary Ann, however, appeared genuinely distressed, so much so that Darla pulled out one of the stools from behind the counter and set it beside her.

"Sit down a minute," she urged, helping the woman onto the seat. "The police haven't arrested her—"

"Not yet anyhow," Jake interjected.

"—and it's probably all a formality," she finished with a dark look at her friend, who merely shrugged. "That whole protest thing was pretty darned stupid on her part, but it doesn't mean Lizzie is a cold-blooded killer by any stretch of the imagination."

Then another thought occurred to her. "Mary Ann, you were there at the counter the entire time. Do you recall seeing Lizzie leave the store, especially when Valerie disappeared that last time?"

The old woman gave her hands a helpless flutter.

"Lord, there was so much going on at the register, I didn't have time to keep up with everyone else. I know I looked over at the signing table a couple of times and saw her helping James, but that doesn't mean she was there every single second."

Then, with a hard look at Jake, she added, "And it doesn't mean she wasn't, either."

"You're right, Mary Ann," the ex-cop agreed, "and that's what Reese is trying to find out. And like I told you, they only took her in for questioning. She's not under arrest."

Yet.

Though the qualifier was unspoken this time, it seemed that everyone still heard it. They exchanged uncomfortable glances before Mary Ann stoutly declared, "Well, you won't convince me that she's guilty. After all, what motive could a girl like her possibly have?"

Darla fleetingly considered explaining about Lizzie's plagiarism claim but thought the better of it. No reason to give Mary Ann something else to worry about. Instead, she smiled and said, "I'm sure the truth will come out soon enough. Why don't you go on back home, and I'll let you know if I hear anything else."

"You're right. No sense borrowing trouble," she agreed, but without returning the smile. Brushing aside Darla's attempt to help, she stiffly climbed off the stool and shook out her skirts. "I'd best go back to the store now. I left Brother all alone there."

Appearing far older than Darla recalled ever seeing her look, Mary Ann made her way out of the store. Darla followed, locking the door firmly behind the woman.

"I'm officially calling it quits," she declared. "I'll let you out the side door, Jake, and then I'm going to go back to the apartment to eat ice cream and watch awful movies for the rest of the day . . . or, at least until lunchtime."

"Sounds like a good plan to me. If you feel like company later on, let me know."

"No offense, but I probably won't. But do me a favor and call me when you hear from Reese about Lizzie. I have a feeling she won't be calling me."

They were headed for the side door when Darla heard what was becoming a familiar sound now: the unmistakable splat of a tossed book landing on the floor.

"Damn you, Hamlet," she muttered.

To Jake, she said, "Ever since that little devil learned how to pull books off the shelf, he's been making a game of it with me."

Darla sought out the source of the sound, and found Hamlet lounging in the drama section near a slender volume facedown on the floor. Turning it over, she glanced at the cover so she could return it to the correct spot on the shelf, and then promptly wished she hadn't. For, just as with some of the other novels that he'd snagged in recent days, Hamlet had pulled down a book that seemed eerily appropriate to the situation.

With an uncertain glance at the cat—what, was he Mr. Psychic Cat now?—she hurriedly shelved the book in her hand, which had just happened to be a copy of the famous courtroom stage play, *Twelve Angry Men*.

 **TWENTY-FOUR**

"ONE NEVER KNOWS ABOUT THESE THINGS, DOES ONE? AH, well, I am certain you will find an appropriate replacement for Ms. Cavanaugh."

James shook his head and took a contemplative sip of coffee. As always, he'd brought his own brew in a thermos from home and drank it from his personal china cup that he kept there at the store. *The only proper way to drink the beverage*, he had told her early on in their acquaintance, not hesitating to inform her about his disdain for the ubiquitous lidded paper cups of the local coffee chains.

It was midafternoon, and the store manager had just arrived for his shift. As threatened, Darla had retreated to her apartment for a couple of hours to indulge in triple-dip ice cream therapy, but by noon she'd grown bored with her bout of self-pity and returned to the store. Now, she barely waited for the door to close behind him to give James the heads-up as to all that had happened that morning.

Though genteelly stunned by the turn of events, he had seemed less dismayed by Lizzie's actions than Darla had expected. Perhaps the recent enmity between them had been more serious than she'd thought, as James seemed well prepared to paint the woman a villain. Even so, he had expressed polite relief to learn that Lizzie in fact had avoided arrest and returned home around lunchtime.

Darla had been equally thankful when Jake called to give her the news.

"That doesn't mean she's off the suspect list," the woman had reminded her. "It just means there's not enough evidence against her right now to issue an arrest warrant. But Reese did find out something interesting when they did a background on her. While Lizzie was still married, the cops went out to her place on a domestic disturbance call."

"Lizzie already told me about that," Darla had replied. "She said she and her husband fought all the time in the six months before they separated, and that one night things got so out of hand that a neighbor called the police."

"That's pretty much what the record says . . . except that it was Lizzie and not her husband who got hauled down to the station that night. The report mentioned something about her threatening him with a big-ass butcher knife."

Jake had rung off after that, leaving a shocked Darla to wonder what she was going to do about her employee now. No way could she risk keeping someone who had no qualms about sabotaging a store event. And with what Jake had just told her about Lizzie's apparently violent history, who knew if her behavior might one day escalate—if it hadn't already? But given all that, what would Lizzie's reaction be when Darla told her she was fired?

She had phoned Jake back a few minutes later for advice. The other woman's response had been blunt.

"Does she have a key to the store? Okay, don't worry about trying to get it back," she'd said when Darla nervously answered in the affirmative. "Ted's brother, Barney, is a locksmith. I'll give him a call and tell him you need him out there before end of business today. Wait until the new locks are on before you call Lizzie to tell her she's out of there. I doubt she'll be too surprised, but this way, she can't come in after hours and trash the place or anything."

"But what about when we're open?" Darla had asked, feeling suddenly vulnerable.

She'd heard Jake's humorless chuckle on the other end. "Don't forget, kid, I'm still your official one-woman security firm, plus you've got all the cameras hooked up to record any problems. Call me as soon as you've told her, and I'll come up to keep an eye on things."

"I'd appreciate that," she'd replied in true relief. "And, yes, send Barney over as soon as possible."

Recalling that conversation now, Darla told James about the locksmith. "And Jake will be hanging out here the next couple of days, just in case."

"Sensible precautions on both counts," he agreed, downing what remained of his coffee. "And now, I had best finish fronting the shelves. That last gaggle of old women wandering the mystery aisle were little better than barbarians."

As James left to tidy the books, the bells at the front door jingled. Darla gave a reflexive start, visions of a knife-wielding Lizzie springing to mind. No weapons were in evidence, however, only a blond bulldog who, judging by his resemblance to Ted the security guy, had to be Jake's locksmith.

"Name's Barney," he said, introducing himself, "and it's your lucky day. You need it picked or changed, I'm the guy for you . . . except when it comes to noses and babies. Badda boom."

Unlike his brother with his finger pistols, Barney punctuated his bon mots with a bit of air drumming. Despite her unsettled mood, Darla couldn't help but smile back as she took him on a brief tour of the store and showed him the various doors needing attention.

Barney completed the job far more quickly than she had expected, though not without sharing additional cringeworthy jokes. He tested all three doors a final time and then handed her a set of keys and a bill that made her gulp only slightly as she reached for her checkbook.

"Pleasure doing business, ma'am. Tell Detective Jake hello for me," he said with a tip of his ball cap. He pocketed her payment and left whistling a tune that sounded suspiciously like "Jingle Bell Rock."

"Seasonally challenged and desperately in need of new material, but efficient," was James's conclusion as the door shut behind the locksmith. Then, with a wry look at her, he added, "Under the circumstances, I will not be offended if you prefer to keep custody of all the keys . . . at least, for a while."

"Thanks, I think I will. And now, I'd better make that call to Lizzie."

She carried the cordless phone upstairs to the break area for a bit of privacy. James was far too polite to stand around and listen to the call outright, but she knew he'd have an ear cocked in her direction. It was going to be hard enough to conduct her first official firing without her remaining employee silently critiquing her performance.

Like the lock changing, however, the call went better than she'd anticipated. Lizzie answered on the first ring, as if she'd had her hand on the receiver all afternoon. Before Darla could get more than a "hello" out, the woman sighed and said, "I suppose you're calling to fire me, aren't you?"

"I am," she admitted, relieved not to have to beat around the bush. "I'm not saying I think you're guilty of anything beside really crappy judgment, Lizzie, but I can't have you work here anymore after what you did, trying to sabotage the signing like that."

"I understand." Another sigh. "Sorry I was such trouble for you. And thanks for the attorney's name. If Detective Reese ends up arresting me, I'll give him a call. I don't suppose I can come by later for my check?"

"Well—"

Remember, they found her with a butcher knife, she told herself as she felt her resolve momentarily waver. That mental image was enough to restore her backbone.

"Not a good idea. I'll have it in the mail to you today. Good-bye, Lizzie, and good luck," Darla finished and hung up the phone before her guilt over canning the woman got the better of her. Then, as instructed, she promptly dialed Jake.

"Good job, kid," Jake said once Darla recapped the brief conversation for her. "It sounds like she took it okay, but I'm still going to hang out with you for the next couple of days. How did Barney work out for you, changing those locks?"

"Easy as changing a baby. Badda boom."

Her reply drew a commiserating laugh from the other woman. "Yeah, he and his brother are something, but believe me, the guys know what they're doing. I'll be up in a few minutes."

The rest of the day proceeded without incident. By the

time Darla closed the store at her usual time, she was satisfied that, if she hadn't made a profit, at least she'd covered the electric bill for the day.

"See," Jake proclaimed from the beanbag. "I told you things would get back to normal soon enough. And even Hamlet behaved himself this afternoon."

"You're right," Darla answered in a wondering tone. In fact, she hadn't seen whisker nor tail of him since his little book snagging incident that morning. Was he still lounging in the apartment, or had he snuck downstairs and tucked himself away in one of his favorite hiding spots? She only prayed that his absence didn't mean he'd been off playing more cat tricks on her.

"So, wanna grab a bite at the Thai place again?" Jake asked.

Darla considered the offer a moment and then shook her head. "Thanks, but after this whole thing with Lizzie, I don't think I'll be good company. I've got a date with a container of yogurt and my pillow."

"Suit yourself, kid." Then, turning to James, who was packing up his coffee thermos, she asked, "What about you, James? Care to go Dutch over some pad thai?"

Darla waited for him to dismiss the invitation in his usual aloof manner, but to her surprise, he said, "I shall go you one better, Ms. Martelli, and purchase dinner for you."

To Darla, who was staring at him in amazement, he added by way of explanation, "My auction last night ended quite favorably, and so a small celebration would not be amiss."

"Well, let's not let that cash burn a hole in your vest pocket," Jake declared with a toss of her frizzy hair. "Darla, if you want to hand over one of your new keys, I'll give the store another look when I get back. And then I'll check in with you, if you think you can keep your eyes open that long."

"Believe me, the idea of you and James out on the town together is enough to keep me awake all night again."

Darla saw them off at the front door, feeling curiously like a parent seeing her daughter off on a date. She resisted the impulse, however, to suggest that Jake take a sweater with her. Instead, she locked her new lock after them; then, finishing the last of the closing process, she set the alarm and went out the side door.

Hamlet was waiting for her behind the newel post at the foot of the stairs. This time, he let her get halfway to the first landing before he rocketed up the steps, using her as a human croquet wicket on his way to the top.

"Damn it, Hamlet," she called after him. "Someday, you're going to trip me, and Jake will find my broken body lying at the bottom of the stairs. And then who do you think will feed you your kibble?"

Hamlet made no reply to this dire prediction, for he was already sitting at the apartment door waiting for her to drag herself up the final flight. As soon as she reached that spot, however, she wondered if she should have had Jake check out her apartment, too, beforehand. Of course, Lizzie didn't have a key to either the downstairs door or this one. But with all that had been going on, Darla decided to let Hamlet enter the apartment first.

He charged inside before she could get the door open all the way. Darla moved more slowly, poking her head around the edge for an experimental look. No hideous caterwauling ensued, and all the books appeared to be in their proper places. So far as she could tell, it was safe to enter.

As always, the first order of business was to feed Hamlet— that, or listen to his official starving-kitty lament that could go nonstop for a good hour (once, feeling in an evil mood, she actually had timed it). That accomplished, she nixed the yogurt and instead made a veggie omelet for herself, which she ate while watching her favorite weekend cable news host expound on the day's issues. She managed to get through almost the entire hour show before the host gave a recap of the Valerie Baylor saga. He mentioned that the private service had been held a few days earlier, and to Darla's surprise she saw a bit of video that obviously had been taken with a long-distance lens.

"No escaping the press," she muttered, scanning the footage for a glimpse of herself . . . or, more likely, her hat. She didn't see either, but the camera had captured a clear view of Morris escorting out his parents.

The sight of Valerie's brother brought back her previous suspicions that the whole Lizzie situation had caused her to put aside as unimportant. Now, however, both Lizzie and Janie had been scratched off the suspect list; neither appeared to have had any involvement with the actual accident leading to Valerie's death. Maybe it was time to put Morris back on the list.

"Yes, yes, assuming that what happened was anything other than an accident," she said aloud to Jake in absentia, since she could almost hear the ex-cop telling her that the whole push-shove question was still up in the air.

Since there was nothing to be done about Morris now, however, given that her one attempt to question him had led to nothing, Darla instead went over to her desk. Feeling virtuous, she accessed the store security software on her laptop. Ted had suggested she make a habit of doing so, at least until she was comfortable that her unknown intruder was no longer a threat. Given what she'd spent on the software, she told herself she might as well get her money's worth out of it.

Once she'd again determined that all was well in the store, she left the screen up and found a nice nonthreatening travel memoir that she'd been meaning to read, and curled up in bed with it. She put it aside only to pick up the phone when Jake checked in a little later, as promised.

"How did your date with James go?" Darla asked her in a bright voice.

The other woman gave a dismissive snort. "Please. We were two friends having dinner together, and it just so happened he was kind enough to pick up the tab. Don't read anything more into it than that."

"Whatever you say," she agreed, grinning to herself at this rare opportunity to needle her friend. She had no doubt that what Jake said was one hundred percent true, but it was far more fun to let her think otherwise. Then, sobering, she asked, "Everything okay down in the store?"

"Locked up tight as a drum, all the alarms are functioning, and there's no one suspicious hanging around. Oh, and only a few hardcore Valerie minions are holding vigil at the flower shrine. No sign of Lizzie or any of the Lord's Blessing Church protesters, so I think you and Hamlet are good to go for the night."

Which hopefully meant that Lizzie was staying put, and that Marnie and company were long since on their way back to Texas in their repaired van.

"Thanks, Jake. I really do appreciate all this. I'd probably be a basket case right about now if I didn't know you were downstairs."

"Just doing my job, kid," the woman replied, but Darla could hear the pleasure in her voice over the compliment. "I'll be back up to the store in the a.m., like I said. Good night, sleep tight, don't let the bedbugs bite," she finished, laughing.

Since bedbugs were currently a scourge in the city, Darla shivered at the very idea. She hung up the phone and picked up her book again. Hamlet deigned to join her in the room, but he made due with the dresser as his lounging spot rather than curl up on the pillow beside her like any normal cat. Darla met the feline's disapproving green gaze with an amused look.

"You know, I don't think a bedbug would dare take up residence here with you running the place," she told him and then settled back into her book.

Interesting as the author's account of his India journey was—so vivid were his descriptions that she could almost taste the boiling chai tea and smell the lackadaisical sacred cows—she found herself nodding over every page. She sprang back to full wakefulness, however, when the sound of a ringing phone had her almost leaping from the covers. She glanced over at her alarm clock. Quarter before ten—too late for polite callers where she came from, but still prime time on the East Coast.

"Oh, thank God you're there, Darla!" Lizzie wailed through the receiver.

"Lizzie?" Darla said. "Why are you calling? I don't think after all that's happened that you and I really should be talking again."

Her rejection launched a dramatic sob from the other woman, while Darla felt the fluffy omelet she'd eaten earlier settle into an uncomfortable lead platter in her stomach. This was *not* what she needed tonight. She clung grimly to the receiver and waited for Lizzie's storm of tears to dwindle to a gentle sprinkle. Finally, when she was certain the woman could hear her, she took charge of the conversation.

"I'm going to hang up now, Lizzie, unless you have a really good reason for calling."

"But I do. I have information about something that happened at the signing."

"Then call Reese. I'm sure he gave you his card, didn't he?"

"He won't believe me," Lizzie complained between sniffles, "but you're a reasonable person, so I'm calling you. Besides, you know me, and he doesn't."

Knowing someone didn't necessarily mean knowing all about them, however, as Darla had so recently found out. She made a noncommittal noise, and Lizzie continued.

"Well, you remember how busy it was during the signing, with all those kids running about, and Valerie with her whole entourage. She was being a big show-off, if you ask me, with all those people hanging around her."

"Cut to the chase, Lizzie," Darla warned, feeling the lead platter morphing into a concrete block now.

"Oh, all right." Lizzie's sniffling took on a distinctly offended note, but she went on, "Maybe I told you this already, but right before Valerie disappeared that last time, I saw her makeup person sneak away upstairs. She came down a minute later wearing a black cape, with the hood pulled up over her head and everything."

"Go on," Darla urged, not bothering to correct the other woman's choice of pronouns when referring to Mavis. Not that she expected anything to come of this; after all, she and Jake had already determined much the same thing from Callie's photos the other day.

Deciding that she'd caught Darla's attention, the woman lowered her voice to a dramatic whisper. "I probably wouldn't have noticed her doing that, except that I made up my mind to keep an eye on her. There was something kind of off about her, if you want my opinion."

So even Lizzie had realized Mavis wasn't quite what she—or he—seemed to be. Darla frowned. "Go on."

"Anyhow, all night long when she thought no one was watching, Mavis had been giving Val the strangest looks. Not exactly mean, but—"

"But like she wanted to kill her?" Darla blurted, unable to help herself.

She heard Lizzie click her tongue in mild reproof.

"Really, Darla, don't you think that's a bit overdramatic of you? It wasn't anything like that at all. It was more a look like she was daring Val to do something."

"That's all?" This revelation was no revelation at all. Why had Lizzie bothered with her dramatic buildup when the payoff was about as compelling as a glass of tap water?

Lizzie, however, was not finished.

"See, that's why I couldn't tell Detective Reese, because I knew he'd say that exact thing," she declared. "You had to see that look on her face to understand what I mean. But Val had the exact same expression the whole time she was signing, except Val wasn't looking at Mavis. She kept staring over at the nice agent lady—what was her name?—Hillary Gables."

 **TWENTY-FIVE**

"SOUNDS PRETTY DARN WEAK TO ME, KID," JAKE SAID THE next morning after Darla had told her about last night's weepy call from Lizzie.

They were eating breakfast back in the little courtyard—the store wouldn't officially open for another two hours—and Darla had been peppering their bagels and coffee with a recap of Lizzie's contention that Mavis had some involvement in matters. She hadn't yet mentioned her own renewed suspicions regarding the author's brother.

"Besides," Jake added, "you know how Reese feels about funny looks."

"Yeah, well the last one panned out, didn't it?" Darla countered, recalling how Hamlet's funny look at one of Valerie's fans had led to their discovering the identity of the Lone Protester. Even as she wondered why she was taking Lizzie's side, she went on, "I like the guy, but I have to agree that Morris has been on my suspect list ever since the memorial service."

"Well, so far as I know, he's not on Reese's list, so the smart thing would be to drop it before you get slapped with a harassment suit. The Vicksons have pretty deep pockets, even without Valerie's book-writing money."

At Jake's words, a thought so outrageous occurred to Darla that she almost dropped her coffee cup.

"Jake," she slowly began, "before we drop it, here's another theory. You know how Lizzie claimed that Valerie Baylor stole her manuscript back in college and got it published before Lizzie could?"

"That's what Lizzie claims," Jake replied with a shrug. "All we have is her word against Valerie's, except that Valerie isn't here to defend herself. Besides, didn't you once tell me that you can't copyright an idea?"

"That's right, but Lizzie is talking plagiarism, which is a whole different thing."

"Fine, but what does that have to do with Mavis, er, Morris?"

"Remember when I introduced Callie to Morris, how he began asking what she thought about the previous *Haunted High* book?"

"Yeah, so what? After all, his sister wrote it."

"But it wasn't just nice little chitchat. His questions were specific, the kind of questions that the book's author might ask."

Jake was staring at her now, a quizzical look on her face. Darla hesitated, certain she finally was on the right track but not sure how crazy her theory would sound out loud.

She took a deep breath and forged on. "Okay, here's the motive. What if Valerie really did steal Lizzie's story . . . and then, later on down the road, what if she did the same thing to her brother?"

"Are you trying to say that Morris wrote the *Haunted High* books but Valerie took the credit?" Jake's curious look briefly morphed into one of incredulity before she frowned and nodded. "You know, kid, you could be on to something. If Valerie had been taking credit for his work the entire time, maybe he finally got tired of getting the short end."

"Wait." Darla held up a hand, for already she'd seen a few holes in her brilliant theory. "Why would he allow her to keep stealing his work?" she mused. "One book, I could see, but three?"

"Maybe he'd already written all three before she stole the first one? You hear about that all the time, unpublished authors with three or four manuscripts stuck in a drawer somewhere. Maybe she ran off with his entire body of work."

Before Darla could answer, they both heard through the open shop door the now-familiar thud of a large volume hitting the floor.

Hamlet! While they'd been talking, he had apparently wandered off to do a bit of mischief. Darla gave an exasperated sigh and headed into the shop, and in the direction of what seemed to be the source of the sound—the reference books.

"You need to figure out some way to break him of that habit," Jake called after her.

Darla spied the wayward book, which Hamlet had dragged from the shelf devoted to books on writing and editing. She bent and picked up the book in question; then, frowning a little, she returned with it to the courtyard.

"Maybe not," she replied and turned the book so that Jake could see its cover. "I think Hamlet is saying he has his own theory."

Jake raised a dark brow as she read the title aloud, *"How to Work as a Ghostwriter."*

The ex-cop folded her arms and pursed her lips in thought while Darla flipped through the book's table of contents. *"When do you need a ghostwriter?" "How to collaborate successfully." "Who gets the royalties?"* Reading the chapter headings, Darla decided that perhaps her new theory wasn't a veritable sieve after all. Maybe it simply needed a bit of tweaking.

"Do you think it's possible—"

"I wonder if maybe—"

They'd started speaking at once and now broke off to stare at each other. When Jake nodded for her to go ahead, Darla tried again.

"Suppose we go with the idea that Morris has something to do with the *Haunted High* books. But maybe Valerie didn't steal the manuscripts—what if they had worked out a deal? Maybe Morris helped write the books, she submitted them to the publisher under her name—"

"And they each took a cut of the cash," Jake finished, her expression of satisfaction matching Darla's. "That's a nice little bit of synchronicity, a ghostwriter writing ghost stories. But I think that would be pretty hard, doing all that work and not getting any of the credit."

"It happens in publishing all the time," Darla told her. "But what about Valerie's death? That's the real issue."

Jake shrugged. "Maybe it really was an accident. If it was a joint project, then he'd have no reason to want her out of the picture." She paused and frowned. "You know, I think we need to take another look at the video we watched the other night."

"I agree. Give me a second."

So saying, Darla went back into the shop, with Jake trailing behind, and walked over to the computer. She pulled up a browser window and after a bit of searching, she located the clip in question. While Jake watched intently beside her, she fast-forwarded it to the spot where the two black-caped figures made their appearances. They ran that portion of the video several times, pausing and winding back during each play as they tried to pinpoint any feature that would clearly identify the pair and clarify their interaction. By about the fifth or six playing, however, Jake gave a disgusted snort.

"Nothing you could take to a judge. But if Mavis really is the second person in the video, I say we pay him a visit and see if we can't learn a little more."

"Do you really think he'd talk to us, after what happened the other day?"

"Trust me, if he saw his sister killed right in front of him, he's going to want to talk to someone eventually. We've got your copy of the business card that Morris gave you, so I'm thinking we try his office. If we go to his house, he'll probably set the dogs on us." She took a quick look at her watch. "It's still early. You wanna go now?"

"Good plan, except today is Sunday. What are the chances he'll even be there?"

"Any entrepreneur worth his salt works weekends," Jake replied. "You should know that. And if he's not there . . . well, maybe it will give us a chance to poke around and find out a little more about how Morris and Mavis fit into this whole sorry mess. You think you can stand opening the store a little late?"

"The church crowd won't be out in force until later, anyhow, and I'm the only one working today, so why not?"

They returned to the courtyard, made quick work of the rest of their breakfast, and then went back inside to do a quick map check online. "Only about twenty blocks to his office," Jake said in satisfaction. "Easy walk."

Darla stifled a groan—she never was going to get used to all this hoofing it about town—but only said, "Let me run upstairs and get a decent pair of walking shoes, and I'll meet you out front."

To Hamlet, who was lounging on the counter, his breakfast long since consumed, she said, "You're the boss for the next couple of hours. Don't let anyone into the store unless they have a credit card with no limit."

Hamlet gave her a stony green glare—he knew patronizing humor when he heard it—and knocked the stack of free newspapers off the counter by way of response. Darla shook her head. The mess could wait until later. Right now, she was in Nancy Drew mode, with a possible killer to catch!

"HE'S NOT HERE . . . THAT, OR HE'S NOT ANSWERING."

Darla and Jake had twice rung the intercom buzzer alongside the tiny brass nameplate frame bearing a handwritten label with Morris's last name and suite number. So far, they'd had no response, and Darla was beginning to feel a bit conspicuous standing on the chilly stoop outside the three-story apartment building that matched the address Morris had written on the back of his business card. This neighborhood had a much seedier vibe than hers. While the place presumably housed Morris's office, Darla had begun to wonder what sort of business he actually conducted there, given the condition of both the building and the surrounding area.

Unlike her own tidy digs, this building, stuck midway down a line of row houses, gave off a distinct air of neglect. The façade's dun-colored brick was pockmarked, as if someone with a grudge had unloaded a few rounds of buckshot at the place. Here and there, the brick was more deeply scarred, as if someone else had followed later with a few judicious blows from a hammer. Above, two rows of three filthy, barred windows each gave a bird's-eye view from the second and third stories . . . that was, if said bird was wearing a blindfold.

Centered between the two equally barred and grimy windows on the ground floor was what charitably could be called a portico, but was in actuality little more than an alcove large enough to shelter a single person. Even though it was morning, a fly-specked bulb glowed from the open iron fixture hanging overhead. Darla didn't need that light to make out the wooden door's peeling brown latex, which revealed a visual account of at least three previous paint jobs, all in similar muddy hues that showed a decided lack of decorating flair. As for the stoop on which they were standing, it looked positively leprous with chunks of concrete missing from the steps. The iron railing gave a definite wobble under hand that spoke of future lawsuits.

It was hardly the sort of place where she expected a man of Morris's apparent money and good taste to conduct business. In fact, she suspected that anyone who worked in that building also lived there, for the other tenants were all listed by a surname and not a business moniker.

Darla gazed nervously around her in time to see a trio of young men sauntering down the sidewalk toward them. In defiance of the morning chill, they were dressed alike in hooded sweatshirts and pants so baggy that they required a hand clutching their crotch to keep their jeans from sliding off completely. All three challenged her and Jake with a look as they drew closer.

"Yo, what's doin', pretty ladies?" one of them demanded, the cold gleam in his eyes turning what might have been a flirtatious question into something far more threatening.

While Darla tugged her wool jacket more closely around her in a reflexively defensive gesture, Jake turned and gave the three her own icy look from behind her mirrored pair of aviators. Her patented don't-even-think-of-jacking-with-me expression combined with her tough-girl outfit of a battered black leather jacket over the usual jeans, boots, and sweater apparently got the point across. That, or it was still too early on a Sunday for the youths to care to indulge in any real harassment.

Watching them keep on walking past, Darla decided that

there were some distinct advantages to hanging with an almost six-foot-tall gal pal who also happened to be an ex-cop. *Even better than owning a Doberman*, she thought with a nervous giggle.

"What do we do now?" Darla asked. "We can't get past the front door if there's no one to ring us in."

By way of answer, Jake gave her a pitying look. "Watch and learn, young grasshopper," she intoned and pressed another buzzer, seemingly at random.

When nothing happened, she chose another. A woman's raspy voice made even sharper by the intercom's distortion asked, "Who's there?"

"Hey, it's me."

"Yeah? Me who?"

"Deb."

"Yeah, well I don't know no Debs. Go to hell!"

Jake gave a philosophical shrug at the figurative door slamming in her face and tried another buzzer. This time, it was a man's disembodied voice that demanded, "Whaddya want?"

"Hey, it's me."

"Yeah? Me who?"

"Deb."

Darla waited for the next round of "Go to hell!" but instead she heard the distinctive click of the door unlocking. Jake gave it a quick push open and gestured her inside. Darla, meanwhile, gave her friend a questioning look. "Deb?"

"Just playing the odds, kid," Jake answered with a shrug as she joined her in the darkened foyer. "Everyone knows five or six Debs. In a larger building, it's even easier. Just punch all the buttons at one time and someone's bound to buzz you in without all the Q and A."

Darla nodded, blinking a little as she tried to accustom her eyes to the abrupt change in light. The inside of the building seemed surprisingly homey. Honey-colored wood on the floor and walls emitted a faint hint of beeswax and linseed oil, as if someone had polished there within recent memory. While the treads and risers of the narrow staircase were covered in ancient green linoleum, the trim and railings were painted a contrasting deep cream color for a look straight from a decorating magazine. Over the double row of brass mailboxes mounted on the far wall, someone had hung a series of flea-market prints featuring nineteenth-century New York City street scenes that completed the urban-vintage vibe.

While Darla was still processing this stark juxtaposition between interior and exterior, the male voice from the intercom demanded from above, "Hey, where the hell's Deb?"

She and Jake glanced up to see a bald, florid-faced man in his thirties leaning over the third-floor railing. He was wearing an undersized wife-beater undershirt that displayed his hairy belly and impressive crop of black armpit hair to distinct advantage. Darla gave a small prayer of thanks that the railing mostly blocked the view of his baggy blue plaid boxers.

Without missing a beat, Jake shoved her sunglasses up on top of her head and opened her eyes wide. "You mean the blonde?" she answered in feigned innocence. "Strange chick . . . she ran off as soon as our friend buzzed us in."

The man muttered a few obscenities that could have been directed at them, the fictional Deb, or women in general, but to Darla's relief he contented himself with that before turning from the railing. A door slammed after him a moment later.

"Nice neighbors your buddy Morris has," Jake muttered as she checked out the numbers on the two apartment doors across from them. "Looks like his little slice of this paradise is number 3, on the second floor."

Darla hurried up first, leaving Jake to make the climb at her own pace. Number 3 faced the street. She waited until Jake had joined her in the narrow hall; then, with a nervous look around first to make sure there were no witnesses, she knocked on Morris's door. Once again, no one answered.

Jake motioned her aside and tried the knob. It turned readily enough, but the deadbolt locking the door kept the latter firmly in place. "Worth a try," she said with a shrug. "You never know, people can get sloppy."

She reached into her pocket and pulled out a key. Inserting it into the dead-bolt lock, she jiggled the key a couple of times while Darla recalled the overhyped news stories she'd seen about lock bumping. Apparently, there was something to the hype, for Jake grinned and tried the knob again. This time, the door swung inward.

Darla gave another uneasy glance about the hall. "Uh, isn't this technically breaking and entering?"

"Technically, yes . . . but only if we get caught. Don't worry, I'll let you be lookout," she said as she all but shoved Darla through the door and then pulled it closed behind them.

The tiny apartment was a studio, with the living and sleeping space all together. Instead of a bed, however, a futon sofa lay fully open. Its crisp white surface was accented with a series of oversized multihued pillows apparently sprung from the earthy loom of some itinerant weaver determined to use every spare color of wool at hand to make those covers.

The only other furnishings were an oversized desk of blond wood with matching chair and overstuffed bookshelf, and a six-foot-tall screen that divided off the section of the room nearest the alcove leading to a bathroom. Constructed of three random doors hinged together, their glass panes now replaced by rice paper, the screen looked as if it had been slapped together in an hour. Darla guessed, however, that it probably had come from some trendy boutique and had sported a four-figure price tag.

A second alcove led to galley kitchen big enough to turn around in, but not bend over. A two-burner stove dating from the turn of the twentieth century held a teakettle of the same vintage. While it was obvious that someone did own the place, it was equally apparent that it wasn't lived in on a regular basis.

While Darla took up her post alongside the window—the three youths who had catcalled them were now sitting on a stoop across the street shouting insults to a passing Asian couple—Jake poked around the place. An empty laptop docking station sat on the desk, meaning that Morris carried his computer back and forth with him. Jake dragged out the stylish wooden trash can from beneath the desk and grimaced.

"I hate compulsive neat fiends," she remarked as she turned it over to demonstrate the can was empty. "It's hard to pry into people's trash when they don't have any."

She pulled open the desk drawers and then glanced at the bookcase, which held mostly reference books and office supplies. Numerous volumes—hardcover and paperback—of the first two *Haunted High* books filled one long shelf.

"Look at this," Jake said, sounding impressed as she pointed down the row. "English, French, Spanish, Russian, Japanese . . . and there's probably five other languages I have no clue what they are. And, aha!"

Carefully, she picked up a large black three-ring binder propped next to the printer on the topmost shelf. She turned it so Darla could see that it was neatly labeled on the front with the words "Last Ghoul Standing."

"It's the next *Haunted High* book," she exclaimed, leafing through the pages. "I thought you said that Hillary Gables told you there weren't any more manuscripts."

"Either she lied, or she didn't know," Darla replied, keeping her gaze on the street below lest Morris abruptly exit a taxi. "I wonder what Morris plans to do with it when it's finished, now that Valerie's gone."

Jake, meanwhile, had put back the binder and wandered over to the divided screen. She peered behind it and then jumped back as if someone had reached out and grabbed her.

"Holy crap, you're not going to believe this!"

Darla felt her stomach plummet. "Please don't tell me that Morris is lying dead back there," she said, wincing over the words. The last thing she wanted to see was another of the Vickson family's cooling corpses.

Jake shook her head. "It's even better than that. Come over here!"

With another look out the window—two of the three punks were now involved in a one-handed shoving match with each other that was hampered by the ongoing threat of pants on the ground—Darla went. With the same caution that she'd using peering into a rattlesnake den, she looked around the edge of the screen.

"Holy crap!" she echoed Jake, adding, "Wow!"

Hidden behind the screen were two freestanding racks filled with women's eveningwear in various lengths and styles. Whether of silk, satin, velvet, or lace, the predominant color was black, though a few jewel tones and pastels were mixed among them. A short wooden shelf stood to one side. She counted on its shelves ten evening clutches stored individually in neat plastic bins, and twice that many shoe boxes with famous designers' names imprinted on their sides. Darla reached reverently for one of the boxes and gently opened the top to reveal a lilac drawstring dust bag. Unfortunately, the pair of pumps nestled inside appeared far larger than the size 7-½ she wore.

She sighed. She'd always wanted to try on a pair of Jimmy Choos.

"Any one of those dresses probably costs as much as my whole wardrobe," Jake observed with a similarly wistful exhale as she longingly fingered a red silk strapless number. "Damn, he has good taste."

Letting the fabric whisper back into place, Jake went over to the bath alcove. "This must be where the magic takes place," she said, indicating a vintage painted iron-and-glass vanity upon which sat several neatly organized trays of cosmetics. "And look, here's Mavis in action."

Photos ringed the lighted oval mirror that hung over the vanity. Most of the pictures were of Mavis and her clients. A few obviously were models, and others apparently actors, including a couple of B-listers whom Darla recognized from television. Also among the collection were a few shots of Valerie Baylor, including one where she appeared to be standing beside a clone of herself.

"Oh my God, it's Mavis dressed as Valerie!" Darla exclaimed, pointing. "In that black wig, he could totally pass for her, no problem."

Seeing the photos prompted her to remember her guard duties. Darla muttered a mild oath and rushed to the door, taking a cautious peek over the railing in case Morris had sneaked in while they were admiring his outfits. Seeing no one, she slipped back inside and made a beeline for the front window.

"All clear," she confirmed a bit breathlessly. "Are we almost finished?"

"Almost," Jake muttered in an absent tone. She wandered back over to the desk and peered again at the shelves. "There's got to be something here."

She paused for a look at the pushbutton phone near the empty docking station. "Let's see who Morris has been chatting with," she said and pressed the "Speakerphone" button, opening the line. "If I can just find the 'Redial' button . . ."

She found it. Darla heard the familiar *beep, boop, bop* of tones as the last number that Morris had input now automatically replayed. Jake put a silencing finger to her lips as the line began to ring, but Darla needed no warning. She was holding her breath and mentally counting the rings as they sounded . . . *One, two, three*.

It was not until the fifth ring that someone picked up. They heard clattering, as if someone were fumbling with the phone, and then a woman's sleepy voice answered, "Hillary Gables."

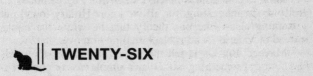

TWENTY-SIX

"THIS IS HILLARY GABLES."

Darla's jaw sagged as she heard the agent repeat her greeting in a sharper tone. Then came a small gasp, and the speakerphone voice demanded, "Morris, is that you? Damn it, don't play games with me. I've got caller ID. I recognize your number."

Getting no response, Hillary stormed on, "Don't think you can threaten me, you son of a bitch! I'm not afraid of you. I can take you down with what I know. So if you want to keep our little secret between us, I suggest you quit the harassment and bring the money to the club tonight like we agreed."

In the good old days, Darla irrelevantly thought, they would have heard the receiver slam down as Hillary ended the call. But since the agent was either on a cell phone or a cordless, the conversation ended with a barely audible click as she cut the connection. Jake hung up the speakerphone with the same one-touch efficiency and then turned to meet Darla's gaze.

"I guess he really did kill Valerie," Darla said, "and Hillary knows all about it. And now she's blackmailing him." She heard the disappointment in her own voice and realized that, despite her suspicions, she really had believed James's theory about twins being unable to murder their siblings. But apparently even the esteemed Professor James James could be wrong on occasion, as Hillary's tirade seemingly had proved.

Jake, however, put up a restraining hand.

"Jump to conclusions much, kid? While I agree this is all pretty damn interesting, for all we know Hillary found out something else—like our theory that he wrote the books instead of Valerie—and is blackmailing him over that."

"Maybe." But Darla felt the venom in the agent's words had hinted at something more than a simple case of ghostwriting. "I guess we need to tell Reese what we found out."

"And what do you suggest we tell him? That we broke into Morris's private office, autodialed Hillary Gables, and heard her say something about money? Remember what I said about thin? Well, we're talking tissue paper here."

"Then I guess we'll have to find this club Hillary was talking abou—oh no!"

Darla had glanced at the window in time to see Morris on the sidewalk below, having just exited a cab. Now, she pointed frantically in that direction.

"He's here. Morris is here," she exclaimed with a panicked look back at Jake. "What if he catches us in here?"

"He won't if we get the hell out right now," Jake replied with a swift look around the apartment. "Okay, everything looks in order, so let's head up to the third floor to visit with Mr. Clean for a bit. Once Morris is safely in the apartment, we'll make our escape."

They slipped out the door, and Jake paused long enough to twist the thumb lock on the inner knob before shutting the door behind them.

"Maybe he'll think he locked the wrong lock last time," she whispered as the sound of the front door opening drifted up to them. She jabbed a finger in the direction of the third floor, and Darla made a swift if silent beeline for the stairs. Over the frantic beating of her heart, she could hear the faint sounds of metal on metal from the lobby, and she guessed Morris was checking his mail, giving them a few extra seconds.

As they reached the third-floor landing, they heard him starting up the steps. Darla shrank back against the far wall and reflexively counted the footfalls, holding her breath when they stopped. Then she heard a key scrape in the lock, followed by a pause, and the sound of a knob jiggling. She could almost hear the question mark in his thoughts as he apparently found the dead bolt open and the twist lock on the knob locked instead. Did he suspect anything other than his own memory?

"Hey! Hey, there!"

The raspy female voice made both her and Jake jump. Darla gazed wildly about for its source and then recognized the voice as belonging to the first woman whom they'd randomly buzzed while trying to get in. As the woman continued to speak, she realized in relief that the sound was coming from the second floor.

"—was real sorry to hear about your other sister," the unseen woman was saying, the words obviously directed at Morris. "I'd of made up a casserole to send around, except I didn't know where to bring it."

"Don't worry, Mrs. Gleason," she heard Morris reply. "Kind thoughts are as filling as food in such situations."

"Well, you just let me know if you need anything, Morrie," Mrs. Gleason said with a comforting click of her tongue. "Oh, and I haven't forgotten about coming around to see that play you told me about. You think maybe Mavis can get me backstage? I'd love to meet that actor fellow who plays Othello. I just love him on that cop show on Tuesday nights."

"I'm sure she can arrange it. Not tonight, but maybe for next Sunday's performance."

"That would be great. I'm going to go call for a ticket right now."

A door closed, and then a second one opened and closed. Mrs. Gleason and Morris both were safely in their apartments, Darla assumed. But Jake gave a warning shake of her head and leaned carefully over the railing to take another look.

Sure enough, a door on the second floor opened again, and Darla heard the sound of shuffling footsteps. "Hey, Morrie," Mrs. Gleason yelled, "which one, three o'clock show or eight o'clock show?"

"Eight o'clock, Mrs. Gleason," Morris patiently called

through his closed door. "The understudy will be playing Othello at the three o'clock performance."

"Eight o'clock it is."

The woman shuffled back into her apartment, the door slamming behind her again. Jake peered over the railing for a few more moments and then gestured to Darla, murmuring, "Come on, kid, let's get out of here."

They made their way down the two flights in silent haste, fortunately not encountering either Mrs. Gleason or Morris on the way. But Darla didn't breathe easy again until they'd made it out onto the street and were a good two blocks back in the direction of Crawford Avenue.

"I'm too old for this sort of thing," she declared with a sigh.

Jake shook her frizzy head and laughed. "Come on, kid, don't be such a cliché. A little bit of adrenaline rush is good for the heart."

"Well, then my heart is good for the next twenty years or so," Darla replied, though this time with a grudging smile. The smile faded, however, as she asked, "So what are we going to do about Morris and Hillary?"

"I was thinking we track them down tonight and see about witnessing this little exchange they've got planned. Now that I know what's going on, no way am I going to let Hillary face off against Morris by herself. It might only be blackmail over a writing credit, but you never know how these things might go down."

Jake's amused expression evaporated as she spoke, and her fixed gaze momentarily reminded Darla of the look she had turned on the three young thugs. As for the unsaid sentiment it reflected, she knew it was *Not again, not on my watch*.

"I see where you're coming from," Darla ventured, "but how do we figure out what club Hillary was talking about?"

"We can do it the hard way"—Jake slanted a look at her over her sunglasses—"which would be to tail her or Morris all day and hope we don't get spotted before we figure out where they're headed. Or, we can do it the easy way."

"I'll put in my vote for the easy way."

"I was hoping you'd say that."

She refused to elaborate, however, until they arrived back at the brownstone.

Once back in the store, Jake picked up one of the free newspapers that Hamlet had kicked aside earlier, and thumbed through it while Darla went to wait on the customer who had followed them into the store as she was unlocking the door. Once assured that her assistance wasn't needed, she casually sidled over to Jake and addressed her in a low tone.

"Okay, spill it. What's the easy way of figuring out which of a few hundred clubs around town is the one where Morris and Hillary will be?"

By way of answer, Jake folded back the paper so that a single large notice was visible. "My money's on this one," she said and tapped her finger on the banner headline.

Eyes wide, Darla began reading the advertisement aloud. *"The Club Theater Presents* Othello *by William Shakespeare, Starring DeWayne Jones and Harry Delacourt."*

Jake nodded. "As soon as good old Mrs. Gleason mentioned her cop show, I remembered seeing this same ad in last week's throwaway. DeWayne Jones is the hunky guy who stars in that show."

"And Hillary said she was going to meet Morris at the club . . . which must be the Club Theater," Darla finished for her.

Jake gave a small, satisfied smile. "We have a winner. So, what do you say, kid, you want to take in an off-Broadway show tonight?"

AS SHE STRUGGLED TO KEEP UP WITH JAKE'S LONG STRIDES DOWN THE sidewalk, Darla—her own feet pinching uncomfortably in the same heels she'd worn to Valerie's funeral—reflected on all the ground they'd traversed the past few days. At least this time, they'd taken the subway part of the way. Even so, she wondered how Jake's bum leg was holding out after their twenty-block walk to Morris's place and back that morning.

That question was partially answered as the ex-cop strode ahead of her, and she saw peeking out from beneath the woman's full-length black leather duster a pair of calf-high, patent leather Doc Martens in canary yellow. Jake glanced over in time to catch her bemused look, and grinned. "Remember how I told you that sitting on your ass is one of the first things they teach you at the academy? Well, so is always wearing a pair of shoes you can run in without falling over and breaking an ankle."

"I'll remember that next time," came Darla's rueful reply as she skipped a little to keep up with her longer-legged and more sensibly shod friend.

Reaching their destination, they stepped through the main double glass doors and into a small lobby already swarming with playgoers. Despite the seriousness of their mission, Darla couldn't help a feeling of excitement at the prospect of seeing live theater. This would be the first theatrical production that she'd attended in New York City. Of course, when various touring companies came through Dallas she had managed to take in a few major musicals—*Cats, The Phantom of the Opera, Les Miserables*—and she was a devoted Shakespeare in the Park fan, but the remainder of her experience with plays had been limited to a brief stint in her high school drama club.

Knowing this, James had once felt the need to enlighten her on the seemingly confusing difference between Broadway and Off-Broadway shows.

"It is not so much where the theater itself is located," he had explained, "as it is the size of the house. Anything under five hundred seats but more than one hundred falls into the Off-Broadway category, but the primary qualifier is whether or not the shows are mounted by companies working under an Equity contract."

This place was definitely Off-Broadway. The Club Theater was a notorious former 1980s nightspot that had started life as a warehouse, and whose latest incarnation was as a trendy three-hundred-forty-seat venue. The new owners apparently had left much of the club's original—and now cringe-worthy—décor intact. The old aluminum-and-mirror bar had literally been divided in two, with half now peddling drinks to customers on one side of the lobby, and the rest serving as a box office on the other. A lighted alcove near the ticket booth led to another pair of doors, both of which were marked "Private."

The "Let's Get Physical" vibe continued with the lobby's shiny black walls, mirrored columns, and large-can track lighting that zipped along the ceiling. A pair of sculptures, each consisting of three giant aluminum cubes piled haphazardly atop one another, flanked the double doors leading into the main theater.

"All that's missing is the disco ball," Jake observed as she shed her long black leather coat and took a look around.

Used as she was to seeing her friend in her usual uniform of jeans, sweater, and boots, Darla had not been prepared for the sight of Jake in a clingy, off-the-shoulder leopard print dress that accentuated her lean body and stopped short of her knees by several inches. Combined with the yellow Docs, the outfit screamed "bad-girl chic" and was drawing more than one admiring set of male eyes in the ex-cop's direction. She was also wearing lipstick, probably the clandestine purchase she had made at Great Scentsations, Darla realized.

Catching Darla staring at her a second time, Jake demanded, "What?"

"Nothing," Darla exclaimed, sadly aware she'd never be able to pull off the same sexy, rough-and-tumble look. "It's just that you look really great tonight."

"You think? I had this in the back of my closet and just threw it on."

She said it with a careless shrug, but Darla could tell she was pleased with the compliment. "Of course, I could have really rocked that red satin number of Morris's, but I figured he probably would have missed it if I'd swiped it." Then, returning the praise, she added, "You clean up pretty good yourself. I didn't think with your hair you could wear red, but it really works on you."

Darla had made do with the same black wrap dress—minus the picture hat—that she'd worn for Valerie Baylor's memorial service. She had vamped it up, however, with a kitschy red velvet rose that she pinned to its neckline and then topped it with a matching red velvet stole, both items that she'd found in Mary Ann's shop. Darla hoped that all her recent purchases there had more than made up for the loan of the vintage cigarette lighter. With her hair pulled back into a loose chignon, she felt like she'd stepped out of an old Katharine Hepburn film.

"Okay, enough with the mutual admiration society," Jake decreed while Darla preened just a little. "We need to get the lay of the land before we take our seats. I'll get the tickets and poke around a little bit. You go find a potted plant or something to hide behind and keep an eye out for Hillary. We need to know where she is sitting in the theater so we can follow her when she gets up to make the exchange."

"How do you know it hasn't happened already?"

"Trust me."

With Darla looking over Jake's shoulder, the older woman flipped through the program she'd picked up just inside the door. She paused at the page headed "Meet the Production Staff" and ran a finger down the alphabetized names. Near the bottom, along with the biographies and photos of the rest of the stage and behind-the-scenes crew, was a listing for one Mavis Vickson.

"*Hair and makeup design,*" Jake read aloud. "*Mavis Vickson has been with the Club Theater since its opening three years ago. She has a bachelor of fine arts degree in theater from Boston University,* blah, blah, et cetera, et cetera."

Tucking the program into her bag—like Darla, she had prudently opted for a small clutch with a long strap that she wore crosswise over her chest—Jake went on, "Mavis is probably in the dressing room right now finishing up the cast's makeup. She'll be tied up until the curtain rises, but then should have some free time until the intermission. If I had to guess, she'll want to do this while everyone is onstage or else watching the action, so chances are Hillary will get up sometime during the first act to go meet her."

"That makes sense," Darla agreed. "Do you think they'll stay inside the building or run out to the alley?"

"Inside. This is Mavis's turf. She'll want to control the meeting and make sure there are no witnesses. In a place like this, especially one that's been remodeled a couple of times, you've always got a rabbit warren of hallways and back rooms. That's why it's critical to spot Hillary before the lights go down, so we can tail her."

"Got it."

Leaving Jake to her own devices, Darla eased her way toward the bar. It was situated near another alcove, above which a garish neon arrow flashed the word "Restrooms." Darla gave a satisfied nod. *Everyone hits the bar or the head eventually*, she told herself. If she kept an eye on both, surely she'd spy Hillary among the other theater patrons.

The crush at the bar had eased for the moment, so she stepped up and ordered herself a club soda with a slice of lime; then, drink in hand, she took up position by one of the mirrored columns kitty-corner to both her targets. She couldn't help but be proud of her undercover skills. Once she spotted the agent, she could turn her back and pretend to use the mirrored column to check her makeup, but she'd still have an eagle-eyed view of the woman's every move.

A few minutes passed, however, and Jake had not returned. Nor had Hillary made an appearance. Darla frowned and glanced at the rectangular aluminum clock posted prominently over the bar. Quarter to eight. The play would be starting soon, and even the drinkers were now abandoning the lobby for the theater. Was it possible that Hillary had arrived there before them and was already in her seat?

Uneasy now, Darla left her post and hurried over to the growing crowd at the double doors. When she reached the front of the line, a smiling young woman in a man's tuxedo held out a gloved hand and said, "Ticket?"

Ticket?

Darla muttered a couple of bad words. Jake had picked up both their admissions from the box office but had neglected to bring one of the tickets back to Darla before heading off who knew where. Doubtless, Jake would show back up eventually, but in the meantime she needed that look around the theater in case Hillary was already sitting down. Trying to spy the agent among the other patrons after the house lights went down would be difficult at best, and a fruitless exercise at worst.

"I'm sorry, my friend is holding my ticket for me," she explained to the usher, trying for what she hoped was a guileless look. "Maybe I can just step inside and see if I see her."

"Sorry," the usher echoed, still smiling. "You have to have a ticket to get in. Why don't you wait for your friend in the lobby so you're not blocking the way?"

"But if she's already inside . . ."

Darla trailed off as the usher shook her head and made a

polite little shooing motion with one gloved hand. Grimacing, Darla stepped aside, even as she reminded herself that she'd gotten past Everest when she'd been denied entry to the church. If she could manage to dodge a professional like him, she darn well could manage a perky little usherette! All she needed was another shield like Morris had been. She had just turned to scout out a potential unwitting cohort when she was all but knocked off her feet by a brunette wearing a pale pink satin pantsuit and matching pink-framed eyeglasses.

"'Scuse me," the woman muttered, not bothering to look Darla's way as she shoved on past her and handed over her ticket to the usher before vanishing into the theater.

Talk about pushy New Yorkers, was Darla's first indignant thought as she stared after the woman. Then she gasped as recognition abruptly dawned, and she realized that the aggressive female had been none other than Hillary Gables.

Darla froze for a moment, unable to believe she'd avoided disaster in this encounter. Now, she had to get into the theater to see where Hillary took a seat.

But barely had she tried to follow after the agent when a restraining hand clamped onto her arm. Darla swung about, ready to loudly protest to the usherette, when she found herself face-to-face with Jake.

"You're gonna need one of these," Jake said with a wry look as she held out a ticket. Then, apparently recognizing Darla's dismay, she demanded, "What's wrong?"

"Quick, Hillary just went inside! Pink pantsuit, pink glasses."

Jake didn't ask any further questions. Handing over the tickets, she snatched the stubs back from the usher and then hustled Darla into the theater.

Immediately before them was a freestanding wall that created a hallway effect and was designed to shield the actors onstage from the patrons' comings and goings to and from the theater. They could turn either right or left as they entered. And so, with a gesture from Jake, the pair split up.

As she peeked around her side of the wall, Darla saw that the layout before her was similar to the older-style movie theaters: an orchestra section only, with the floor sloping toward the raised, curtained stage. The slick black walls of the lobby remained here as well, and the disco balls that Jake jokingly had mentioned hung above them like a dozen mirrored clouds. A broad center block of rows seated the majority of the play-goers, with the rest settled into two narrow sections separated from the main block by aisles.

The houselights began a slow dim as Darla frantically scanned the place. How could Hillary have eluded them in such a relatively small venue? Then a flash of pastel color caught her eye, and she gave a relieved sigh. Joining Jake on her side of the wall, she whispered, "There, about halfway down the center, aisle seat on the left-hand side."

Jake followed her pointing finger and nodded as she, too, gained their target. Pretending to confer over their ticket stubs, they clandestinely watched as Hillary settled into her chair. Once seated, the woman glanced about a couple of times, the glow from the remaining houselights glinting off her glasses.

"We'd better sit down, too, before she notices us," Jake softly told her. "Our seats are right here, best in the house."

She indicated the aisle seat and one next to it in the final row, just a few feet from where they stood. The show wasn't quite sold out, and Darla saw that several choicer spots still remained open.

"Hope you got us a discount," Darla muttered back as they took their places. "I guess I should be glad we're not stuck behind a column."

"Hey, kid, we're not actually here for the show," Jake reminded her as the last of the houselights flickered out.

The green velvet curtains parted to a polite rumble of applause, revealing a stark stage setting of scaffolding and gilded columns meant to represent a Renaissance Venice canal front. Roderigo and Iago took the stage, and the action commenced.

Darla was oblivious to what happened next onstage, her attention held by the solitary figure seated twelve rows down from them. Whether she liked the woman or not, Darla knew they couldn't let Hillary come to any harm this night. She only wished she could ask Jake what, if anything, she had learned as she prowled about the theater before the show had started. Unfortunately, sound carried readily there, so she didn't even dare strike up a whispered conversation.

She did, however, turn her attention to the stage at the second scene of Act I long enough to discover the reason why Mrs. Gleason enjoyed her Tuesday night cop show so much. DeWayne Jones, the actor portraying Othello, had been costumed to show off his muscular chest and arms to advantage. Darla hadn't paid enough attention to judge how good an actor the man was, but she could honestly report back that he looked damn good on stage.

Act I became Act II, and Hillary still remained in her seat. Darla shifted impatiently in her own chair and gave Jake an anxious look.

What's taking so long? she mouthed, getting a headshake back in return. By now, Iago had begun his soliloquy that would conclude the first scene of the second act. Despite herself, Darla kept one ear cocked toward the spoken lines, for she knew this portion of the play. Here, Iago revealed his perfidy, though his motives were still hazy, even in his own mind.

'Tis here, but yet confused: Knavery's plain face is never seen till used.

She wondered if that was how it was with Morris, and if that meant that she and Jake still might be able to stop whatever plan would be carried out this night.

As she pondered this, Iago's final words died away, replaced by the sound of polite applause as he exited the stage . . . which was when Hillary Gables abruptly rose from her seat and started toward the back of the theater.

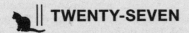 **TWENTY-SEVEN**

JAKE'S TOUCH ON DARLA'S ARM MEANT THAT SHE HAD also noticed Hillary get to her feet as the scene ended. "That must have been her cue," the ex-cop murmured. "Sit tight a little longer, let her get out the door, and then we'll follow."

Darla nodded, trying to keep an eye on the agent while not appearing to do so. Though the woman had been seated several rows down and house left of them, she would be passing just a few feet from Jake and Darla as she exited the double doors to the lobby. And while the houselights were still down, enough illumination came from the stage that, should she glance their way, Hillary might well recognize them.

On the other hand, she had smacked right into Darla there in the lobby and never made the connection.

A faint squeak of hinges behind them told them that Hillary had left the theater. "Let me take a look first," Jake softly cautioned as they reached the double doors. Inching one of them open, she gestured Darla to join her. Through that gap, she could see that Hillary was headed for the alcove near the empty ticket booth.

"Morris must have told her which way to go," Darla whispered back. "Did you get to see what's in there?"

"Besides a couple of offices, there's a stairway that heads

down to the basement. That's probably how the cast and crew get to the dressing rooms and backstage without going through the theater. I didn't get very far, though. A couple of stage-hands caught me, and I had to pretend I was looking for the ladies'."

She waited until Hillary's pink pantsuit had vanished around the corner of the alcove, and then whispered, "C'mon!"

Glancing over at the bar to make sure they were not being observed—the crew that earlier had been pouring drinks was apparently on break until intermission, leaving only a door-man gazing forlornly out into the street—they made their swift way to the alcove. Just as Jake had said, two doors marked "Private" were visible from the lobby. It was only after they'd ducked inside that arched recess that Darla saw the dimly lit entry to her left opening onto a narrow wooden staircase.

Hillary's pink pantsuit flashed like a reluctant beacon at the bottom of the stairs.

Jake started down the steps after her, moving with pan-therlike silence despite her boots. Darla tried to emulate her, but her pumps were not designed for stealth. After her first couple of steps, which resulted in hammerlike blows against the wooden treads, Jake swung about and wildly gestured for her to stop.

"Lose the shoes," she hissed.

Darla swiftly pulled off her heels. Clutching them in one hand and the handrail in the other, she negotiated the remain-ing steps silently—and, of necessity, slowly. While several bare bulbs were strung from the electrical wiring above her, only one was lit, and most of its yellow light was absorbed by the rust-colored brick walls.

Major OSHA violation, she told herself, wondering how many actors and stagehands had taken a header down those poorly lit steps before.

Fortunately, she managed to avoid such a fate. Reaching the bottom unscathed, Darla took a moment to glance about her, squinting a little in the dimness as she tried to form a mental floor plan of where they were beneath the theater.

Jake was waiting for her in what appeared, at first glance, to be a corridor. A second look showed it to be nothing more than a narrow stretch of open basement between the outermost wall and the first in a series of rows of brick support columns that ran parallel to it. The electrical wire continued on its path like a sagging tightrope above them, its few lit bulbs reminding her of fallen high-wire walkers clinging to it for dear life. The remainder of the basement was thrown into the sort of shadow that would have required Jake's official police flashlight to pierce. Someone had taken a roll of black and yellow floor-striping tape and made the open passage a formal walkway with the built-in caution not to step outside its bounds—not that anyone would want to deviate off that path on purpose.

For what surrounded them was the original nineteenth-century brick building, untouched by any trendy attempts at renovation or camouflage. A mazelike collection of rusty iron girders intersected the thick brick columns and formed a secondary skeleton that supported the four stories above. The mortar that once had held the outer walls together with crisp precision was crumbling in some places and missing altogether in others, while the years had rounded the bricks' sharp edges so that they more closely resembled oversized cobblestones. The ceiling here was so low that, had Jake's boots been a bit taller, the top of her frizzy head would have brushed the subflooring over them.

To her left, Darla could hear the periodic clang and hiss of steam over the distant sounds of speech and applause from the theater above. This section of the basement was strictly functional, serving as combination boiler room and storage space. Beyond the boiler, she could see barrels and crates piled high, along with what appeared to be fixtures from the old club, and random machinery likely left over from the days when the place had been some sort of factory. For all she could tell, Jimmy Hoffa might have been stuffed in some far corner, too.

The floor was cold beneath her stockinged feet, but she didn't dare pull on her pumps again lest the echo of her footfalls against the rough stone signal their presence. Feeling the nylon beneath one foot snag on an uneven spot in the flooring, she accepted the fact that her twenty-dollar pair of pantyhose was not going to survive the night.

Of course, all that mattered was that Hillary did.

Jake, meanwhile, put a finger to her lips and pointed up toward the stage above them. Perhaps thirty feet directly ahead was a second entryway, its interior faintly glowing against the shadows that crept from beyond the boiler and other forgotten equipment.

"She went in there. C'mon."

Darla barely could hear Jake's low whisper, but the swift jabbing of her finger in that direction got the point across. She fell into quiet step behind her friend, grateful for Jake's unflappable presence and feeling unwilling admiration for Hillary, who had traversed the basement alone. An uneasy air clung to the place; the brick columns that revealed the building's mechanical underbelly also served to conceal. Perhaps that black and yellow caution tape on the floor was there for reasons other than mere workplace safety. Maybe the theater workers knew that something worse than an OSHA breach lurked beyond the stripes.

Darla felt her scalp tingle as she pictured some unknown being lurking in the shadows ready to pounce from behind a column as they passed. She wouldn't have been surprised to hear that the theater's actors had encountered unexplained activity late at night when they ventured down there alone. Neither could she shake the odd feeling that she'd been in this particular basement before.

Then it abruptly occurred to her that, in a manner of speaking, she had.

She realized she was walking her way through virtually the same basement that was found on the other side of the Janitor's closet in the *Haunted High* books.

Scenes from the most recent novel flashed through her mind. In one, Lani discovered phosphorescent footprints that hinted the Janitor had survived his exorcism in the second book. In another, a squad of ghouls dressed as cheerleaders captured one of Lani's living friends and held her hostage, threatening to devour the terrified girl if Lani did not surrender to them. And, in still another, Lani learned that the new vice principal had a taste for both handing out detentions and sipping fresh blood.

These and several other of the book's more chilling incidents had all taken place in a fearsome subterranean level that

lay somewhere beneath the fictional Lani's high school. Some
of the book's characters believed the spot to be a portal to
hell; others claimed it was simply a way station for the dead.
Accessed by way of the Janitor's closet, that supernatural
basement had become Book Three's battleground where Lani
and the Janitor squared off as each sought to gain control of
the school's various paranormal entities. Nothing good happened there, and the physical description of the place—at
once terrifyingly otherworldly and laughably mundane—
described this theater's basement as well.

So who would they encounter tonight, she wondered with
a shiver: Morris, the kindly old Janitor, or Morris the sharp-
toothed demon?

They halted at the entry, and Jake peered cautiously around
the splintered jamb. The dialogue from the stage above was
more distinct here, and Darla could follow the actors' progress by the sound of their footsteps atop the boards. She
waited until Jake gave an all-clear signal, and then joined her
to take a look.

The area was larger than she expected. As best she could
judge, it ran the width of the entire basement and encompassed not only the basement space under the stage but also
that beneath the entire backstage area. Practical rather than
architecturally stylish, this section had been walled off from
the remaining basement by means of a sturdy wooden frame-
work covered in bare sheetrock. The lighting here was only
marginally better, but sufficient to make out the storage
room's layout.

Plywood had been laid over the stone floor to provide a
more stable surface for a series of vertical racks, and had also
been used to create shelves and pallets. These storage sys-
tems, which took up large segments of the available floor
space, held all manner of old backdrops and stage props, from
furniture to statuary to artificial trees. Under other circum-
stance, Darla would have enjoyed the chance to poke around
there, but the seriousness of their mission did not allow for
exploring this veritable graveyard of plays past.

Had they kept walking straight ahead, they would have
found themselves on a ramp that rose to stage level and likely
led right past the main stage to the backstage area. Dressing

rooms and costume storage would be up there, along with areas for the props and set decorations used for the current run of plays. Would they find Hillary and Morris there, or were the two of them together somewhere here in this nether-world of theatrical discards?

"Damn it, Morris, where are you?"

The sound of Hillary's peevish voice answered the question as to her location. The voice came from somewhere beyond the large vertical rack just inside the doorway where Darla and Jake had swiftly concealed themselves. They could hear the sound of her impatient heels tapping as she paced the plywood floor. Darla peered through one of the gaps between the canvas and wood-framed backdrops standing on end like books on a shelf. She could see a flash of pink as Hillary walked past. *Yes, where* is *Morris?* Darla wondered, aware that her palms had begun to sweat a little in nervous anticipation. She shifted her shoes from one hand to the other and blotted her free palm on her skirt.

"Damn it, Morris!" Hillary called again, "I'm not going to play games with you. Let's finish this."

"Let's not."

The sound of a second voice made Darla jump, even though she had been expecting it. The speaker was Morris. His words came from what seemed to be a spot well beyond where Hillary waited. Darla could hear a man's faint yet solid footsteps crossing the plywood floor, though she could not spy him from her vantage point.

She exchanged a look with Jake, who signaled her to hold tight. She nodded and peered again through the slatlike gaps in the backdrops. Now, she could hear Hillary moving in the direction of where Morris seemed to be, her staccato steps revealing her agitation.

"Where are you? What do you mean, 'let's not'?" she demanded. "We had a deal."

"I've reconsidered."

Morris's voice seemed a bit more distant, as if he were leading her deeper into the basement. Looking grim, Jake gestured Darla to follow behind her. They moved softly in the same direction as Hillary's footsteps, using the props and backdrops as cover. The sounds from the actors above masked any noise the two of them made, though Darla suspected that Hillary's only focus was Morris.

"Damn it, Morris," she repeated, "quit running away from me. I want that money, or I'm going to reveal everything."

The woman's footsteps stopped abruptly. Jake and Darla halted, too, crouching behind a small grove of fake bushes that served as a handy screen for them. The light here was dimmer and seemed to flicker. Peering between the leaves, Darla frowned a little in surprise.

They had stumbled into what appeared to be the stage crew's private lounge. Someone had arranged armchairs and a small love seat around a glass coffee table. Two accent chairs covered in red velvet sat a short distance beyond this cozy scene, pulled together as if the previous sitters had been involved in a tête-à-tête. An abandoned paperback novel lay open on one of the seats, while a couple of fast-food-chain drink cups sat on the table.

Hillary flung herself onto the love seat. "Five seconds, Morris," she snapped, "and if that money's not in my hand, I'm out of here."

"I wouldn't leave just yet, Hillary . . . not until you hear me out."

The lights began to flicker again as Morris's voice continued, "You think you hold all the cards here, but I assure you that you don't. You think you have the ability to ruin me, to keep me from carrying on my sister's legacy now that she's dead. You think the readers will abandon the series if they find out that someone besides Valerie actually wrote the *Haunted High* books. Someone like me."

Darla and Jake exchanged quick looks. So the threats that Hillary had been making weren't about Valerie's accident. Darla allowed herself a moment of cautious relief, for this likely meant that Morris hadn't killed his sister. Still, it seemed she'd been right about Morris being the true author of the book. The deception didn't much bother her, but apparently Hillary saw it as a game changer, an issue worthy of blackmail. Darla wondered why.

The agent quickly answered Darla's unspoken question.

Hillary's voice took on a nasty edge as, leaping to her feet again, she shot back, "Just who do you think your readers are, Morris? Most of them are teens, impressionable children. What do you think will happen when their parents find out these bestselling young adult books were written by a man who spends his nights dressed as a woman? Your books will be in the remainder bin faster than you can say Kate Gosselin."

She snorted at her own joke and added, "It doesn't matter to me . . . I've made my money off you, and I can always find another Valerie Baylor somewhere. But what about you?"

Her tone grew even harder.

"Oh, maybe I'm wrong. Maybe the parents won't care that little Susie and Jimmy are reading books written by a cross-dresser. And maybe I'm wrong about the fans, the thousands who dressed up in black capes and stood in line for hours for an autograph in every major city. Maybe they won't feel betrayed because the author they worshipped never really existed. And all those major review publications who gave Valerie Baylor starred reviews? Maybe they won't feel like idiots for praising a woman who once stole other writers' work because she couldn't get her own published. And maybe Mr. Pinter won't feel like you and Valerie pulled a fast one on his company, putting her out there as the brilliant talent that came up with the *Haunted High* series. Maybe all of them will forget, and you can keep on writing those books of yours forever.

"But, then, you know what that means, Morris?" She gave a cold, tinkling little laugh—the kind of laugh that, to Darla's mind, could have come straight from the Janitor's closet. "It means that you'll have to face your biggest fear. You'll have to make all the public appearances, do the television interviews, show up at national conferences and speak in front of hundreds—even thousands—of people. You'll have to do all the things that Valerie did for you. Oh, yeah, she couldn't write a shopping list if her life depended on it, but she loved the limelight, craved it, while you hate it. That's why you dress up as a woman, so you can hide your true self from everyone . . . even from yourself!"

Darla exchanged swift, troubled looks with Jake. Hillary was far more intelligent than she'd ever given her credit for being, Darla realized. Now that the agent had put it out into the open, the whole Morris-Valerie collaboration with the *Haunted High* books made for an odd if understandable symbiosis. One twin had the talent, while the other had the looks, the presence. Together, they were Valerie Baylor. And Hillary had seen what Darla had guessed at: that the Mavis persona was Morris's way to walk among the living, so to speak, rather than keep himself locked away from the world in some personal Janitor's closet.

But what didn't make sense—at least, from what Darla had heard—was why Hillary had such great enmity toward the pair. No matter the deception, hadn't she managed a sweet cut of their pie?

"Morris, why don't you answer me?" the agent demanded, sounding peevish now. "Oh, that's because I'm right, isn't it? So if you want me to keep your secret, I need some quid pro quo. Maybe I'll even put in a good word for you with Mr. Pinter, tell him you're just as talented as your sister, so you can keep writing under Valerie's name. And I'll even write you a juicy new contract that says you never have to make a public appearance if you don't want to."

"But why should I pay you anything," came Morris's voice in reply, "when your secret is far more damning than mine?"

"Wh-what do you mean?"

The spiteful tone abruptly fled her voice, replaced by uncertainty as she straightened in her seat and gazed about her, looking for Morris. "I don't have any secrets."

"To the contrary, I think that you do."

The sound of his footsteps grew louder now, though Darla still could not see him from her vantage point.

"You found out that I wrote the *Haunted High* books, not Valerie, and you thought you could use that and my personal life to your advantage." His voice took on a faintly mocking tone. *"Morris is rich . . . he'll pay me to keep my mouth shut, to keep the status quo.* But you forgot that rich people hate to part with their money, just like everyone else. And you also thought that Valerie didn't know about the blackmail. But she did."

He paused a beat and then added, "And she didn't like it."

The lights that had been flickering almost imperceptibly as he spoke now abruptly blinked out. As they were plunged into darkness, Hillary gave a little scream.

"I know what you're trying to do, Morris!" she shrieked, while Darla choked back a reflexive gasp of her own. The woman's tone was so shrill that Darla wondered if she could be heard through the stage floor. "You're trying to scare me into going away. But it won't work. So turn the lights back on and give me my money!"

Then a few things happened simultaneously. A light slowly flickered on near the two red velvet chairs tucked away in the far corner, while the pungent odor of cigarette smoke abruptly wafted toward Darla. The surrounding air seemed colder all at once, so that Darla hugged her stole more closely to her and wished she dared pull her shoes back on. Even the sounds from the theater above seemed suddenly muted, as if even the cast had halted to learn what was happening there beneath their feet.

And then a woman's voice—not the agent's, but uncannily familiar—spoke.

"Hillary, you always were a greedy little bitch."

The lights near the chairs flickered again and dimmed, while a figure wrapped in a hooded black cape abruptly materialized. *Morris?* Darla thought in confusion, squinting for a better look. Surely this was some sort of trick that the man was playing to unnerve the agent . . . except that the figure before them was oddly transparent. Staring at the phantom image, Darla felt the hair on the back of her neck leap to attention. A bit desperately, she reminded herself that she didn't exactly believe in ghosts, herself . . . that was, if she didn't count the strange footsteps that had wandered her store and the unseen force that had stacked books into nice neat columns on her living room floor.

Then the figure reached graceful hands up to push away the concealing hood, revealing a spill of black hair and a pale face with bright red lips that was straight from the author's photo on the *Haunted High* books.

"V-Valerie?" Hillary quavered, taking another step back. Then, seeming to rally, the woman protested, "I don't believe it. That's you, Morris, dressed up like your sister! Don't think for a minute that I'm going to fall for your silly disguises."

The figure chuckled, the soft sound of amusement edged with what sounded like anger. Still, his—her?—tone was conversational in reply. "What, aren't you happy to see your favorite client again? And here I dragged myself out of that nasty coffin just so we could have this little chat."

In a casual move, the figure sat upon one of the red chairs . . . except that instead of sitting, she hovered a good two feet over the cushion, the lines of the chair still visible through her transparent form. The sight of the floating image seemed to drain the last of the fight from Hillary. In a small voice, she said, "I don't want to see you. Turn on the lights so I can get out of here."

The phantom Valerie shook a reproving finger.

"Not yet, Hillary. Not until we talk about how you followed me out of the store the night of the autographing. You thought I was Morris, didn't you? You'd been harassing him for money to keep the secret. But Morris had told me what you were trying do. I didn't want to believe him, so I told him I wanted to hear your threats myself."

"I-I really didn't mean it," the agent whimpered. "I just needed a little cash. My mom is sick, and—"

"Bullshit," the ghost replied in a distinctly earthly manner. "Morris checked. Your parents are fine back in Ohio, and they had no idea that their darling daughter has a nasty little habit involving white powder."

"That's not true! I might have tried it once, but—"

"Can it, Hillary. You're hooked, and you know it. But your drug of choice doesn't come cheap. So you've been digging in other people's pockets to support your drug habit."

Darla shot an astonished look in Jake's direction, wishing she could make out the other woman's expression in the dark. So it wasn't only money, but drugs that made Hillary's world go around. Maybe this explained the agent's apparent affection for her old rich boyfriend at the memorial service. She'd found yet another cash cow—or, likely in the old man's case, cash steer—and was going to hang onto him for as long she could, no matter what it took.

Darla swiftly turned her attention back to the scene before her, however, as the phantom Valerie continued speaking.

"Your habit and your greed made you stupid, Hillary."

The ghost gave a disgusted snort as she stood again and paced, walking through the velvet chairs now. The odor of cigarette smoke was growing stronger, and Darla could swear this part of the basement was growing even colder.

"You forgot that Morris was my brother—my twin—and I would do anything for him. I wasn't going to let you hurt him. I even grabbed that stupid sign some girl left lying in the trash bin so that he wouldn't accidentally see it. You were surprised, weren't you, when I pulled off my hood and you saw it was me and not him out there on the street with you. And then when I told you I didn't care about keeping Morris's identity a secret anymore, that I was going to have you arrested for attempted blackmail, you were furious."

Her voice lowered, she finished, "Furious enough to . . . kill."

"The whole thing was your fault!" the agent wailed, sinking back onto the sofa again. "You said terrible things to me. You said you were going to fire me. You said you'd have your lawyers break our contract so I wouldn't get any more money off your books. It wasn't fair! You were rich already anyway, and you kept getting richer. I wanted that. You were my way to the big time!"

"The big time," Valerie echoed, her light voice filled with disgust. "I guess we were, weren't we? And I have to give you credit. You were lucky enough to be the agent's assistant who found Morris's manuscript in the slush pile, and you were clever enough to talk your boss into promoting you to a full-blown agent because you knew you'd stumbled over something good. And Morris was so thrilled that someone wanted to represent him—someone who didn't know our family, someone who valued him for his work and not his bank account—that he barely even looked at the contract. He didn't notice that you'd changed the commission rate from fifteen percent to twenty-five, or that you had locked him into a five-year agreement."

"That's not my fault," Hillary huffed. "You could have said no."

"I signed it because he asked me to. I'd already promised him that he could submit his manuscript under my name. He knew that if it sold, he could never deal with the pressure of doing all the things an author is forced to do these days to get his name out there. But I'd done it before and liked it, and so I agreed to be his public face. We made a good team, don't you think?"

"You wouldn't have been anything without me. I worked hard for my money."

Hillary had regained her earlier aggressive attitude and was pushing back—at least, as much as one could against a phantom. "Everyone wanted vampires. No one wanted ghosts. That book was a hard sell, and I—"

"You had four major publishers bidding for it the first week," Valerie cut in, "and it was a free ride for you from there on out. But you weren't satisfied, were you? You thought you deserved a bigger piece of the Valerie Baylor action, and when I wouldn't give it to you, you tried to poison my brother against me. That's how you found out that he wrote the books and not me, wasn't it? You thought you'd hit an even bigger jackpot then, until you found out we weren't going to play your game."

The ghostly author's voice dropped now to a purr. "So tell me, Hillary, had you planned to kill me off all along, or was this one of those spur-of-the-moment things?"

Hillary shifted guiltily in her seat now. "It was an accident, all of it. I, I wasn't in a right frame of mind!"

"Tell it to the Janitor," the author softly said. "You see, Morris and I aren't going to let you get away with what you did to me."

At that, the remaining lights flickered out.

They flashed on again a few heartbeats later, illuminating the area where Hillary huddled on the love seat. Darla gasped despite herself as she saw that the phantom Valerie now loomed over the frightened agent. Then the ghost leaned closer, and in a scathing voice demanded, "Oh, for Chrissakes, Hillary, just admit you deliberately shoved me into traffic and killed me."

"All right, I did!" the young woman shrieked. "You deserved it for the way you treated me, and if it makes you feel any better, I'd do it again just to shut you up. The only thing I'm sorry about is that you died right away. I would have laughed to see you squirming around on the street for a while before you croaked!"

The distant roar of applause from the theater above greeted

her confession as the agent cowered in her armchair, her head covered with her hands as if to ward off a ghostly attack.

The second act must be over, was Darla's first irrelevant thought as she stared wide-eyed through the fake foliage at the scene before her. Her second, more pertinent realization was that the phantom Valerie now looked as real as she had the night of the autographing. She stood preternaturally still, her visage twisted into a look of horror and outrage as frightening as anything Darla had ever seen. The figure slowly raised a fist over the huddled woman, and Darla saw something else she hadn't noticed before.

The phantom Valerie wore a large gold puzzle ring on her right hand.

"Don't do it, Morris." Jake's voice, clear and firm, rang out from beside her. "You don't need to do anything more. You've got two other witnesses here to Hillary's confession."

"I didn't confess to anything!" the agent shrieked, even as she crouched lower in her seat. Darla heard a faint intake of breath from the ghostly figure hovering over her. And then, a man's familiar baritone replied, "I've got videotape as well. Come out, please, and make yourselves known."

Morris's voice sounded weary as he lowered his hand and tugged off his long black wig, revealing spiky blond locks beneath. He raised his other hand, which had been concealed beneath his cloak, and Darla could see he was holding what appeared to be a remote control. He gave it a couple of clicks, and the remaining basement lights flared on again.

Darla stiffly rose from her crouched position and gratefully slipped on her shoes. She and Jake came out from around the bush. Morris gave a small sad smile as he caught sight of them.

"Darla, Ms. Martelli," he greeted them with a formal nod. "I rather expected I might see you two tonight. Mrs. Gleason told me that she'd seen two women enter my apartment before I arrived. Since she was watching through the peephole, she'd thought the tall one was Mavis in a curly black wig. It wasn't until a bit later that she wondered if she'd been wrong. Her description of you two was quite accurate."

"But how could you know that we knew you were meeting Hillary here tonight?" Darla asked in confusion.

He shrugged. "The two of you had been painfully persistent in questioning me when I stopped by your store the other day to see the lighter—which was just a ruse to get me there, I presume? Since you said Ms. Martelli used to be a police officer, I made the leap and assumed she looked about my place for some obvious clues. As you know, there were a couple of saved voice mails from Hillary that confirmed our plans for tonight."

"It's a trick . . . a trap," Hillary weakly protested. "You can see how he can pretend to be someone else. He, he imitated my voice."

Darla, meanwhile, was giving Jake a pointed look. It was the latter's turn now to shrug as she pulled her cell phone from her purse and powered it on. "Oops. Guess we did it the hard way. Remind me next time to check the voice mail, kid."

Addressing Morris again, she said, "If you and Darla will keep an eye on Hillary, I'm going to go upstairs and call for some official backup. I can't seem to get a signal down here."

While Jake made her way back through the maze of props, Darla joined Morris where he stood looking at the agent, still huddled on the sofa and now loudly weeping. Tentatively, she touched his arm.

"I am so sorry about your sister, Morris."

He flinched a little but did not pull away. Staring down at Hillary, he softly said, "She could have done anything she wanted to me, and it wouldn't have mattered. But to take my sister from me . . . she's cut me in two, and I'm afraid I won't survive it."

"You will survive it, Morris, I promise," Darla rushed to assure him, emotion clogging her throat. "You'll be scarred, but you'll carry on. Wouldn't you want Valerie to do the same if your positions were reversed?"

"I suppose so."

Tears trickled down his face, sluicing trails in the white face paint that he wore. Then he raised his head and gazed around him, as if seeing the place for the first time. His words were little more than a sigh as he said, "Welcome to life beyond the Janitor's closet."

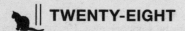 **TWENTY-EIGHT**

JAKE'S PHONE CALL BROUGHT TWO POLICE CRUISERS WITH lights flashing, though since the immediate emergency was long over with, they had refrained from turning on their sirens. One of the four cops who rushed in through the theater's front doors turned out to be Officer Hallonquist, the same patrolman who had cited Darla at the coffee shop a few days earlier. He shook his head a little at recognizing her, but made no comment as he and his partner hustled the handcuffed agent outside and loaded her in their car for the trip to jail.

Reese had shown up right after the uniformed officers. "Yo, Fiorello," one of the younger cops had called with a grin and a wave at the detective.

Reese gave the rookie the old finger-across-the-throat gesture, but it was too late. Darla had overheard. With a delighted grin of her own, she stared at him and said, "Wow. Fiorello is your first name?"

"Yeah," the rookie interjected, poking his forefinger to his cheek to form a dimple. In a simpering voice, he added, "It means 'little flower.'"

"Correction," Reese snarled back. "It means 'he who kicks ass.' So shaddup already, if you don't want your butt handed to you."

The rookie snickered but obligingly shut up. Then Reese turned to Darla. "Yeah, so sue me. My dad was German and my mother was Italian. I got his looks, and she won the baby-naming contest. But we don't use that name, got it?"

"How about this?" Darla replied, trying to keep a straight face but failing miserably. "If you don't call me 'Red,' I won't call you 'Flower.' Deal?"

"Deal. Now, forget about me. What the hell is going on here?" he demanded with a stern look at both her and Jake.

Quickly stepping back into serious mode, Darla waited quietly by and let Jake explain what they'd been doing at the theater in the first place. Then Darla gave Reese a quick run-down of the private conversation she'd had with Morris in the basement after Jake left, and before the police arrived.

Morris told her he had followed Hillary and his sister down the sidewalk that fateful night, and so had witnessed Valerie's death. He had been the caped figure who had rushed into the street to help her, and who Reese had pushed aside. Realizing there was nothing to be done for his sister, Morris's next thought had been to pursue Hillary, who had already melted back into the crowd.

He'd had little doubt that Hillary's actions were deliberate. Despite his grief, however, he'd also realized that, under the circumstances, it would be his word against hers should he accuse her of a crime. And so, he had made the difficult choice to pretend that he'd seen nothing. Instead, he had returned to the store, determined to find some way to later pry a confession from the agent. Hillary had not been content with murdering Valerie, however. A day later, she had contacted Morris with another blackmail threat, and that was when he'd had the inspiration for staging the ghostly intervention.

In the time it took for Darla to make her explanations, Morris had changed back into his street clothes and comman-deered the theater's offices for further interviews. Darla won-dered how a lowly makeup artist had managed such a feat, until Morris explained with a wry smile, "I don't think they'll mind, considering that I own the place."

Once the statements had all been given—according to Reese, Morris's official account had squared with what he had told Darla—Reese rejoined Darla and Jake in the lobby.

The play had ended, and most of the theatergoers had already departed, leaving behind a handful of curious employees to finish closing up the place. Morris reappeared as well. He gave a few whispered instructions to the same tuxedoed female usher who'd politely demanded Darla's ticket. The girl nodded and made hasty work of rushing the other employees out the door.

By then, the remaining patrol officers had driven off, leaving the three of them alone with Morris. He gave Darla and Jake a tired smile.

"Detective Reese was asking about the ghost illusion," he said. "Perhaps all of you would care to see how it was created?"

At their eager nods, he led them back down to the basement. There, he demonstrated how he had conjured Valerie's ghostly appearance.

"It's an old theater trick called Pepper's Ghost Illusion," he explained as they stood in the lounge area where the phantom Valerie had confronted Hillary. "If you've ever been to Disney's Haunted Mansion, or even one of the professional haunted houses that spring up each year for Halloween, you might have seen this effect before. We use it here at the theater on occasion. I had some of the stage crew set this up for me a few days ago."

He showed them how the space beyond the lounge area actually formed an equilateral L, with the lower portion of the L blocked from their view by a wall of shelving. A sheet of glass sat across the elbow of the L at a forty-five degree angle, with the red velvet chairs positioned behind it. The unseen portion of the L had been where Morris in his ghostly disguise had been hidden. That area was curtained in black fabric that formed a backdrop on all three sides and was empty, save for what appeared to be a set of freestanding steps that were also draped in black. Like a good host, he gestured them to sit on those stairs.

"When the lights are dim here and bright there," he said, pointing toward the chairs, "all the audience sees from the outside is exactly what's in that space."

With his remote control, he adjusted the lights so that a cheery beam illuminated the red velvet chairs, while the light in their half of the L dimmed.

"But if you lower the lights there"—he again indicated the chairs and turned down the illumination—"and raise the lights on this side, whatever's here reflects on the glass and looks like a ghost on the side to the audience that's watching."

As he spoke, a light came on overhead. Now, the four of them were reflected with almost mirrorlike precision in the glass, their transparent images seeming to hover over the chairs, just as Valerie's ghost had done.

"Pretty cool," Jake muttered, while Darla nodded her agreement.

Reese grinned a little, like a kid figuring out a new trick. "It's like when you have a lamp on in your house, and you look out the window at night. You can see everything behind you—and even yourself—reflected in the glass, so it kind of looks like you and your room are outside on the street."

"Exactly," Morris said with an approving smile. "The lighting is crucial, as is the black backdrop on this side. It's a simple enough effect, but very powerful if the audience is in the mood to believe."

And it seemed that all of them had been in that mood, Darla told herself, remembering the chill she'd felt at her first sight of the ghost. Probably, Morris had tinkered with the air-conditioning down there, too, and had lit the cigarette to further trigger the connection to Valerie.

Reese remained behind at the theater awhile longer, while Darla and Jake made their good-byes and returned to the brownstone. It was after midnight by the time the taxi they'd commandeered at Darla's insistence left them off on the curb. As she stepped out onto the sidewalk, Darla noticed in surprise that the Valerie shrine with its guttered candles and dead flowers had been cleared away sometime during their absence, leaving the sidewalk bare once more.

Jake followed her gaze and nodded.

"Our sanitation department at work," she observed. Then, noting Darla's troubled expression, she added, "Don't feel bad, kid. That mound of flowers couldn't have stayed here forever, you know."

"I know. It just seems a shame that all those poems and letters and tributes that Valerie's fans left for her ended up in the back of a trash truck."

"Actually, I think Mary Ann gathered all those things up this morning. She thought the family might want them, so she was going to package up everything and give it to you to forward."

"I'm sure Morris and his parents will appreciate that," Darla agreed, relieved and yet feeling a bit guilty that she hadn't thought of doing the same thing.

They parted after agreeing to meet back at Darla's apartment when Reese finished at the theater and stopped by to update them on the situation. Yawning, Darla went upstairs to change out of her theater clothing. Hamlet was waiting for her, his expression disapproving.

"Sorry, boy, we were chasing down ghosts and murderers," she explained, earning a spit and a hiss from Mr. Anxious Parent Cat for her trouble.

Once snuggly attired in sweats, she flipped on her computer and did her official scan of the store. Everything appeared in order, so she left the screen up and turned on her favorite all-news television station. Within a few minutes of watching, she discovered that word of Hillary's arrest had already hit the media.

"And in breaking news," the jowly broadcaster proclaimed, "a twenty-nine-year-old New York City woman has been arrested in what is now considered to be the murder of best-selling author Valerie Baylor last week."

Snippets of video from the autographing rolled as he described what little the police had released to this point. Darla was glad for Morris's sake that, at least for the moment, no reference was made to Mavis or ghosts. And a fleeting shot of Hillary doing the perp walk made Darla smile in grim satisfaction.

A knock sounded at her door a few minutes later. It was Jake and Reese, the former having exchanged her chic leopard-print dress for a pair of sweats and a T-shirt like Darla's, and the latter wearing his usual leather motorcycle jacket and bearing a chilled bottle of sparkling wine.

"Hey, I had it in the fridge and thought we should celebrate," he said, popping the cork before Darla even had a chance to chase down the proper glasses. Then, with a mock disappointed look, he added, "Of course, I'd been planning on drinking with a couple of hot broads, and not two kids ready for a pajama party."

Jake gave him a friendly punch in the shoulder, though a smiling Darla wasn't sure if it was for the "hot broad" comment or the pajama party reference. Once she returned with glassware and the surprisingly good champagne had been poured, Darla offered up a little toast toward the ceiling.

"To Valerie."

"To Valerie," her friends echoed and raised their glasses, as well.

"I guess she wasn't quite the witch she pretended to be," Darla observed after they'd settled on the horsehair sofa, displacing a miffed Hamlet in the process. "But the way she treated Mavis at the autographing . . ."

"Pretty much an act," Reese said. "Morris and I had another informal chat after you two left. Apparently, the whole Valerie-as-diva thing was a put-on. They figured it was best to have the public Valerie Baylor be something of a bitch. That way, if a fan or an interviewer asked her a question about the books that she couldn't answer, she could blow them off, and people would figure that's just how she was. It also helped protect Mavis. They were afraid if the two of them got too chatty together, it would call attention to her, er, him. And that was what Morris was trying to avoid from the start. Social anxiety disorder is what he said it's called."

"Jeez, you'd think the guy was rich enough to afford counseling, or at least a bottle of antidepressants," Jake broke in.

Darla gave her friend a disapproving glance. "It's not always that easy. I once worked with a woman who refused to go out to lunch with the rest of the department. We all thought she was a snob. Then one day she told me she just was afraid to eat in front of anyone, couldn't swallow a bite if anyone was looking at her. I'm sure Morris does the best he can."

Jake appeared unconvinced, but she dropped the subject of the author's brother for the equally confusing motivation surrounding Hillary.

"Her, I don't get, either," she said of the agent. "Wasn't killing off Valerie basically killing off her golden goose?"

"Not necessarily," Darla answered. "If Valerie's death really had been an accident—or if Morris had thought it was—Hillary could have cut a deal with Morris directly. They could have said that Valerie had a couple of finished manuscripts sitting around and then put them out posthumously under her name. And once everyone got used to her being dead, Morris could have officially been authorized by the estate to keep writing under her name. It's been done with a lot of authors before."

Then another thought occurred to her, and she sat up straight in her seat.

"Lizzie's manuscript!" she exclaimed, drawing looks of surprise from the other two. "Jake, remember in the basement how Hillary claimed that Valerie had stolen other authors' books, and that she couldn't even write a shopping list? It sounded like maybe other people had the same thing happen to them that Lizzie said had happened to her. So Lizzie probably was in the right, even though she tried proving it the wrong way."

"You think?" Jake said with a snort. Then, turning serious again, she said, "But I still don't understand why Hillary hated Valerie so much. The way she was carrying on, it sounded like something personal between them."

She turned to Reese, who shrugged and said, "That'll probably come out in the trial. I can make a couple of guesses, but that's all they'd be. It's not like a cop show on television, where the perp spills her guts as soon as she's arrested. You should know that better than anyone, Martelli."

"Yeah, so I like my murders tied up in nice red ribbons. So sue me."

Darla gave her friend a commiserating look. She liked things tied up in nice red ribbons, too. She'd also read somewhere that greed was the number one motive for murder, closely followed by fear and jealousy and rage. All of them seemed likely reasons for the agent to have snapped. But perhaps it was something even more basic. Maybe Hillary, suffering from paranoia because of her drug use, had felt betrayed on a personal level when she learned Valerie was not who she had claimed to be and had felt compelled somehow to punish the woman.

Before Darla could ask what would happen to Hillary next, an ear-searing yowl from Hamlet made her jostle her champagne. She turned to see the cat sitting on the chair in front of her laptop, pawing at the screen. Alarmed, Darla rushed over to see what had caught his attention. The screen was displaying the interior of her store, along with a dark figure as it slid through the shadows past the cash register and then disappeared somewhere near the locked case of collectible fiction.

"Jake, Reese, come quick," Darla called, barely able to keep the panic from her voice. "Someone's in the bookstore again!"

Her cry was unnecessary, for the pair had already rushed up behind her. With no more movement to trigger it, however, the single channel view already had subsided back into the usual six-segment display.

"What did you see, and where?" Reese demanded, leaning in closer.

Darla pointed, leaving a champagne fingerprint on the screen. "There. Whoever it was went behind that shelf."

"Can you switch views and show that part of the store?"

Darla shook her head in frustration. "That's one of the blind spots Ted told me about. None of the cameras catch it."

"What about sound?" Jake prompted. "Didn't he set up some audio, too?"

"You're right, I forgot."

Fingers shaking, Darla pulled up the on-screen menu and found the audio option. Turning up her computer's speakers, she could hear the hiss of an open microphone . . . and then, the soft sound of stealthy footsteps. Then came a sharp *thud*, which Darla recognized as a book hitting the floor. That noise was followed by what sounded like a gasp and a small voice saying, "Oh my gracious!"

Darla felt her mouth drop open. She turned to gaze at Jake, who appeared equally astounded. As one, they chorused, "Mary Ann?"

"Mary Ann?" Reese echoed with a frown. "You mean Ms. Plinski, the nice little old lady I met at the autographing, looks like everyone's granny?"

"That's her," Darla choked out, dragging her gaze back to the monitor.

She saw another flicker of movement, and the channel that caught it abruptly blew up to a full-size screen. Now, Darla spied a small figure dressed in what appeared to be one of those baggy tracksuits popular among the over-seventy set. The figure turned in profile, and she made out the distinctive silhouette of hair styled into a neat bun. Definitely Mary Ann.

"Guess she didn't get the memo about Darla's new security system," Jake said with a wry shake of her head, leaning in for a closer look. "But what the hell is she doing?"

"She's looking for something," Darla replied. Indeed, she could see now a tiny beam of light emanating from the miniature flashlight that the old woman held in one hand. "But why is she sneaking around in the middle of the night when she could just ask me for whatever it is she needs?"

"What I want to know is how she got into your store without tripping the alarm," Reese answered. Then, sighing, he added, "Hell, guess I'd better go down and arrest her."

"Oh, no, I don't want to press charges," Darla exclaimed in horror. "She's old, and she was Great-Aunt Dee's friend."

"Okay, I won't arrest her, but I'm going to bring her up here so she can explain why she's been breaking into your place." Turning to Jake, he added, "You've got the key and the alarm code, right?"

"Got it," Jake said. "I guess I'm backup?" At his nod, she gave Darla a commiserating look. "Ma is going to kill me if she ever hears about me arresting a nice little old lady like Mary Ann," she said in a resigned voice.

Darla trailed them to the door but Reese shook his head firmly when she made as if to follow after them. "Old lady or not, a crime is being committed. We'll be back in a few minutes. You wait here and keep an eye on the monitor."

"I will, but only if you swear to me you won't frighten her," Darla insisted, clutching his arm. "She's totally harmless."

"Yeah? Well, remind me sometime to tell you about the nice, harmless old lady who once about carved out my liver with a spatula when I tried to arrest her grandson."

Jake gave Darla a reassuring pat on her shoulder before she followed Reese out the door. Darla closed it after them and then rushed back to the computer. The security video had split back into six smaller eyes again, meaning that Mary Ann had moved out of camera range once more . . . that, or else she had vanished as mysteriously as she had arrived.

A few seconds later, the screen again switched over to a single-channel view, this time of the store's side door as it slowly opened. Reese and Jake slipped past it and then carefully closed the door after them.

Darla stared more closely at the laptop, straining her ears to hear any sound from the store. She saw Reese gesture Jake to move in one direction while he took another. The screen flashed from image to image as they passed each of the downstairs cameras. Then she heard Reese's voice break through the silence to say, "Ms. Plinski, this is Detective Reese. We know you're in the store. Stay right where you are. We're going to turn on the lights."

"Oh my gracious!" she heard Mary Ann exclaim again as someone—presumably Jake—flipped on the lights closest to the inside stairway.

The camera angle changed again as Jake came striding past and headed for the spot behind the shelves where they'd last seen the woman vanish. Darla heard murmured voices, though she couldn't make out the words. A few moments later, Reese was walking toward the camera. One leather-clad arm supported Mary Ann, whose wrinkled visage reflected both fear and embarrassment. Jake followed after them, stopping to gaze up at the camera and wave in Darla's direction.

"We've got her," she called. "Reese is bringing her up. Once they're out, I'll hit the lights and lock the store, and then head up myself."

Darla kept an eye on the screen, watching as the shop's bulbs dimmed again. She saw Jake make her way back to the door, which opened and closed again. Then the screen subsided into the usual six-segment view and remained that way.

She shut down the sound option just as a knock came at the door. She rushed to open it, finding a teary Mary Ann clad in a purple tracksuit, and a rueful-looking Reese. Jake was right behind them, looking equally dismayed.

"Oh, my dear," the old woman cried, wringing her hands as Darla ushered her inside, "I am so sorry. Truly, I didn't mean any harm."

"I know that," Darla assured her as she settled the trembling woman on the horsehair couch. "Here, let me make you a cup of tea, and then you can explain everything."

By the time she returned from the kitchen with a pot of boiling water and a teabag in a cup, Mary Ann was looking calmer. She stroked a docile Hamlet, who lay sprawled across her bony knees. The cat shot Darla a reproving glare, as if blaming her for the situation, and then sprang off Mary Ann's lap to stalk his way over to the window overlooking the street.

"Thank you, my dear," the old woman said, her voice stronger now as she accepted the cup and began dunking the teabag. Her glance encompassing all of them, she sighed and said, "I suppose I had better come clean."

They waited while she took a sip and then set the cup on the table before her.

"I'm afraid this is most embarrassing," she began, once more clutching her hands together. "You see, a few months before Dee passed away, I found myself in something of a financial pickle. Normally, I would have gone to Brother for help, but business had been poor over the past year, and he was in monetary straits of his own. But Dee was—pardon the expression—rolling in dough from all her ex-husbands, so I asked her for a small loan."

She reached again for her teacup and took another steadying sip.

"Of course, I insisted on giving her some collateral. I had a very old book—well, technically, it was Brother's, too, since it had come from our parents' estate—which was of some value. And then, silly me, I discovered an old insurance policy that I'd forgotten about. I cashed it in, intending to repay Dee, but she refused to accept the money. She said that I should consider the loan a gift, from one friend to another."

"But what's wrong with that?" Darla asked, confused.

Mary Ann gave a helpless wave. "Oh, yes, it was kind of her, but what I really wanted was my book back. It was something of a family heirloom, and I knew that Brother would eventually ask what had happened to it. I tried to explain that to her, but you know how stubborn some old folks can be."

"Stubborn as some young folks," Jake said with a smile, earning a grateful nod from the old woman.

Mary Ann went on to tell how they finally had compromised. Dee would accept half the money she had loaned Mary Ann as payment in full, but she wanted to finish reading the volume before returning it to her friend. Seeing no other recourse—"Really, your great-aunt was quite strong headed about the whole situation"—Mary Ann finally had agreed to her terms. The only problem was that Dee had suffered a stroke and passed away before she'd gotten around to giving it back.

"And ever since then," Mary Ann finished with a sigh, "I've been trying to find my book."

"But how in the world did you get in without setting off the alarm?" Darla wanted to know. "You don't have a key or the alarm code."

Now, the old woman's expression grew sheepish.

"I suppose, not being from here, you don't know much about row houses, do you, Darla?" she asked. "Well, most of the homes on this block were erected around the turn of the last century. Your brownstone, mine, and the apartments on your other side were actually all built at the same time."

Darla nodded. She'd known this much from some of the legal papers she had signed when she inherited the place. Her building (and presumably the others around it) dated to about the 1880s.

"Since the same workers were doing all the construction," Mary Ann went on, "it didn't make sense for them to be constantly running out of one house and into the next. So, they very cleverly put in several doors connecting all three houses from the inside. Of course, when they were finished building, the workers bricked up all the connecting doors again, and that was that."

"Unless someone opened them back up again," Reese countered with a slow nod. "Are you trying to say that there is still a door between your place and Darla's?"

"I'm afraid so," the old woman admitted, her cheeks turning pink. "I don't know if Dee ever mentioned it, but my father used to own both of these buildings. My family lived in the side where Brother and I now live, and my grandparents lived here in Darla's brownstone. So you can see that it made sense to keep them connected. After my grandparents died, Papa sold your place to someone else, but no one ever got around to bricking up the doorway again."

"But I've never noticed any extra doors before," Darla protested. "This hidden one, where is it?"

"It's in that little alcove under the stairs on the second floor in your storeroom. The door looks like part of the paneling, and the knob is just a wooden latch, so you wouldn't even see it unless you knew to look for it." The old woman paused and gave a small chuckle. "You had stacked several boxes in front of it, so I had a doozie of a time getting through there the first time I tried."

"Sorry," Darla replied with a contrite smile. Then she narrowed her eyes as she recalled yet another incident, and Mary Ann's reaction to it. "Wait. What about the night I found those books in neat piles in my living room? Was that you in my apartment, too? You're the one who stacked the books?"

When Mary Ann gave an abashed nod, she went on, "But I thought you said there was just one door between us. How did you get in?"

"Why, through the dumbwaiter, of course."

When Darla stared at her in astonishment, Mary Ann continued, "Dee and I were both old ladies who liked a visit, but we couldn't be running up and down two flights of stairs all the time. It's far too hard on old knees. So I showed her what Brother and I used to do when we were children—we'd ride up and down the dumbwaiter. How else do you think your aunt made her way down to the store and back every day at her age?

"Oh, perhaps it's not perfectly safe," the old woman admitted as Darla continued to gape. "Nothing fun these days is! But it is rather thrilling. And I did insist that she always carry a cell phone with her in case something went wrong and she got stuck. But I promise you, I will never do it again . . . at least, not on your side of the house."

Jake was grinning outright by now. Reese was attempting a stern look but failing miserably at it. As for Darla, she took another swig of champagne. Really, this was all a bit much for one night!

"All right, Mary Ann," she replied, raising her hands in surrender, "you've explained everything, except why in the heck you just didn't tell me about the book! I would have been happy to let you search as much as you wanted until you found it."

"Oh, I couldn't have done that," she protested, her pink cheeks now turning bright red.

Darla frowned. "Why not?"

"Well, my dear, I am mortified to admit it, but this is not just any book. It's filled with etchings of, er, people in the altogether, doing terribly naughty things."

"You mean, Victorian porn?" Jake broke in with a terribly naughty whoop of her own.

Darla burst into laughter and leaped off the sofa. "Wait right here, Mary Ann. I think I can solve this problem for you."

So saying, she headed to her bedroom, returning a few moments later carrying a small cardboard box, which she handed to the old woman. "Is this what you're looking for?"

Veined hands trembling, Mary Ann pulled off the lid and then gasped. "Oh, my dear, this is it," she cried, pulling book from box and clutching it to her like a favored child. "Wherever did you find it?"

"In the most obvious place of all—Great-Aunt Dee's bedside table. I must admit, I was a bit shocked when I found it. I knew she was eccentric, but this was bit too—"

"Kinky?" Jake cheerfully supplied, earning a disapproving look from Mary Ann.

"Really, Jake," the old woman chastised her, "there is nothing wrong with enjoying something naughty so long as it is in the privacy of one's own home."

"I'm with you on that, Mary Ann," Reese spoke up with a broad wink for Darla.

Feeling herself blush almost as bright as Mary Ann, Darla forged on, "—a bit too . . . spicy to sell in a store like Pettistone's Fine Books. I thought about having James put out the word to his collectors, but I didn't want us to get the reputation for selling, well, you know—"

"Victorian porn?" Jake once again filled in the uncomfortable blank, this time earning a disapproving look from Darla.

"Erotica," she firmly finished. Then, turning to Mary Ann, she said, "Believe me, I'm thrilled to give the book back to its rightful owner. And if there's anything else of yours that Dee had here . . ."

"Oh, no, that was it," Mary Ann assured her with a prim nod.

Darla smiled and settled back onto the sofa. "You know, for a while I was afraid that Great-Aunt Dee actually *was* haunting the place," she confessed with a rueful laugh. "Not that I wouldn't be happy see her again, but I think I prefer my ghosts on stage and in books."

Then, grabbing up the champagne bottle, she added, "Now, how about one last toast?"

She poured the last of the sparkling wine among the three of them. They raised their glasses again, while Mary Ann lifted her teacup, as Darla proclaimed, "To Great-Aunt Dee . . . one heck of a broad."

"To Dee," the rest of them chorused before everyone took a celebratory sip in the old woman's memory.

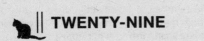

TWENTY-NINE

SINCE IT WAS MONDAY, PETTISTONE'S FINE BOOKS WAS closed as usual that next day, but around lunchtime Darla went down to the shop to do a bit of work. The news of Valerie Baylor's murder at the hands of her agent currently filled the television broadcasts, though that story was almost topped by the revelation that her twin brother, Morris, was the true brains behind the *Haunted High* franchise, which would now continue. Darla had a feeling that sales of all the *Haunted High* books would skyrocket come Tuesday morning when she reopened. She intended to have a huge new display ready to go in anticipation. Hamlet had elected to join her downstairs and supervise from his spot near the register.

"You know, we should have toasted you last night, too," Darla told him as she unboxed another carton. "All those books you snagged were pretty much on track. I bet if you'd had a little more time, you could have solved this entire case by yourself."

She grinned as Hamlet gave her a cool green look that dared her to call him a clever kitty. So of course she did, earning a hiss in return. Her grin broadened and then abruptly faded as she glanced at the book she held and noticed something that she hadn't before.

The author photo on the back cover of *Ghost of a Chance* was similar to the one of Valerie that had been on the promotional poster, and likely had been taken during the same photo session. It was the same sweep of long black hair partially obscuring the cameo features, the same broad forehead and slash of crimson lipstick. But this time, rather than clutching the scarlet fountain pen, her pale hands were folded together in an almost prayerful attitude as she gazed demurely downward.

And on one long finger, the author wore a heavy ring made of twisted metal strands that formed what appeared to be a Celtic knot.

A sharp rap on the door glass made her jump.

"Not another of Valerie's fans," she said with a groan as she set down the book and headed for the door. "Well, this time, they're going to have to wait for regular store hours, no matter how hard they beg."

And once she'd shooed off the person at the door, she'd make a quick call to Jake and let her know that Morris seemingly had taken his rightful credit as author of the book, after all.

But it was no fan girl standing out on the stoop. Darla flipped back the curtain to find herself staring through the glass at Mrs. Bobby Jennings, aka Marnie. The woman smiled and called through the windowpane, "Please open up, Darla, I need to talk to you."

Darla stifled another groan. Though she'd hoped that the woman had already left town days before, it would have been an even bigger surprise—more likely, a miracle—if the repairs to the van had been completed that quickly. So finding Marnie on her stoop wasn't quite the shock it could have been. Not that she ever wanted to see the woman again, but if she didn't face her now, Marnie likely would continue to dog her until she'd said her piece. Best to get it over with.

"Hello, Marnie," she said in a cool tone as she opened the door. "Actually, the store is closed today, and I'm pretty busy right now. Is there something I can help you with?"

"Well, I think you would do better to be closed on the Lord's day, instead," Marnie replied, the smile tightening as she gestured to the sign on the door with the shop's hours, "but I suppose that's how they do business in this sinful city."

"I suppose it is," Darla agreed, her smile equally forced. "Speaking of which, shouldn't you and your friends be headed back to Dallas by now? Or is the van still in the shop?"

"Why, that's what I came to tell you. May I step inside for a moment?"

She didn't wait for Darla's invitation but stepped past her. Once again, she was wearing the pink suit, jacket buttoned all the way up, and looking like a confection with her teased crown of blond hair. Heels clicking on the wood floor, she made a quick perusal of the shop, halting when she saw the shelves devoted to religious readings.

"All is not lost if you feature the Lord's word among these other heathen writings," she declared, nodding her approval before returning to where Darla waited. "And speaking of heathens," she went on, "I saw the news last night about Valerie Baylor. It was appalling. Why, that agent of hers used me to commit murder! I may never recover from this."

Darla was tempted to point out that Valerie Baylor definitely would not recover, but once again she saw genuine pain in the woman's eyes. Self-righteous as Marnie might be, she was suffering under the burden of being responsible for another person's death; and guilty as Darla felt given her own peripheral involvement, no way would she be cruel enough to kick Marnie when she was down.

Instead, she said, "Don't be too hard on yourself, Marnie. I've spoken to Valerie Baylor's brother, and the family blames no one but Hillary Gables for her death."

"Why, thank you for that, Darla. In fact, that's what I came to tell you."

Marnie reached down the front of her jacket and proceeded to pull out a wad of cash large enough, as James would put it, to choke the proverbial equine. Cinching the bills was one of those thick red rubber bands from a head of fresh broccoli, a money-handling technique that was a supposed trademark of a certain well-known crime organization.

The Barbie version of a made man, Darla thought in amazement, wondering if Marnie had seen that trick on an episode of *The Sopranos*. Not likely, though, given that the TV program was certainly banned by her church.

"It's five thousand dollars," the woman declared, slipping

off the band and fanning the bills so Darla could see she spoke the truth. "I swear, it was like a Christmas miracle."

She went on to explain how a local television reporter had located her soon after the news had broken about Valerie's murder, hoping to get a statement from her. Marnie had obliged, venting her outrage that she had been made, in her words, "the Devil's unwitting tool." She'd also told the reporter that she and her fellow church members were stranded in the city waiting for their van to be repaired and that they had been forced to borrow the money for that work.

"So what do you think happened this morning?" she exclaimed. "First, I got a call that our van was ready, after I'd already been told it would be a few days more. The shop said the repairs had already been paid for by an anonymous donor and that I didn't even have to come get it . . . their driver would be dropping it off within the hour. Then, while I was saying a prayer of thanks, a courier showed up at the house where we've been staying. He had a big envelope for me, and when I opened it, I found all this cash inside it. I fell to my knees right there on the doorstep and thanked the Lord."

"Sounds pretty miraculous to me," Darla agreed. "Any idea who sent the money to you?"

"A note inside said that it was a donation to the Lord's Blessing Church from the Valerie Baylor Memorial Foundation so that we might continue our good works." Marnie smiled. "It seems that, in death, Valerie Baylor has finally renounced Satan and found the Lord instead!"

Darla suspected that Morris, and not Valerie or the Lord, had done the donating, but she merely said, "Well, congratulations, Marnie. I'm sure your congregation will put the money to good use. And in the meantime, you can all go home."

"Not yet," she declared, giving Darla a momentary heart attack before she added, "not until after I give you back your money."

With the expertise of a casino cashier, the woman counted out ten hundred-dollar bills. Handing them over to Darla, she said, "Our work here is done. I'll say hi to your sister for you when I get home."

"You do that. Have a safe trip now."

She hustled Marnie to the door and waved her down the steps to the curb, where the church van was double-parked, and then hastily closed the door after her. The satisfying click of the lock turning served as a final punctuation to the end of this particular acquaintanceship.

"Look, Hamlet," Darla said with a grin, waving the money at him as he leaped from the counter to saunter her way. "The loan's repaid, so I can keep you in kibble for a while longer. And, even better, we'll never have to hear from Marnie again."

With a little celebratory whoop, she tossed the cash skyward and let it cascade back down on her. Then, just because, she allowed herself a little victory dance.

Hamlet had paused and was watching this frivolous human display with the greatest of feline disdain. The dance, however, was apparently the last straw. He gave his black whiskers a flick; then with another scornful look, he flopped onto the floor and flung one hind leg over his shoulder to give the base of his tail a quick lick.

FROM THE AUTHOR OF *A KILLER PLOT*

ELLERY ADAMS

Wordplay becomes foul play . . .

A Deadly Cliché

A BOOKS BY THE BAY MYSTERY

While walking her poodle, Olivia Limoges discovers a dead body buried in the sand. Could it be connected to the bizarre burglaries plaguing Oyster Bay, North Carolina? The Bayside Book Writers prick up their ears and pick up their pens to get the story . . .

The thieves have a distinct MO. At every crime scene, they set up odd tableaus: a stick of butter with a knife through it, dolls with silver spoons in their mouths, a deck of cards with a missing queen. Olivia realizes each setup represents a cliché.

Who better to decode the cliché clues than the Bayside Book Writers group, especially since their newest member is Police Chief Rawlings? As the investigation proceeds, Olivia is surprised to find herself falling for the widowed policeman. But an even greater surprise is in store. Her father—lost at sea thirty years ago—may still be alive . . .

penguin.com